I0785071

AS A BRIDE IN THE WILDERNESS

By E.J. Ashmore

ISBN:978-1-968792-49-7

I remember the devotion of your youth,
Your love as a bride,
How you followed me in the wilderness, in a land not sown.
Jeremiah 2:2

E.J. ASHMORE

Acknowledgements

First and foremost, I thank God for putting this story on my heart and seeing me through this. It's been a rough ride, but enjoyable every step of the way. I'd like to thank my dad, Greg, as well as Melissa and Allison from church for pushing me to publish. Thank you, Jed, from Scribophile for teaching me all about "telling" and going through each of my books line by line *twice* to sharpen and improve my writing and believing in my story. Thank you, Lynne from ACFW Scribes, for teaching me about close third person vs distant third person, for your great recommendations, and for cheering me on. Thank you, Doug from ACFW Scribes, for being my cheerleader and encourager. Thank you to my editor, Sarah, for your meticulous work on both books. Thank you, Cynthia Hickey, for giving my beloved books a chance. And thank you, Joel Richardson, for showing me the big picture of God's beautiful love story and redemption plan, all your teachings, and your patience with me as I hounded you for publishing advise.

E.J. ASHMORE

Dedication

To my husband Shawn and my precious sons, Adam and
Zackary

<u>Terms</u>
<u>Ima</u>: Hebrew for mother.
<u>Abba</u>: Hebrew for father.
<u>Mwt</u>: Ancient Egyptian for mother.
<u>Jt</u>: Ancient Egyptian for father.
<u>Hebrew</u>: How outsiders referred to the Israelites
<u>Israelite</u>: How Israelites referred to themselves.
<u>Avaris Group</u>: small town at bottom of Goshen where Eliza lived. They are the last to leave Egypt and the stragglers of Deut 25:17-18.

<u>Important Characters and Places</u>
<u>Seti</u>:18 years old. Egyptian.
<u>Eliza</u>: 16 years old. Hebrew.
<u>Sabu</u>: Seti's 18-year-old best friend. Egyptian.
<u>Nala</u>: Sabu's 18-year-old-wife. Egyptian.
<u>Adam</u>: Eliza's 17-year-old brother. Hebrew.
<u>Zechariah</u>: Eliza's 15-year-old brother. Hebrew.
<u>Miera</u>: Eliza's 11-year-old sister. Hebrew.
<u>Twins</u>: Eliza's toddler twin sisters. Hebrew.
<u>Sarah</u>: Eliza's mother. Hebrew.
<u>Jeremiah</u>: Eliza's father. Hebrew.
<u>Rahel</u>: Eliza's best friend. Hebrew. Yehudite.
<u>Sena</u>: Eliza's second cousin and nemesis. Hebrew.
<u>Yuval/The Lank</u>: musician who crushes on Eliza. Hebrew.
<u>Hoshea</u>: (Yehoshua). Friend of Moshe, Seti, Eliza, and Adam. Hebrew. Ephraimite.
<u>Kabelo</u>: Seti's brother. Egyptian (referred to in memory).
<u>Lumeri</u>: Seti's ex-betrothed. Egyptian. (referred to in memory).
<u>Ameneten</u>: Seti's father. Egyptian. (referred to in memory).
<u>Homan</u>: Sidonian merchant traveling with the Hebrews.
<u>Moshe</u>: Moses.
<u>Aharon</u>: Aaron.

<u>Order of stops:</u>
<u>Red Sea</u>: The ultimate defeat of the Egyptians. Also holds chaos/order symbolism.
<u>Sweet waters</u>: ("Waters of Marah").
<u>Elim</u>: the oasis (often symbolized as Eden because of its contrast with the desert).
<u>Desert of Sin and Rephidim</u>: manna, quail, battle of Amalekites.
<u>Horeb</u>: where the split rock is, still a good distance from Sinai.
<u>Sinai</u>: still in the Horeb region so is also referred to as Horeb. The multitude arrives here in stages after the battle. (Exodus 17).

Chapter 1

Eliza peered over her shoulder at her family. They hadn't even noticed she'd gone. She'd rarely seen them all together, let alone arguing over a biscuit. The sight brought a smile to her face. She'd be back. Besides, she would spend the rest of her life with them.

With fading voices and crackling fires at her back, she let Seti lead her into the dark hills rimming the Red Sea—away from her people. Away from the light and warmth of her God, manifest as a pillar of fire near the sea. Only the drone of desert bugs and the crunch of gravel beneath their feet filled Eliza's ears.

Her stomach knotted into a ball of nerves, no longer rumbling from the sweet aroma of roasted unleavened dough. She had only been alone with him twice before, one of those times not by choice. Seti, the son of her Egyptian master, led her away during the gnat infestation, one of ten plagues God had sent upon Egypt to coerce Pharaoh to free her people from slavery. Then, and the one time they ventured off just after leaving Egypt were no less inappropriate.

She cleared her throat. "Where are we going?"

Orange light from the Fire Pillar illuminated the contours of his muscles as he pulled himself onto a large rock.

He peered over his shoulder, a hint of mischief in his eye. "Where no one can find us."

That look was all too familiar—one he'd exchange with his friend, Sabu, back in Egypt, but not with Lumeri, the girl to whom he was once betrothed. Eliza took his outstretched hand and joined him on the rock.

The hill steepened, and Seti let go of her to grab hold of a crevice as he continued to climb. His long legs and arms drew him up the hillside with an agility and speed she couldn't match.

Though the light of God illuminated the camp, it only sharpened the contrast of the dark hills and shadows surrounding them. Seti was right: no one would find them up here. Eliza pressed her lips together and heaved herself farther up, unwilling to fall behind.

After Seti hoisted himself onto a flat rock atop the cliff, he reached down for her hand, just as he'd done in the clearing by his house back in Egypt. Only this time, when she took it, he didn't let go. The pride in his smile set her heart aflutter. He pulled her onto the ledge with ease. She wiped the dirt from her legs and stood beside him, gazing at the view.

"Look." He stretched out his arms and turned about.

The entire congregation of newly freed slaves spread before them all the way to the Red Sea where the Fire Pillar burned. Its bright oranges and reds reflected on the water, transforming the shoreline into a shining golden gate between them and utter darkness. The camp started far inland. Was that their choice or God's?

"It's kind of poetic, isn't it?" Seti faced the desert.

Eliza searched for the Avaris group in which her family camped at the far rear of the multitude. A mountain shadow obscured them except for the flicker of their fires, faint like the more distant stars in the sky. She turned to Seti in astonishment. It hadn't felt like they had sneaked off so far.

"Poetic, like our future. And the past is behind us. Gone." His voice trailed off as he dropped his hand and stared far off, a pensive look in his eyes.

His words sank deep into Eliza's heart as she drank in his presence. This was why she had fallen in love with him long before he had given her a thought. His poetic eloquence elevated his already rugged handsomeness far above that of the average Egyptian man.

Yes, his deep, spellbinding eyes, broad shoulders, and lean but strong stature had often rendered her useless in her work in Egypt. Slavery kept her eyes lowered until she could scamper out of sight and watch him undeterred. Observing his effortless transformation from the reckless, arrogant high priest's son to the soft, doting servant whenever his betrothed came near had entranced her.

Further, he distinguished himself from other young men in that strong drink or sensual pleasures didn't rule his heart. Instead, he found contentment in the quiet peace of a sparkling night sky, the mystery of an open scroll, the sweet melody of strings and lutes, and devotion to the gods he loved—a devotion that rivaled her own.

She had prayed for his love, but only if he'd come to love her God first. And here he stood, a walking miracle if he ever knew it.

In fact, God heard all her seemingly insignificant prayers. Her family, whole and healthy, free for the first time. Her people, a nation birthed from the midst of another, and on their way to a place they'd call home. And God, manifested as the Fire Pillar by night and a Cloud Pillar by day, leading the way.

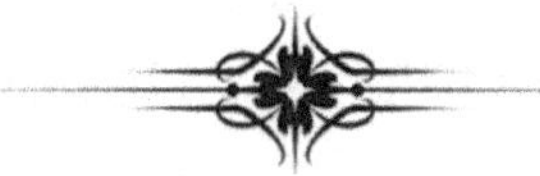

Complete blackness engulfed Egypt. Seti drew in a breath. Try as he might, he couldn't bury the haunting thoughts of his family. When he turned to Eliza, all such thoughts melted away. She stood there, bashfully unaware of the power of her presence—at least over him. How could he have overlooked her all those years? Untamed brown curls lifted in every direction, a stark contrast to her reserved demeanor. Despite the timidness in her stance, a fiery boldness shone in her deep eyes. The fading scar stretching across her face from his mother's whip testified to her bravery and nobility, adding to her beauty.

He'd take her in his arms and kiss that scar, but instead he sat and dangled his legs over the ledge of the rock slab. Eliza followed suit and hugged her cloak tight against herself. Her legs swung off the ledge, her bare feet caked in dirt. Seti had promised to get her a pair of sandals. No such girl should walk barefoot. He owed her everything after she had saved him in Egypt from the wrath of Pharaoh as well as the wrath of her God. His God.

Seti pulled his sandals from his feet and tossed them into the air.

"What—" Eliza paused, watching them bounce down the cliff-side.

"I won't wear any until you do. I can't believe you climbed up here barefoot." Seti touched her hand, but she shied away. He leaned in front of her until their eyes met.

"You led me up here," Eliza said, her cheeks blushing in the light. "I wasn't going to stop just because I'm barefoot."

He reached again, and his hand closed around hers. Her warmth proved a breath of fresh air amid the chaos of guilt, shame, and relief that had swirled through his mind the past few nights. He had abandoned his mother and brother, and he should have died along with his father. Yet here he sat, alive, a stranger amid a people who hated him. His only reminders of home were Eliza, her sister, and his horse. Her presence gave him the reassurance he craved. His thumb gently caressed the inside of her wrist.

She tensed.

"What?" he asked.

She pulled her hand away. His heart fell. Every moment of every day, somebody from her family watched him. To appease them, he kept his distance. When they walked together, he kept his hands tucked in his cloak pockets. Circumcision may have made him acceptable, but to the Hebrews, he remained the enemy. But now that he finally had Eliza to himself, she pulled away.

"Eliza." He kept his voice gentle. "You're not a slave anymore, and I'll never be a priest."

She wouldn't look at him. "That's exactly it, Seti. What's to restrain you now?"

Laughter escaped from him, though nothing about this was funny. "What do you think I'm going to do?"

She closed her eyes.

Wrong question. Seti sighed. He drew a leg halfway up so he could face her. The Fire Pillar burned silently in the distance, illuminating her profile. She stared into the darkness. Once her apprehension had been sweet, but not so much anymore.

"You can trust me." He had done nothing to prove otherwise.

She lowered her gaze to her folded hands. "I—I do trust you."

"Obviously not."

The silence was awkward. The breeze tossed her curls, and the orange glow intensified the shadows on her face. She could be difficult all she wanted, but he'd never stop loving her.

Seti pulled a blade of grass from a crack in the rocks and wound it around his finger. He drew in a deep breath. Only one thing could pull her out of her shell: talking about her God.

"I spoke with Hoshea," Seti tried. "Did you know Moshe calls him Yehoshua and thinks he's going to be the big savior you all keep talking about?" Hoshea denied it, but Eliza wouldn't know that.

Her head shot up, and she laughed, covering her mouth with her hand. It worked.

He raised an eyebrow. "What's funny about that?"

"I don't know why Moshe would think that about Hoshea. He's no savior." She laughed again. "Yehoshua? How? He told you that?"

"Yes." Seti drew up his other leg and rested his arms on his knees. He buried his chin into his arms to hide his smile.

"The savior will come from the clan of Yehudah not Ephraim. You must have heard him wrong. Look at the heavens, Seti," Eliza said, pointing. "God wrote His plan of redemption in the sky for us. The year begins with the Virgin and ends with the Lion of the tribe of Yehuda. At least, until we left Egypt..." her voice trailed off.

Seti's jaw dropped. "What—"

"Which would mean it's not Hoshea. Or Moshe." She sighed and passed a hesitant glance toward the Fire Pillar.

Seti gave her a moment before saying, "You lost me at the stars."

Weren't the stars the long-dead gods in the new life? The Hour Priest would track them and chart them, ultimately mapping the path of each god in his temple for all to know. In turn, the gods would warn of future calamities. It was they who instructed the design of the vast Saqqara, they who placed the pyramids and the temples. Of course, they didn't see the Hebrew God coming. Even Ra obeyed Eliza's God and shut off his light. Or perhaps none of the gods had ever existed, and the stars were nothing more than inanimate objects. A shiver ran through Seti. And to think, he had once wanted to become an Hour Priest.

"You mean the stars—"

"The year ends with the Lion of the tribe of Yehudah, but Moshe said that God is starting the new calendar with this month." She put a finger to her lips. "According to the great Yacov: 'The scepter will not depart from Yehudah, nor the staff from between his feet until Shiloh comes, and the allegiance of the nations will be his.' Shiloh is the seed of the woman, the savior. God will return everything to its proper place." She paused and glanced at Seti, as if just remembering he was still there. "My abba told me that long ago."

This girl never ceased to amaze him. Her honey-brown eyes shone with wonder.

"Which tribe does Moshe belong to?"

"He's a Levite, like my family."

"Is there a tribe of Yehudah?"

"Yes. It's one of the twelve. Yehudah was one of Yacov's sons."

"So Moshe isn't the Shiloh—seed of the woman?"

"No." She pulled her legs up and folded them beneath her.

"Then what's special about the Levites that Moshe should come from them?"

Eliza shrugged. A sadness clouded her face, though the wonder hadn't yet gone from her eyes.

Seti had to understand this people if he wanted to understand her. He would study the tribes, the history of the patriarchs, and especially this Yacov and his twelve sons. "Nothing? What tribe does Hoshea belong to?"

She tucked a strand of hair behind her ear. "Ephraim, from Yoseph."

Wasn't Yoseph the savior of Egypt? Zaphnath-Pananeah, the vizier? That must be why Moshe called Hoshea the savior. He was referring to his forefather.

"So Shiloh hasn't come yet? This isn't it? The big exodus from slavery isn't it?" How many promises and covenants had this God made with His people? There was something beautifully complicated about the Hebrew God that separated Him from all other gods. Even His own people couldn't grasp Him.

Eliza rested her face in her palm. "No."

"You thought it was Moshe, didn't you?"

"Yes, but the more I think of it, the more he's not." She let out a long sigh and stared into the distance, brows furrowed.

The Fire Pillar was God, or part of God, or a manifestation of God. Eliza's mother had said so in so many words but emphasized that God was everywhere at the same time. The Pillar's fingers of oranges and yellows spiraled upward in constant motion, converging in the heavens as one, ringed by halos of gold and jade. A flame, dancing among the stars. Seti had tried to catch up to it once on his horse, but like the rainbow—another mysterious phenomenon from this God—the harder Seti tried, the further it moved. As if its magnificence would vaporize flesh, it—or God—kept its distance.

"Yehoshua means 'God saves,' not 'Yehoshua saves'," Seti muttered as his soul tangled in the winding motion of the Pillar.

Before returning to Egypt, Moshe had spoken to God on a mountain. Rumor had it that he was leading them back to it. Mountains connected the terrestrial to the celestial, man to deity. If the Hebrew God wanted them at that mountain, then He must have something more to say.

All the whys to life's questions swirled in a mass of twisting flames in Seti's mind. He must get close to God, or at least to Moshe.

Time stilled until Seti forced his gaze away from the Pillar, only to catch Eliza ogling him like a lion ready to pounce. A shadow darkened her face, but her enchanting eyes rivaled the allure of the Pillar behind her. Then those eyes softened to the innocent demure look he'd often seen, the look that had confounded him when she dared make eye contact for the first time. The look that held him captive when he nearly opened her door in Goshen to the Angel of Death as it slew the firstborn. He'd be dead three times over if it weren't for her. He must make her his wife.

"Let me kiss you," Seti whispered.

Eliza's eyes widened, and he grabbed her around the waist, drawing her in, before another word escaped her perfect lips. His fingers lingered at the back of her neck, exploring the depths of her wild curls. He tightened his grip to the point of losing all distinction between their bodies. Her taste, so sweet—like buttermilk and honey—proved delightfully overwhelming, exactly as he imagined. No, better. Like cinnamon—

She squirmed, and he let go.

"Seti!" she gasped, jumping to her feet. "I am not an Egyptian woman!"

"Precisely." He stood, wiped his mouth with the back of his hand, and reached to pull her from the ledge, but she slapped his hand away.

"You told me I could trust you!" Eliza's open hand came at him, but he caught her wrist before it made contact with his face.

He pulled her in for one last taste before releasing her with a chuckle.

"No!" She shoved him. "That's not funny!"

He stepped back, catching himself. Her fiery glare pierced straight through him, slicing his heart. Guilt swept over him like a sudden burst of cold wind, freezing him solid. What had he done? She was right. With the boundaries between them lifted, what was to keep him from making her his wife this very moment?

Honor.

He'd honor her and betroth her properly, the way of her people, whatever that may be. He'd prove her value. She was no longer a slave and would never again live like one.

"I'm sorry," he stammered, dropping his gaze.

"Seti?" Her voice trembled.

"I'm sorry, Eliza. I shouldn't have done that." He held out his hand, hoping she'd take it.

Instead, she pointed past him.

Toward Egypt, firelight filled the blackness. Torches moved in a procession toward the Hebrew camp. Pharaoh had sent his army, trapping them in the valley against the Red Sea.

"They've come for us," Eliza cried behind him. "I—"

Stones broke loose, and Seti spun, but Eliza had vanished. He ran to the ledge, and his breath caught. Halfway down, her motionless body lay in a heap on a rock.

"Eliza!"

She didn't answer. She didn't move.

Chapter 2

Seti dropped over the ledge, sliding down the slope toward Eliza. He grabbed a protruding rock to catch himself and skidded to a halt beside her. Warm breath escaped her mouth in regular increments, but her eyes remained closed. She lay sprawled on her back, her cloak tangled beneath her.

"Eliza."

He slid his hand beneath her head.

"Eliza, wake up." He couldn't lose her.

She moaned, and her eyelids fluttered open.

Seti released the breath he'd been holding. "Eliza."

"Seti?" she mumbled, her gaze unfocused.

With his voice forcibly calm, he said, "It's me. I'm here." A warmth moistened his hand, and he pulled it from behind her head, revealing blood. His breath caught in his throat. Kneeling over her, he fished through her matted hair for the source.

She grabbed his arm. "Leave me be."

"You're bleeding." He turned her chin to the side for a better look, but she pushed him away.

"Please," she muttered, trying to sit.

Her eyes rolled back, and Seti caught her head before it hit the rock. "Eliza!"

Heart pounding, he shook her gently until she refocused on his face. He glanced toward the camp below, then at the approaching army. Nobody would hear him if he called out, and leaving her wasn't an option. This was his fault.

"Seti!" She gripped his arms with both hands, face as white as wool. "They're after us!"

"We're safe here." His panic matched hers, but he wouldn't let her see.

Pharaoh's army would massacre the unarmed Hebrews, and if spotted, Seti and Eliza would die too.

"My family. We have to warn them!"

Though the dark impeded his view, screams rose from the valley. "I think they already know."

In the light of the Fire Pillar, the multitude scrambled to collect their belongings, making the desert floor appear as if it crawled with locusts. The Pillar remained unmoved, like a spectator of death. What was God doing? He must have known about the army. Why go through the trouble of releasing their bonds only to have them annihilated in the desert?

"He led us here to kill us, Seti. It's a trap! So we'd be buried in the wilderness, because of the frogs. Because there's no room to bury us in Egypt. He left us for the vultures. I saved you for nothing!"

"No, Eliza!" Seti yelled.

Her face resembled that of a corpse. "It's because of our lack of faith. God's angry with us, and we will die as an offering to your gods."

Seti gripped her shoulders. "Eliza, stop!"

"Why would God trap us then? Without food or water? And with the gold and silver? He brought us to Migdol to be looted. Sacrificed. Buried in the sea. He's punishing us!"

With a thunder-like roar, the Fire Pillar swooped over the congregation, creating a gust of wind so intense that Seti fell back against Eliza. The air sucked from Seti's lungs in a whoosh, caving in his chest. The Pillar halted at the rear of the camp, between them and Pharaoh's army.

Seti gasped as his lungs re-opened. He gaped at the

Pillar, now blocking his view of the torches. Like the blood on the lintels, God protected them.

"I knew it!" Seti cried, springing to his feet. He punched the air. "I knew it!" He turned to Eliza. "God's protecting us." He knelt beside her and pointed. "Look."

She slowly peered at the Pillar before slumping against Seti.

He took her face in his hands. "I'm sorry." With the army blocked, he could give her his undivided attention. "Don't close your eyes." If he let her sleep, she may never wake. "It's all my fault. If I hadn't kissed you, then none of this would've happened."

"No, it's not your fault." She gripped his wrists, her eyes glassy.

"Can you see me?"

She nodded. Tears streaked through the dirt on her face. "I'm sorry."

"For what?"

"For pushing you and getting angry. You may kiss me...if you want." Still that slave mentality, afraid of disappointing him.

"I think I'll wait on that." Seti smiled. "You're right. You're not like the Egyptian girls. You're far better. A treasure. I should have treated you as such."

The melee below faded. A light breeze cooled the sweat beading on his forehead. With the Fire Pillar closer, the wind warmed, and a yellow light reflected in Eliza's tears. Abrasions and scratches covered her arms and legs. What would her family say when he returned her to them? They'd never let her marry him.

"Don't sleep, Eliza. We have to get down. Can you stand?"

"I don't know."

She clutched Seti's shoulders, and he eased her to her feet, but when he let go, she slumped to her knees.

"My head keeps spinning," she whimpered.

She sat on the slope and cried. Seti's mind whirled. Blood could leak from her ears and nose at any moment, signaling impending death. At home, he'd have taken her to the temple where the priests would immerse her in potions and myrrh. A Sau Priest from Giza might have invoked the power of Isis and Imhotep. He shook his head. Why was he thinking of Egyptian gods now?

"I'm sorry for crying. I hate it. It seems like it's all I ever do."

He knelt in front of her, taking her hand in his. "You saw me cry." When the Angel of Death spared him, he had blubbered like a fool in her arms.

She nodded with a sniffle.

A thought popped into his head. "Can you pray for help?" How did one pray to the Hebrew God? If sacrifices were required, they were doomed.

"I—I don't know. I accused God. I—" Her fingernails dug into his arm. Tears streamed down her face, and she looked away in shame. She had blasphemed God with her accusations moments ago.

Defeat washed over him. He slumped on his knees before her. What god would honor the requests of a blasphemer? It was against Maat. Did the Hebrew God enforce the same rules? Seti might lose her. He bent over and buried his face in his trembling hand.

"Seti, say something." Her soft voice broke through her staccato of sobs. "Please."

"I don't know how to pray," Seti muttered into his hand.

"You were praying when I found you."

He had spoken to the Hebrew God on the mesa, told Him to take his life. Was that a prayer? He peeked through his fingers at the Fire Pillar. Its brightness obscured Pharaoh's army. Seti balled his fists and whispered toward it, "You heard me before. Will you hear me again? Save us. Save Eliza. Make her whole again. And thank you for protecting us."

He lifted his head. "I'm done."

The tension in his muscles eased, and his mind cleared. He crumpled beside Eliza against the slope and gazed at the sky. Her grip loosened. She rested her head on his shoulder but continued to sniffle quietly. No miracle manifested. Just exhaustion.

White light beamed from the Pillar in rays. Its halos, now much closer, resembled the tiny rainbows on the glass baubles in the temple windows. How could Seti ever take such beauty for granted?

Eliza's quiet voice broke the silence. "I used to pray for you."

He sat up to face her, astonished.

"And He heard me."

"In the field by my house?"

She nodded, eyes closed. "I never prayed before Moshe came, but now I pray every night."

He gazed at her, remembering the night he had chided her for leaving the property to pray, the first time he'd really noticed her eyes. She had tried to save him then, too. What did she see in him? Words wouldn't form. He fought the urge to take her face in his hands and kiss her, to kiss all the tears away. Instead, he gently dabbed those tears with his finger. Why would God entrust such a beautiful soul to him? Speechless, he grasped her hand and leaned against the slope.

Chapter 3

A cold mist settled on Seti's face, and he awoke to a continuous, low rumble. Rubbing his eyes, he re-oriented himself. How long had he slept? Loose stones rattled around him and Eliza, some tumbling down the cliffside in a dust cloud. An earthquake? The rumbling intensified, like the thunderous pounding of a thousand antelope on the run, coming from the sea. Then, as if rent by some invisible hand, the surface of the Red Sea ruptured down the center. And with a resounding boom, the water suddenly exploded along the rupture, shooting skyward as if slamming headlong into an invisible wall. Seti flinched. The sea split, creating two violent surging walls of water on either side of a narrow path cut straight through the middle.

Seti inched forward, mouth agape. He wiped moisture from his face, suddenly aware of the mist filling the air. It smelled fresh, like the garden sprayers at the temple. Fresh and cool. The earth continued to tremble, its rumble competing with the thunderous roar of the raging sea walls.

As if to confirm he wasn't dreaming, the multitude exploded into a panic. The sun had not yet breached the horizon, though it was close, but the Fire Pillar, still behind them, illuminated their frenzied packing and fleeing.

Trembling, Seti turned toward Eliza.

"Eliza?" He shook her hand. "Eliza, we have to go."

Her eyes cracked open.

"Look." Seti pointed toward the sea.

She squinted.

"We have to go." The urgency in his voice betrayed any attempt to stay calm. "Now."

She sat up.

"How are you feeling?" he asked. "Can you climb down? Are you still dizzy? How's your head?"

Eliza steadied herself with both hands on the rock. "My headache's better. But I see two of everything."

Seti glanced at the camp. "Everyone's leaving. They're going through the sea."

"What?"

"You can't see that?" He pointed again.

She looked harder, concentrating.

God hadn't healed her. And sleep hadn't helped. Seti's chest tightened. The Avaris group—on the tail end of the camp—now headed toward the shoreline, leaving a valley littered with housewares. The multitude of people, wagons, and animals jammed at the path's entrance, forced to slow and squeeze in. God wouldn't keep the sea split forever. Seti examined the cliffside. The steepest part would be difficult, but then it leveled out toward the bottom. Still, there was no way they'd catch up to the others without his horse, Chewy. Even if they ran. And Eliza was in no condition to run.

"Everything's double. That's all." Eliza's hand slid to the lump on the back of her head. She winced.

Seti scooted off the ledge, sending a cascade of stones tumbling.

Eliza gripped the rock, steadying herself. "What are you doing?"

"I have a plan," he said. "We slide down on our bottoms. If we go slow, we can stay in control. I'll go first." The morning shadows obscured his view as he scanned the empty valley. If her family had taken Chewy with them, he and Eliza would never make it. He prayed God wouldn't close the sea.

He flashed Eliza a hopeful smile before easing himself lower.

"Now?" she asked, her voice trembling.

"Yes, now. Your family is going into the sea. We couldn't see it from the camp, remember? They're gone. It's just the two of us. We must hurry." He didn't want to scare her, but they were out of time.

More stones loosened as Seti slid farther down. His cloak caught beneath him, and he almost lost it. It was steeper than he expected. He flung his hands out but found nothing to grab. His foot hit a jutting rock, jolting him to a stop. Seti let out a breath through his teeth and looked up to Eliza. "Slowly, now."

She inched forward off the ledge, feet first.

"Careful with your cloak. Lift it so it doesn't get stuck beneath you."

She crab-crawled a short distance before she slipped and yelped, splaying her limbs to stop herself.

"Take it slow. If you slip, I'll catch you."

She laughed. "Then I'll end up taking you down with me."

Seti sighed. She still didn't trust him. Or was he overconfident? They had a ways to go before reaching safety. The uneven rock beneath his foot jabbed him, and he wished for his sandals.

Eliza inched lower, sliding and grasping for handholds. Seti covered his head as stones rained down. On the climb up, he hadn't considered the descent. Foolish. The Fire Pillar hadn't moved. Good. But how long would the sea remain parted?

Eliza whimpered as she picked up speed. Seti looked up.

"I can't stop!"

Stones pelted him just before Eliza slammed into his chest. He gritted his teeth and caught her, but the impact sent them both down. Sharp rocks and thorny desert plants snagged his clothes and tore his skin. They hit grass and rolled to a stop, Seti still cradling Eliza.

He exhaled and gazed at the morning sky. His feet and back stung. Eliza lifted her head and met his eyes.

"Success," he whispered, releasing her so she could sit.

"I told you," she said, settling beside him.

"You told me what? That I'd catch you?"

"Well…"

"See? I told you," he said proudly.

"We were both right," she conceded.

Her family must be worried sick, or they thought they had gone ahead. Sunlight breached the horizon, glistening on the walls of water. Nothing remained of the camp but scattered linen and utensils.

Yet, something else sprang into view, coming from the direction of the sea. Two horses, moving fast. Seti squinted as he stood. Chewy had been the only horse to leave Egypt. Who was this?

A fierce wind picked up, driving mist hard into his face as he studied the approaching animals.

"What is it?" Eliza steadied herself, rising beside him.

"I don't know. Someone's coming, but I can't tell who." A warm trickle of blood ran down his back. Eliza clung to him as he hurried to the base of the hill. The horses drew closer—one rider on each? No. Only one had a rider. Two riders on one horse.

Seti gaped. No. It couldn't be. He paused, heart pounding in his throat.

"I think…." His mouth went dry. Sabu and Nimrod? He suppressed the urge to sprint forward. His best friend's smiling face came into focus, and Seti thanked the Hebrew God as he pulled Eliza forward. He laughed aloud as Sabu reached them on his horse, his wife Nala seated behind him, and Chewy trotting close behind.

"Sabu!" Seti shouted.

Sabu leaped from Nimrod and rushed toward Seti with

arms wide. They collided in a fit of laughter, and Sabu lifted Seti off the ground. Nala stayed mounted, smiling.

Sabu set Seti down and clapped him hard on the back. "Well, if it isn't the son of Ameneten!"

"How?" Seti gasped, straightening to relieve the fire in his back.

"It was Hoshea." Sabu gestured toward Nala. "We left for Goshen after the locusts came." He looked Seti over. "What happened? You're a mess."

Eliza caught up, and Seti turned to her with a grin. "I thought I'd take her on one of my adventures."

"Are you well?" Sabu asked.

Seti nodded, still stunned. He could easily kiss Sabu's feet. Thankfully, the damp air masked the wetness in his eyes. He peered over his shoulder at the Pillar, which now morphed into a cloud spinning around the Fire. "It's the Hebrew God."

"I know." Sabu's lopsided smile stretched across his face. If only he knew how much Seti missed that smile. "My time with Hoshea and his men convinced me. I tried telling you. When the locusts came, they desecrated my land. That was the final straw. They even ate some of the flax in the stable. We left after that."

He glanced back at Nala. "I took my mwt and sisters and what remained of the flax to my cousin's house. We made it to Goshen just as the darkness hit. I found Hoshea, and he told me it was another plague. I asked him to tell you we'd gone."

"You gave him a map, right?"

"Yes. He found you?"

"No, he gave it to Eliza. She delivered the bovines and followed the map to the mesa. She came for me."

"The bovines?"

Seti slid his arm around Eliza's shoulders and pulled her close. "She saved me."

Sabu's gaze flipped between them. "I don't

understand. Why would he … bovines?"

"She found the new Api bull and delivered him and four others in the darkness. Hoshea told her about them and gave her the map." Pharaoh had placed a price on Seti's head for accidentally leaving the sacred bull exposed during the livestock plague.

Sand stung Seti's face, whipped up by the cold wind. He shielded it with his hands.

"Sabu, we have to go," Nala called, her face buried in her cloak.

Sabu's gaze lingered on Eliza. "The firstborn…"

"I told you, she saved me, Sabu. Because of your map. She found me on the mesa. If it wasn't for the bovine, and you, and Hoshea. And the map. Sabu—" They'd parted on the mesa before the locusts came. So much had happened since. Seti didn't know where to start.

Nala nudged Nimrod forward. "Sabu, you found him. Let's go."

Sabu shook his head. "I—I didn't know about the firstborn until afterward. I thought you … All I did was give him the map and tell him. I didn't know what he'd do. We fled …"

Seti gave his shoulder a firm squeeze. "Their God knew what to do."

Mouth open, Sabu ran a hand through his hair. He started to say something but looked away. It was not like him to show such emotion.

The wind blew Sabu's cloak against his legs. He turned back toward Seti. "I thought you were gone. Then I saw you racing Chewy a few nights ago. I—I …We should go now."

"Right." Seti nodded. They'd have time to talk later, to say everything. But first, they must cross the sea. He whistled for Chewy.

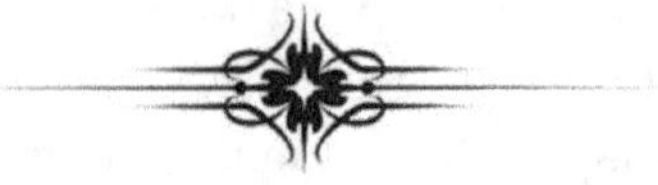

Eliza had never looked Sabu in the eye, and his scrutinizing stare didn't make it easy. She fought the urge to hide behind Seti. Without warning, Seti swooped her into his arms and hoisted her onto Chewy's back, making her head spin. She grasped Chewy's neck, fumbling for the reins, which danced in circles in her double vision. Seti mounted behind her and grabbed the reins. She tilted, and his arm encircled her and pulled her back against him.

"You think you can hang on even when Chewy's moving?" Seti asked in her ear when she tensed.

"I don't know," she muttered, heart pounding.

"Well, I'm not taking that chance. You're just going to have to trust me." With one arm around her waist, he led Chewy into a trot. She sighed and relaxed against him. Sabu and Nala blurred by on Nimrod, and Chewy sped up.

The last of the camp had entered the path between the parted sea. The height of the water didn't look like much from the cliffside, but seeing the people in comparison took her breath away. They were like ants in a rock crevice. Wagons and carts appeared as toys. Seti's grip on her tightened as they bounced on Chewy's back at a full gallop.

Eliza swallowed against the bile rising in her throat and closed her eyes. Her fingers dug into Seti's arm, not knowing where else to grab. Finding her family would be impossible, at least until they reached the other side. Seti was her eyes, and Chewy her legs.

"Are you seeing this?" Seti cried into Eliza's ear, but she gave no response.

The roar of the sea swallowed his voice and rattled his bones. His heart sped as they neared the entrance.

"Here we go," Seti said, following Sabu.

He spat strands of Eliza's hair from his mouth and wiped water from his face. The mist soaked their cloaks and tunics, but the ground was dry. Seti's neck strained as he attempted to find the top of the massive walls of water. Only a strip of blue sky was visible above. Ahead, the multitude strolled through in a never-ending procession, the other side out of sight.

Seti let go of the reins long enough to stick his hand out and feel the pressure of the water forcing his arm up. Amazing. He grabbed Eliza's hand and stuck it out. It was a once-in-a-lifetime event, and he wouldn't let her miss a thing. She laughed and tilted her head back to see him, still gripping his other arm.

Seti glanced back in time to see the Cloud Pillar lift from the ground. He snatched the reins to steady himself as it soared above them toward the front, the waters surging in its wake.

"Seti, look!" Eliza yelled, pointing.

A resounding gasp rippled through the multitude, and people began to run.

The pounding of hooves, and the clamor of armored Egyptian chariots echoed between the walls of water. Seti yanked on the reins, spinning Chewy to face them. Eliza lurched forward with a yelp. Charioteers, horsemen, archers, and foot soldiers charged between the parted waters, gaining ground on the Hebrew procession. Seti wiped the water from his face and tightened his grip on Eliza. Was this the Hebrew God's plan all along? To lure Pharaoh's army between the sea walls and crush them? Drown them? Egypt would be left desolate, with broken families and a defeated Pharaoh. For the first time in history, they'd be open and vulnerable to their enemies.

"He's going to drown them!" Seti yelled over the roaring sea.

Terror propelled the people forward, their cries muffled by the waters. Children ran from their parents. Men tugged at mules and oxen, urging them onward. Women dropped their belongings amid screams and wails, horror etched on their faces. The mesmerized procession had turned into a chaotic scramble.

Seti's mouth dropped open. There wasn't much time. The entire rear of the camp hadn't yet reached the opposite shore, and Eliza's family was somewhere in the chaos.

"What are you doing?" Eliza cried. "Go!"

"Wait." Seti jumped to the ground and darted for a wailing child amid the stampede. He snatched up the tot, tossed her behind Eliza, and mounted.

"Hang on!" He snapped the reins and gripped Eliza tight, squishing the child between them. Chewy reared then lunged into a full sprint.

Chewy burst from between the walls of water and climbed a steep hill toward the shore, plunging into a heap of wagons, animals, and Hebrews. Seti squinted in the bright sunlight. A warm wind hit his face, and he breathed deeply. Further inland, the Cloud Pillar swirled.

Sabu and Nala waved from a small hill overlooking the shoreline, and Seti headed toward them. A screaming mother chased after them until Seti handed her the child. The last of the Hebrews emerged from the waters, breathless and fear-stricken. Pharaoh's army, insects in a tunnel of water, were about halfway through.

Moshe stood on a large rock. The wind whipped his robe and long white beard, like a beacon over the sea. A throng of people huddled beneath him. Seti held his breath, eyes locked on the great man of God.

Moshe raised his hands, and with a mighty wind that forced the people back, the waters fell. The sea collapsed in on itself, roaring so loud that the crowd covered their ears and crouched. The sound rippled through Seti's veins. Chewy stepped backward, Eliza closed her eyes, and Seti watched in horror. The Egyptians were gone, swallowed by the churning, foaming sea.

Silence swept over the vast multitude. The waves calmed, order restored. The morning sunlight lit the distant Egyptian hills they had come from. Seti let out the breath he'd been holding. His surging adrenaline diminished, leaving him weak. He dismounted Chewy, helped Eliza down, and stumbled forward. Some of the people fell to the ground in shock, others in worship.

The water became so still that he second-guessed what had just happened. Yet he stood, on the east side of the Red Sea with Sabu, Nala, and Eliza at his side. Sabu sat, Nala nestled in front of him. Seti succumbed to his trembling legs and dropped onto the sandy hill. Eliza joined him.

Song broke out near the shore with lutes and tambourines. Eliza slid her arm around Seti's and nestled her head against his chest.

"Seti," she whispered, watching the dancing group below. "I love you."

He tilted her chin up with a finger.

"And I do trust you," she said, gazing into his eyes.

He smiled. "It's about time."

Her face lit up with a radiant grin. "You may kiss me if you want."

He chuckled. "You mean I get a do-over?"

"Yes."

He cupped her face with his hands and kissed her gently, slowly, carefully. Her eyes sparkled, and he melted. Seti kissed her again amid the song and music, pulling her onto his lap.

"I want you to be my wife," he whispered.

Eliza wrapped her arms around him. "I want to be your wife."

He pecked her on the forehead where the scar met her hairline. The sea resembled a chasm between their old and new lives. They had survived the great exodus together. Because of each other. Because of the great and powerful God who had carried them through. The only God Seti would ever worship.

Eliza's love for him was evident in her eyes. He'd make up for his wasted life by devoting himself to her for as long as God allowed him life on this Earth. God had loved Seti enough to pull him from the depths of Egypt, and Seti owed Him his life. The God of the Hebrews had shown Himself to the world. What God would do such things? Not just any god—not a weak, manipulatable god, or a demigod—but the God of gods.

Chapter 4

"There they are! I see them!"

Eliza's eyes popped open at the excited squeals of her younger sister in the distance, jolting her from sleep against Seti's chest. A kaleidoscope of blurred colors and the bright noon sun blinded her. Since the fall from the cliffside, her head had become a flaming warzone, aggravated by even the slightest noise or light, and it sapped what little energy remained after three days of rationing food.

"Well, that idea worked. It's about time." Sabu huffed beside them. "Who would've thought they'd revert to being last again?"

Once the spinning in her head subsided, the multitude of Hebrews came into focus. Miera had broken from the sluggish group trailing the line of people and animals. She bounded toward Eliza, followed by their frantic mother. Behind them, the remainder of her family stepped out from the crowd and halted.

Tears sprang to Eliza's eyes. She squirmed against Seti's hold in an attempt to jump from his horse and run into their arms, but he tightened his grip. "We'll meet them. You're in no condition to run."

The struggle tired her aching body. She stilled against him as he guided Chewy forward. Sabu and Nala followed on their horse. For three days since leaving the Red Sea, they had searched the multitude for her family. Upon approaching their second oasis, Seti had stopped a good distance away to scan the people as they entered the greenery. Though the odds of spotting her family in the dense crowd were slim, their two horses stood out like sphinxes in the desert, making them beacons for her family.

Seti dismounted and helped Eliza down. Miera barreled into her with open arms, making her wince and stumble back against his arms.

"Careful, Miera. She's hurt." Seti steadied her.

"You're hurt?" Miera stepped back, looking Eliza over.

Those candid eyes and her bubbling energy had indeed been missed. Eliza knelt to her sister's level. "I hurt my head at the Red Sea …"

"Eliza!" Her mother skidded in the dirt and fell to her knees before her. She pulled Eliza into a tight hug. "My daughter, where have you been?" Her voice broke into sobs against Eliza's shoulder.

"We lost you after crossing the Sea. Everybody mixed together—"

"I thought you were left behind!" Her mother squeezed the breath from Eliza's lungs. She gripped her shoulders and shook her. "You have much explaining to do, young lady."

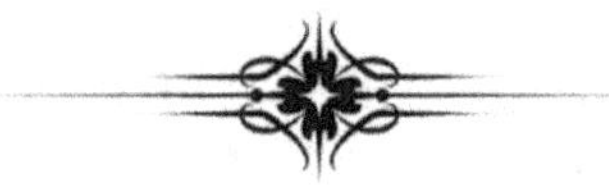

Blueberries burst in Seti's mouth with each chomp, their juices a haven against the dryness of his tongue. He moaned, savoring the juicy sweetness. Almonds came around in a basket, freshly gathered from somewhere nearby, but he'd wait on those. A day without water had diminished his appetite for anything dry.

Apparently, after leaving the Red Sea, Eliza's family had rejoined those from their town of Avaris, at the back of the Hebrew caravan. One would think they'd opt for the middle or possibly the front near Moshe. Yet they moved as they did when leaving Egypt, like a wounded antelope falling behind the herd. Perhaps it was the comfort of traveling with familiar faces. Beyond that, it defied all logic.

Seti sat back in the shadows of the evening sun, leaning against the wagon with Sabu and Nala while Eliza told her family everything that had happened since parting from them at the Sea. She mentioned falling from the cliff but kept the details vague, sparing Seti the wrath of her father and brothers, though glares shot his way periodically. If they knew her fall stemmed from a squabble over his unwelcome kiss, he'd be ousted at best, a dead man at worst.

"… Sabu found us, and he had Chewy. So we caught up just before the Egyptian army reached us." Eliza nodded toward Sabu and Nala. "That's Sabu and his wife, Nala."

Miera bounced from the rock she had been sitting on. "I know them!"

"Great," Eliza's older brother, Adam, muttered. "More Egyptians."

Her father, Jeremiah, stood and crossed his arms. He pinned Seti with a look of caution before facing Eliza. "No more sneaking away." He leveled his gaze at each of his children. "We are a family, one afforded a second chance by God's grace. Never again shall we be separated. Nobody leaves our camp. I will not risk losing any of you."

A chorus of "Yes, Abba" rumbled from Eliza, her two brothers, and three younger sisters.

Seti shrank deeper into the shadows with the weight of Jeremiah's words. Before a week ago, the thought of Eliza having a family never crossed his mind. And to think, she was more fortunate than most Hebrew slaves.

"I thought I lost you," her mother, Sarah, admonished, her voice trembling.

Jeremiah glared at Seti. "That goes for you, too. No more galivanting like a wild youth. This isn't Egypt. If you want the protection of our God, you'll obey and stay within

His presence."

Seti nodded, shame knotting in his belly. He glanced at the Fire Pillar in the distance. Earning the trust of Eliza's family would be harder than expected, but if that meant reining in his free spirit, then so be it. After all, the one time he'd sought alone time with Eliza, she'd nearly died. They might never have crossed the Sea if it weren't for Sabu showing up.

God bless Sabu's soul. Not only was he Seti's best friend—a partner in crime and accountability—but he proved to be a pillar of common sense when Seti's heart led him astray. Not to mention, his shared ethnicity offered a measure of comfort in this newfound loneliness Seti had never fathomed, until now.

The differences between them and the Hebrews grew by the day. Seti caught himself glancing back often, as if to see Egypt, or even the Sea. Curious eyes followed him, and Eliza's brothers watched him like hawks. Was it distrust? Curiosity? Perhaps both. God had plucked him from a life of ease and planted him in an unstable world among a hostile people. For once, Seti would have to work for acceptance. But as long as he had God and Eliza at his side, it would be worth it.

At nightfall, Seti joined Sabu in a nearby stream to bathe. He'd never gone so long without a bath. A thick film of grime coated his skin. He scrubbed the dirt, sand, and sweat from his only tunic on a rock and rinsed the cloak Eliza's father had given him when they'd fled his homeland. While Sabu and Nala changed into clean tunics and slept in their small tent to the side of the main camp, Seti shivered against Chewy, covered only by his wet cloak.

After giving the people two days to replenish their stores and stomachs, the ever-spinning pillar of cloud picked up and moved into the wilderness. At this pace, they would arrive in Canaan within a week. It had barely been a month since leaving Egypt. With jars refilled and baskets overflowing with grapes, pomegranates, and whatever else could be found, the multitude packed their things and left the safety of the oasis.

Either the Hebrew God manifested as the Cloud Pillar or resided inside it, but as Eliza's mother had said, He was everywhere at the same time. The winding gray clouds spiraled upward, then fanned out over the multitude like a canopy, offering a cool shadow in the heat of the day. At night, the fire within shone through, drowning out the glitter of the stars and offering its warmth as the desert temperature dropped. God led His people in this way. When He moved, they moved. There was a peculiar nurturing sense about it that reminded Seti of an eagle sheltering her little ones. Now, if only God would feed them.

Word had spread that God had led His people through the wilderness instead of along the highway, with the purpose of stopping at the mountain where He had first spoken with Moshe. Seti kept his gaze fixed on the horizon. So far, only mundane, flat desert floor stretched in all directions, speckled with the occasional shrub.

"Something about these water jugs brings back bad memories," Sabu grumbled as he and Seti led their horses on foot, jars slung over their shoulders. Both horses were heavily packed, and none of it belonged to Seti.

Neither the water nor the newly gathered fruit would last long.

"I'm talking about the Nile," Sabu said when Seti didn't reply. "When the water turned to blood."

"I know what you meant." Seti's stomach ached. In Egypt, as long as the people pleased their gods, they remained safe and provided for. Any calamity they faced would be their own fault. But to rely purely on faith? The heavy undercurrent of distrust filtering through the air proved he wasn't alone in his thinking. These people didn't know their God any more than he did.

At nightfall, the Cloud Pillar halted, stopping the multitude in the middle of the barren wasteland. The stony ground lay flat against a starry sky in every direction. Seti sucked in a breath. Any other day, he might have found the view beautiful, but this was the desert—the realm of the dead. What if Eliza's blasphemous thoughts at the sea were correct? That this God had merely dragged these people out here only to turn on them? Leave them as a prize, a living sacrifice for the wandering spirits too lowly to make it to the heavens?

He gazed at the people, setting up camp in a rumble of low chatter, completely oblivious to their vulnerability. He exchanged a careful glance with Sabu then turned toward the Pillar—now a twisted fire reaching the sky—before clamping his eyes shut in shame.

This God couldn't read his thoughts, could He?

Then God should know how ridiculous it was to trust with no guarantee. Yet Seti, like everyone else, had no choice. They couldn't go back. He flung the hood of his cloak over his head in a sorry attempt to hide himself then sauntered toward Eliza's family to help set up camp, before quickly retreating so as not to impose.

After her friend Rahel came by to visit and sing a lullaby to the twin toddler girls, Eliza mumbled goodnight and disappeared into her tent.

Seti curled into a ball beneath his cloak. For the five years Eliza had worked for his family, she had kept to herself, reserved and mysterious. But after leaving Egypt, a different side of her had emerged: feisty and full of giggles. It had amused him.

But the injury changed everything. She'd become quiet and cranky—another reason he kept his distance.

He had ruined her.

Chapter 5

The Fire Pillar morphed into a cloud with the coming of dawn. It remained stationary longer than usual, as if waiting for the people to starve to death. God was about to do something, Seti could feel it in his aching bones. He had missed the miracle with the sweet waters; he would not miss the next. While Eliza slept, he grabbed Sabu, and they left the Avaris camp in search of Moshe.

The multitude resembled a large harbor city but without buildings. The Avaris group had been quiet and kept to themselves, save for crying babies and a small band that played every morning. But the drastically larger camps brought more congestion and noise. Loud, angry voices permeated the air. Merchandise, wagons, and carts piled around makeshift tents. Restless livestock filled the spaces between. The odors of animal dung, campfire smoke, and matted, soiled hay assaulted Seti's nostrils.

Foreigners, mostly imported slaves, scattered outside the clusters of Hebrew camps. A small group of Egyptians made eye contact with Seti, giving him a nod of familiarity.

He dismounted some distance from Moshe and his brother Aharon to avoid unwanted attention. Heaven forbid Moshe recognize him. He and Sabu left the horses with a herd of cattle and hurried the rest of the way on foot.

The grumblings among the people had begun a few days earlier, intensifying to their current state of threats and complaints. Rumors spread of returning to Egypt. But Egypt couldn't be in any better shape than out here—except perhaps for Goshen. Yet that would have been raided a month ago. If this were a test of faith, they clearly had failed. But what did their God expect?

"At least my family has food left from the harvest," Sabu said as they meandered around several rowdy children.

As out of place as Seti felt, going back would be absurd. "Don't be a fool. This has to be a test or something. Like at the first oasis. God didn't sweeten the waters until after Moshe's intervention."

"That's the rumor …" Sabu scoffed. He had followed the Hebrews after working alongside Hoshea for five days in Egypt. Whatever words Hoshea had spoken then had long lost their luster. Starve the flesh, and the spirit would soon falter.

This game God played with His people didn't make sense. Their hearts needed His daily dose of reassurance, and so did Seti. The thought shamed him. His faith shouldn't rely on miracles. Yet, it wavered with each passing day.

At the sound of Moshe's voice, Seti waved his hand at his friend. He hadn't seen the man of God so close since that dreadful day at the palace. Sabu ducked behind the gathered men, peering over their shoulders. Moshe chastised the crowd with Aharon beside him, clutching his famous staff.

Moshe's strong stature betrayed his eighty years—no hunch of the back or sag of the shoulders. He had lived two different lives of equal length: forty years as an Egyptian prince, and another forty in the wilderness as a nobody.

Seti smiled. Moshe was the epitome of Hebrew heritage. A full head of gray hair framed a leathery face and passionate gaze. A long beard hung in a neat wave of white curls. His deep voice commanded silence and stirred Seti's heart. Despite the anger radiating from this strange man, a peace washed over Seti.

Moshe continued, "… and come morning, you will see

the Lord's glory. He has heard your grumblings. For who are we that you should grumble against us?"

"What?" Sabu whispered.

"Yahweh will provide meat tonight and bread in the morning. You are grumbling not against us but against Yahweh."

Seti shook his head. "Who's Yahweh?"

Sabu shrugged.

"We're getting meat?" a man beside them asked.

It would have to be another miracle. The crowd stirred, their murmurs growing louder. Several began to depart.

Aharon opened his mouth to speak when a loud thunderclap shook the assembly, sweeping through Seti like a wave. Several people collapsed. In one motion, they turned to face the Cloud Pillar, which had sneaked up on them as if eavesdropping. The glory of God shot out in rays of light from the swirling cloud. Though beautiful, its proximity arrested Seti's heart. Another thunderous boom made even Moshe flinch.

An urge to step back—better yet, to run—overcame Seti. Instead, his knees weakened, and he fumbled for Sabu's arm. The sovereignty of God pushed down on his shoulders until he collapsed, the breath leaving his lungs. His body trembled as God spoke as if only to him. All the questions and yearnings that had tumbled through him the in past month dissolved. Yet his flesh screamed and begged God to move away.

The sound vanished, and the Cloud returned to its usual distance as if nothing had happened. If it had remained a second longer, Seti would surely have burst. He filled his lungs with air, placed a hand on his chest, and opened his eyes. But he couldn't move.

Seti willed it to come close again, to speak. His flesh couldn't handle it, he couldn't breathe in its presence, but he had never felt more alive.

Eliza's eyes shot open at the rumble of thunder. The second clap shook her to the core, and she gasped. Images of the hailstorm in Egypt flashed through her mind. She waited alone in her tent, listening, but minutes passed, and not another sound came but the grumble of her belly.

Heart still pounding, she stepped outside. Her mother and the twins huddled together at the firepit, staring into the clear noon sky. An eeriness stilled the air. Others had stopped their business, eyes turned skyward.

Seti wasn't in his usual spot beside Sabu's tent. Eliza pushed through a dizzy spell as she made her way over and peered inside. Nala slept alone, a drool spot on her pillow. Eliza straightened and checked around for Nimrod or Chewy. Her stomach sank. Seti had left the camp against her father's demands. That didn't take long. Lips pressed into a thin line, she crossed her arms. In the distance, familiar music broke the uncanny silence, and though she'd heard it before, a spark of curiosity ignited within her.

She followed the strum of lyres and string instruments to a group of tents set in a circle on the outskirts of the Avaris camp. The family who had played at Moshe's meeting back in Goshen gathered with their instruments, the family with the rowdy boys who had proudly showed her their scars.

A beautiful rendition of Miriam's song flowed from a harp, stopping Eliza in her tracks. Her heart fluttered, and she nearly broke into a twirl on her toes, but a sharp voice spoke from behind her.

"Where's your special friend?"

She spun to face a group of girls approaching, two of them cousins from her father's side. She'd recognize the sisters anywhere. Though Levites, Sena and Samara stood out with their long blonde hair and blue eyes inherited from their mother, a foreign slave from the north. Sena in particular resembled an exotic goddess with those perfect curves and dark olive skin contrasting her yellow braids and piercing sky-blue eyes. What few memories Eliza had of her weren't fond. Sena marched over, the other four close behind.

Eliza masked her surprise with ignorance, knowing full well who she referred to. "Special friend?"

Sena lifted an eyebrow and tilted her head. "The Egyptian."

"I don't know. Why?"

"He's very handsome," one of the other girls said, cheeks flushed.

The others giggled, but Sena merely lifted her chin, lips pressed in a smug line.

Eliza shifted her weight and glanced toward the musicians. Sweat pooled in her hands. A pang of insecurity rose.

"How does somebody like you end up with somebody like him, anyway? What's your story? Aren't you the Frog Girl?"

One of the girls made a throaty frog sound, followed by more giggles. Eliza's head throbbed, either from the fall at the Red Sea or the reminder of the giant scar crossing her face. She had gained a reputation among the slaves of On after poisoning Seti's mother's stew with a dead frog and spewing unbridled words. Seti had stepped in to save her from his mother's wrath, but not before she was whipped across the face.

Eliza searched Sena's eyes. She would not respond to their Frog Girl taunt. "He came out here with me. With my family."

"Oh." Sena glanced off into the distance then back at Eliza. "How does someone like him end up with someone like you? He's Egyptian."

Hadn't Eliza just answered her? "My parents let him."

"That's not what she meant," Samara sneered.

The true meaning of Sena's words sank in. Eliza should have known. She squinted at the musicians again while searching for a smart retort, but nothing came to mind.

Sena stepped closer. "What's his name?"

Swallowing, Eliza lifted her chin. "You've never talked to me before, Sena. What do you want?"

"His name."

"Then ask him yourself," Eliza said coolly, immediately regretting it.

"I'll do just that." Sena whipped her sleek braid behind her shoulder and smiled.

Giving in to the urge to run, Eliza bolted toward the musicians, laughter breaking out in her wake. She ducked into the crowd of onlookers and crouched low to conceal herself. Fool. She had fled like a fool, hiding like usual.

With a deep breath, she inched through the audience toward the front, the uplifting cadence brightening her downcast heart. Five boys and several adults bounced to the beat, their hands full with lyres, lutes, man-sized harps, tambourines, trumpets, a cymbal, and a sistrum. Even a set of foreign drums. A small boy, no more than a tot, drove the beat with his clappers.

Miera appeared from nowhere and plopped down beside Eliza just as a pouch of water came around. They each took a swallow, but little was left, and it did nothing for the gaping pit inside her.

One of the older boys with a lute knelt beside Eliza, the boisterous teenager with the crazy whipping stories from the brick farms.

"You want to try?" he asked, extending the lute toward her.

Mouth agape, Eliza stared at it.

"Do it!" Miera waved her hands excitedly.

"I'm Yuval, son of Yobach" He helped Eliza position

it so she could use her right hand to strum the strings, but instead, she dropped it.

"Sorry," she said.

"Try this." Unaffected by his instrument hitting the ground, he picked it up and guided her fingers on the strings.

When she copied him, the beautiful chord emanating from her fingertips sent shivers rippling through her. She flashed Yuval a surprised smile before strumming again.

"Go ahead and play this. I have something else." He stood and reached for a large harp leaning against a rock.

Impervious to Eliza's amateurish strumming, the musicians' lively song continued, joined by clapping hands and bobbing heads all around. Laughter, long buried, bubbled up from Eliza's heart, and the weight on her shoulders seemed to float away on the notes. She stood and joined the group, unfazed by the watchful eyes of the audience.

Chapter 6

Seti's eyes grew heavy early that evening as he leaned against a log, willing the hunger pains to subside. After nearly dying in the presence of God, he had stumbled back to camp and collapsed at his spot near Sabu's tent, all energy drained. Thankfully, Eliza still hadn't woken. Curling beneath his cloak, he clutched his abdomen and mulled over the afternoon's miraculous events to distract himself from the constant gnaw of food.

Just when on the verge of sleep, a sudden wave of darkness swept over him so quickly his eyes snapped open. A thick cloud of quail blanketed the western sky, reminiscent of the locust plague from the Hebrew God. Sabu burst out of his tent.

"Of course! Birds!" he shouted, hands raised in amazement.

Nala threw her arms around him, and the two danced with joy. Cheers and shouts rippled through the somber camp as Hebrews spilled from their tents, overcome with sudden hope.

As if on command, the birds changed course and nosedived into the camp, sending people scattering with hands covering their heads. Sabu and Nala dove into the tent, and Seti ducked under his cloak. Quail beaks pelted the stony ground and hammered against wagons. Tables crashed, spilling belongings. Campers screamed as tents collapsed around them. Livestock ran wild. Seti recoiled, flinching each time a sharp beak struck him.

When the chaos ebbed, laughter and singing rose up in its place. Seti peered from beneath his cloak at the bloody scene, stunned by the rise of music across the camp.

To the Hebrews, everything was cause for celebration. Feathers floated like ash, clouding Seti's view of the aftermath. Bloodied quail flopped helplessly, their beaks pinning them to the ground. Others lay motionless, killed on impact. As Seti sat up, a limp bird slid from his shoulder into his lap.

The rich, smoky aroma of burning dung wafted through the air as fires sparked to life. Children chased each other with feather-stuffed hemp sacks in fits of squeals and laughter. Seti watched, speechless.

Sabu crawled from his collapsed tent, holding an empty sack. "Get a fire going," he called to Nala, who fumbled beneath the canvas. "We'll collect the birds." He tossed Seti a sack. "Let's go."

Nerves twisting into knots, Seti paced in front of Sabu's tent, hands on his hips. Only upon bringing a plate of quail to Eliza's tent did he realize she was gone, which meant she had left before he returned to camp. His stomach churned from worry. The overabundance of quail he'd eaten and his unbearable thirst didn't help. Unable to quiet his mind, he dropped to the ground and stuffed a sack with feathers for a pillow.

"Seti!" Miera yelled from her tent.

He turned, hoping for news of Eliza.

"You should hear Eliza play!" Miera started toward him but halted when her mother called her back to eat.

"You should hear Eliza. She's playing a lute."

He blinked. He'd never seen her with an instrument. The thought made him smile, yet only laughter and chatter drifted through the air.

"I'll show you." Miera grabbed his hand and said over her shoulder, "I'll be back, I promise."

Miera tugged him along, skipping in her new sandals, a wide smile on her face. A few belches escaped Seti's gut as he jogged beside her. When the soft hum of lyres and lutes reached his ears, he paused. A crowd had gathered around a group of musicians. Then he saw her. His heart leapt, and he broke into a sprint, weaving through the back of the crowd.

Eliza's fingers melodically strummed the lute strings. Her eyes were closed, a gentle smile on her lips. She appeared angelic—more radiant than any treasure in Pharaoh's palace.

Seti had to get her a lute. But how? Anything to see her like this again. Not wanting to break the spell, he stood still, awed.

The final notes drifted through the silent crowd, mingling with the savory scent of roasted quail. When Eliza's gaze found his, her eyes lit up, and warmth flooded his chest. A tall, lanky boy set his harp against a rock and lifted Eliza's free hand into the air.

"Eliza, the Frog Girl!"

Her face flushed crimson, and Seti's stomach dropped. The boy released her hand but continued to gaze at her. Her blush deepened. Similar in age to Eliza, with long, dark curls, a stubbled jawline, and wide-set brown eyes, the scoundrel was so tall he had to look down at her.

Jealous heat propelled Seti to his feet and around the crowd. He grabbed Eliza's hand and pulled her away. She giggled, waving at the admiring musician.

"Time to eat," Seti said flatly.

"Did you hear that?" she asked as she hurried to keep up with his stride. "Did you hear me play? Wasn't it all so beautiful? The most amazing sounds I've ever heard!"

Seti spun and swept her into his arms, hoping the musician saw. Eliza clung to his shoulders, struggling to find her footing as he dipped her backward, one arm snug around her waist, the other caressing her neck. His irritation blurred into a surge of sensations, every nerve buzzing.

He bent toward her lips but stopped short of making contact, the unwanted kiss on the cliff flashing through his mind. It took all he had to pull away. He set her on her feet and cleared his throat. "You're amazing."

"Seti!" Eliza's hands trembled as she stepped back. But a mischievous gleam in her eyes hinted that she rather enjoyed it.

He laughed.

The crowd dispersed, casting curious glances as they passed.

"I … I apologize." His flesh proved stronger than he'd like to admit.

Eliza's mouth hung open. She regained her composure and straightened her tunic. "Seti, we aren't even betrothed yet."

He shook his bangs from his eyes and squared his jaw. "May I kiss you, Eliza?"

"Not here in front of everybody."

"Why not?"

"It's not right."

He smirked. Of course it wasn't. Any other girl might have leaped at the chance, right or not. But Eliza wasn't any other girl. "Sorry," he whispered.

Eliza smiled sweetly but gazed at him provocatively. "Tonight?"

He'd do it her way, even if it tortured him. He nodded and walked beside her, their hands entwined. "I watched you play, and it was like the old you had returned."

"The old me?"

"The you from before. Pre-fall you."

"Well, I'm back. I think. It was the music. I love it. Like Rahel's singing, it's rejuvenating."

"I'll find you a lute." Idiot. With no money and

nowhere to buy one, he'd better stop while he was ahead.

"How?" she giggled, swinging their joined hands in wide arcs.

Seti smiled. "See? You're laughing again."

Eliza stopped, tugging Seti to a halt. She cupped his face in her hands and leaned in. He reached to stop her but hesitated. Heat rushed through his body as her warm, soft lips pressed against his.

When she pulled back, Seti wouldn't let go. "Eliza, you don't need to please me …"

"I love you," she whispered.

Startled by her seriousness, he stared, speechless. The strange longing he'd felt when they had first spoken on the road by his house returned. He'd find her a lute. And sandals. And he'd make her his wife.

Roasted quail wafted on the breeze as Eliza ate the last of her family's haul. The sun straddled the horizon, its reds and oranges a visual display of the people's newfound hope. Children scattered a flock of sheep. Laughter from all directions lifted her heart.

On the hilltop behind Sabu's tent, Seti waved her over. The smile on his face sent her heart cartwheeling. Not long ago, the feelings weren't mutual. But God had heard her silly prayers and fulfilled her heart's desire. Seti sat in the grass with his arms resting on his knees, Sabu beside him in a similar pose, and Nala sat like the lady she was.

Eliza plopped onto the ground next to Seti in no ladylike way, but it didn't matter. He made her feel like the prettiest girl in the desert. The view stole her breath away. Between the sunset, the Fire Pillar glowing orange in the distance, and the landscape tightly packed with tents and animals, it was a scene to behold. A barren desert brought to life.

"Glad you joined us." Seti put his arm around her shoulders.

She leaned into him.

"We just got up here a little while ago." He leaned his head against hers, breathing in the scent of her hair. "I was showing them the mountains ahead. Can't be too far."

"Mountains?"

Beholding a mountain with her own eyes would be a wonder. Egypt was mostly flat, save for the small hills dotting eastern Goshen. But the farther east they traveled, the rockier and hillier the terrain became.

"Look." Seti pointed east.

If he hadn't pointed them out, she might have mistaken what lay ahead for shadows or clouds. But yes, peaks serrated the horizon. The darkness lent them an air of mystery.

"That's our direction," Seti said. "I remember from my world studies that there are mountains toward Midian and in East Asia, which is where Canaan is. I think. It means we're almost there."

Sabu leaned forward, gazing around Seti at Eliza. "Seti was saying that God made this." He swept his arm in front of him. "That it's not by chance or from Ra or Osiris, or anything else. The Hebrew God made the world like molding clay and laid the stars in the sky like a canvas or something like that. Is that true?"

The fact that Seti remembered her words warmed Eliza's heart and set the butterflies aflutter. "You're learning."

"Only from the best."

Eliza laughed.

Seti, Sabu, and Nala looked at her, waiting for an answer.

"God isn't boring. There's only flat land for so long

before He starts something new. Everything's a reflection of Him."

"I don't understand." Sabu's brow knitted. "He's a world?"

"Just listen," Seti said.

"Well, no." Eliza folded her hands on her lap, thinking. "The world reflects Him—or shows something of Him. I mean, how do I explain it?" She paused, a finger resting on her lips. "Let's say Seti were to build a house."

A sparkle gleamed in Seti's eye.

"From what I know of him, he'd build it on a high place, like a cliff, overlooking a beautiful valley. He would have lots of windows because he loves the sunshine and never shuts his curtains. He'd maybe even sleep on the roof, gazing at the night sky. The floor would be marble or granite, like that of the palace. Scrolls and books about history and the gods would fill his library. There would be lots of different shades of blue and a mural of trees. His love of music would require a room full of instruments. These things reflect who he is, and visitors would recognize it as the house of Seti."

Seti's mouth hung open, and his eyes shone. Eliza had come to expect this look from him every time she spoke of God. Sabu raised one eyebrow, a smirk tugging at his lips. Nala stared, brow furrowed.

"Well, you've got Seti figured out." Sabu punched Seti in the arm, knocking him out of his trance.

"But it's true, look at it." Eliza pointed to the now purple and pink sky in the west. "No sunset is ever the same, nor is a storm. God is a God of beauty and of detail. He gave us the ability to experience beauty through all our senses. Everything good about life—creation—it all began in God's heart." She smiled at Seti. "But humanity is His special creation, and nothing compares. Seti would fill his house with everything that brings him joy, but he would cherish his wife and children above all else and give them the world if he could."

Seti escorted Eliza to her tent well past dark, her hand in his. After assuring her family wasn't around, he paused and gazed into her eyes. "You fascinate me. I want to kiss you so badly, to make you my wife, and live together in that house I'm going to build in Canaan."

Eliza's face warmed. "It's not me that's fascinating, Seti. It's God. El Roi."

"It's both. I don't know. I just know that I—I want to kiss you now."

He folded his trembling hands. His next words caught on the edge of his tongue. The love this God had for His people was so foreign, deeper, and more intense than anything he could imagine, as if this God would stop at nothing to gain the love of His people.

The same could be said of Seti's love for Eliza. It defied explanation, sometimes overwhelming. Each time she spoke of God, her words on the cliff before the Red Sea echoed in his mind. She had prayed for him, even before he had given her a thought.

Eliza glanced around before rising onto her toes, leaning toward him, and gripping his arms. He cupped the back of her head, letting the silkiness of her hair slide between his fingers. Wrapping his arm around her waist, he lifted her slightly, losing himself in the softness of her lips. A long, passionate moment passed.

When she tensed, he reluctantly released her.

"Wow, Seti," she whispered, her chest heaving.

Seti smiled. "We can't keep sneaking around like this. We must marry."

"Indeed." She clasped her hands behind her back and

looked everywhere but Seti's eyes.

He couldn't tear his gaze from her.

"Good night now," he said, forcing himself to turn away before he'd lose it.

"Good night."

Seti sprawled on his hay pile beneath the cloak Eliza's father had given him. He glanced at the stars and the glowing Fire Pillar in the distance.

"You're smitten for trouble." Sabu's head peeked from his tent flap.

"What?" Seti startled.

"You'd better not ruin this one."

"I've never ruined *any* of them," Seti scoffed.

"All but Lumeri. Don't let this one go. She's different from the others, fits you well. You're going to scare her off. Remember, she was a slave."

"Seriously, Sabu? Like I haven't thought of that!" Seti yanked the cloak over his head.

He willed his friend to go to sleep. Was he too intense for Eliza? But she'd seen him with girls. She knew what he'd been. Sabu shuffled closer. Seti sighed, peering out.

"How did we miss this?" Sabu gestured toward the Fire Pillar. "This God. He's not just the God of the Hebrews, He's *the* God. How could we not see it? And you, the priestly boy with all your studies." The Pillar's glow outlined Sabu's rugged cheeks and shaggy black hair.

The same question had burned in Seti's heart for some time now. Yes, his schooling had blinded him. But God had to reveal Himself with extravagant shows of power for anybody to truly believe. Even the Hebrews.

"So this God speaks in thunder," Sabu went on. "Is He a storm? And somehow, I understood part of what He said. Not like words—but inside. I just knew."

"I think thunder is just one of the ways He speaks."

"Has any god ever spoken to you?"

"No. Never." Seti brushed his hair from his eyes. "Not even when I consulted Ptah. Not even in my dreams."

"Same. But you were almost a priest. What about your jt? Did any god ever speak to him?"

"If one did, he never spoke of it. We looked for signs just like everyone else. Favor or no favor. That's how it's always been."

"But this God actually speaks!" It was rare to see Sabu so serious.

God knew their conversations and thoughts, that much Seti understood. The Hebrew God challenged and humbled him, not like a master punishing a servant, but like a father who cared about the man his son would become. Seti missed his father.

Chapter 7

Seti pulled the cloak from his head the following morning, and a fluffy white substance landed on his shoulder. He shuddered and instinctively sprang to his knees, remembering the gnat and locust infestations. Sunlight pierced his eyes, and he lifted a hand to shield them. The white material coated the stony ground in every direction, making the morning brighter than usual.

He sifted some between his fingers. Though finely powdered, it had a grainy texture and smelled sweet.

"Sabu, wake up!" He shook the rest of it from his shoulders.

Children giggled as they frolicked through the powder, kicking it into the wind. Seti sauntered toward Eliza's tent, his bare feet sinking slightly into the strange substance.

As he rounded her tent, Miera bounded out and bumped into him. "She's still sleeping." She took Seti's hand and pulled him away.

He glanced over his shoulder as Sarah emerged from the tent, squinting in the bright morning light.

Miera tugged Seti's arm. "Ima says we have to gather an ephah each. She said that Moshe said that we can only get enough for a day."

Seti watched the oxen graze on the substance. "What is it?"

"Food. Here." She shoved a basket lined with cloth into

his hand and pulled a linen pouch from inside it. "You can fill Eliza's."

This was the miracle food Moshe spoke of? Seti knelt by the firepit beside Miera and tasted it. Like honey … or cinnamon. Sweet, either way. To see Eliza's face at the new provision would be a treat, and he glanced continuously at the tent, but she never showed. Sabu appeared gazing about with wonder, before locking his gaze with Seti.

"It's food!" Seti yelled.

After filling several more pouches, Seti joined Sabu. Nala had emptied their containers and sacks and now followed them toward a small mound.

The substance didn't last long. It melted with the morning dew.

"It's melting!" The Hebrews hurried to fill their baskets.

Seti avoided the frenzied crowd by retreating to Chewy among a yoke of oxen.

"Don't worry, Chewy. Look." He pulled a handful of the stuff from his pocket and let the horse nibble it from his open palm.

"I told you God would feed us." He scanned the hillsides.

Adam and Zechariah stood on a nearby rise, mingling with a group of boys their age, each carrying baskets. Their loud jesting caused him to pause, reminding him of his friends back home.

He sucked in a breath and patted Chewy on the nose, then headed up the hill to catch Eliza's brothers in an atypically good mood. But as he approached, their banter died down to whispers, and all but the brothers scattered. Zechariah lowered his gaze, while Adam scowled.

Seti ignored the scowl and faced Adam. "I have a question."

Zechariah laughed and punched his older brother in the arm, then hurried to catch up with the others. Adam balled a wad of the fluff in his palm and tossed it in his mouth before turning to Seti. "What?"

A tinge of jealousy crept through Seti. His relationship with his own brother had been strained, as their personalities seemed to clash. Even so, he missed him. Pushing the thought aside, he said, "I want to take your sister as my wife."

Adam's eyes widened, and he choked.

"I'm serious," Seti said. "Don't act surprised. You knew this was coming." He didn't dare ask Eliza's father yet, but Adam, on the other hand, might warm up if approached for advice.

After a series of hacks and finally swallowing the remainder of the substance, Adam wiped his mouth with his hand. "What does that have to do with me?"

"I—I don't know how to go about it. I need your advice. How does a Hebrew get married?"

Adam ran his fingers through his thick brown curls, looked away, then back at Seti. "I don't know if my abba will allow it."

Seti shrugged. "Why not?"

"Well." Adam jutted his chin, eyes narrowing. "Who are you but a lost Egyptian with nothing? Can you provide for her? Do you have a *mohar* or a *mattan*? You don't even belong to a tribe. Eliza's his first daughter. How can you prove you're worthy?"

His words hit deep. Every one of Eliza's family members seemed to affect him so intensely. But Adam was right. What father would give his daughter to a man with nothing to offer? That's why marriages were arranged.

"What … what's a mohar?" Seti asked, unable to conceal the strain in his voice.

"The dowry." Adam didn't bother hiding his condescending tone. "The groom's abba gives it to the bride's abba in exchange for the bride. If you die or divorce her, it'll sustain her as a widow. It's no different from what your people do. And it separates a bride from a concubine. My abba won't let her marry without one."

Seti nodded, swallowing hard.

"And the mattan is your betrothal gift," Adam continued. "Then, sometime after the betrothal, the groom and his father prepare a place for her. After that, the marriage is consummated with a ceremony, and the groom takes her home." He crossed his arms. "But you, you sleep outside on the ground like an animal."

Seti ignored the insult. "I just want to get betrothed for now. We can officiate the wedding when we get to Canaan."

"Israel. We're calling it Israel."

"Israel." Seti looked away as heat crept up his face.

"But you still have the same problem. My abba won't let her live like a concubine."

"She won't live like a concubine!" Seti caught himself. He needed to stay calm. Adam held the upper hand, and Seti couldn't afford to ruin anything good with him. "I'll have a dowry—mohar. And a mattan. You can be sure of that."

A satisfied grin crossed Adam's face.

"She deserves nothing but the best." Seti straightened. "I will prove myself worthy. I guess saving her from the whip and setting her free meant nothing."

"Don't get all mad, now," Adam replied, his tone softening. "I'm just warning you what my abba will expect. When you're ready, let me know, and I'll tell you the right time to ask him."

Seti nodded and turned away, fists clenched.

To Seti's disappointment, Eliza woke only to eat, as if the previous day's normalcy had drained her. The joy of playing the lute had long waned.

Her mother, Sarah, baked cinnamon cakes and muffins with the miracle substance, using the last of their water. Nala's rolls and loaves were equally delicious, giving Seti more than enough to satisfy his hunger. The sweet aroma of warm olive oil and honey drifted through the multitude.

After a late dinner—and after Eliza had returned to her tent, having barely eaten—Seti lingered by the firepit, where her father, Jeremiah, conversed with neighbors. Speaking with him would prove far more difficult than with Adam. In Egypt, everything had come easily. Women had lined up for the privilege of marrying into the Ameneten family. Not here. Not among these people. Not with nothing but a horse, a donated cloak, a sack of feathers, and his gold arm cuffs.

The gold cuffs!

Jeremiah acknowledged Seti with a nod, then rose and strolled toward the tents, announcing his agreement with the neighbors to share goat's milk each day. Did he really think they'd need to resort to that? The animals wouldn't last. They'd dry up. But God had fed them this morning, provided meat the night before, and water from the oasis before that. If God loved them as much as Eliza claimed, even as much as Seti loved Eliza, it wouldn't be long before the next miracle.

Milk would be a welcome treat. Dinner had left Seti's mouth as dry as sand. He sighed and shuffled to his spot near Sabu's tent. According to Eliza's parents, a name had been given to the miracle powder: *manna* or "what is it." Moshe had called it "bread" the day before, but "manna" was the chosen word. It sounded more like a joke than a blessing.

Sabu peeked his head from the tent flap. "Where's your leftover manna?"

Seti nodded at the pouch beside his feather pillow.

"Good. We're hiding it in the tent." Sabu darted out, snatched the pouch, and disappeared inside. Seti followed.

Clothing and linen lay scattered across their bedding in a heaping mess. Sabu plopped down and combined his, Nala's, and Seti's manna into a clay jar.

"We were only supposed to gather enough for one day," Seti blurted, despite having gathered extra.

Hands clasped behind his head, Sabu reclined and rolled his eyes. "And wait until we starve again? I don't know where you heard that, but have you looked around? Everyone gathered more than a day's worth."

True. Seti could wager his one pillow that every tent contained a stash of manna. The sweet water had been a one-time occurrence, and the oasis had only appeared after relentless pleading. God seemed to play an odd game, waiting until the people nearly turned violent before providing. Seti had questioned Jeremiah's faith after watching him bargain for milk, but even he had gathered and eaten more than enough of his share of manna.

Like the famed Hebrew vizier who'd saved Egypt four hundred years ago, Seti would save a portion of his daily allotment, preparing for the next shortage. That wisdom had kept Egypt at the top of the world as nations came from all over to buy grain during the eastern famines. It had given Egypt leverage. Genius. Now, he would have leverage, and the Hebrews would come to him. He'd no longer be the lost Egyptian.

A piercing screech jolted Seti awake. Nala stumbled out of the tent, pulling it down with her to the cries of Sabu trapped inside. Seti sat up, squinting against the bright morning sunlight reflecting off fresh manna. God had provided again.

"Get this off me!" Sabu cried.

Nala pulled at the collapsed goat-haired canvas, but it wouldn't budge. "Seti, help."

He dusted manna from his hair, grabbed one end of the tent, and tugged with Nala. A disheveled Sabu sprang from a pile of bedding, swatting his clothes and hair.

"What?" Seti yelled.

"Maggots! Everywhere!"

Seti jumped back, snatching up his cloak and pillow.

"Burn it! Burn it all!" Nala cried.

Locusts were terrible. Flies and gnats, defiling. But maggots were an abomination. Sabu tore off his tunic and flung it aside. Nala did the same, then she dropped to her knees, sobbing. Seti pulled a tunic from the sand, shook it out, and draped it over her while Sabu kicked the bedding away. The jar of manna they had buried beneath teemed with maggots. Vomit rose in Seti's throat.

With no way for Sabu and Nala to cleanse themselves, Seti inched backward, distancing himself from the horror. What would the Hebrew God think of them now? His stomach knotted at the thought of being cast out, though surely half the camp had done the same. Seti swallowed the bile in his throat, wincing at the chaos surrounding him. Screams rang out. People stumbled from their tents, rolling in the sand, and swatting each other.

While Nala sat, crying, her knees pulled to her chest, Sabu placed the maggot-ridden jar and infected linen in a blanket and wrapped them into a ball. Seti grabbed a stick to help him bury it but hesitated before drawing near again.

"Just burn it," Nala whimpered.

"We should have buried it to begin with. Maybe it's extra sensitive to the heat or something," Sabu muttered. He wiped his sweaty brow with the back of his arm and took to hand-digging in the sand.

"I think we angered the Hebrew God," Seti bemoaned.

Sabu found an empty pouch and tossed it toward Nala. "Get more before it melts."

"I can't."

"It's either that or starve. It's clean, Nala. Hurry and gather it while we take care of this."

She huffed and stood, then snatched the pouch from Sabu.

"Let's finish this, Seti. Half of it's yours," Sabu snapped.

"What do you think I'm doing?" Seti shot back.

"What are you doing?" Miera's voice came from behind. Two baskets of fresh manna dangled from her shoulders. Her twin sisters stood beside her. "You kept some from yesterday?" She gasped. "You're in trouble."

Sabu rolled his eyes and continued digging.

Laughter erupted from Eliza's tent, and Adam peeked his head out. Seti sighed.

"You'd better not bury that," Adam called. "Moshe has men coming around for the delinquents. The walk of shame is by his tent. There is to be no rotten manna in the camp."

Seti paused. "Walk of shame?"

"Don't even think about pretending you're innocent. He knows." Adam said, his tone thick with derision. He nodded toward the Pillar.

Heartbeat speeding, Seti locked eyes with Sabu. Miera shrugged and strolled away with her sisters. Far ahead, the all-seeing Cloud Pillar swirled in place, drawing the higher clouds into a funneling canopy. Did God expose all those who disobeyed to Moshe?

"I guess we're going to Moshe," Sabu muttered.

Seti swallowed hard. Dread filled his chest at the thought of meeting the man of God under such circumstances. But what else could he do with the stuff? People were everywhere, and God saw everything. Seti threw his hood over his head and followed Sabu, who tucked the linen ball of maggots beneath his arm.

Several groups of people huddled near a tent near the front of the camp. Seti stopped at a distance from Moshe's tent. Sweat dripped beneath his cloak in the morning heat. He eyed the Cloud Pillar in the distance. Would it ever come near again? That might be a disaster. He had failed the Hebrew God.

A line of offenders wove around a city of tents and wagons. Moshe and Aharon stood at the front, speaking to each person before directing them toward a small hill where they carried their abominations to the valley on the other side. The walk of shame.

Seti couldn't face Moshe or Aharon. His last encounter with them had been humiliating enough, when they'd witnessed Pharaoh unleash his wrath on Seti, right in front of them. And before that, he'd mocked them aloud while Sabu pelted them with stones. His heart thumped against his chest. He glanced around, desperate for a way out.

Sabu flagged down a boy of about twelve and asked him to take the blanket to Moshe.

"Ha! No! What if my abba sees?"

Seti stopped a young girl. "I'll give you a ride on my horse if you take this to Moshe."

Her eyes widened with horror.

After several more failed attempts, Seti groaned, grabbed Sabu's arm, and pulled him into a nearby herd of cattle. "There's no way I'm joining that line."

With a sly grin, Sabu held up a finger then ran behind a tent, returning empty-handed.

Did he just dump the maggots?

Sabu smiled, shrugged, and slipped his hands into the pockets of his cloak.

After glancing around, Seti leaned close to Sabu and said, "Go back and get it. I have a better idea."

"No."

"No innocent Hebrew should suffer because of us. Go!" Seti shoved him with both hands.

Sabu stumbled. "Alright, I'm going." He sauntered behind the tent, retrieved the sack, and thrust it toward Seti. "You want it? You take it."

Already defiled and unable to cleanse himself or make amends, Seti grabbed the sack of soiled linen and nodded toward the path they'd come from. "We're going back."

At the outer edge of the Avaris camp, Seti halted beside a cluster of tents, having filled Sabu in on the musician from the other day. Hiding behind a large bull with Sabu crouched beside him, he pulled up his hood.

"Which one is he?" Sabu whispered, peeking over the bull's back.

Seti popped his head up, ducked, and swatted at the swarm of flies circling the bull. "The tall, lanky one by the fire."

A younger boy sat beside the curly-haired musician, poking at the logs with a stick. A harp leaned against a wagon loaded with Egyptian furniture, but no other instruments were in sight. The manna had long since melted, and women and children bustled around nearby fires, preparing the noon meal.

"The Lank," Sabu whispered, wiping sweat from his face, a lopsided grin forming.

"What?"

"Look at him." Sabu nodded toward the musician. "All lanky and such."

They waited patiently, shifting with the bull's movements. The sweet scent of warm bread teased Seti's empty stomach. He had missed breakfast. He licked his chapped lips. A jar of goat's milk had never sounded so good. Hopefully, Eliza's family had saved him some.

"Psst," Sabu whispered. "The Lank is on the move."

The Lank removed his cloak, revealing a back crisscrossed with scars. He walked like a gazelle. He slipped into a tent and emerged a moment later without the cloak. He picked up the harp and carried it to a rock, sat, and positioned the instrument between his long, hairy legs. With a sharp whistle, he beckoned a group of boys to join him.

Would he offer a lute for Eliza if Seti asked? No. She wasn't getting anything from The Lank. Seti would find another way. There had to be more lutes out here.

A pleasing melody filled the air as The Lank plucked

the harp's strings.

"He's pretty good," Sabu whispered, swaying to the rhythm.

Seti elbowed him, though he had to admit, the sound was beautiful. Images of the temple musicians flashed through his mind.

"Cover me," Seti said.

Sabu nodded.

Seti darted behind another bull, then ducked into a flock of sheep, keeping low until he reached The Lank's tent. Snores came from one direction, a baby's cries from another. A group of men laughed and talked around a fire. Seti's pulse raced.

Sabu nodded from behind the bull. Seti bit his lip, rounded the tent, and in one swift motion, tossed the maggot-filled jar and linen inside, then bolted. A loud crash from inside made his breath catch.

He dove behind the neighboring tent, tumbled in the dirt, and rolled over, one hand clamped over his mouth to muffle his laughter. The music and chatter continued, unabated. After a steadying breath, Seti crept back to the bull where Sabu crouched with his face buried in his arm, shoulders convulsing. They hurried through the maze of tents until finding cover in a cluster of cattle and oxen. Once concealed, they howled with laughter.

Chapter 8

A scolding from Moshe rippled through the congregation, followed by instructions for gathering manna for the sabbath, but nothing on how to atone for their disobedience or cleanse themselves. As the days passed, nobody dared defy God's rules again. Though Seti could feel the eyes of Adam and Zechariah on him, appraising, waiting for a reason to find fault, he refused to give them the satisfaction.

Despite her lingering lethargy, Eliza managed to continue to walk with him in the evenings and to help her mother prepare the manna for the meals. Someone donated a sickly lamb to her family for her to snuggle. Taking it on walks gave both her and the lamb a chance to gain strength. Once, she led Seti to where the musicians had camped, only to find they'd packed up and gone. A twinge of guilt tugged at Seti's conscience. What if they'd left because of him? But they couldn't have known. There was no way.

He had to find a lute. His gold cuffs would suffice for the dowry, but he still needed sandals for a mattan. Proving his worth, though, would be the real challenge. Then again, maybe these little Hebraic traditions weren't even upheld anymore. They had been slaves for almost four hundred years, after all. But that was unlikely. Hardship often deepened cultural customs, not erased them. Or perhaps it was a ploy to discourage him from courting Eliza.

Even more puzzling was how the Hebrew God had allowed His people to plunder Egypt and drag their treasures into the desert yet forbade them to hoard food. He was inconsistent, giving instructions then changing them. At least the Egyptian gods were predictable. No strange rules that changed on certain days of the week. No guessing if one would starve the next day or not.

Never had he experienced such vulnerability, not even when the Hebrew God decimated Egypt. One would think manipulation of the human heart would be hard. The absence of food and water was one thing, but threaten one's pride and need for love and even the strongest of men could be brought to their knees.

Seti's fears were unfounded, right? The Lank posed no threat, Adam's words meant nothing, and Eliza loved him. He did have purpose. Yet his heart whispered otherwise.

Logic prevailed in the daylight, but under the brilliant spread of stars, the battle between his heart and mind began anew. God had led the Hebrews into the desert and provided for their needs, yet they quarreled, complained, disobeyed, and unraveled. Seti was no different.

After the people gathered manna the following morning, the Cloud Pillar lifted and moved toward the mountains.

The multitude had traveled through the heat of the day, sheltered beneath the Pillar's sweeping canopy, until late evening when it came to rest atop the jagged mountains in the distance, creating a stunning silhouette against the star-strewn sky. But to Seti's disappointment, the Avaris group—lingering at the rear of the multitude—never came close to the mountains. The flat land, though easier to traverse, felt all too familiar. He longed for diversity of terrain, specifically mountains. Weak and thirsty, the people dropped their things and slept in heaps, not bothering to set up camp.

Seti's mind reeled as he lay in the sand against Chewy. Earlier, an Egyptian stock-wagon had rumbled past, straight from the loading docks of Menf, with "For Sale" painted in Hebrew over the original hieratic lettering. Trinkets, utensils, linen, and other Egyptian wares overflowed from it, and from the rear dangled a fishing net stuffed with sandals. The man leading the oxen sported a smooth face, long blond curls, and a knee-length leather Egyptian kilt. He'd be easy to find come daylight.

When sunlight pierced the horizon, Seti was already awake. A carpet of white covered the desert floor, untouched while the multitude slept. Chewy stirred, shaking his head and flinging manna in all directions. Sabu and Nala remained curled in their blankets, undisturbed by the manna shrouding them. After one last look at the tranquil scene, Seti mounted Chewy and set out to find the light-haired merchant.

"Eliza, get up. You need to help." Miera shook her shoulders.

Eliza squinted at Miera's face, barely visible with the morning sun blazing behind her.

"Ima's getting milk, and we have to gather manna. You have to help. Ima said so." Miera pulled Eliza's hand.

With a moan, Eliza sat up. She pried her eyelids open with her fingers. Her swollen, dry tongue peeled from the roof of her mouth. "Has Ima collected any yet?"

"Milk? Not yet. There's not much." Miera tossed a basket toward Eliza. "Come with me."

With no water or milk, they'd resort to eating the manna raw, which would dry Eliza's mouth out even more. It left little motivation to force her body to move. She bent to pick up her cloak and nearly fell over from dizziness.

Adam and Zechariah slept near the family's unpacked wagon in the dawn's cool, dry air. Eliza peeked under the wagon for dew on the grass but found none. She sighed and straightened.

Sabu and Nala chatted quietly as they set up their tent, but Seti and Chewy were nowhere to be seen. He had left camp again. Eliza shook her head, tightened her cloak around her waist, and followed Miera into the horde of gatherers.

Not wanting to interact, she remained on the edge of the crowd. Kneeling, she cupped her hands, scooped the weightless manna, and blew it from her palm, mystified as it dispersed and floated to the ground.

A striped cat nuzzled her ankles.

"Hey, little one." She lifted the cat and tucked it inside her cloak, settling it on her lap. How many cats had she befriended in the Ameneten stable? Or snuggled in the outhouse, seeking comfort when she missed her family? With eyes closed, the cat purred until Eliza stiffened at the mention of "Frog Girl" behind her.

"I don't know what he sees in her anyway. She's not even pretty." Sena's voice dripped venom.

Eliza peered over her shoulder. Her nemesis stood in a circle with several others, unaware of Eliza's presence. Flipping the hood of her cloak over her head, she remained crouched, watching from the corner of her eye.

Another girl drew her finger across her face. "You can still see that nasty scar on her face."

Sena laughed. "That'll never go away. We should call her Scarfaced Frog instead."

Nods and laughter followed.

"She walks like a boy, and her hair is out of control," Samara said, still giggling.

"Watch." One of the girls pulled her hair from its bun, fluffed it with a handful of manna, and shook her head, sending it flying in every direction. "Like this!" She strutted with a masculine gait.

They cackled so loudly that nearby gatherers stopped to look.

"Shhhhh! Her family's right over there," one of them hissed, pointing toward the tents going up.

Eliza's heart rattled like a chariot over a rock bed.

Another girl sighed. "I think Seti's exotic."

"Oh, for sure. You ever watch him on his horse?" Sena wiggled her eyebrows.

Their gasps and squeals sent heat raging through Eliza's veins.

"I dare you to ask him for a ride, Sena," a tall, skinny girl with braided hair said.

"I've never been on a horse," Sena replied. "It'd be the perfect excuse to snuggle against him."

They all sighed, as if imagining themselves with Seti.

"I'll bet you a handful of almonds he will leave Eliza for you," Samara offered.

"That's too easy. Don't waste your almonds."

"Exactly," another nodded. "His standards couldn't get any lower."

They laughed with no restraint, and Eliza struggled to remain calm, biting her lip.

She stood, and the cat scurried away. Her knuckles whitened around the basket handle as fury surged through her. Every fiber screamed to storm over and drive a fist—no, a foot—into Sena's smug face.

Instead, she bolted in the opposite direction. If she remained, the entire camp would hear about her losing it, including Seti.

Rage propelled her legs until weakness took over. She stumbled up a steep hill where the manna remained untouched. At the top, she dared look back. The girls huddled in their tight group, unfazed by the abrupt departure of the hooded stranger.

After scanning the valley for her sister and not finding her, Eliza descended the far side of the hill. Alone. She collapsed in tears, sending up a billow of manna. It fell silently upon her heaving shoulders. Seti had never courted an ugly girl, much less one with a scar across her face. And yet he'd settled for her. Egyptian girls were beautiful, graceful, and clean, with sleek hair in perfect form.

Lying on her back, Eliza stared at the cloudless blue sky. The thought of Seti's shining eyes and dimpled smile steadied her breaths. Handsome—even for an Egyptian—he would be unequally yoked with her.

"There she is!" Miera's voice snapped Eliza back to reality.

She wiped her tears with the back of her hand as a rumble of footsteps neared.

Moments later, Rahel appeared above her, hands on her hips. "I didn't recognize you in that cloak."

Eliza gazed at her friend as Miera tumbled by in a cloud of manna, giggling.

Rahel leaned over. "You were crying?"

A trembling sigh slipped through Eliza's lips. She could hide nothing from her best friend.

"What is it?" Rahel asked. She sat, cradling her basket in her lap.

Eliza's chin quivered. "My cousins. Sena and the others …" Her voice shook. She nodded toward the crest of the hill.

Rahel placed a gentle hand on her arm, her kind eyes urging her on.

"They were saying Seti lowered his standards for me and talking about ways to get on his horse with him …"

Rahel squeezed Eliza's hand.

"They called me ugly. Said I walked like a boy, and my scar is hideous."

"You can barely see your scar anymore," Rahel said. "But you do walk like a boy."

Nodding, Eliza wiped her nose with her hand.

"But that doesn't mean he lowered his standards. You're different, but not lesser. Actually, you're better than them. Which of those girls would've risked her freedom for him when he didn't deserve it? Or run into Egypt during the darkness plague to save him?"

"I know," Eliza whispered, tears streaming down her cheeks. "But he has a thing for pretty girls."

"He has a thing for *you*." Rahel hugged her.

Eliza nodded. "None of them could care for him like I do."

"That's right."

While Rahel's sweet and gentle words were comforting, Eliza craved the safety of Seti's arms. She'd never tell him what happened. He might confront Sena, and that would only make things worse.

"Don't tell Seti. Or anybody."

"Who would I tell?" Rahel shrugged. "I barely speak to him anyway."

Eliza worked the manna in her hand into a ball until Rahel's breath caught. She followed Rahel's wide-eyed gaze to Miera standing far down the slope, speaking with a strange man. They stood alone in the empty valley, his stocky frame towering over her. He rested a beefy hand on Miera's shoulder as he spoke, too far away for Eliza to understand.

Heart pounding, Eliza jumped to her feet. She whipped off her hood and ran toward her sister, Rahel at her heels.

"Miera, what are you doing?" Eliza demanded as she reached them. She grabbed the man's hand and tore it from Miera's shoulder, stepping between them.

"Eliza, he's nice." Miera tried to get around her, but Eliza wouldn't budge.

She recoiled at the man's imposing stature. His

shoulders were nearly twice the width of her father's. Deep creases lined his face as he smiled; veins bulged in his thick neck. His curly brown hair hung wild around his shoulders. A long black cloak flapped behind him in the wind, and a leather vest covered a broad bare chest speckled with curls of hair.

This man was no Hebrew. And no Egyptian either. He was a stranger, a wilderness wanderer.

"Stay away," Eliza demanded.

The man chuckled. "I come in peace," he said, his voice deep and grave. "I noticed your camp and asked her about it."

"He just wanted to know who we are and where we're going," Miera added.

His smile softened, and his eyes lit up when Rahel arrived. He started toward her, but Eliza blocked him again.

"Who are you?" she demanded.

"I am passing through, on my way to the land of Midian. I came across your camp and merely asked this young lady about it. Surely you wouldn't turn away a sojourner, would you?"

"Leave!" Eliza snapped, pointing away from the camp.

His smile faded to a frown.

"Eliza, don't be so mean." Miera struggled to get between them, but Eliza held her back.

"Leave us! Go to Midian but stay away from our people!" Eliza yelled.

With a final glance at Rahel, the man said, "As you wish, my lady."

Eliza remained still as he walked away.

"You could've gotten more information out of him," Rahel said after a moment.

Eliza spun to her. "You want him to stick around?"

"No, but he didn't look like someone just passing through."

"You saw the way he looked at you!"

Rahel folded her arms. "You know what he is, don't you?"

"What he is?" Eliza frowned, watching the stranger head south, away from the camp.

"He's an Amalekite. A descendant of the Nephilim."

"A what?"

"A giant, Eliza. You've never heard of them?"

"No. How do you know of them?"

"I learned a lot on the brick farms. Amalekites rule these parts. They make war with everyone—and usually win. They're part of the Rephidim. Brutal. No one crosses them and lives. They even sacrifice children to their gods."

Miera gasped and grasped Eliza's hand. Eliza gulped. How had she never heard of these monsters? "Are they even human?"

"Yes, but they're descended from the Nephilim. The Nephilim were part human, part god."

"Like Pharaoh?" Miera asked.

"Maybe. Though Pharaoh's no giant. Then again, maybe he's a runt."

Eliza searched the hills for more Amalekites. Why would he be alone? Goosebumps prickled her skin. She gripped Miera's shoulders and shook her with such vigor that her sister's hair bounced out of its bun. "What did you tell him?"

Tears brimmed Miera's eyes. "Not much. I don't know. He asked me some questions."

"What kind of questions? What did you tell him?"

"He asked who we were and where we were going. I told him we were Israelites headed to Canaan." She sniffled.

"You said that?"

"Yes. And I told him we were slaves in Egypt and escaped because God saved us. He already knew about the Red Sea and the Egyptian army. He asked if that was us, and I said yes. Then he showed me manna in his hand and asked what it was. I said it's how God feeds us. Then he asked who our leader was, and I told him Moshe."

"He's a spy!" Rahel blurted.

"He's a spy, and you told him everything, Miera." Eliza shook her head.

Tears streamed down Miera's cheeks. "What's going to happen now?"

Eliza knelt in front of her and gently held her arms. "Nothing will happen. God protected us at the Red Sea, and He'll protect us now. He will see that we finish this journey, though we should tell Abba."

Rahel clutched her basket with both hands. "Let's get out of here."

Taking Miera's hand, Eliza led her up the slope with Rahel closely following. A shiver shot down Eliza's spine at the possibility of the man seeing her crying earlier. Had he been watching?

Chapter 9

There was no mistaking the overpacked cargo wagon tucked into a crowded valley of tents, wagons, and animals just beyond the Avaris camp. Several wooden tables formed a square in front of the extra-long wagon, with shelves standing at either end.

After dismounting, Seti surveyed the spread. Utensils, fabric, dishes, and jewelry piled in bins on a table near the wagon. Clay jars, woven baskets, papyri, and writing utensils filled another. Silk gowns, leather cloaks, and white kilts hung from a line stretched between a pole and the wagon. He paused, adding papyri to his mental list. A small monkey hopped onto a table and greeted him.

"A monkey!" He hadn't seen one since traveling the border towns with his father. He knelt and extended a finger, smiling as the monkey gave it a shake.

Leather sandals adorned with gems sat on the rear table, still enclosed in the fishing net. Perfect. Except he didn't know Eliza's size. Her feet were larger than Lumeri's but smaller than his.

From behind the wagon, the blonde man appeared and paused mid step upon seeing Seti. "You're Egyptian."

Seti straightened. Middle-aged, tanned skin, wearing only a loincloth, with his long hair twisted in small braids pulled into a ponytail—one of Egypt's foreign slaves. Perhaps he worked along the Nile or in the palace courts.

"You're Phoenician."

How did a Phoenician end up a slave? Unless his own people sold him …

The monkey scrambled onto the man's shoulder.

"What brings you into the wilderness?" the merchant asked, scrutinizing Seti.

"The Hebrew God saved me. Now I follow Him wherever He leads."

The man glanced at the Cloud Pillar, furrowing his brow, then faced Seti.

"I could ask the same of you," Seti said.

"Not all slaves were Hebrew."

Seti nodded.

"I escaped when the Hebrews left. It was my only chance." The man's jaw twitched.

Seti gestured to a shelf cluttered with figurines of various gods. "Do you really think anybody will buy those?"

The man crossed his arms. "What do you want, Egyptian?"

"My name is Seti, son of Ameneten. And you?"

"Homan. I belonged to the Kalibri family in Menf."

The name wasn't familiar. Enough jabber. "I'm looking for a pair of women's sandals and …" Seti pointed to an adjacent table. "That bolt of blue cotton and some papyri. What would you take for them?"

"What do you have?" Homan asked.

Seti held out his hands. "I don't have money, but I can offer you my services."

"And what can you do?"

What could he do besides academic things that no longer mattered? "I can winnow barley."

"Does it look like I own a farm?" Homan gestured at the tables.

Seti rubbed the back of his neck. He should have given this more thought. "What is it you need? Someone to keep your logs? I can write Egyptian and Hebrew script."

"What I need is water, and unless you've brought a well with you, you're of no help. It appears you have nothing to offer."

Seti swallowed the lump in his throat. "I can watch your setup while you come and go as you please, and help pack and unpack—"

"That bolt is cotton. The gems in those sandals are genuine. Both imported. You're getting none of that unless you fetch water for me, my oxen, and him." He nodded toward the monkey.

"I have no more water than you."

"You have a horse."

Seti sighed. There was no hiding Chewy. It didn't help that he and Sabu raced around without a care. He couldn't stay obscure if he tried. "I'm not giving you my horse."

"I don't want your horse, you idiot. What would I do with it? I have enough mouths to feed, though I'd welcome a cow. Take that fancy horse of yours and ride to Elim. It's a day's journey at most. Bring back water, and I'll give you the sandals and cotton."

Seti laughed. "Elim? You want me to leave camp? You do know God will supply water, right? He's given us manna and quail. We just have to wait. He won't abandon us. I'm not leaving here. Who knows what's out there? And besides, God won't be with me outside the camp."

"For an Egyptian, you have a lot of faith in the Hebrew God."

This man was something else. "How could I not? As I've said, He saved me. I'm a firstborn. He led me here. You're here because of Him too. And you doubt Him? Selling worthless idols like those?"

Homan glanced at the figurines, then back at Seti. "Then don't go. I'll have other buyers."

"There must be something else you need."

Turning away, Homan dismissed Seti with a flick of his hand.

Anger and desperation clenched Seti's chest. "If you want water so badly, why not go back to Elim yourself. You clearly aren't interested in following the Hebrew God. You'll have all the food and water you want there."

Homan turned to Seti. "I don't want to live in an oasis. I'm going to Canaan, and from there, Sardis. I have no interest in hanging around these kinds." He waved toward the tents around him.

Seti stared. Homan was merely surviving, tagging along under the protection of the Hebrew God until beyond the danger of the wilderness. How many others did the same? And why would God allow it? Regardless, Seti needed those sandals. "I'll be back."

Though Homan didn't look up, a slight smile tugged at his lips. Seti huffed, mounted Chewy, and headed back toward the Avaris camp. With little work to be done, no currency, and nothing to trade, he was out of options.

The brilliant blue hue of Homan's high-end cotton shimmered with an unusual sheen, suggesting it came from East Asia. It would look as beautiful on Eliza as his mother's turquoise earrings had. No bride of Seti's would marry in rags, even if it meant finding water before God supplied it.

"Sabu?" Seti peered inside his friend's tent.

Sabu snored lightly while Nala nestled against him with a pillow over her head.

Grabbing the thin blanket covering them, Seti tore it off. "Sabu, wake up!"

"Seti!" Sabu yelled. He pulled the blanket back.

"What are you doing still sleeping? It's past midday."

"Unfortunately," Sabu muttered, burying his face into his pillow.

Nala sat up and shot Seti a fiery glare.

He gestured outside. "There are still cakes left, if you want some."

She narrowed her eyes and muttered something under her breath before saying, "I'm a woman, Seti, not a dog. Just say you want a moment with Sabu."

"May I have a moment with Sabu?" Seti asked in the politest tone he could muster.

She let out an exasperated groan.

"Thank you," Seti said as she exited the tent, flicking her hand at him.

Seti flopped onto the bedding beside his friend, snuggling into Nala's spot.

"Leave me!" Sabu shouted, pushing Seti away.

"I need your help." Seti laid on his back, hands folded on his chest.

"Here we go." Sabu turned away.

"I'm serious! I really need your help. Why are you still sleeping, anyway?"

"Dying of thirst."

"Perfect. Then come with me to Elim to get water."

Sabu faced him. "What?"

"I need to go back to Elim to get water for a Phoenician merchant who's selling sandals and other things. It's for the betrothal, for Eliza. I have nothing to trade except the gold cuffs, and those are for the dowry. But I still need the other items. Listen, he'll give me everything if I just bring him some water. But I can't do it alone. I need you."

"Why not wait until we reach Canaan to get married?" Sabu asked, yawning.

"I can't wait that long."

Sabu pulled the blanket over his head. "You can control yourself a little longer. You have your whole life to lie with her."

True, and he managed to stay pure for this long. "Well … yes, but that's not it."

Sabu peeked from under the blanket, urging him on.

"Her family won't take me seriously unless I secure a proper betrothal." It was the truth. Insecurity gnawed at Seti like a plague—foreign and unwelcome. If he could secure one thing out here, it would be his future with Eliza.

"This is meaningless," Sabu groaned. "I don't know the Hebrew God that well, but I do know that leaving His presence is a bad idea. What if He doesn't allow us back?"

The thought of being barred from following God and losing Eliza knocked the wind from Seti. He gulped and turned away from his friend. "I think He knows this isn't about faith. I wouldn't be leaving otherwise. I'm doing it because I'm a poor, desperate fool."

"Finally, something we agree on."

Seti wiped the sweat from his forehead. How could Sabu sleep in this tent in the middle of the day? It was sweltering. How could Eliza?

"You know evil beings lurk out there, right?" Sabu asked. "We're protected here with that big cloud thing. I'm all for an adventure, but I don't know about this one."

"Then do you have anything I could trade?"

Sabu sat up, concern etching his features. "Really?"

"We've got horses and knives, and it wouldn't take long. A night at the most. And you owe me anyway, for taking the blame for you throwing rocks at Moshe."

"That saved your life, temporarily," Sabu reminded him. "Be thankful."

The goatskin canvas seemed to close in. Adam's taunting words echoed in his head: *The lost Egyptian who has nothing and sleeps outside like an animal.*

"I know," Sabu said with a grin. "I'll distract the merchant while you steal the sandals or whatever you need."

Seti laughed. "And he won't know who did it? Some Egyptian youth wants the sandals, and the next day they're gone? It wouldn't be hard to find me. How would that look to Eliza's parents?"

"Sounds like your life in Egypt," Sabu gave his signature lopsided smile.

"Not exactly." Closing his eyes did nothing to stifle the

growing claustrophobia.

Sabu flopped beside him with a sigh. "When do you plan on doing this?"

"As soon as possible. I want to deliver the water before God supplies it."

"Tonight?"

"No one will see us leave."

"I want water, so I'm coming. But you owe me."

Seti took a deep breath and whispered, "Thank you." He sat up, knowing that if he didn't leave tonight, he'd back out. "Be ready by nightfall, after Eliza goes to sleep."

When he pulled the tent flap open, Nala blocked the way. "Absolutely not!"

"Don't worry, I'll protect him," Seti told her.

Sabu sprang up. "Oh, no. If anything happens, it's me saving your hide."

Nala narrowed her eyes at Seti. "Time for you to go."

A reminder of how he saved their farm would suffice, but instead, he shot Sabu a pleading look. His friend had a way with the woman that disarmed her. Seti left the two alone, confident in Sabu's charms.

Outside, the Cloud Pillar cast a shadow over the nearest mountain and most of the multitude. The knots returned to Seti's stomach. Surely God knew of his plans.

"It's nothing against You, God," he whispered. "Please protect us and try to understand my reasons."

Chapter 10

The clanging of clay dishes and the scent of baked manna stirred Eliza from her nap. The morning's encounter had left her more lethargic than usual. She joined her family at the firepit for the evening meal, but Seti was nowhere in sight. It wasn't like him to miss a meal. He didn't leave camp again, did he? Her knees weakened, and her head ached. She fought the urge to lie down right there in the dirt.

After helping her mother clean up, she spotted Seti sitting alone on the hilltop—the same one she'd hidden behind that morning. His arms rested on his knees as he gazed solemnly at the somber, grumbling camp. How long had he been up there?

As Eliza climbed toward him, his face lit with a smile, and he rose to his feet, dusting the sand off his rear.

She motioned for him to sit. "Don't get up on my account."

"No, I want to walk." He took her hand.

Her heart sped. Had Sena approached him?

She followed him down the other side of the hill. With the manna long gone, only sand, stones, and weeds spread before them. Seti led her in the opposite direction of Miera's small footprints beside the set of enormous ones. He halted in an undisturbed area, taking both her hands in his.

"What is it?" Eliza searched his eyes, forcing herself not to scan the horizon for more spies.

"Do you still want to marry me?"

She blinked. "Of course I do."

His smile widened, and she melted, having craved his presence all day, especially after the morning's events. More than anything, she wanted to hold him, to feel his strength beneath her hands, to rest her head against his chest and listen to the steady beat of his precious heart.

"I was thinking we should do it soon," he said. "I asked Adam about the betrothal process. If we do it now, we could marry in Canaan. I already have the mohar—my gold cuffs, from my Father of Old. Will that be sufficient? Will your abba accept that?"

The uncharacteristic apprehension in his voice pained her. "You're really worried about this, aren't you?"

Seti nodded, his gaze distant.

"We don't have to rush," she reassured. "I'm not going anywhere."

"But I want to. It's just … I feel like your parents are wondering what I'm doing, and they won't take me seriously unless I have a plan. And I'm tired of sneaking around just to kiss you."

Despite his trepidations, a weight lifted off Eliza's shoulders. Sena would back off after the betrothal, and Seti would be hers forever. His worries over her abba's acceptance were unfounded. Her mother cared for him like an orphaned child, and her father not only respected him after the circumcision but didn't miss how Seti tended to her needs. Seti was everything she had known him to be back in Egypt. His good looks, charm, and love for adventure had drawn her in, though his compassion and loyalty made her stay.

"Sooner than later would be preferable," she said. "And yes, the cuffs will be sufficient. Though, if it were up to me, I'd be happy with just you."

He smiled, pulled her into his arms, and pressed a gentle kiss on her forehead. "Very funny."

She wrapped her arms around his waist and leaned in, soaking up his warmth. The tenseness in his muscles didn't ease up. She let her hands travel up his back, to caress away whatever anxiety gripped him.

"Footprints," he said suddenly, startling her. He pointed toward the valley floor. "We're not the only ones who come out here."

She followed his gaze. "Those are mine, Miera's, and Rahel's, from when we gathered manna."

"The manna reached this far?" He turned toward her. "You were awake this morning?"

Eliza scanned the horizon, then zeroed in on the giant prints beside Miera's. "Yes, to help Miera."

Gripping her shoulders, Seti looked her square in the eyes. "Did something happen?"

Her heart snagged on the compassion in his voice. While his doting observance unnerved her at times, maybe, for once in her life, she could be vulnerable and let her guard down. After shaking the thought away, she carefully chose her words. "Somebody was spying on us."

He smirked. "It was probably one of your brothers."

"No, it wasn't. Miera found him. A giant of a man, not one of us. He was spying on the camp."

"What?" His brow furrowed. "What do you mean she found him?"

"I don't know. I saw her talking to him. He asked her questions that she stupidly answered. And the way he looked at Rahel—"

Seti's eyes swept over her, sharp with concern. "Did he touch you?"

Her voice rose a notch. "No. I told him to leave us alone, and he did. But I think he might return with more of his kind. Rahel said he was so big because he's part god."

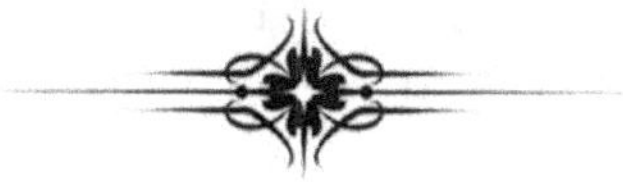

Seti stepped back. Part god? Pharaoh immediately sprang to mind. "Like a demi-god?" If God was the only god, how could someone be part god? Unless more than one kind of god existed, like in Egypt, and the Hebrew God reigned above all.

Eliza's eyes scanned their surroundings. "They sacrifice children to their gods."

Did she say what he thought she said? "What? Since when did God accept human sacrifices? That doesn't sound right. Are you sure?"

"Seti!" The frustration in her voice grounded him. "Of course He wouldn't! They aren't sacrificing to Him. He's the only God, but those people don't know that. I don't know what Rahel meant, but that man was huge."

The stranger had come close. Were they standing outside of God's protection? How could they be in danger with the very presence of God hovering over them?

"Let's go back." Eliza grabbed his hand, tugging him toward the slope.

Seti set his feet. "Are you afraid?"

"Yes. Aren't you?"

"A little." He forced a smile. "But you know we'll be safe, right?"

Eliza nodded and met his gaze. The moisture in her eyes tore at his heart. He gently cupped her face and gazed deep into her troubled soul. "God destroyed the strongest army in the world. He protects us, feeds us, and He'll give us water. Look, He shields us from the sun. No one can harm us, not while we're under His cover."

She exhaled with a slight nod.

With his thumbs, Seti brushed the tears from her

cheeks. Going to Elim would be more dangerous than he thought, but he'd risk anything to see her smiling and laughing again.

After saying goodnight to Eliza, Seti found Sabu sitting against a rock in front of his firepit, stirring dry ashes with a stick.

"Sabu!"

Sabu looked up through droopy eyelids as Seti approached.

"We need to go. Pack up!"

"Why?" Sabu continued stirring. "What's the hurry?"

"I don't want to go in the dark." Seti pulled his dagger from a woven bag near his pillow. "You have any more knives? Daggers? Other weapons?"

Sabu laughed as Seti strapped the dagger to his thigh and covered it with his tunic. "I have a sword. How about a spear?"

Seti turned. "Really?"

"No! Where would a farmer like me get a sword or a spear?"

Seti rolled his eyes and crawled through the brush toward Sabu's tent, sweeping the sand with his hands.

Sabu sat forward. "Now what are you doing?"

"I need string or something," Seti said. "Grab your canteens." He found a piece of twine tied to the tent, tore off a length equal to his forearm, and stuffed it into his cloak. After cinching one of Sabu's leather belts around his waist and adding another dagger, he turned to his friend, who hadn't yet moved.

"Sabu! Let's go! Get ready. We're leaving."

"How is it you have so much energy?" Sabu asked, rising with a groan and cracking his back.

Seti paused. If it weren't for the intense heightened awareness pulsating through him, he'd probably be asleep.

He'd have to make up for it in the morning, but it would soon be dark, and he couldn't waste any more time.

"I have to go measure Eliza's footprint. When I get back, you'd better be ready."

Shaking his head, Sabu ducked into the tent. Seti ran toward the hill.

He had deliberately led Eliza to where the sand lay undisturbed. When he reached the top, he scanned for spies, took a deep breath, and located their footprints. Kneeling beside them, he pulled out the twine and dagger, measured it against the smaller set of prints, and cut it to length.

Seti urged Chewy into a trot as the sun skimmed the mountain tops, its bright oranges already deepening to red. Nala stood with her arms folded, watching him and Sabu depart. She'd sworn to secrecy, and if they weren't back before dawn, she'd get help. How Sabu had managed that, Seti didn't know and had no desire to find out.

After passing the last set of tents on the outskirts of the camp, Chewy and Nimrod picked up the pace. Empty pouches bounced against their sides. Seti longed to break into a full gallop but didn't want to overwork the already thirsty horses. They could run on the way back.

The desert heat blasted against Seti's face, hotter than he remembered. The Cloud Pillar truly did shelter them from the heat. Only after leaving it did it become so apparent. He cringed. How foolish could he be, traveling with his back to God?

The difference in travel time while on horseback as opposed to on foot was less than Seti had anticipated, and they arrived at Elim as the sun disappeared below the horizon. Like entering Goshen after plagues destroyed Egypt, the contrast hit him like a dunk in a cold pond. The sweet scent of desert rose and grass filled his lungs, and the gentle trickle of water calmed his nerves.

He rode Chewy into a shallow stream, dismounted, and knelt in the cool water, slurping it from his cupped hands. Beside him, Sabu stumbled into the flow and dipped his face into the water, lapping it like a dog.

After wiping his mouth, Sabu sat back, leaning on his hands. "This is the best idea you've had in a long time."

Seti smiled. The coolness soothed him, easing the knots in his stomach. A week without water when the Nile turned to blood was one thing, but wandering in the wilderness with nothing but warm goat's milk? He sprawled on his back and let the current wash away weeks of sweat and grime from his skin. Never had he felt so filthy.

"This makes it all worth it." Sabu lay beside him.

Seti could've lain there all night. And why not? Even with dehydrated horses, the trip had been quick, but now he, Sabu, and the horses were replenished. Only one thing dampened the bliss—the threat of danger. With renewed energy, Seti grabbed the pouches from Chewy and got to work.

"Thank you, God," he whispered, his heart sinking at the absence of the Fire Pillar. God was everywhere, right?

"Seti! Berries!" Sabu had climbed out of the stream. He bounced between berry bushes like a giddy girl in a flower patch. Small trees swayed in the breeze along the banks, and high grass grew around the roots and stones, reminding Seti of the stream near the mesa. Pomegranates should be ripe by now. He had missed the evening meal. With heavy pouches hanging from his shoulders and neck, Seti wandered through the shrubs, searching for pomegranates while Sabu dug through the berry bushes.

A tree heavy with fruit stood in the brush a few paces from the stream. What a sight to behold. Seti plucked a pomegranate, sliced it in half with his dagger, then returned the blade to his belt. He bit into the juicy red fruit, closing his eyes as the juices dribbled down his chin. Eliza's family would be overjoyed if he returned with water, pomegranates, and berries.

A twig snapped. Seti's eyes popped open. A burly man towered over him, clad in leather armor beneath a black cloak, its hood casting his face in shadow. A long, braided beard rested on a barreled chest, and the hilt of a sword jutted from under his cloak. Seti's eyes widened. He slowly stood, mouth agape, dwarfed by the man's size. Mocking laughter erupted, first from the man, then from behind. Seti spun. Two more emerged from the shadows. The pomegranate slipped from his hand and hit the ground.

Sabu stood frozen near the berry bush, three hooded figures surrounding him and another holding the reins of the horses. His wide eyes met Seti's just before one of the men shouted, with a fist in the air, startling him.

Seti darted to his left, dropping the pouches. A massive hand clamped down on his shoulder and yanked him backward. The man yelled in a foreign tongue, and before Seti could react, another hand grabbed his arm and twisted it behind him.

"Get off!" Seti cried.

The first man shoved him into a bush and barked a taunting laugh. Seti hit the ground hard. He scrambled to his feet and ripped the dagger from his belt. Panting, he backed away, waving his meager blade. "Stay away!"

The giants glanced at each other, then at Seti, and laughed. Their mysterious darkened figures sent a cold dread coiling down his spine. The men edged closer, backing him deeper into the brush.

Seti turned and bolted onto a path, only to be tackled. The air whooshed from his lungs, as the full weight of his attacker crushed him against the ground. When the weight lifted, he choked and gasped. Before he could turn over, his arms were wrenched behind his back and tied, the dagger ripped from his grasp. They yanked him to his feet.

"Sabu!" he cried, spitting dirt, searching every direction. The darkness had swallowed up Sabu and the horses.

While the giant pushed him toward the stream, Seti's feet dragged, and he stumbled. One of the men grasped the back of his neck and set him on his feet, nudging him along, while the others followed.

Seti ducked out of the man's grasp and spun in the opposite direction, back into the brush. Thorns ripped at his flesh, slowing his progress. Just when he thought he might get away, a massive hand caught him and flung him to the ground. He cried out as the world spun and his vision blurred. He tried rolling away, but somebody grabbed his neck and lifted him into the air, holding him at arm's length.

His legs kicked uselessly. The man dangling him laughed, bathing Seti's face in the pungent odor of his hot breath. Once released, Seti hit the ground, choking. As he struggled to his feet, an enormous fist struck him across the face. Everything went black.

Chapter 11

Seti awoke when he hit the hard ground on his left side. Pain jolted through his torso like a spear. Only his right eye would open. A coarse, woven hood covered his head, cutting off all visibility. Every breath tightened with pain. Panic arose as the memories of what happened came rushing back.

"Seti?" Sabu's voice pierced the darkness.

"Sabu?" Seti's own voice cracked against his sore throat.

Something struck him in the chest, making him gasp.

"Sorry," Sabu whispered.

Attempting to sit up proved futile, as searing pain stunted Seti's movements. He relented and lay on his back, gasping. "Where are we?"

"We're still in Elim. They threw us in a pit."

Seti took a moment to pace his breathing and slow his racing thoughts. "Is your head covered?"

"Yes. We're not far from where they caught us. They tried to make sure we couldn't see, but I glimpsed firelight. It looks like they've set up some kind of camp out here."

"You weren't knocked out?"

"I didn't try to run," Sabu patronized. "I figured we'd have better chances of escaping later if I stayed alert. Thank goodness too, or I'd sound like you right now."

Seti sighed, recalling the final minutes before the

punch. Sweat beaded on his forehead and stung his eyes. "At least we drank first."

"You have got to be the most optimistic idiot I've ever met. Are you serious right now?" Sabu scoffed. "I can't believe I let you talk me into this."

"I'm thankful you came, but I'm sorry too," Seti rasped. "You'd be angry, though, if I had gone alone."

"And you wouldn't have gone alone."

"Maybe."

"Well, maybe. When you fall in love you do stupid things."

"Like you don't?" Seti shot back, then coughed.

"No. I don't let girls cloud my judgment."

"I can think of plenty of times," Seti retorted, shifting to find a comfortable position but failing.

"Hey, I had to work to impress girls. They didn't flock to me like they did to you."

Seti tilted his throbbing head back, taking shallow breaths. He stretched his legs and tried again to sit up. Midway, a sharp pain jabbed his ribs, halting him. Holding his breath, he gritted his teeth and pushed through the pain until he was upright. The rope binding his wrists looped tightly around his neck—a slip knot. Panic set in. His panting exacerbated the pain in his torso, in turn, stunting his breathing.

"Seti." Sabu jarred Seti from his reeling thoughts.

Lightheaded, Seti turned toward Sabu's voice, the woven hood trapping the heat of his breath.

"Seti, you have to calm down. You're going to pass out again."

The harder he tried to slow his gasps, the worse it got. His head throbbed, pulsating his left eye. The head covering tightened, worse than the claustrophobia of Sabu's tent midday. It'd be impossible to escape like this. And if by some miracle he did make it back, there'd be no hiding his battered face from Eliza. Would God even accept him back?

He had betrayed his faith in God. That had to be unforgiveable. The Hebrews would enter the promised land without him, including Eliza.

Even in pitch black, the world spun. Like at the temple, the darkness clung to him like a smothering black sheet. Hopelessness gripped him. The taunting memories from those three nights in Egypt came back as real as ever. He had failed his best friend. Failed his parents. Even Eliza. Most of all, he had failed the Hebrew God.

"Seti. Seti, get a hold of yourself. I need you coherent." Sabu's words echoed in his ears, bringing him to the present.

"God, please help—" Seti fell onto his back, and a fiery pain exploded in his side.

God, please help. Take me back.

Hoshea's gentle words whispered above the panic: "*Seth, it means 'appointed.' The significance will come to you later.*"

As Seti clung to those words, his breathing slowed, and he stared into the fabric with his good eye. God must have a purpose for him despite his mistakes.

Then, clear as day, a thought broke through the fog. His captors had taken one of his daggers, but the other might still be strapped to his thigh.

"Sabu," he whispered, pacing his breaths.

"Are you all right?"

"I think." Seti rolled, carefully, until the hilt of the blade jabbed him. *Thank you, God!* "Are your hands tied?"

"I thought I lost you a second time," Sabu said, a flicker of hope in his voice. "Yes, behind my back, with a rope looped around my neck."

"Are you hurt?" Seti asked.

"A little sore from the landing, but fine," Sabu said. "Whatever you do, don't pull on the rope. You'll choke yourself."

"I noticed." Seti took a breath. "Get the dagger strapped to my leg."

Sabu let out a laugh of disbelief and sidled against him.

"You have anything on you?" Seti asked.

"I had some knives on my belt, but they took them."

Seti inched his leg upward to bring the dagger closer. "That's it."

"Got it!"

Relief spilled from Seti's lungs. "Now cut my rope." He turned his back to Sabu's.

The sound of wood scraping rock froze Seti solid. Sabu dropped the dagger between their hands. An orange sliver of firelight came from above, piercing the thread holes in Seti's hood.

"They're awake," a voice said in Egyptian.

Several others spoke at once in a different tongue, husky and deep.

The Egyptian speaker shouted over the cacophony, silencing the others. "Who are you? Egyptian?"

"Yes," Sabu muttered.

"Louder, boy, I can't hear you from up here."

"Yes, we are from Egypt."

"And what brings you to the desert? You're not with those Hebrews, are you?"

"They took our women, so we're going after them," Sabu answered.

Seti's mouth dropped open, but he stayed quiet.

"Is that so? We happen to know where they are. Maybe when we capture them, we'll throw your women in the pit with you." The other voices erupted in laughter as the Egyptian speaker shouted in a foreign tongue.

"We can help you!" Sabu yelled over the noise. "We can help you."

They quieted.

"And why would we need help from the likes of you two scrawny Egyptians?"

"Our cloaks—they're Hebrew," Sabu said. "If you give them back, we can infiltrate their camp, learn their weaknesses, and find out who their leader is. That way, your attack is certain to succeed."

Silence. Then the man spoke in his native tongue, shifting aside to allow firelight to stream in.

"No," Seti whispered in Hebrew. "We'd lead them right to them."

"Shhh!"

The pit darkened again before the man spoke in Egyptian, voice cold. "You'd warn them. Besides, we already know who their leader is."

Sabu sighed loudly. "We have a common enemy. Let us be your spies."

"And how exactly were you planning to rescue your women from a camp of a million people?"

"What do you think the Hebrew cloaks are for?"

The man laughed, and the others followed suit. Their voices faded to a distant mumble. Seti was about to urge Sabu to continue cutting when the voices returned.

"No, we do not need you," the man said in Egyptian. "You'll stay down there until we decide what to do with you."

Wood scraped rock again, plunging the pit into total darkness.

"So much for that," Sabu muttered as he grabbed the blade and resumed sawing. "How would they know who our leader is?"

"They sent a spy. Eliza's sister told him everything."

The sawing paused. "Wait. You knew they were out here and didn't tell me?"

"I found out right before we left when I spoke with Eliza. That's why I wanted to leave before dark."

Sabu sawed faster. "Why didn't you tell me?"

The dagger jabbed Seti's palm, making him wince. "It wasn't going to change anything."

Sabu yanked the rope, choking Seti. "I'm going to kill you when we get out."

Seti fell sideways, struggling to breathe. He tried to slacken his arms, but it made no difference. One final tug from Sabu, combined with a strong cut, and the rope gave way. As soon as his hands fell free, Seti tore off the hood, loosened the noose, and gulped air. He pounced on Sabu, throwing him onto his back.

"No, you don't!" Sabu rolled and kicked him in the side.

Engulfed in pain, Seti keeled over. He clutched his side, his lungs heaving. After catching his breath, he scrambled to his knees, fumbling in the dark for Sabu.

"Looking for the dagger?" Sabu taunted.

When Seti's hand touched Sabu's foot, he lunged, pushing him against a wall and feeling for the rope. His fingers closed around it, and he yanked. Sabu fell against him, choking. Seti groped the dirt until he felt the hilt of the dagger. He punched Sabu in the stomach, then slashed his rope.

"There," Seti choked out, falling back on his heels and returning the blade to its sheath.

Sabu pulled the hood from his head and tossed it to the floor. He collapsed against the wall, gasping. "Just wait," he rasped.

"You just wait!" Seti shot back.

Neither moved.

After what felt like hours, Seti's mind sharpened. He forced himself to focus on escaping. The lid had sounded like it was made of wood, thankfully lighter than the stone ones in Egypt. They were trapped in a dry cistern, and outside flickered torches or a fire.

He gathered his strength and whispered, "Do you remember a cistern when we camped here?"

"No."

"Where are Chewy and Nimrod?"

"I had a hood over my eyes, remember? How would I know?"

"Well, what do you remember?"

After a moment, Sabu replied, "We're in a wooded area. They were eating something from the trees when they hooded us. Seven of them. More in the distance. I think all men. When we stopped, they took our cloaks, told me to jump in, and tossed you in after."

"Do you remember any weapons?"

"Swords. Knives. Big ones. Before they hooded me."

"What about animals? Horses? Chariots?"

"No. Nothing. They walked. It wasn't far from where they found us. You weren't out long."

"How deep is this pit?"

"Deep enough we can't climb out."

Seti looked up. From the little light that had leaked in earlier, the hole appeared narrow, especially when the giant's body blocked it while speaking. But at the bottom, he and Sabu had enough room to squabble.

"What are you thinking?" Sabu asked.

Seti pushed himself to his feet, one arm braced across his ribs. He dragged his hand along the wall, tracing the circumference, until he tripped over Sabu.

"It's circular, and I think it widens at the bottom." He stepped into the center and spread his arms, but only one hand touched the wall. "I need you to lift me."

"You think you can reach the top?" Sabu grunted as he rose. "It's deeper than that."

"Maybe. I just need to feel it out. Let me stand on your shoulders."

Sabu bumped into him. Seti placed a hand on his shoulders, then one foot into Sabu's cupped hands and climbed up. He thanked God for Sabu's lifetime of labor, which had honed his strength as he unwaveringly held him.

Breathing deeply, Seti let the pain in his ribs subside before saying, "Now, walk around the perimeter slowly. I want to see how wide it gets."

Carefully, Sabu turned with him balanced overhead. Seti stretched out his arms, feeling the wall with both hands. "I have an idea."

He crouched until his fingertips lost contact with the wall and made a mental note of that point in relation to Sabu's head.

"Now what?" Sabu asked.

"Let me down."

Back on the ground, Seti searched the dirt for the ropes, tied them together, then looped the length loosely around his neck.

"Up again," he said, rubbing his hands together. "It's wider down here and narrows as it goes up, like a perfume bottle. I think I can shimmy up."

This time, Seti climbed onto Sabu's shoulders. As Sabu stood, Seti braced himself with one hand on the wall.

"Back me up," Seti directed, facing the opposite direction from Sabu.

"What do you mean?"

"Walk forward until I tell you to stop."

Sabu gingerly stepped forward until Seti's back touched the wall.

"Stop." He took a deep breath and winced. "Okay, brace yourself."

"Brace myself?"

Seti pressed his back against the wall and placed one foot against the opposite side. With a deep breath, he gingerly lifted his other foot into place. His ribs screamed in pain.

"How—"

"I'm right here," Seti moaned. "I can shimmy to the top."

"Good, but what about me?"

"When I get up there, I'll throw the rope down."

"What if it's not long enough, or there's nothing to tie

it to?"

"I'll find something." Seti inched upward, pausing after each movement to let the pain subside. The rock-hard dirt wall cut into his back. When his head hit the wooden lid, he sighed out a long-held breath.

With both hands, he pushed. It wouldn't budge. He shoved harder. His feet slipped, and he froze, heart pounding. Groping for handholds or hinges, he found a small hook on the underside of the lid. Carefully, he looped the rope through it, then dropped it to Sabu.

"Can you reach the rope?" he asked.

Sabu gave it a tug. "Got it."

Seti pushed again, moving it slightly, letting in a sliver of torchlight. "I think there's something on top of the lid. I need your help."

When Sabu tugged on the rope again, the lid slid back into place, cutting out the light. Seti gritted his teeth. But with Sabu's strength, they might be able to move it enough to squeeze through. He counted his breaths, willing the pain to subside as he waited for Sabu.

The sound of Sabu shimmying upward stopped when he bumped into Seti. Perpendicular to each other—with Seti on top and Sabu below—they braced their backs and feet against the wall and pushed. The lid moved. Light streamed in again, illuminating Sabu's smiling face. They heaved it again, this time getting it halfway off. Fresh air swooped in. With a final push, the lid toppled from a stone ledge and landed with a dull thud. A large log that had weighed it down rolled away.

Chapter 12

Seti peered over the rim of the cistern. They were inside a tent, lit by three flickering torches. He hauled himself onto the rock ledge, nearly crying out in pain. Clutching his side, he rolled onto the dirt floor. Sabu pulled himself out while Seti crept to the two cloaks on the ground and searched the pockets for knives. No knives, but the cut twine remained. He tossed Sabu his cloak and slid the cover back over the pit.

"We're clear," Sabu whispered, peeking outside.

After placing the log on top of the lid, the two peered out the tent flap.

Shadowed figures gathered around a towering fire that shot sparks high into the night. Several men danced, creating ominous, shifting shadows. Shouts and chanting rose to a crescendo, accompanied by rhythmic drums.

The drumming and chanting abruptly stopped, and the sudden stillness enhanced the fire's crackle. Fists shot into the air, and a war cry tore through the trees, shattering Seti's nerves. His knuckles whitened around the tent flap. Sabu's wide eyes met his.

"They're celebrating something," Sabu whispered as the cry faded, and the drumming resumed.

Seti bit his lip. "No. They're preparing for something."

"Calling their gods?"

"Let's find our horses and go."

"I hope they didn't eat them," Sabu muttered.

They slipped outside. Darkened tents scattered across the camp, blending into the shadows. Something snorted nearby, startling Seti. He took a deep breath, composed himself, and drifted toward a group of camels. He whispered Chewy's name, not daring to whistle, even over the blaring drums. With his good eye, he made out the shapes of camels, sheep, and goats resting between the tents. But no horses.

The drums halted again. Another war cry split the air. This was no settlement. This was a war camp. Predators.

Seti's stomach gurgled at the rich aroma of roasted meat, even as a chill ran down his spine. Was it human flesh? Horse? He eyed the fire, searching for the aroma's source, but the horde of men blocked his view.

Please God, don't let it be.

Beyond the fire sat a pile of what looked like treasures surrounded by restless animals. Seti nodded at Sabu and inched toward the gathering.

"Where are you going?" Sabu whispered.

"There are more animals over there." And treasures. If he didn't return with water for Homan, he'd better return with something better. "You stay here and search. I'll be back."

Sabu hesitated before nodding and continued toward the first group of animals.

Seti crept to a stand of trees near the fire, keeping to the shadows. Crouching behind a trunk, he surveyed the scene. Men huddled in groups while others danced naked, screaming and throwing items into the fire.

A small baboon, tossed into the flames, screamed violently. The men roared louder. Seti stared, horrified. The drummers to the left stopped, their beastly hands held high. The entire gathering stilled before erupting again with a cry aimed at the blaze. Seti's fingers dug into the warm bark of the tree. The wrenching sounds tore through him. He glanced over his shoulder for Sabu, only to see darkness. Pressing one hand against his ribs, he forced his breathing to slow and focused on the treasure beyond the fire.

Darting from one tree to the next, Seti made his way toward the far side.

Hundreds of men stood in a line, facing the flames, their bulging eyes glowing orange. With feet tapping to the beat of the drums, they raised their left arms, palms facing the fire. An enormous man came forward, holding a woven sheet. His blood-curdling scream pierced the night before he fanned the flames higher.

The drumming shifted from a rhythmic pounding to a soft hum, joined by a flute. The atmosphere's chaotic energy transformed into a hypnotic trance. Seti edged closer, involuntarily swaying to the music.

The flames resembled the Fire Pillar—intense and violent—but without the colors or awe-inspiring sense of protection. And it didn't move as Seti approached. He emerged into the open, eyes fixed on the dancing flames.

So this was what it looked like—Osiris blazing from the heart of the earth, sending the dead adrift into new worlds to rule in righteousness and watch over the living.

Thousands of souls scattered into the expanse of the afterlife, their glow fading as they ceased to exist. At least in this realm. How many had ascended during the last plague of Egypt? Did they shoot into the sky like these, without a burial, mummification, or entombment? Lost with no god to guide them? Did his father's soul wander aimlessly, his light snuffed out in some lost orbit?

A lion's roar shattered Seti's trance. He gasped, standing among the naked men. As one, they raised their knives and sliced their upstretched arms, unflinching, then returned the blades to their sides, arms dripping red, eyes transfixed on the fire. Not one noticed him.

Behind them, a lion, bound to a tree, fought against the rope. It paused, met Seti's gaze, then continued its struggle.

Heart pounding, Seti dashed into the shadows and dove

behind a tent. He stifled a moan as pain shot up his side. What just happened? The Hebrew God protected His people, but this fire, or whatever it was, did no such thing. It would have consumed him if not for that lion.

Was it the fire? The music? Seti's feeble mind? The way it so easily swayed him shook him to the core. He pressed his singed face into the dirt, wishing he could sink into the ground, wanting to grab the feet of the Hebrew God and beg for mercy.

"God, what did I do? I'm so sorry," he prayed.

Nothing made him feel further from God than this debauchery surrounding him. Trembling, he sat back on his heels. He craved the safety of the Fire Pillar and Eliza's gentle touch.

With new resolve, he set his eyes on the treasure ahead. He'd finish what he started and return to the Hebrew camp. If God refused to let him back in, he'd follow behind.

The horde of men continued their ritual, slicing into their flesh to the hypnotic beat, unfazed by the stranger who had run from their midst.

Now was the perfect time. Seti sprang toward the treasure pile, scattering chickens, donkeys, and camels. He rounded the far side. More camels, a small drove of pigs, but no horses.

"Chewy," Seti whispered, scanning every direction. "Nimrod."

He whistled in sync with the tantalizing drums.

Once beyond the treasure pile, he paused. Weapons and clothing mixed with fine instruments, sparkling jewelry, and heaps of gold and silver. He planted his feet and dragged a massive sword from the mound. Hoisting it over his head, he held his breath until no longer able to bear the pain. Grasping his side, he dropped it. Everything here was huge. Did these men battle only those of equal size?

Seti scanned the pile for something he could carry: a knife or a dagger. A harp caught his eye, tangled in canvas and surrounded by drums and lutes. Lutes! Seti climbed through the trove and grabbed the nearest one, but it was nearly as long as he was tall. Another jutted from beneath a set of drums, but its strings were broken. An ivory lute, still large but more manageable, came out intact. Seti rummaged for more but only found tambourines and flutes, all oversized.

The drumming stopped. Seti straightened, lute in hand. Cheers erupted. Shouting followed. Then the roar of the lion. What were they doing? Seti hurried to the ground, looped his rope through the lute, and secured it to his back. Something shimmered ahead at the foot of the mound.

Half unsheathed, a golden sword fit for a giant lay in the dirt, stuck out from a tangled rug. Seti pulled the blade free. Smooth as still water, the golden edge glistened in the moonlight. He ran a finger down the edge. Who would fight with a gold sword? A dull one at that. Of all the weapons lying around, this was the only gold one. Inscribed in the hilt were four unfamiliar silver symbols.

He gritted his teeth and struggled to lift it with both hands before setting it down and gasping for breath. Fighting with it would be impossible, but Homan might trade for it.

Another round of cheers broke out, followed by a drum-roll. Seti sheathed the sword and tied it to the lute, swung them over his shoulder, and hurried into the trees.

Even after Seti's good eye adjusted to the dark, the tents all looked alike. The cool air refreshed his face, and adrenaline surged through his veins as he searched for Sabu or the horses.

A pig dashed past, nearly tripping him. Pulse racing, he paused in the brush, wondering if he had gone in the right direction.

"Psst!"

Seti ducked behind a thick tree trunk, holding his

breath.

"It's me. Over here." Sabu stepped out from behind a tent, Chewy and Nimrod in tow.

How? Were they just fortunate or did the Hebrew God guide them in the right direction? Seti hurried toward them.

"Chewy!" He wrapped his arms around the horse's neck and squeezed, whispering prayers of thanks.

"What about me? Aren't you glad to see me?" Sabu whispered.

Seti chuckled and embraced Sabu. "Where'd you find them?"

"By the tent. Right after you left. I've been waiting the whole time. What'd you get?"

If God truly had a hand in this, then He'd accept them back into the camp. That would be the answer. Seti removed the sword and lute from his shoulder and handed them to Sabu, breathing easier without the extra weight.

"This is gold." Sabu drew the sword from its sheath and ran his thumb along the blade.

"Yes."

"The whole thing. Even the hilt." Sabu pointed it straight ahead, his arm shaking from the weight. He gripped it with both hands and raised it overhead, then tried a downward swing, letting the momentum spin him. "Is it one of theirs? It's huge."

"It was in the treasure pile. Everything's big. Who fights with a gold sword?"

"I don't think it's for fighting." Sabu stabbed the air again. "It's a trophy." He stuck the tip in the dirt and let it stand. "What are you going to do with it?"

"Hopefully, the merchant will take it."

Sabu glanced at the horses. "Right. The pouches and canteens are still at the stream."

Seti took the sword and sheathed it. "It's time to leave." He gingerly mounted Chewy. "This place is full of evil."

Once a safe distance from Elim, Seti glanced back. The trees stood black against the starlit sky with no trace of the ceremonial fire, no rumble of cheers.

The stars twinkled, unmoving. Not gods. Not the afterlife. Just the constellations and the vast canvas Eliza had spoken of. A shooting star crossed the sky, and he shuddered, recalling his trance near the warrior's fire.

Sabu rode ahead. "Which way?"

"This way." Seti turned Chewy north, knowing Elim lay south of the Hebrew multitude.

"How do you know?"

Pointing to the brightest star in the sky, Seti said, "Thuban is always due north. Pharaoh Khufu aligned his burial chambers with it to guide souls to the afterlife." Soaring orange sparks rising into the darkness flooded Seti's mind.

What would Eliza say about Thuban?

"What am I going to tell Eliza?" he muttered.

"About what?"

"Look at me."

Sabu rode up close and scrutinized Seti's face. With a grin, he said, "That you're a fool. That I saved your hide just like I said I would. Tell her it was me who blackened your eye—after I saved you, of course."

"I can't lie. She'll find out sooner or later." Seti's head throbbed from the mess he'd made. Add to that the dreadful prospect of being denied re-entry into the camp. And if he were allowed in, would Homan even accept the trade?

Chapter 13

Sunlight beat against the goatskin canvas, heating the tent like the outhouse in Egypt, though at least there, Eliza had been able to sweat. She sat up on her mat, wiped her brow out of habit, and waited for the spinning in her head to subside. Two baskets of manna sat near the tent flap. Miera had woken her earlier to help collect breakfast, but Eliza had nodded off again.

The heat she could take, but with no water—not only would her head never heal, but she'd probably be the first to die. Her carcass would be left in the desert for the buzzards. She blinked away the thought and peeked outside. The manna had long since vanished, and nobody sat around the firepit. The dryness in her mouth stifled her voice as she called for her mother and Miera.

She cleared her throat and tried again. "Ima? Miera?"

"The girls are sleeping," came her mother's hushed reply from the other tent.

The morning milk ration remained on the wagon bed, shaded by a shelf. Eliza rose to get some but paused at the sight of the lump outside Sabu's tent. Seti never slept this late. She started toward him but stumbled, her head pounding. She steadied herself against a tent post until the spinning subsided, then tried again.

"Seti?" She knelt and pulled his cloak aside, revealing a black-and-blue face so swollen his left eye was nothing but a slit. Eliza gasped and fell back on her heels.

A crooked grin lifted Seti's pitiful face, and he opened his good eye. "You're a sight to behold when waking." He pushed himself up but winced and fell back.

Eliza leaned closer, inspecting the red marks and raw gashes across his neck. Who could have done this to him? Who would dare? "Seti, what happened? Who did this to you?"

He tried again, this time holding his side as he sat up and leaned against a log.

"What happened?" She reached for his cheek but hesitated, afraid of hurting him.

He averted his gaze, his smile gone.

Eliza gently moved the dark strands of hair from his eyes, revealing the bruises in full. The contrast was shocking—one side of his face held only traces of his once chiseled jaw and beautiful cheekbone; the other was a swollen, discolored mass, leaving his mouth askew. When he blinked, his left eye only twitched.

"Seti, tell me."

"I had to get your gifts for the betrothal." His voice broke, and he cleared his throat.

"What?"

"I went back to Elim with Sabu to get water to purchase the gifts."

"You went to Elim? You left the camp?" Her tone rose, sharper than she intended.

He winced as if she'd slapped him.

"You told me not to leave God's protection, and then you did it yourself?"

He nodded and dropped his gaze, rolling a piece of grass between his fingers. Sabu peeked from his tent but quickly ducked back inside when Eliza glared at him. The pounding in her head synced with her racing pulse.

"Eliza," Seti said softly, reaching for her hand, but she pulled it away. "Eliza. I can't marry you without a betrothal gift. You deserve the best. And I found the perfect one but had nothing to trade. The merchant wanted water, so we went to Elim."

She looked away, crossing her arms. He could be reckless, stupid even. Especially when it came to girls. But this time she was the girl. The thought settled over her, and her anger softened. "What if you never came back? Nobody would know where to look for you. I could have lost you."

"Nala knew. We told her to get help if we didn't return by morning."

"Sabu told her, but you couldn't be honest with me?" Her voice rose again.

Seti sighed, looking down. "He wasn't going to tell her, but she overheard us."

"What about me?" Eliza stood and turned away, but he caught her hand. Dizziness swept through her, and she stumbled into his arms. Annoyed, she pushed away but was too weak. Her dramatic exit had faltered.

"Don't run away from me, Eliza." He placed her hand on his heart. How could he do this—take advantage of her weakness? Use sweet words and pitiful gestures to pacify her?

"It's not fair," she whispered. "You're the one who left camp, put yourself in danger, but you get the water while the rest of us suffer." She closed her eyes as he brushed the dark curls from her face.

"We couldn't bring any back," he said. "Though we did have a drink, but then we got captured. And I did suffer, obviously."

"Captured?" Of course he was captured. His face didn't get like that from the ride. She pressed her lips together to keep them from quivering, unable to think straight or control her wavering voice. If there were any tears left, they'd come pouring out.

"They were the same men you saw. I'm sure of it. They threw us into a pit, but we escaped. All is well." His words were quick and clipped, as if avoiding the details. He ran a gentle finger down her cheek. She should be comforting him, not the other way around.

"No, Seti. All is not well."

Seti started to say more but stopped and felt her forehead. She was burning up. He shifted against the log, then leaned her head against his shoulder. Why hadn't he searched for the pouches in Elim and brought back water? He had been so focused on making it out alive that the thought had eluded him.

Finding his way back from Elim had been easy once the Fire Pillar came into view, and nothing prevented him and Sabu from re-entering the camp. Once his adrenaline had faded, exhaustion set in, and Seti evidently slept through the morning.

"Did you get milk today?" he asked, masking the worry in his voice.

Eliza shook her head.

"I should find some. You don't look well."

"No. Just have somebody bring it."

Seti gently rested her against the log, his muscles and ribs screaming in protest. "I'm going."

"I'll be fine, Seti," Eliza murmured, reaching for him. "I'm just tired. Got up too fast."

He smoothed the hair from her face. "I'll be right back."

He hurried to her family's tents. The larger one stood open, breeze filtering in through the flap. Inside, Sarah and Miera sprawled on a mat, the twins sleeping between them. Sarah traced circles on one of the girls' foreheads, humming softly. Not wanting to disturb them, Seti looked in the other tent, but it was empty.

"Seti?" Sarah gasped. "My dear, what happened?"

She started toward him, but he turned away, embarrassed. "Is there any milk left?"

She sighed. "Some. Not much, I'm afraid. Yours is on the wagon."

"Thank you."

Nine cups lined the wagon's ledge. Seven were empty. Seti combined the remaining two into one, filling it half full, then returned to Eliza.

"Eliza." He knelt beside her and lifted her chin. "Drink."

She took the cup and drained it in three large gulps.

"That's all there was," he said.

Eliza nodded. Her brow crinkled as if seeing him for the first time. Her mouth opened, but nothing came out, and her shoulders slumped. Seti sat beside her, resting her head again on his shoulder.

In the distance, Adam crouched among the livestock, tugging at udders with a small bowl in his hand. Seti sat up and rubbed his eyes. That greedy scoundrel. But Adam was alone, and now Seti had the upper hand. He gently lifted Eliza's sleeping face from his shoulder. He must've nodded off as well. How long had he been out? His body ached, begging for rest, but he helped Eliza back to her tent, then set off through the herd until coming up behind Adam working on a goat.

With arms crossed, Seti watched. Only a few squirts joined what little was already in Adam's bowl. "Cow and now goat's milk? What about sheep?"

Adam startled, dropping the bowl and spilling half its contents in the dirt. He cursed and glared at Seti before gulping down the little he'd salvaged.

"Eliza's sick," Seti said evenly. "She could've used

that."

"We're all sick!"

"She's worse than just thirsty, Adam."

Adam wiped his mouth with the back of his hand and stood eye to eye with Seti. He lifted his finger to poke Seti's swollen cheek. "You lose a fight?"

Seti swatted Adam's hand away. "Over water. Better than stealing."

"That looks like more than a fist fight." Adam rubbed his neck and stepped back.

The raw burning on Seti's neck returned. "I need your help."

"Now what?"

Seti stepped past him. "Walk with me."

With a scoff, Adam followed, the empty bowl in hand.

"I want to talk to your abba," Seti began. "I'll have the mohar and mattan soon. Do I ask him casually? Is there a formality? How do I arrange the betrothal?"

"Seriously? I thought you were in some kind of trouble. You made me spill my milk over a stupid betrothal?"

Seti stopped, his hands balling into fists. He'd make Adam's face match his if he weren't Eliza's brother. "You told me to come to you first. I'm respecting your wishes, but clearly you've changed your mind."

He turned on his heel and started back when Adam spoke. "Fine. Yes, I wanted you to come to me first. Eliza's my sister, after all, and I don't want her embarrassed." He muttered something under his breath.

Seti ignored it, faced him, and raised a brow.

"Ask my abba when he's relaxed, preferably with the whole family around. If he accepts, Ima will invite the guests and organize the gathering."

"When? How long will it take?" Seti didn't care about guests.

"Depends on how they take the news. But it's only a

day."

"I thought it was seven," Seti said.

"No, that's the wedding. The betrothal only takes a day, usually starting midday and lasting until evening." Adam paused and looked at Seti. "But don't get me wrong. It's more important than the wedding. Everything is set during the betrothal, and the wedding is just a celebration. That and the consummation."

"Consummation?"

"You know."

"No, I don't."

"Don't make me say it."

"Say what?"

Adam sighed loudly and strode ahead. "I thought you were educated. Consummation. You know, where you take her home and make love, two become one."

Seti smirked and shook his head. "Never heard that word before. Why didn't you just say 'make love'?"

Rolling his eyes, Adam waved a hand. "Anyway, the betrothal is the business transaction. The wedding comes later—the seven-day party that ends with the consummation."

"Business transaction. Got it." Seti pushed past a stubborn sheep. "What happens at the betrothal? What else do I need?"

Adam slowed, forcing Seti to do the same. "The transaction is made at the betrothal, right? Gifts exchanged, ketubah read, witnesses present, then we eat. Maybe dance. Afterward, life goes on as normal until you're ready for the wedding, when you have a place prepared for her."

"What's a ketubah?" Seti asked before Adam could make a snide remark about him being homeless.

"The contract. You write it, read it out loud—I mean, sing it—so all witnesses can hear, and then all parties sign it, including her. Like a covenant. She agrees in everybody's hearing. Another thing that distinguishes a wife from a concubine."

"Sing it?"

"Yes. Singing formalizes it. It's tradition. Everybody sings it now."

Seti turned to head back. "How do I know what to put in it?"

"I don't know. I'm not married. Ask somebody. Don't forget to blow the ram's horn too, before singing it. It ensures everyone's awake and paying attention. The more witnesses, the better."

"What?"

"More tradition. Very important. If even one person is nodding off or distracted, it's a bad omen."

Seti arched a brow. Since when did Hebrews care about omens? "That sounds like an Egyptian—"

"If you don't like our customs, then don't marry a Hebrew." Adam snapped. "You were circumcised, were you not? You must follow every tradition of our people. Speaking of which, you must declare your allegiance to our tribe in the ketubah. We are Levites, if you didn't already know. That matters."

Seti nodded.

Adam put a finger to his lips. "Maybe I should write it for you."

"No. I can write my own ketubah. I know Hebrew script." Adam's sudden willingness to help stirred Seti's suspicions. "So that's it. Your abba makes the announcement, I blow the horn and sing the ketubah, everyone agrees, signs it, I give her the gifts, and that's it? What should I wear?"

"Something clean, obviously."

"Obviously."

"Consecrate yourself the night before."

"Consecrate myself? Like Egyptian priests?" Finally, something that made sense.

"Exactly. Bathe and shave. Leave nothing behind. Not

a single hair. God is a witness, you know." Adam tapped an eyebrow. "Brows too."

"Does Eliza shave too?" Though most women in Egypt were bald, Seti couldn't imagine Eliza without her big hair.

"No, only the groom."

"I can't bathe without water," Seti said, his mind whirling.

"Of course." Adam glanced around as if searching for someone.

Several donkeys brayed as Seti stopped where he'd started, the sea of tents beginning only a few paces away. His gaze drifted uphill to Sabu's tent. The position not only allowed him to oversee the Avaris group, but was strategic, considering the threats from both within and without. With Eliza asleep, now would be a good time to meet Homan. Then, maybe Seti could catch a nap before supper.

Chapter 14

The group Homan had joined dismantled their camp in a quiet frenzy, as if the Cloud Pillar had taken off. Children lay about in the dirt with restless livestock, while adults crammed wagons full, not bothering to fold their linen or organize their wares. Their urgency sent Seti's heart racing. He scanned the horizon for giants but found none. To his relief, Homan hadn't left yet, though he'd packed away his tables and shelves. Several sacks of goods sat behind the wagon, and the net of sandals already hung from the back. The Sidonian covered his wagon with a canvas, tying it down as Seti approached on Chewy.

Seti dismounted and cleared his throat.

"Whoa!" Homan recoiled.

Seti rolled his good eye. He should've hidden his face behind a turban.

"What happened?"

"I went to Elim for water." He kept his gaze hard on Homan, refusing to let the embarrassment or desperation show.

Homan squinted, scrutinizing Seti's face. "I thought you weren't doing that."

"Well, I did."

"And?" Homan spread his hands, glancing at Chewy.

"I found water but got caught and had to escape, losing it in the process. But I did bring back something." Before

Homan could protest, Seti opened his cloak and drew the golden sword from the sheath strapped to his shoulder. He pointed the sword skyward, the gold gleaming in the afternoon sunlight.

Homan's eyes widened.

"I found it in the camp where I was captured. They are giants, hence the size of the sword." Holding the sword across both hands, Seti offered it to the merchant.

Homan took it by the hilt, his lips parting. He ran a finger down the edge and touched the point, then angled it toward the sunlight, watching it shimmer as he turned it. A smile crossed his face, revealing broken teeth.

Seti gave him a moment. "I don't know if it's solid gold or just overlaid. It might have been a trophy or something."

"By the weight, it's pure gold," Homan said, examining the etchings in the hilt. "Your captors were descendants of the Nephilim. Must be the Zamzummin. Or Amalekites."

"The what?"

"The Nephilim. Demigods. Giants who ruled the world before the great flood. Only a few continued after but much smaller in stature. These men might have been large, but nothing like their ancestors."

The great flood? The one that brought the rainbow? "Demigods…like Pharaoh?"

"Perhaps, though Pharaoh is likely more human than he'd admit." Homan extended the sword, the muscles in his arm bulging as he held it steady. "It's a wonder you escaped. I've never met anyone who crossed paths with a giant and lived."

"They didn't seem very bright for demigods." Seti shifted. The only things that lived out here, according to the temple scribes, were evil spirits.

The little monkey appeared on top of the wagon and *oohed* at the sword, coming near with arms spread. Homan ignored him. "Or you were protected by your God. Those kinds are beyond evil. That's why they roam the deserts. They'd been cast out here by the gods to fight each other to the death."

"Do I look like I was protected?" Seti's voice caught as he tried to hide the impact of Homan's words. Despite the retort, the lion at the ceremony roared in Seti's mind. Did God have a hand in that? Seti shivered at his stupidity. If he'd known the giants were reputed to be so evil, he wouldn't have risked everything—especially Sabu's life—for a couple of gifts.

Homan nodded, then motioned for the sheath with his hand. "There's always a price, even when you're protected."

Seti handed him the sheath. "What can I get for it?"

A peculiar glance passed between Homan and the monkey before he turned back to Seti. He ran his hand over the blade again. "Three items."

Perfect. Seti blew air from his cheeks and pulled the twine from his pocket. "I want the sandals with the turquoise gems in this size, the blue cotton I picked out earlier, and a stack of papyri."

Three pairs of turquoise-adorned sandals landed on the ground with soft thuds. Seti measured them against his twine while Homan searched for the rest.

"You seem revived," Homan said. "Must've had a drink before getting caught?"

"I did."

"Rumor says Moshe found water in Horeb with the tribal leaders. We're to catch up." Homan dropped the large bolt of fabric beside the sandals and opened one of the sacks.

Seti's head shot up. "In Horeb? Where's that?"

"A day's walk northeast. Sounds like you were right about your God."

"Of course I was," Seti muttered, placing the pair closest to Eliza's size under his arm. "Do you have any pouches or jars?"

"I'll give you three pouches as your third purchase."

The papyri would have to wait. "That'll work."

Homan's lips twisted as he studied Seti before fetching three large leather pouches from his wagon. "Your people must be way in the back, I presume."

"The very back." Seti threaded his rope through the sandals and around the fabric bolt, then laid them across Chewy's back with the three leather pouches. He patted the monkey's head, thanked Homan, and mounted Chewy.

The desert hills gradually transformed into mountainous terrain as Seti rode north. Though brown and lifeless, they held a certain beauty against the bright blue sky. Still, a faint disappointment settled on him. Greenery covered the mountains he'd read about, and cold streams tumbled from their white peaks, rushing toward the foothills. He hoped Canaan had such mountains. For now, he'd have to settle for the desert version.

Loose rocks, tumbleweeds, and drab bushes dotted the valley ahead, where the front of the multitude materialized. Seti made quick progress on Chewy, but it would be a long walk for the Avaris group, and he questioned if they'd even make it this far by dusk. If he ever managed to acquire a tent of his own, he'd keep Eliza near Moshe, never again to let her decline the way she had.

A small group of men strolled ahead of the multitude toward a pile of stone and rock, topped with a giant boulder. But as they ascended the formation, its size became apparent as they appeared as ants. This was no pile but a hill.

Seti grabbed the leather pouches and left Chewy with a drove of donkeys. He flung the hood of his cloak over his head and continued toward the group on foot.

Two men reached the summit first and addressed the others below. Seti paused to listen among a group of onlookers. Moshe stood confidently, his long white beard blowing in the breeze and his robe buffeting against his legs. His deep voice rang out, but the wind stole his words away.

Aharon moved around Moshe, closer to the enormous rock towering over them. He tilted his head back, surveying it, one hand on his staff, the other on his hip. The crowd around Seti grew, shielding their eyes and clasping their cloaks closed against the hot wind.

Moshe lifted his hands high before taking the staff from Aharon. He struck the rock hard with the staff. An earth-shattering crack echoed off the surrounding mountains, startling Seti. The boulder fractured straight down the middle. Water burst through with such power it sprayed well beyond the hill, forcing the men with Moshe and Aharon to jump aside. The deluge settled into a steady, frothy flow, sparkling in the sun.

Seti stepped forward, awestruck. Cheers erupted. Bystanders broke out running. The intensity of the flow dislodged rocks and earth with it, sending a torrent rushing into the valley toward the mountains where the Cloud Pillar hovered.

Seti bolted, his hood flying off, pouches dangling from his hand. The jarring pain in his ribs nearly made him stumble.

Gasps and laughter filled the air as people splashed into the flow in the valley where its force had waned. Seti gingerly stepped in, letting it wash the dried blood from his legs. He knelt, lowered his face into the current, and flinched as the force stung his wounds. He filled a pouch and poured it over his head, letting it run down his face and over his swollen eye, plastering his hair against his cheeks. It tasted sweet, like the waters of Marah when God had transformed the water from bitter to sweet. A vibrant energy swept through his body and out his mouth in uncontrollable laughter.

The Great God had provided. Why He'd waited so long, Seti didn't know and no longer cared. They had water.

Cool, refreshing, cleansing, sweet water. Enough not only to drink, but to bathe in.

The crowd rushed in, filling the rapids until there was little room to move. Singing and hilarity erupted as the people filled their pouches and jars, dipped their heads, and splashed each other. Moshe and Aharon had long since departed the strange rock, but the water continued to gush. As the animals pushed their way into the swelling river, Seti filled his pouches then shouldered through the crowd to get out.

Once free of the congestion, Seti shot a "thank you" toward the Cloud Pillar. It took three whistles before Chewy emerged from a herd of cattle downstream. The water in Elim paled in comparison to the energy and strength this water provided. Like the manna, it carried something special. Something divine. He slung the pouches over Chewy's back and mounted, anxious to return to Eliza.

Chapter 15

Seti dismounted and hid the gifts with the lute behind the log.

"Guess what I have?" He flung open the flap to Sabu's tent.

Nala sat up, her face flushed and sweaty.

"Take Nala to the mountains. Moshe and Aharon brought water out of a rock. Lots of it!"

"What?" Sabu sat up, rubbing his eyes.

"Let's go." Nala nudged him.

"Are you serious?" He scrunched his face. "After all we did last night?"

"I told you God would provide," Seti said.

"Did you get what you wanted?" Sabu asked, slipping on his sandals.

"I sure did! They're behind the log." Seti held up the pouches. "And I brought some water for Eliza's family. Take Nimrod. It'll take a while to get there. At the mountains."

Sabu and Nala exchanged excited glances.

"I'm not packing anything." Nala crawled toward the flap. "I just need a drink."

"Let's go, fill up, and come back." Sabu crawled after her.

"Better yet, take a bath. You both need one!" Seti called as he headed toward Eliza's tent.

Miera peeked out from her tent. "What's happening?"

"I have water!" Seti hurried over and handed her one of the water pouches.

She stared, mouth agape, but Sarah snatched the pouch from her. "How? From where?"

"Moshe and Aharon went ahead to the mountains. They made water come out of a rock. I brought some back." He opened Eliza's tent flap.

"Oh, Seti." Sarah poured a little into her hand and looked at him with an expression of endearment and joy so intense he thought she might throw herself on him.

He turned away, cheeks warming. "Where are Jeremiah and the boys?"

"I don't know. Somewhere. I'll give them this one, and we'll keep the other." She hurried to where the twins slept.

A mixture of rank body odor and sweaty feet wafted from Eliza's tent. Seti took a breath and stepped in. Heaps of dirty linen filled the small space. He let out a slow exhale. Eliza sprawled out on a sandy mat, her hair covering her face.

Thankful Sarah hadn't followed him inside, Seti let the flap close. He dropped to his knees beside Eliza and moved her hair aside to feel her forehead. Same as before. He ran a hand through his hair, checked the flap behind him, then folded his hands, and knelt over Eliza.

"Oh, God," he whispered. "Yahweh, is it? I know I haven't been very good to you lately, but this isn't about me. Please make Eliza better. Completely better this time. Please—"

"Seti?" Eliza opened her eyes and lifted her head. Her voice came out groggy. "What are you doing in here? What if my parents see you?"

Seti released a breath and smiled. "Look. I have water." He held up the remaining pouch.

Her brow furrowed, and she stared, eyes glossed over, before grabbing it and tearing it open.

"How are you feeling?" he asked. "Did you get any sleep?"

Eliza gasped at the contents, then chugged it.

Seti smiled. "Don't forget to breathe."

She guzzled, tilting her head back. Seti was sure she'd drain the whole thing. Instead, she suddenly lurched forward, spewing water everywhere. The pouch dropped from her hands, and she doubled over, trembling, tears streaming down her pale cheeks.

"Wha—?" Seti's gaze darted between her and the pouch. "Eliza?" He reached to touch her face, but she shot up a hand.

"What happened?" he squeaked, heart racing.

She stared at the mess, shaking.

The flap opened, and Sarah rushed in, dropping to her knees beside her daughter. She cupped Eliza's face, glanced at the pouch beside her, then back to Eliza. "You drank too much too fast. You must take it slow."

Seti inched backward, not wanting to leave but feeling intrusive.

"Seti." Sarah turned to him, eyes gentle. "I'll take it from here. You did well, but give it some time, and she'll feel better. Now, if you please, I don't want my husband finding you in this tent."

Seti nodded and glanced at Eliza, whose hand went to her mouth as if to vomit again. She gripped her mother's shoulder, not once looking at Seti. Why had God let her get so sick? What if Seti had never gone to Homan? The Avaris group would've been the last to learn of God's provision, and Eliza would have never reached the mountains.

He blew air from his nostrils and left.

Sabu and Nala were gone.

Seti knelt by the log and clawed at his hair with a groan. There was no privacy in this place. Nowhere to vent his frustrations without making a show of himself. The

Cloud Pillar tugged at his heart, though he refused to look at it.

He had barely collected his thoughts when Miera bounded his way. She skidded in the dirt, nearly crashing into him. He drew in a breath as she threw her arms around his neck.

"You saved us!"

He grunted and pried her off—careful of the raw gashes around his neck. She knelt in front of him, eyes round with wonder. "What happened to your face?"

"I got punched," he said, wishing he'd hidden in Sabu's tent.

Miera gasped. "You were in a fight?"

"Sort of."

"I didn't know you did stuff like that." She tilted her head, chin in her hand as if he were a peculiar object. "Did you win? Well, obviously not. What happened? Who was it?"

Miera and her endless questions. Seti ran his fingers through his hair. "I'll tell you if you keep it a secret."

With a squeal, she plopped down beside him. "I'm ready. I promise I won't tell a soul."

He looked sideways at her, a smile forming. "You won't? Because you already gave important information to a complete stranger."

Miera's mouth opened, and she dropped her gaze. "I didn't mean to. Really, I didn't. Plus, no one said anything was a secret. I thought everybody knew about us. That man didn't seem like a bad person." She twisted the hem of her tunic. "He fooled me. Seti, I swear, I didn't mean to."

He started to speak, but she rushed on. "Nobody knows but Eliza and Rahel. They're both angry with me. And now you." She turned away.

"I'm not angry."

Her damp eyes met his, stirring his heart like her mother had earlier.

"I'm not upset. You didn't know. And what we're doing isn't a secret, but you must be careful who you talk to. Next time a stranger approaches, come get Eliza or me. He could have taken you. Bad people usually pretend to be friendly at first."

"I know, I know. I'm sorry," she whispered.

"It's a lesson learned. Now you won't do it again, will you?"

"No. I promise I won't."

"Good. Now, you ready for my secret?"

She nodded with a slight smile and inched closer.

He pulled the sandals and linen from behind the log and shook the sand from them. After a quick nod toward Miera, he stuffed them back into hiding.

Miera's gaze darted between him and the log.

"I want to marry Eliza, and they're for the betrothal. Sabu and I went to Elim to get water so I could purchase these. But a group of men like the one who approached you caught us." He pointed to his face. "One of them did this."

Miera grimaced, pulling her knees to her chest. "How did you escape?"

Seti shoved back Homan's eerie words echoing in his head. "They were too distracted to see us leave. And I found a gold sword at their camp and used that to purchase the sandals and cloth."

"They took you to their camp?"

"Yes. At Elim."

"Wow!"

"But it's a secret. Don't tell anyone." Seti put a finger to his lips. "And the betrothal's a secret too."

Miera nodded, face beaming. "Not a word!" She stood and dusted off her tunic.

"Not even your ima," he said.

"Nobody. I promise, Seti. You can trust me."

"And no wandering off on your own, either. We may move toward the mountains soon, so stay close to the camp."

He pointed to his face. "I should know."

"I only left because I was looking for Eliza. She left first."

"She did? Why?"

"She … well, that's another secret." She quickly dropped her gaze, her spark dimming.

Seti narrowed his eyes. Eliza was keeping secrets too? Manna only appeared within the camp, so she hadn't actually left, which meant the spy had breached the boundary.

"I'm going to help Ima now. Bye, Seti!" Miera waved and skipped toward the tents.

She bounced down the hill, and Seti whispered a "thank you" to God that she'd approached him. He and Eliza were overdue for a walk and an honest conversation. Head pounding, Seti rolled onto his back against Sabu's tent. The sun had moved westward, taking the tent's shadow with it. He must have slept a while. Though his body begged to go back to sleep, his mind reeled. Was this what a head injury felt like? A pounding skull, exhaustion, and pain pulsating with every breath? Or was this simply the healing process? He wiped the sweat from his forehead and sat up.

"Look at that face!"

Seti jerked as a strange girl knelt beside him. How long had she been there? He flinched at her overpowering flowery fragrance.

"Did I surprise you? I saw you earlier and just had to bring some balm." Long blonde hair framed her face, fluttering in the breeze. She dipped her fingers into a deep-blue ampule then reached for his cheek.

He caught her hand roughly before she made contact. "What are you doing?"

She lifted her blue eyes to his and smiled, revealing a row of straight, white teeth. "I'm only trying to help."

He eyed the balm on her delicate, smooth fingers. "You weren't a slave?"

She looked too poised, too polished to be a slave. Her

pale pink tunic enhanced her eyes and accented her olive skin in an exotic way that reminded him of the girls who fanned Pharaoh's throne. Her silky hair was no wig either. She couldn't be Hebrew and definitely wasn't Egyptian.

"Of course I was a slave, silly." She touched her chest as if surprised.

Maybe the balm would help him heal faster. Smirking, he released his grip and allowed her to apply it. She gently smoothed the concoction over his cheek in small circles. There was a coolness to it.

"Eucalyptus and spearmint, if you're wondering." Her gaze locked onto his as her fingers drifted downward, tracing the gashes around to the back of his neck. Tingles shot down his spine, and his chest warmed. Her soft pink lips parted, and her breath brushed over his face.

"I'm Sena." Her voice held a childlike quality. "I'm akin to Eliza. Our fathers are cousins. I couldn't help but notice you on your horse. You have quite the control over that beast. Beautiful, if I must say."

Seti struggled not to react to her boldness and tried as he might to ignore the shivers shooting from where her fingertips teased his skin.

"Eliza must be sleeping like usual, yes? She sleeps a lot."

That snapped him from his trance. He pushed her hand away. Sena was no different than the Egyptian girls back home. He glanced around for a flock of giggling friends. Sure enough, three heads ducked behind a bull nearby. Annoyance replaced his intrigue as he squared off to face her. "She doesn't sleep well at night. She's parched and sick. We'll marry when she's better."

Sena placed the ampule into a small hemp sack tied at her waist, unfazed. She flashed a sultry gaze through her lashes and twirled a lock of hair with her finger. "I heard Moshe found water and was wondering if you could take me there."

Seti laughed. "You are something else. You want me to take you to Horeb? I just got back from there. I'm not returning until we pack up and leave."

Grabbing Seti's hand, she pleaded with wide eyes. "Oh, please. I haven't had a drink in so long. I even brought a pouch to fill for my family." She nodded toward a small leather pouch on the sand.

She hadn't come for water. That much was obvious. Even in the middle of the desert with a bruised and battered face, he couldn't escape the fawning. "You want me to take you all the way to Horeb for water?"

Her resolve fractured slightly, and she straightened. "I was hoping you could." She lifted a hand to her forehead as if on the verge of fainting. Her kohl-rimmed eyes rounded, and her luscious bottom lip stuck out.

Seti pulled his hand away and hesitated. If he took her, he'd be falling straight into her trap. Yet something inside him longed to go. Besides, Eliza could use more water.

Chapter 16

The last thing Eliza remembered was Seti's bruised, pitiful face staring at her after she vomited. Her mother had limited her to small sips of water at a time. She sat up on her mat and threw off her blanket, bracing for dizziness, but it never came.

"Are you better now?" Miera asked, sitting cross-legged beside her.

Eliza nodded. "I think so. Where'd the water come from?"

"Seti brought three pouches and said there's more, but we have to go there to get it."

"Go where?"

"To Moshe, by the mountains."

Sweet, precious Seti. Eliza found a comb at the foot of her mat and ran it through her hair. The past week had drifted by like a dream. Had Seti really gone to Elim? Really gotten caught and beaten? She tied her hair back with a strip of cloth as Miera watched silently, chin in her hand. A small giggle escaped Eliza as she rummaged through the linen for a clean tunic. It was amazing what a little drink could do.

"I need more water," she said as she pulled the sweaty tunic over her head and donned a clean one.

Miera dashed out with the cup but returned just as fast, the cup empty, face pale.

"What is it?" Eliza paused at her ghostly pallor.

Miera shook her head.

"Out with it, Miera."

"Water's gone," Miera whispered.

There had to be something more to elicit that face. Eliza's throat tightened. "What is it?"

Miera shook her head, and Eliza grabbed the cup from her hand. She opened the tent just as Seti boosted Sena onto Chewy. Her breath caught, and the cup hit the ground with a thud. Seti mounted in front of Sena, three pouches dangling from his shoulder. His face was bruised and swollen. It hadn't been a dream. He had really gone to Elim. Sena slipped her arms around his waist and pressed herself against him, letting out a little yelp when Chewy moved.

Eliza sprang to her feet but stopped short of bolting after them. The air left her lungs. Seti rode away with Sena clinging to him. The world spun, and Eliza's headache returned with a vengeance. Her legs gave out, and she crumpled to the ground at the tent's entrance, chest heaving.

"Eliza?" Miera's voice trembled.

Sena was on the move, doing exactly what she said she'd do, and Seti had fallen for it. She'd enslave him in no time. He'd cease to be him, never leaving her side, fawning over her every word. No more sunsets, adventures, or horse races.

His faith was new and fragile, and Sena could easily rip him away from God. She was not innocent. Seti had never let girls come between him and his dreams before, but Sena could charm a man to wrestle a crocodile if she wanted.

Eliza had been a pathetic mess—unbathed, hair matted, neglecting their walks. All she'd done was cry, sleep, and complain. Her runaway emotions had pushed him into Sena's arms.

Tears stung her eyes and spilled down her cheeks as she hugged her knees. The only boy she ever loved was beyond reach. Now he'd found someone on his level.

"I'm going to get Rahel." Miera's voice broke through

Eliza's spiraling thoughts.

Reeling from the torment, Eliza shook her head. "No."

"You need somebody."

"Please," Eliza choked, not bothering to look at her sister. "Leave me. I want to be alone."

"Eliza—"

"No. Just go."

After Miera stumbled from the tent, Eliza collapsed onto her mat, curled in on herself, and convulsed as she sobbed.

Though most of the multitude remained in the Desert of Sin, the crowd at Horeb had grown. The rock on the hill continued to spew water, swelling the stream into a river that sliced through the desert floor, its end no longer in sight.

Seti cracked a smile as Sena gasped at the wonder. He guided Chewy along the water's edge to a spot without many people. As he dismounted, the rock Moshe had struck caught his eye, entrancing him. A rainbow arched in the misty spray, tugging at his soul.

"Seti, help me," Sena called.

His thoughts interrupted, he took a deep breath. When had he told her his name? He scanned the crowd. No one else paid any attention to the majestic rock—as if it were an everyday occurrence. Seti shook his head and turned toward Sena.

He helped her down, and she hurried toward the stream, splashing into the water in a fit of squeals and giggles. "Come in, Seti!"

"No thanks. I might take a ride to that rock." Seti pointed.

"No, don't leave me. Stay here!"

Seti sighed. He'd climb that mound, touch the rainbow, feel the force of the spraying water, and circle to the back to find its source.

"Fill your pouches, Seti. Come get a drink." His name on her lips grated him. Sena sat chest-high in the water, her hair floating on the surface like an open fan.

Several children raced in, laughing and screaming. Parents called after them from where they relaxed in the dirt near their possessions. As fresh groups arrived, the gasps and laughter persisted, and people left the water rejuvenated and refreshed.

"Hi, Sena!" A group of young men waded by with smiles and flushed cheeks, stopping to chat with her.

Her seemingly exaggerated hilarity could be heard above everybody as she frolicked with them, pushing and splashing in playful banter. Seti shook his head in disbelief, then turned his attention back to the rock on the hill.

"The Rock of Horeb," he said to himself, thankful the young men distracted Sena.

"That's him over there. He brought me here on his horse. Seti, don't leave me all alone."

Heat crept into his face. He turned his back and mounted Chewy, wishing for a cloak to hide beneath.

"Oh, look, he's shy. You fellows should leave before he ditches me."

The young men moved on, leaving Sena to focus on Seti again. Coming here with her was a mistake. With a final look at the Rock of Horeb, he dropped to the ground, pain tearing through his side. He moaned—half from the pain and half out of regret—and grabbed the pouches before nearing the water's edge, keeping his face lowered.

"Seti, come in with me." This girl was beyond annoying.

When he lifted his face, she splashed him. He immediately stood, dropping the filled pouches in the dirt. Sena covered her mouth with her hand to stifle her giggles, the setting sun creating an array of orange sparkles around her. She tipped her head back and laughed. Her toes broke the glittery surface.

Seti's anger wavered, and he wondered how aware she was of her provocative pose. As he waded in, the cool water invigorated his aching body. He returned the taunting laugh and kicked water toward her.

"That's more like it." She smacked the surface, sending a cool spray his way.

"Oh, that's how you want to play?" He darted after her.

Seti grabbed her ankle when she tried to scramble away and pulled her toward him, then dunked her head beneath the surface. She came up, hacking, and pushed Seti away before spattering water into his face with a barrage of kicking feet. Seti blocked the spray with one hand and grabbed her ankle with the other. He wrestled her and held her down while she struggled in a fit of screams and giggles. Noticing the stares she drew, Seti let her go and stood, hands on his hips, laughing. Sena lunged at him, wrapped her arms around his neck, and pulled him down with her. His neck burned as if his skin was tearing.

He yanked her hands off and pushed her away, then backed toward the edge. "That hurt!"

The sunlight reflected off the droplets on Sena's skin, and her pale pink tunic appeared transparent where it clung to her slender body. Her ample chest heaved against the thin fabric. She pinned him in place with a look of contrition.

Seti couldn't look away if he tried.

After a moment, she asked, "You can swim?"

"Of course I can."

A slight grin curved her lips. "Eliza can't."

"She can't?"

"No, silly! When would a slave learn to swim?"

The idea had never occurred to him. The sudden desire to bring Eliza here and teach her distracted him from Sena's spellbinding gaze. He peered back at Chewy, the urge to leave gripping him.

Touching his neck, he asked, "Then how do you know how to swim?"

"My master had a pool."

Seti chuckled. "A pool? Who was your master?"

"Hapnir. I served his guests, often in the pools. They taught me to swim."

A chill ran through Seti's bones, and his jaw dropped. Hapnir, the vizier to Pharaoh, no doubt used his pools the same way as those in the temple. The lack of shame in her tone spoke volumes. It was time to leave.

"What are you doing, Seti?" came a voice from behind.

Seti jerked upright. Sabu and Nala, both soaking wet, stood near Chewy with Nimrod.

As Seti struggled to answer, Sena squealed, "Look, it's your handsome friend! Come join us!"

Sabu gave a nod but kept his eyes locked on Seti.

"Yes, and his handsome friend's wife, might I add," Nala said, hands on her hips.

"Where's Eliza?" Sabu asked, arms crossed.

Sena's tone, her greeting, the way she said "your handsome friend"—all of it amassed into a pit in Seti's stomach. He grabbed the water pouches from the dirt and trudged toward Chewy, unable to look at Sabu. He should leave her here. She had plenty of food, water, and men to tend to her every need. But her footsteps padded behind him, too close for comfort.

"Leaving already?" she asked.

"It'll be dark soon," Seti muttered, looping the pouches across Chewy's back.

He pounded a fist against his forehead before helping her onto Chewy. Sabu and Nala rode ahead while he followed, Sena chattering nonstop in his ear about who knows what. He didn't care. His mind reeled with Eliza and her haunting words. *All is not well.*

Chapter 17

Dusk settled across the camp, but Seti still had not returned. Eliza stood atop the hill that Sabu's tent sat on, waiting, watching. Below, the Avaris families quietly packed their belongings in the light of their fires. Word had spread of God's water provision. Her family, rejuvenated by the water Seti had delivered, would leave with the others at dawn.

Eliza descended the back of the hill where she wouldn't be seen. She dropped to her knees and grabbed her tunic to tear it but lacked the strength and resorted instead to covering her head with dirt.

Leaving the camp and putting himself in danger proved Seti's independence and carelessness. Any attempt to rein him in would only drive him away further. Who was she to tame his free spirit?

God had blessed her with a small portion of Seti's life that she'd cherish forever, even if he never returned. She'd lift him in prayer as long as she lived—for his protection, the building of his character, and the strengthening of his relationship with God.

She groaned in agony. If God had heard her prayers in Egypt, certainly He'd hear them now.

"Oh, El Shaddai!" she cried, voice trembling. "I don't even know what to pray." Her fingers clenched the stony dirt. Tears streamed down her cheeks. "I want the best for him, and Sena doesn't. I love him, God. Oh, God …" She covered her face and wept.

After what felt like hours, a horse's whinny and familiar voices reached Eliza's ears. She straightened, her face having been pressed to the ground. The tears had long ceased, but the sorrow weighed heavily on her back. As she processed her surroundings and brushed the dirt from her cheeks, Sena's screechy voice jolted her back to reality, and a searing rage coursed through her veins.

With fists clenched, Eliza marched up the hill. At the top, her eyes zeroed in on the four people on two horses approaching Sabu's tent halfway down. Sena straddled Chewy with her arms around Seti's waist, Sabu and Nala close behind. A harrowing scream clawed at Eliza's throat, but she stifled it and charged down the hill, stopping behind Sabu's tent as Seti helped Sena down.

Sabu's head shot Eliza's way, but before he could say a word, she rounded Chewy, grabbed a handful of Sena's hair, and yanked. Sena yelped as Eliza spun her around and slammed her face into Chewy's flank.

Seti yelled, but Eliza jerked Sena to face her. The girl's eyes widened in horror before Eliza's fist crunched into her nose. A punch to the jaw snapped her head to the side. As Sena's legs gave out, Eliza lunged, but Seti's arms wrapped around her, pulling her back.

The stifled scream erupted. She drove her elbow into Seti's ribs. He doubled over, releasing her.

"Stay away from me!" She raced up the hill.

"Eliza!"

Hearing him yell her name caught her heart momentarily, and she stopped and turned. He barreled after her. Her breath caught, and she scooped up a handful of sand and bolted. As he grabbed her tunic, she spun and hurled the sand into his face.

He halted in his tracks as it hit him, stones and all, and squeezed his eyes shut in shock. Then, with teeth clenched, he charged forward.

Gasping, Eliza scooped up another handful, but before she could hurl it, he caught her wrist and shook her arm violently until the sand dropped.

"Enough!" He held her at arm's length. "What's wrong with you?"

Tears welled in her eyes as she yanked her arm free and backed away. "What's wrong with me? What's wrong with *me*?" Her voice rose to a shrill. "You run off with her and have the nerve to ask what's wrong with me?"

"You're a madwoman!"

Eliza turned to run but stopped mid step. "You tell me not to leave the camp, but you leave whenever you want, putting yourself in danger, after I told you what happened the other morning. After you told my abba you wouldn't leave camp. You knew I'd care, so you left after I slept. Why not just lie to my face? Then you leave with—with her!" She pointed at a blubbering Sena being helped to her feet by Sabu, blood coating her face. "Am I nothing to you?" She turned and started up the hill.

Seti followed. "This is ridiculous. You're acting like a jealous child. Her family needed water."

Eliza whirled on him. "I'm jealous?" She poked her chest. "I'm jealous? Maybe I am. But not of her. I'm jealous for you, Seti. For your love. You know very well her intentions. The girls you fall for will bring you down and wither you to a fraction of who you are now. And you'll let them. Because they're beautiful. And you won't even see it happening until it's too late."

"What?" Seti drew back, as if slapped. "You're overemotional."

Eliza shook her head, one hand planted on her hip. "Am I? I love you, Seti. And we were going to be betrothed. How could you say that?"

"You love me? Then how could you throw sand at me? And stones."

His pathetic retort hit with unexpected force, laced with pain. The realization that she'd hurt him knocked the breath from her. She fought the pull—the urge to run into his arms, to clean his face, and to kiss the pain away.

"You're a beautiful soul, Seti. Drawn to high places with spectacular views. You love to feel small beneath the night sky. Your passion for truth—for God—touches the depths of my heart. But when it comes to women, you're a fool."

Seti stared, dumbfounded. He stepped toward her but hesitated. "I see you're feeling better."

Eliza narrowed her eyes, then continued up the hill. To her relief, he didn't follow.

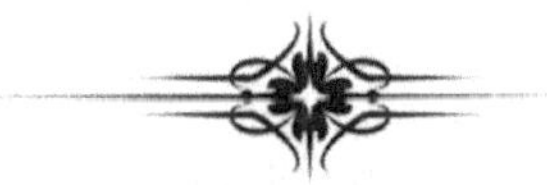

Seti let her go. She disappeared into the darkness beyond the hilltop. He clenched his fists, forcing himself not to run after her, take her in his arms, and passionately kiss her until exhaustion rendered her helpless beneath him, vile words long forgotten. No, that would be unfair. He loved her like no other. Let her seethe. They'd talk—really talk—after she'd cool off.

Sena was long gone. The water pouches lay in the dirt at Chewy's feet. Seti wiped the remaining sand from the balm on his face and averted his eyes from the stares of Eliza's family, neighbors, and his best friend.

Nala disappeared inside her tent, leaving Sabu standing with arms folded, scowling.

"What?" Seti asked as he sauntered toward the pouches.

"You're a fool."

"Why does everybody keep calling me that? She needed water. What did I do wrong?" Seti kicked the dirt.

Shaking his head, Sabu retreated inside his tent.

"I did nothing wrong," Seti muttered, carrying the pouches toward Eliza's family. Noticing their glowering eyes, he dropped the water near the firepit. No reason to go any closer. Miera rushed past him toward the hill, and Seti reached for her instinctively, but let his hand fall. He sighed, watching her disappear over the crest.

"Be careful with Eliza's heart," Sarah's voice startled him. "You're her first love." She picked up the pouches.

Seti opened his mouth, but no words came out. He glanced at the hill again. *And her last.*

Eliza huddled in the dune grass, wrapping her arms around her knees to make herself as small as possible. Though laying into Sena brought a long-overdue sense of satisfaction, the implications of her actions festered in her mind beneath the whirling mixture of pity and pain for Seti. She flexed her aching hand. Seti judged her as an over-reactive, jealous child. Did he speak the truth? Had he innocently taken Sena for water? Yet Sena had an agenda, and he failed to guard his heart.

"Eliza?" Miera's wet eyes glowed in the moonlight.

"You don't need to cry for me, Miera."

"But I want to."

The absurdity. Who in their right mind would want to cry? Yet despite her distaste for showing weakness, Eliza had made a habit of it lately.

"Come back with me," Miera whimpered. "You can't stay out here, especially in the dark. Seti says—"

"I don't care what Seti says."

"It's dangerous. Come back to the tent. You can hide under the blankets."

Besides Rahel, Miera was Eliza's closest friend. Such a sweet girl, a treasure. And she was right. The chilly breeze and daunting darkness sent shivers through Eliza.

She stood, took Miera's hand in resignation, and let the girl lead her to their tent.

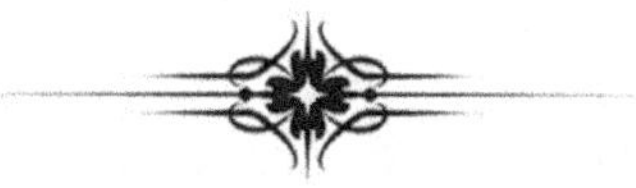

Seti lay on his back in the dirt, head resting in his hands, watching the night sky, and contemplating how everything Eliza said was wrong. He refused to acknowledge her when she passed with Miera, then watched her with a longing desperation, only to look away when her gaze flashed his way as she entered her tent.

Rahel scampered over moments later and scowled at him before ducking into Eliza's tent.

At her arrival, Adam and Zechariah stumbled out with their blankets, mumbling unintelligibly. Adam lay his mat near the embers while Zechariah snuggled against the side of the tent. Seti leaned on his elbow and smirked as he studied Zechariah. If he wasn't mistaken, that boy was eavesdropping.

He shook his head and turned his attention to the night sky. Its serenity stood in stark contrast to the drama below. The sovereign Hebrew God, thankfully, removed His canopy-cloud at night, allowing the stars to be savored.

The love of Seti's life had a powerful scream and an even more powerful punch. She'd clearly recovered from her injury. It wasn't like her to have temperamental outbursts. The frog guts she'd squeezed into his mother's soup, her smart mouth that earned the lashing across her face, and how she dared wear his mother's jewelry while his family celebrated the Nile's recovery were all out of character. Or were they? Hadn't she called his mother a weakling to his face? But all that came after Moshe's return to Egypt. Before that, nothing stood out.

The image of her tied to that pole, awaiting the whip, tore his heart anew. He pushed the compassion aside and returned to wallowing. The fact that she knew him so well and he barely knew her irked him. But if she really knew him, she'd trust him. After all, they were talking about marriage just the day before. And she thought he'd throw it all away for Sena? Maybe she really didn't know him.

Still, her words rang truer than he wanted to admit. His draw to beautiful views and the vast night sky meant nothing to anybody before. Never had he taken a girl to his mesa—except Lumeri, and that was after a year of courting. And she had no appreciation for it.

Seti's anger ebbed. If Eliza wasn't praying for him or orating mysteries that pulled him into her world, she was screaming, throwing sand, or punching girls. When she wasn't sewing his curtains shut and earning herself extra work, she was saving his life.

Again, Seti propped himself on his elbow and peered at her tent. An orange glow from the hearth illuminated the dark lump of Adam, while Zechariah's shadowy figure rolled over and fluffed his pillow. Should Seti apologize?

The excruciating ache in his heart overpowered his physical injuries, and he dropped his head, sighing. The stirring livestock beyond the tents mirrored the turbulence inside his soul.

Eliza lay awake in the sheer blackness of the tent. Rahel's rhythmic breathing suggested she was fast asleep, as was Miera beside her. Rahel's wise counsel and beautiful rendition of Miriam's song had once again soothed the sting in Eliza's heart. What was worse: Seti's insensitivity or the pain in his eyes when she left him standing on the hill?

She yearned to go to him, to spill her churning emotions on his comforting shoulder. But how many times had she done that already? No wonder he traded her for Sena.

And yet, Seti had returned with water, proving she was on his mind. He'd tended to her every need since the Red Sea. The least she could do was sneak out and apologize, mend his wounds—inside and out.

Shifting to her other side, Eliza lifted the canvas wall to peek out, but stones and plants blocked her view. Did he lie awake, brooding like she? He could sleep on a bed of stones only a few hours and wake replenished for a full day. Not her. This was going to be another long night. Sighing, she rolled onto her back, closed her eyes, and willed her mind to clear.

Footsteps outside snapped her eyes open. Seti? She held her breath, listening. The snores of her brothers continued, unabated, as the sound of shuffling feet grew closer. Such sounds in the middle of the night weren't unheard of, but never this close. She closed her eyes again, drew in a deep breath, and pulled the blanket to her chin.

The blankets lifted, and Eliza bolted upright. Moonlight spilled into the tent through the open flap, outlining an enormous figure. Rahel slid out from beside her without a sound. Eliza gasped. Gleaming eyes locked with hers. The figure smothered Rahel with something in his hand then flung her over his shoulder and disappeared outside as another ducked in, reaching for Miera.

Eliza tried to scream, but her voice caught. She grabbed her sister's arm as the stranger's massive hand clamped onto Miera's ankle.

"No!" Eliza cried, voice cracking.

Miera yelped as the man yanked her from Eliza's grasp

and disappeared from the tent, muffling her screams with a giant hand.

Chapter 18

Seti sprang up as a monstrous form ran from Eliza's tent. Shadowy silhouettes looming among the tents halted. Nala's shrill cry spun him around as a massive figure in full leather armor tore away Sabu's tent with one hand, a shining sword in the other. Nala and Sabu clung to each other, staring up at the giant in horror. The brute ripped off their blankets, grabbed Sabu by the throat, and lifted him into the air. Nala screamed again, crab-crawling backward. After tossing Sabu aside, the man stepped toward her, moonlight glinting in his ravenous eyes.

Seti grabbed one of the tent's bronze support rods and slammed it into the man's side. The giant turned with a grunt, reaching for the weapon. Seti side-stepped and struck the rod against the brute's legs, causing his knees to buckle. By the time the man regained his footing, Sabu pounced, knocking him to the ground and punching him furiously. The warrior yelled and grabbed Sabu's tunic. Seti brought the rod down on his head, and the giant crumpled in a heap at his feet. Sabu rolled off, panting, and gave Seti a grateful nod.

Screams erupted across the camp. Giant warriors tore through tents and wagons, all stealth abandoned. Sheep scattered between them, and a flock of chickens awoke in a squawking billow of feathers nearby. Adam had vanished while Zechariah and his father fought off a lurker, but nobody tended to Eliza.

Another monstrous man ripped into her tent.

"Sabu, help me!" Seti yelled.

Gripping the rod, he raced down the hill, vaulted over the firepit, and crashed into the tent, bringing it down over her and the intruder. As the giant struggled within the canvas folds, Seti delivered a crushing blow to his head, forcing him to his knees. Sabu rushed in behind and thrust a sword straight into the giant's back. With his foot planted on the giant, Sabu pulled the sword free and kicked him to the ground.

Seti stumbled back, mind reeling. "Where—"

Another giant grabbed Sabu in a headlock, spewing guttural words. The bloodied sword dropped from Sabu's grip. Ignoring the pain shooting down his side, Seti dove for it.

"Seti!" Miera's voice pierced the melee.

The distraction muddled his focus as he swung the heavy blade at Sabu's attacker, knocking him off balance.

Sabu kicked and gasped for air, dangling in the giant's grip. The giant laughed and leveled his weapon at Seti. Clutching the hilt with both hands, Seti swatted the giant's sword from his grasp. Zechariah rushed to retrieve it. The opening allowed Seti to slice through the giant's free hand. The man dropped Sabu and recoiled with a piercing roar.

Before Seti could finish him off, Miera collided with him, wrapping him in a hysterical embrace. Thankfully, the maimed giant stumbled away in a defeated stupor. Sabu gasped for breath where he had landed.

Eliza scrambled out from beneath the collapsed tent, catching Seti's eye.

He dropped his sword to unlatch Miera.

Adam appeared, waving her toward their parents, having finished off her kidnapper.

"Go to your brother," Seti demanded.

"I can't!" Miera buried her face in his chest.

Without a glance toward Seti, Eliza dashed into the

ensuing chaos. His jaw dropped. He started after her, but Miera weighed him down. He pried her arms off. "Let go!"

Adam shot Seti a look of disdain. He pointed to the ground at his feet. "Miera! Come. Now. Seti's busy."

She sobbed as Seti spun her around toward her brother. He then reached for the sword, but Sabu seized it first as another giant came barreling their way. With an exasperated groan, Seti grabbed the bronze rod and bolted after Eliza. He raced past a mound of wounded Hebrews and tripped over a collapsed tent canvas, scrambled up again only to fall into an ashen firepit.

"Eliza!" Seti yelled, glimpsing her in the fray. He struggled upright and made it only a few paces before a giant slammed into him.

Eliza rounded an overturned wagon, paused, then raced away, clutching a long-bow.

After returning to his feet, Seti broke into a furious sprint. "Eliza!"

She skidded to a stop and turned just as Seti plowed into her. He wrapped his arms around her before hitting the ground, his shoulder taking the brunt. They rolled, coming to a stop with Seti on top.

"What are you doing?" she gasped.

"Where are you going?" He pinned her shoulders down despite the pain shooting through his torso.

"They took Rahel!"

Seti froze, chest heaving.

"They took her, Seti!"

"And what are you going to do? Shoot him?" He glanced at the bow, then back at her. "You don't have any arrows!"

Eliza held up an arrow.

"One arrow. One. And that's a giant's bow!" It was a reckless, stupid move—much like his own choices of late.

"He's getting away." Eliza struggled beneath his weight.

Seti relaxed his grip. Her eyes widened with terror, and he instinctively rolled to his back and snatched the rod as a sword came down on them. He blocked the strike, its clash ringing in his ears and vibrating through his arms.

Eliza rolled clear as Seti parried another blow. She scrambled to her feet and glanced back to see him on his feet, stumbling backwards to avoid the giant's slicing blade. The giant edged forward, driving Seti back with an endless barrage of strikes. Seti lunged to the side, but the brute blocked him, sneering. He towered over Seti, his dark, black braids streaming from his head, intertwined with his beard.

A hand grabbed Eliza's ankle. "My babies. Get my babies," a man pleaded from the ground, eyes bulging.

Unable to speak, Eliza tore her ankle from his hold. No babies were in sight. She gauged the bleeding gash on his side, then surveyed the scene. People lay everywhere, moaning and screaming, giants hunting. And yet the Fire Pillar stood far in the distance in a peaceful glow, unmoving.

Seti's cry snapped her focus back to him. He had backed against an upturned wagon. She gasped as the giant's massive blade cleaved the wagon in two, sending Seti diving to the side. She searched the ground, frantic for a weapon. The bow she had dropped lay useless in the dirt.

The giant stepped around an undisturbed wagon, cutting off Seti's escape. Without another thought, Eliza ran, jumped on the wagon, and onto the warrior's back. He stumbled forward in surprise, but she clung to his braids. After hurling herself onto his shoulders, she wrapped her legs around his thick neck and squeezed.

"Seti, the bow!" she screamed as the warrior seized her legs with his free hand.

Seti sprinted for the bow, then sifted through the dirt for the arrow.

Claws dug into Eliza's leg. Gritting her teeth, she pressed her palms to the warrior's forehead and dug her thumbs into his eyes. The giant unleashed a horrendous scream that momentarily silenced the melee around them.

Seti stumbled back at the scream, catching himself against a table. With the giant's vise grip on Eliza's leg, she wouldn't last long. Seti found the arrow and snatched it up but struggled to draw the oversized bowstring.

Eliza screamed as the warrior pried her off and flung her aside with a sharp growl, blood dribbling down his cheeks. She landed with a thud and a whimper at the feet of another giant. The braided giant let out a satisfied grunt before turning again to Seti, lips twisting in stubborn resolve. He took a swing at Seti, forcing him back. The table collapsed, and Seti hit the ground hard. Planting his foot on the curved wooden bow, he nocked the arrow and drew the string back with both hands. He honed in on the snarling face of the braided giant charging him.

The second warrior smiled down at Eliza. He clamped his massive hand around her neck as she tried to rise. Seti drew in a quick breath, pivoted the bow, and released. He shut his eyes and rolled as the braided giant's sword came crashing down. Searing pain surged through his arm, but the blade clanged against the stony ground.

A resounding thud rippled through the earth against Seti's ear, followed by a familiar war cry. Not like the one he'd heard in Elim … but like the one from his father's pyramid back home. Seti opened his eyes. The giant's braided head rolled past him in a tangle of blood-soaked hair.

It came to a rest beside him, its bloodshot eyes staring lifelessly.

Seti grimaced as he pushed himself up. The giant's body lay in a crumpled heap. Hoshea stood over it, bloodied sword in hand. He pinned Seti with a hard look before rushing to Eliza and heaving the dead warrior from her, revealing a well-aimed arrow protruding from the warrior's face.

Eliza filled her lungs with air. Hoshea grabbed her arm and pulled. She cried out in pain, and he paused.

He let go. "Are you hurt?"

She grabbed her throbbing shoulder. It had better not be broken. Not now, after finally feeling better.

"Yes, but I'll fare." She winced, then locked eyes with Seti's. Seti, whole and perfect. Safe. Except for his bleeding forearm.

"Eliza." Hoshea's voice commanded her attention.

He held out a large rough hand, bringing back flashbacks of the giant's hand in her tent.

"Hoshea," she said urgently. "They took Rahel."

His gaze darted between her and Seti.

"You have to get her," Eliza begged. "Please, Hoshea. You have to save her!"

"The Amalekites? They have your friend?"

"Yes, they took her from our tent. Please, save her!"

Hoshea pressed his lips together, jaw twitching, as fighting men poured in from all directions with war cries that echoed his. They snatched fallen swords, spears, and arrows, flooding the valley like a great army. The air pulsed with clashing weapons and shouting as the beastly giants welcomed the challenge with savage delight.

Eliza grabbed Hoshea's hand, and he pulled her to her feet.

"Where?" he shouted over the commotion.

Gathering her strength, Eliza stared toward the dark expanse behind the camp. "That way. I'm sure of it. You're going to find her, aren't you? Promise me you'll find her."

"I'll go." Zechariah stumbled upon them, breathless and clutching a large spear. Adam came in close behind, wiping sweat from his brow, wide-eyed at the rush of men streaming past.

Creases formed on Hoshea's forehead as he assessed Zechariah. "No. Stay with your family. Tend the wounded."

"Take me with you." Zechariah nodded toward the horizon.

Hoshea studied Zechariah. "What are you, twelve? You're a child."

"I'm fifteen," Zechariah shot back. "And I've already had my first kill, Hoshea."

"Go back to your family."

Zechariah opened his mouth as if to counter but closed it and glared.

"We're wasting time!" Eliza grasped Hoshea's arm.

Adam stepped forward. "Eliza, I've got Miera. Hoshea will get Rahel. Let's go."

With a quick nod, Hoshea sprinted into the darkness.

Legs weak and heavy, Eliza stumbled toward Seti and collapsed on her knees beside him.

Seti reached out to steady Eliza as she dropped to her knees, her tunic muddied and wrinkled. Strands of hair bounced from her loose headwrap. Her jaw hung slack. She grasped his arm and stared at the seeping blood. The giant's finger marks on her neck quickly faded. She seemed unfazed by them, focusing more on Seti, instead.

"You hurt?" he choked.

She shook her head and untied the wrap from her hair. Cradling his arm in her lap, she wiped it clean with the edge of her frayed tunic. Her hands worked with the care and precision born of experience. Time stilled. Heat flooded Seti's insides. Her rough, nurturing hands warmed Seti's soul in a way Sena's never could. After she knotted the headwrap below his elbow, he reached for the curls framing her face. She stilled with a swift inhale. He smoothed the hair from her forehead and gently lifted her chin, gazing into the large brown eyes that had captured him long ago.

"My brave little kitten." He leaned in to kiss her parted lips.

A dust cloud shrouded them as a Hebrew fighter skidded to a halt beside Seti. He spat sand from his mouth, leaned on his giant shield, and bowed his head, panting. "Master Ameneten. It's an honor to see you alive. Are you in need of assistance?" He pointed to Seti's arm.

Seti wiped sand from his eyes. Like the others pouring into the valley against the giants, this man bore a head full of dark brown curls and a neatly trimmed beard. His dirt-streaked white kilt displayed Pharaoh's emblem, signifying he'd once belonged to the Egyptian government.

"Master?" The man nodded toward Seti's arm, eyes shining beneath thick caterpillar brows.

Seti's jaw dropped. These men who came out of nowhere, echoing Hoshea's war cry, were none other than his father's pyramid slaves.

"I—I'm fine," he muttered, turning toward the battle still raging before him.

Muscle and metal glistened in the moonlight as the men fought in seamless unity, overwhelming the giant warriors and driving them back. A trail of devastation marked their path. It made sense. These men moved as one, just as they'd cohesively constructed his father's pyramid and harvested the wheat and barley before the hailstorm.

The young man bowed once more, then disappeared into the pandemonium.

"Eliza, let's go." Adam stepped forward and reached for her arm, but she shot up a blocking hand.

"Careful," she warned.

The interruption snapped Seti back to the moment, and Hoshea's disappearance into the wilderness returned to the forefront of his mind. He jumped to his feet. "I know where they're taking her."

"Rahel?" Eliza rose beside him.

A mixture of disbelief and irritation crossed Adam's face. "What?"

Seti made a quick assessment of their surroundings before whistling for Chewy.

"Wait—" Eliza began.

Adam's eyes narrowed. "How do you know—"

"I know where they're taking her." Seti whistled again, hoping Chewy would hear him above the racket.

"What do you mean? Where?" Zechariah demanded from behind Eliza.

"You're going to save her?" Her eyes rounded with desperation.

Expression softening, Zechariah nudged Eliza aside. "Take me with you."

Seti glanced in every direction, searching for Chewy, but the thick dust from battle obscured everything. He moved away from the others and whistled again.

As Chewy materialized from the darkness, Zechariah jumped in front of Seti. "Take me with you."

"I don't have room for an extra body, and I need to find Hoshea. Give me your sword."

Zechariah clenched his jaw and exhaled sharply through his nose. "That's what happened to your face, isn't it? What did you do with those people? You led them to us, didn't you?"

Seti met his glare and replied with forced calmness, "I did not. Now give me your sword." He extended his hand.

The scowl crossing Zechariah's face pit a sour knot in Seti's stomach. First, Jeremiah's angry—but expected—reaction to Seti's presence, hopefully now resolved, then Adam's stubborn resistance. Now Zechariah? Seti held his ground, hand outstretched for the sword.

Nostrils flaring, Zechariah handed it over. Adam and Eliza stood by. Her hand covered her mouth, eyes filled with worry, while Adam watched Seti with suspicion.

With a deep breath, Seti gave Zechariah a reassuring nod, hoping it would suffice for now. He mounted Chewy. Rescuing Rahel would be easy compared to the ongoing challenge of winning the approval of Eliza's family.

Chapter 19

Seti reined in Chewy, finding Hoshea at the edge of the camp, alone, staring into the darkness, the battle of Avaris at his back. A gallant, heroic air shrouded him. His cloak flapped in the wind, accentuating his powerful build. With a sword at his side, he epitomized manhood. Seti's sheltered, priestly upbringing no longer held any glory but shrank into the past with the rest of Egypt's arrogant antiquity of lies. This was the man Seti strived to be. Yehoshua, the one who saves.

He pushed back his shoulders. "Hoshea."

Hoshea spun, eyes afire, brow furrowed.

"I know where they went."

Hoshea opened his mouth, but no words came out.

"I know where they went. Get on." Seti held out a hand.

Trepidation flashed across Hoshea's face as he assessed the horse. He ran a hand down his beard. "How do you know this?"

"Trust me. Come on!"

Hoshea had never ridden a horse. Gallant, fearless Hoshea. Seti suppressed his amusement as Hoshea grasped his hand to hoist himself up.

With one arm awkwardly encircling Seti's waist and a hand steadying his sword, Hoshea remained silent as Chewy started forward. His grip tightened when Chewy broke into a gallop.

Aside from the few giant warriors herding the Hebrews' livestock into the darkness, the wilderness remained empty. With the noise of battle fading behind them, the silence of the desert assailed Seti's ears. Memories of his previous ride away from the Fire Pillar arose, whirling with Zechariah's accusation and the dread of confessing his rendezvous in Elim to Hoshea. He set his jaw.

He hadn't led the enemy to the camp, had he? No. They'd sent spies even before he went to Elim. The distance stretched before him, and Seti wondered how far a giant could run with a girl on his back. What if he stopped somewhere? Dropped Rahel and joined the fight? Was Seti taking Hoshea far from the camp for nothing?

"Where are we going?" Hoshea's voice broke into his whirling thoughts.

"Elim. Hopefully, we'll catch him before he gets there."

"How do you know they're taking her there?"

The dreaded question. Seti swallowed the lump in his throat, sifting for words.

"How, Seti?" Hoshea demanded.

"Sabu and I went back there for water—"

"To Elim?" Hoshea's voice echoed off the desert rocks, and Seti cringed.

"It's a long story…"

"I don't suppose that's what happened to your face too?"

"It is."

The whole endeavor reeked of stupidity, pummeling Seti with shame. Hoshea would never look upon him with respect again. Gone was the idea of appointment—the name *Seth* that Hoshea once deemed fitting. He'd forever remain Seti, the naïve Egyptian named after an enemy god.

"You led them to us," Hoshea muttered.

"No," Seti burst out. "We didn't. They'd already scouted the camp before Sabu and I went—"

"What do you mean, scouted the camp?"

"Eliza found one spying. Her sister told him everything, and that was before we left."

Hoshea released a drawn out sigh, prickling the hairs on the back of Seti's neck.

"I needed water to trade for the betrothal gifts. It was the only thing the Phoenician would accept."

"Why wasn't I told of this spy?"

Seti didn't know. He had left for Elim not long after finding out himself, then barely rested once he returned, let alone had time to think about telling anyone. Why should he report to Hoshea anyway? Who would've thought the man had built an army out of pyramid slaves? If Seti were to inform anyone, it'd be Moshe. And that would never happen.

"You were aware of spies and didn't think to tell anyone? Then you and Sabu left anyway? And you were captured?"

"Yes," Seti muttered.

After a harrowing silence, Hoshea shouted into Seti's ear, "How'd you escape?"

Seti slowed Chewy so they could talk more easily. "They were distracted. Some kind of ritual sacrifice or something." He kept it short, hoping Hoshea would drop it.

"Why is it, Seti, that you and Eliza's family were the only ones of the entire Avaris camp able to defend yourselves? What did you do?" Though nearly a whisper, Hoshea's words carried sharp accusation.

"You ask me like I did something wrong."

"Not wrong. But I know you enough to know you had something to do with it. Did you bring water back from Elim?"

"No. We couldn't. I got water from the Rock of Horeb and brought pouches back for her family."

Hoshea sighed again. "It gave you enough stamina to hold them off until I arrived."

Yes, Hoshea had saved him. Again. And Eliza. Seti shuddered at the thought of what might have happened if Hoshea hadn't shown up when he did.

"Yet the only one they took was her friend," Hoshea muttered.

"Or so we think. But Eliza said something about the spy eyeing Rahel. Maybe it was the same one."

A figure materialized ahead. Hoshea shifted, hand moving to the hilt of his sword. The giant had covered a lot of ground, and Seti welcomed the distraction. He slowed Chewy even more, closing in on the lone figure running at a steady pace. Rahel appeared unconscious, bouncing on his shoulder.

Hoshea leaned forward and spoke low into Seti's ear. "Let me off."

"You'll need my help."

"I'll take care of him. Your job is to take her back. My men are on their way."

"We can defeat him easier together."

"You're not of age. Now let me off. I'll sneak up on him."

Seti twisted on Chewy to meet Hoshea's gaze. "Not of age? I fought off two giants before you showed up, and I escaped their camp, remember?" Anything to gain a sliver of respect from the man.

Hoshea flashed a hard glare, then slipped from Chewy's back and landed silently. He broke into a ferocious sprint toward the giant. No! Seti huffed a frustrated groan and yanked the reins. Rearing, Chewy let out a loud whinny.

The giant spun, dropping Rahel. He drew his sword and planted his feet.

"Wait!" Seti yelled, leaping from Chewy.

The giant warrior charged. His sword skimmed Hoshea's cloak as Hoshea jumped back. He countered with a cross swing. Metal clashed against metal. The brute spewed incomprehensible words while Hoshea moved in stealth silence, save for the occasional grunt.

Rahel's head lolled as she pushed herself upright, her eyes unfocused.

Hoshea exchanged blows with the giant, then drove his elbow into the brute's jaw, despite the height difference. Leaping, Hoshea's foot slammed into the giant's throat. The warrior stumbled back, clutching his neck and gagging. With a defiant cry, Hoshea thrust his blade toward the giant's chest, but the giant parried, still gulping air.

Clashing metal shattered the desert silence as the combatants battled on, their flashing swords and valiant forms ominous against the starlit backdrop. Dirt clouded at their feet. Seti ran after them, sword in hand.

Hoshea's blade sliced into the giant's arm. The brute howled, staggering backward.

Seizing the moment, Hoshea turned to Seti and pointed at Rahel. "Get her out of here!"

"You need my help!" Seti dashed behind the warrior and struck him, but the thick cloak absorbed the blow. The warrior spun on him, and Seti's eyes widened. He backpedaled, wishing he'd stabbed straight through instead.

"Seti, you imbecile!" Hoshea charged.

The giant swung at Seti, spittle flying as he yelled in his native tongue.

Jumping backward to dodge the blade, Seti tripped on his cloak and fell. Laughter bellowed from the giant as he raised his weapon, but Hoshea darted between them and blocked the strike. Seti scrambled to his feet as Hoshea sliced into the giant's shoulder. The brute stumbled in shock and grabbed his arm. His sword bounced on the hard ground.

Keeping his sights locked on the giant, Hoshea growled, "Seti, if you're still here when I finish him off, I'm going to kill you next."

The giant warrior grunted low and picked up the

sword. Even with one arm limp at his side, he lunged, clashing blades with Hoshea.

With an exasperated groan, Seti backed away. He'd become a liability.

As Hoshea gained the upper hand, Seti hurried toward Rahel, his sword tip dragging in the sand. She clung to him, her hand on her forehead, as he steadied her and whistled for Chewy. Once she was settled on Chewy's back, he glanced at Hoshea. His hero's fluid moves contrasted the giant's flailing, off-balance attacks, making giant-fighting look easy. How did a slave learn to fight like that?

Seti huffed and mounted. Rahel gripped him from behind, silent as he turned Chewy away. In Hoshea's eyes, he had gone from admirable to foolish to killable in a single night. Zechariah blamed him, Sabu and Eliza called him a fool, and Sena's face got punched, thanks to him.

When the Avaris camp and Fire Pillar appeared in the distance, Rahel spoke with a weak voice, "Seti."

He sighed, eyes forward, lips pressed shut, defeat washing over him.

"Seti?" Rahel said again, more forcefully. "Please go easy on Eliza. She knew Sena's plan. You're her first—"

"Sena's plan?"

"She overheard Sena wagering on how fast she could win you over. Sena said you lowered your standards for Eliza."

Seti smirked. "Lowered my standards?"

"Because, you know, the way you are and the way she is."

"No, I don't know."

"Sena claimed that because Eliza is ugly and scarred, you could do much better."

Seti slowed Chewy. "Eliza heard that?"

"She made me promise not to say anything, especially to you. When you took Sena out, it confirmed what she feared."

His heart sped as Miera's words repeated in his mind. *"That's another secret."*

"When did this happen?" he asked, though he knew.

"When we were collecting manna. The day Miera found the spy."

He ached to get back to Eliza, to hold her face in his hands and tell her how beautiful she was. To apologize for everything. His brave little kitten. The girl who gouged the eyes of a giant. The one who nursed his wounds. How foolish he had been. The other girls wagered over him like he was a trophy to be passed around, lured like a weak fool with no will of his own, no conviction. Is that how everyone saw him? But it had worked. The cunning Sena had easily snared him in her trap, proving Eliza's very words.

Chapter 20

Hoshea's men had chased the giant warriors into the wilderness, leaving behind scattered animals, downed tents, overturned wagons, wandering livestock, and trampled possessions. Stunned Hebrews meandered in a listless daze or lay wounded in the dirt. Children and babies cried, separated from their parents.

Eliza rocked a crying baby she had found squirming beneath a downed canvas. Rahel's parents huddled nearby in anxious silence, waiting for news of their daughter. Eliza's imagination ran wild with the horrors Rahel might have suffered, while worry for Seti gripped her heart. Mouth dry, her stomach knotted so tightly it hurt.

Her father had demanded she and Miera stay close, fearing losing his daughters as well. The request seemed silly, considering how sleeping in a tent near his hadn't made a difference. If not for Adam, they'd be weeping over Miera too, and maybe Eliza herself. A shiver shot through her at the thought. The urge to gather every lost child warred with the desire to honor her father's weak attempt at control.

Her bouncing and cradling of the child had no effect on his wails. How could she be angry at her father? He couldn't have prevented any of this. No, her anger was displaced. She and Miera had told no one about the spy. Though Eliza had intended to tell her father, waiting for his presence at the campsite had proven to be a mistake, possibly a tragic one. Not only was Rahel gone, but Seti too. The entire Avaris camp suffered loss, thanks to her.

Eliza wrapped the child in a blanket, her hands trembling, and held him to her shoulder as tears blurred her vision. "I'm with you, little one. We both long for our loved ones. If only I had your innocence—unable to imagine what might be happening to them."

Hours passed. A cry from Rahel's mother startled her. Eliza sprang to her feet, still clutching the child. Seti approached on Chewy with Rahel behind him. His weary eyes met hers.

Rahel slid from Chewy's back into the safety of her parents' arms. Eliza quickly handed the baby off and stumbled toward Seti. The flood-gates behind her eyes broke forth, and the knots loosened in her stomach. She barely made it three steps when he caught her and squeezed so tight the air whooshed from her lungs in a sharp gasp. His hand pressed her face against his chest, muffling her broken sobs. She gripped his shoulders, fearing she'd crumble to her knees.

Moments passed before she regained control and tried to push away, but his grip tightened, and his breath staggered.

"Seti," she managed.

He released her enough to look into her eyes and smiled.

Eliza glanced toward Rahel, but her parents concealed her in their enveloping arms and cloaks.

Rahel's father straightened and acknowledged Seti with a nod. "Thank you."

Seti's grip on Eliza loosened, and he faced Rahel's father. "It was mostly Ho—"

"You saved her, Seti!" Miera slammed into him, wrapping her arms around his waist.

Patting her head, Seti gave Miera a moment before he pried her arms off.

"Seti and Hoshea worked together," Rahel said softly, eyes fixed on Eliza. "Hoshea fought the giant while Seti helped me."

Tears spilled down Eliza's cheeks as she met Rahel's gaze, unspoken words passing between them. Adam stepped forward, stealing her attention. His brow knitted as his gaze flicked between Rahel and Seti. "Where's Hoshea?"

"He wanted me to get Rahel to safety. He'll be here soon." Seti pressed his lips into a thin line as if holding back a retort and glanced toward Eliza. What did he want to say?

"You left him?" Adam's tone was more accusing than inquiring.

Seti inched back. "Hoshea can handle himself."

"How did you find her?" Rahel's father asked.

All eyes turned to Seti. His head dropped as he rubbed the back of his neck. "It's … it's a long story."

Rahel's father stepped toward Seti and scrutinized his face. "It must have been a fierce battle. How can we ever thank you?"

Adam smirked as the man enfolded Seti in his arms.

With his arms pinned at his sides, Seti stared straight ahead, waiting out the long embrace. Once released, he quickly clarified. "This isn't from saving Rahel. It's from before. Hoshea did most of the fighting. I just knew where he was taking her." The piercing gazes gave him pause. "As I said, it's a long story." His hand found Eliza's, and he tugged her toward Chewy.

"If you ever need anything … anything at all …" Rahel's father came at him with arms outstretched again, but Seti sidestepped, pulling Eliza.

Eliza let out an awkward laugh as Seti hoisted her onto Chewy. She glanced at her brothers, then at Rahel, who remained in her mother's arms, beckoning her with her eyes. Eliza needed to talk with Rahel. But Seti mounted and turned

Chewy, leaving Rahel's father staring with his hands on his hips.

"Where are we going?" Eliza whispered, gripping Seti's waist.

He peered over his shoulder toward Nala, who watched from the mess of scattered clothes, torn canvas, and broken jars where her tent once stood. "Where's Sabu?"

"I don't know. He left without a word." Nala's voice trembled. She hugged herself tightly and shuddered. Her typically neatly tied black hair hung in a tangled, stringy mess.

Seti turned Chewy again, shielding his eyes against the sliver of sun cresting the horizon as he scanned their surroundings.

"Seti, let me off," Eliza said.

"What? Why?"

"I need to talk with Rahel." She slid off Chewy before he could object.

The landing sent a jolt of pain from her shoulder to her head, and she stifled a moan. She gripped her upper arm, looking up at Seti. His wide-eyed expression mirrored the betrayal she'd seen on him when she left him on the hill. She couldn't give in.

"I haven't spoken with Rahel yet," she said. "And you owe my family an explanation about the other day and the water and your face. Everything. Besides, we just got raided by an army of giants, Seti. My family needs me. I can't leave them. And my arm hurts. I don't really feel like riding Chewy like this."

"We don't need to ride Chewy. We can walk." But even as he said it, he looked toward Nala, clearly torn between staying or searching for Sabu.

Eliza glanced toward her parents' lingering gazes. "You're not understanding. Just go without me. You always do what you want anyway."

His brow narrowed and mouth gaped. "What's that

supposed to mean?"

Her heart broke at his tone, but she held her stance. He could be both deeply empathetic and entirely oblivious at the same time.

"You've got to be more thoughtful than that, Seti. You can't just pull me away and leave everyone with no answers. And you didn't even ask me."

Seti lifted his chin, unwilling to show any semblance of pain under the watchful eyes of Eliza's family.

"Eliza," he said evenly. "Will you come with me so we can talk privately?" He dared to look at her, only to catch her shaking her head. "I'm asking you."

"I will, but first I must speak with Rahel and help my family clean up."

A tug on Seti's chest urged him to join her. Help her family recover, show himself as one of them. But that would mean confessing to his foolishness with the giants in Elim. Besides, Sabu might be in danger. Nimrod was gone, and the look in Nala's eyes begged him to find her husband. If Eliza hadn't dismounted when she did, he'd have taken her to search for Sabu, putting her in harm's way. Still, he longed to resolve everything left hanging between them.

The rising sun illuminated the ongoing battle in the distance and cast shadows from the hills over the camp. The ground whitened with manna—not falling from the sky but forming from nothing, like the dew.

Having made up his mind, Seti inhaled deeply and turned Chewy toward the wilderness. He didn't linger, not wanting to appear hesitant. A quick glance over his shoulder revealed Eliza shuffling toward her family. Rahel and her parents had already gone.

Great. She had missed comforting her friend because of him. Her words hung at the forefront of his mind as he realized the impact of his selfishness. But Sabu…

Maybe joining the battle would be good for his restless soul anyway. And he'd prove to Hoshea that he was capable, no matter his age.

Chapter 21

Rahel had come and gone without a word or embrace from Eliza. Her parents couldn't wait a little longer before whisking her away? Gutted, Eliza slumped in defeat. Her only friend—nurturing and compassionate, steadfast—needed her for once, and Eliza hadn't been there. Hoshea and Seti had snatched Rahel from the jaws of death. No wonder her parents rushed her off. They must think Eliza a danger, or at least this portion of the camp. She pressed back the tears threatening to fall, feeling more alone than ever.

Wait. She had demanded Seti save her friend yet expected him not to save Sabu? Eliza glanced at Nala, who swept shards of clay jars in the dirt, eyes fixed on the horizon. How selfish of Eliza to make Seti choose between pleasing her and saving Sabu.

"Eliza." Her father's barreling voice shook her from her thoughts. He stood near the wagon with his hands on his hips.

With a nod, Eliza ceded to his reminder not to wander, then joined her mother and the twins where their tent once stood. The canvas was gone, their belongings strewn and mixed with others, as if a stampede had torn through the place. Her father and brothers heaved the wagon upright, only to have one side crack and collapse. The boys grumbled and complained while he ordered them to find something to tie the sides back on, while he searched for the mules.

After gathering the nearby clothing and personal items, Eliza widened her search while remaining within her father's line of sight. Exhausted, but mind whirling with guilt and worry for Seti, she paused to rest. Miera bounced between untouched patches of manna, filling several baskets and humming softly, seemingly unaffected by the morning's chaos. How? Eliza's stomach still hadn't unknotted from the endless what-ifs.

Darkness abated as the sun rose, though Eliza's heart remained shadowed. She sighed. In the distance, the sun glinted off a sword protruding from a giant's chest.

Surprised no one had claimed it yet, she made her way over. Who knew when another attack would come? God had done nothing to protect them. She stepped on the fallen man's torso, grabbed the hilt, and pulled. Blood gushed from the wound as the blade slid out with ease. Heavier than anticipated, it pulled her off balance, and she fell, catching herself with both hands. Lightning bolts ignited in her shoulder. She grasped it, moaning.

Fresh blood soaked the manna beneath the giant. Eliza turned her head, pressing the back of her hand against her nose, and squeezed her eyes shut at the sudden gore. He may have been the enemy, but he was still human. Mostly.

"Thank you." Zechariah retrieved the sword from where it landed. "We're leaving. Abba wants to camp closer to Moshe and his men."

"Did you see where Rahel went?" Eliza kept her face averted, unwilling to let her brother see the tears in her eyes.

"They're packing up too. Everyone's leaving. For some reason, we were not protected. Maybe it's because Moshe moved to Horeb, and we didn't. I'm not sure, but I know one thing— none of us will be last anymore."

"Seems right," Eliza muttered.

Zechariah stabbed the ground repeatedly with the sword, the slicing of dirt and stone making Eliza cringe. "You hurt?"

She mustered a relaxed face and swiped the tears away before looking at him and changing the subject. "Did you kill this man?"

"A couple, but I don't recognize this one. Give me your hand."

She let him take her good hand and help her to her feet. Dusting the manna from her tunic, she fought the urge to throw herself on Zechariah in a fit of tears. No, he wouldn't see that side of her, not if she could help it. Her family rarely saw her break down, no matter how emotionally and physically battered she felt. That part of her stayed buried. Except with Seti. Every moment with him chiseled at the façade of strength and control she had worn all her life.

"See if he has daggers or anything on him. We need all the weapons we can get. Get his armor too. And the leather."

Eliza nodded, wiping her nose with her arm before clearing the manna from the man's body. The task would keep her busy and productive until Seti returned. As she searched for weapons, Zechariah moved to the next body, doing the same. She stripped off the warrior's thick leather kilt, then removed his metal shin and arm guards. The cloak, a thick, tanned leather, came off next. Only the vest remained, which required rolling the man to pull it off— something she couldn't do.

While the Avaris group gathered their things in a daze, Eliza worked with purpose. Making piles of weapons, cloaks, and armor, she channeled her frustration and sorrow into the work. Some giants had tunics beneath their vests and kilts, made of a strong cotton that she cut with their daggers. Some wore helmets laced with gold.

After each new pile, Eliza glanced toward the hills for Seti. When the sun peaked, Adam and Zechariah joined her with a cart. Hairy, naked bodies lay everywhere. Eliza wiped the sweat from her brow and tied her hair back with a leather strap from a shin guard, a detail that brought Seti's injured arm to mind.

"There she is!"

Eliza spun at Sena's nasally voice. A man seized her injured arm and yanked. She cried out in pain, stumbling.

"You hit my daughter?" Sena's father snarled. "You think you'll get away with it?" He yanked her again, and she fell at his feet. His scraggly black beard glittered with spittle.

"Make her pay!" Sena yelled behind him.

Eliza's father jumped between them and broke his cousin's hold. "Get away from her."

Sena's father shoved him back. "Look what she did! Your daughter did this! Sena, show him!"

Sena pulled down the printed scarf hiding her crooked, purple nose and grinned, revealing the gap where her two front teeth had been.

No. Eliza covered her mouth in shock. She did that?

"She'll never be the same again. Let me at her, I want her teeth knocked out too!"

He lunged, but Jeremiah held him off, shoving him back toward Sena. "Impeccable timing, cousin, just after an ambush. You plan this out?"

"We're in the same camp, you foul dog! I came before you'd mix with the rest. She ruined my daughter."

"Stop it, both of you!" Sarah rushed in, arms waving. Adam and Zechariah followed.

Sena's father swung at Jeremiah, striking him in the face, and Sarah screamed. Fists flew as the men scuffled, yelling obscenities. Sena's father hit the ground and gasped for air, clutching his chest. He rose to his feet with a sluggishness that exhibited the all-too-familiar weakness of dehydration. Jeremiah readied his fists, giving his cousin time to recover.

"What's happening?" Miera came running, leaving the twins on the hillside.

As punches rained once more, Sarah reached in to separate them, but Eliza pulled her away. Adam wedged between the brawling men but was knocked off his feet. He jumped up and tried again. "Stop!"

This was Eliza's fault. She had to do something. She grabbed Sena by the shoulders and spun her around to face her. "Quick, Sena. Hit me!"

Sena stared, her forehead wrinkled above her swollen nose.

"Hit me!" Eliza demanded, fists clenching her tunic in anticipation.

With a slow nod, Sena set her feet and drew back her fist. Eliza squeezed her eyes shut. Every muscle tensed. Flesh cracked against flesh—but not hers. When she peeked through an eyelid, Zechariah had caught Sena's fist a handbreadth from her face.

"Nobody is hitting Eliza."

"Get out of the way, Zechariah!" Eliza shoved him aside.

Sena lunged, slamming into her. Eliza flew off her feet, smacking her head on the hard ground. Her mother yelped at the thud. The men paused. The camp fell silent. Head spinning, Eliza sat up and felt the back of her head. No blood.

Her vision blurred, but she returned to her feet. "I said punch me, not push me down. Now knock my teeth out."

Sena went for the punch, but Zechariah caught her arm, spun her around, and shoved her hard, sending her backpedaling to the ground. Sena's father started toward him, but Jeremiah yanked him back.

"Stop!" Adam yelled, throwing himself between the men. "All of you!"

"He hurt me!" Sena wailed as she rolled in the dirt.

"Good!" Zechariah yelled.

"Zechariah!" Sarah stepped toward him but stopped and covered her face with her hands.

"Everybody, stop. Now!" Adam shouted, struggling to keep the men apart.

Sena pointed at Eliza. "She ruined my life."

"You should have stayed away from Seti!" Eliza fired

back.

"I didn't do anything wrong. You should be blaming him."

Stepping toward Sena, Eliza pointed. "I heard your plan, Sena. You're nothing but a harlot!"

"Eliza!" Sarah gasped.

Eliza stared at Sena's wide eyes, waiting for a response.

Glaring at Jeremiah, Sena's father growled, "This is how you raise your children?"

"Stay out of it."

"Some family."

"Everybody, shut up!" Adam roared.

All eyes turned to him. "We will take this to Moshe."

Zechariah shook his head. "Nobody is hitting her."

"I'm fine," Eliza hissed, shooting him a glare.

"Moshe will settle this," Adam repeated, staring his brother down.

"Why bother?" Zechariah muttered. "You know what he'll say."

"He'll take her head injury into consideration," Adam told him.

Sena's father shook his head and raised a finger. "No. He will see it as clouding her judgment. The attack on my daughter was premeditated, head injury or not. She deserves punishment."

"You try, and you'll suffer the same fate." Jeremiah leaned forward, but Adam held them both at arm's length.

Sena's father shot his cousin a glare. "Ironic, Jeremiah—beat up a man dying of thirst, but heaven forbid your scheming daughter gets what she deserves."

Jeremiah pushed forward. "You laid hands on her and threw the first punch!"

"Stop! This is ridiculous!" Adam braced himself between them. "You're acting like children. All of you. I'm barely an adult but more so than you. We're on our way to

Horeb. Once there, we will consult Moshe.”

"Moshe is not God," Sena's father spat.

"He's the judge!" Adam snapped, fists clenched.

"We can settle this right now, right here, and not waste his time."

Adam blew air from his nostrils. "No. It's not that easy."

"She should have thought of that before hitting my Sena."

"No," Adam said firmly, pinning his uncle with a fiery glare. "We'll meet you at Horeb. Now go."

"Oh, no," Sena's father retorted. "I'm not letting you out of my sight. For all I know, you'll mix in the multitude only to delay justice. We'll stay behind you, and the moment we arrive, we are marching to Moshe, even before setting up camp. Your daughter ruined my Sena's face, and she'll pay."

Crossing his arms, Jeremiah stepped back and nodded toward Adam. "Good. Follow us. I want this settled as much as you do."

Sarah took his hand and pulled him away. Sena stood, dusting off her bright yellow tunic, keeping her eye on Eliza. She sauntered toward her father, pulled the scarf over her nose, and wrapped an arm around him as he led her away in a huff.

Chapter 22

The battle between the Hebrews and the giants raged on, where the hills flattened near the Wilderness of Sin, a familiar place Seti wished to never see again. He stood on the ridge of a low hill and scanned the scene below for Sabu. Men and giant warriors spread across the desert floor in a storm of clashing blades, flying arrows, and hand-to-hand combat. Sunlight glinted off metal shields and sword blades. Amalekite bodies, stabbed through or with limbs severed off, filled the area between Seti and the fight.

One of the benefits of becoming a priest had been to avoid scenes like this. How ironic that he now felt compelled to prove his valor to Hoshea. He'd have to stomach the human gore first.

Seti weaved Chewy through the dead, searching for a weapon to replace Zechariah's sword, which he had dropped to embrace Eliza. He gazed again at the ensuing battle, looking for Sabu. In the daylight, the vastness of the fighting became apparent, spreading beyond sight. The giant warriors towered over the hundreds of pyramid slaves, yet the Hebrews had amazingly pushed the enemy back beyond the Avaris camp. Seti's shoulders slumped. It'd be impossible to find Sabu within the melee, even on a horse.

A giant moaned at Chewy's feet, and Seti pulled the reins. The man's bloodshot eyes pleaded for Seti's help, reaching out a trembling hand. He attempted to speak but managed only a wet gurgle as foam seeped from his mouth.

Seti leapt from the horse and crouched beside him, his gaze drawn to the three stab wounds in the giant's torso, one gushing blood. How long had he been lying here? As Seti reached for a sheathed knife tied to the warrior's leather vest, the giant's hand seized his cloak, startling him.

"Ve-vermin," the giant choked in Egyptian before his hand dropped.

"Vermin?" Seti frowned.

He grabbed the knife, thinking to end the giant's suffering. But the gurgling stopped, and the man's contorted face relaxed. His eyes glazed over, vacant and still.

Stunned, Seti sat back on his heels, never having witnessed the moment life abandoned its body. A pang of sadness pricked his heart. No spirit emerged from the gaping mouth, no chariots of fire descended from the heavens— only the instantaneous shift from life to death. Though giants were the offspring of demigods, none came to retrieve him. The man's comrades would have to collect his body and send it to the afterlife, either by boat or coffin like any other man, otherwise his spirit would forever drift in the unknown. Images of Seti's father rose unbidden. What did the Hebrew God do with His dead?

He gulped, pushed the thoughts aside, and stood to survey the carnage. Endless gray sand painted red. Buzzards descended, gorging themselves on soft flesh. Seti covered his mouth with a fist, his stomach churning. A solemnness washed over him.

The blast of a ram's horn tore him from his thoughts. As if a renewed wave of vigor swept through the Hebrew fighters, cheers and shouts rang out, and the clashing intensified. Seti's fingers tightened around the hilt of his blade. To join the fight with only a knife would be madness. He quickly checked around for a sword but paused when something else caught his eye.

On a distant hill, silhouetted against the late-morning sun, a figure sat on a rock with arms held aloft by two men. Seti shielded his eyes, squinting. Moshe held Aharon's staff high above his head, facing the battle below. Aharon and another man braced Moshe's arms like stone columns. Behind them, from the peak of the tallest mountain, the Cloud Pillar loomed, as if a spectator. No, not a spectator but the source of power itself.

Competing urges to run to Moshe or to fall to his knees where he stood warred within Seti. His strength left him. He reached for Chewy to steady himself, grabbing the horse's mane with shaking hands, but still dropped to the ground. The battle belonged to the Hebrew God. His divine power flowed through Moshe. The sight melted Seti's heart, and he wanted nothing more than to be consumed by it.

"Over here," Seti whispered, overcome with a deep yearning for God to look upon him with favor. God had looked directly at him once, but not with favor. No, that was the Angel of Death, as Hoshea had said. Had God ever set his face toward him?

"Use me, too."

Where once Seti despised being used by the Hebrew God, he now longed for it. One time was not enough. He would do God's work the rest of his life.

His mind cleared as the minutes passed. The last bit of tension in his muscles gave way to exhaustion. His ribs throbbed anew, as if hitting the bottom of the cistern all over again. With a groan, he clutched his side. The Cloud Pillar spun upward in a blaze of white, reaching the canopy above. The same canopy that sheltered the congregation but hadn't protected them. Seti narrowed his eyes.

"Why fight for us now but not last night?" he whispered into the breeze. Had God waited for Moshe to wake, unwilling to disturb the old man's precious sleep? Or was He angry with the Avaris group? Perhaps Seti had angered Him by leaving for Elim.

Seti had assumed they were safe as long as they remained in the presence of the Pillar, indicated by where the manna appeared. He'd even instructed Eliza and Miera to stay within its limits. But God allowed the enemy to attack in their safety zone when they were sick and vulnerable.

He turned from the mountain toward the battle, frustration bubbling inside him. Why hadn't God blown the Amalekites away, sparing Hebrew lives? They shouldn't have to fight. He blinked and shook his head, already questioning the awe he felt moments ago.

A horse caught his eye in the distance. Sabu!

Seti pocketed the knife and mounted Chewy, grimacing through the pain. He slapped the reins and raced toward the battle line where several Hebrews lay among the Amalekite dead.

Please, not Sabu.

Shouts and the clash of metal rang in his ears as he reined in near Nimrod. Sabu lay on his back, an arrow protruding from his thigh.

Seti sprang from Chewy and ran to his friend. "Sabu!"

Sabu's eyes opened, and Seti let out an exasperated breath as he skidded in the dirt beside him. "You're alive!"

"Barely," Sabu rasped, pushing himself up to examine his wound.

"I, as well!" a man cried nearby.

"Over here!" another voice called.

Wounded Hebrews mixed with the Amalekite dead, the desert strewn with bodies. Seti squinted at the Cloud Pillar, heart pounding. People were dying in a fight that should never have happened. He stifled his anger, focusing instead on the bloody arrow in Sabu's thigh.

When Seti reached for it, Sabu's hand shot out. "No, no, no! Don't touch it!" He dropped back, groaning.

"What do I do?" Seti wrung his hands, forcing himself to look at Sabu's pale face rather than the pooling blood.

"Weren't you trained in the healing arts?" Sabu choked out between ragged breaths.

"I was trained to be a priest, Sabu. The closest thing to healing was embalming."

"Then get me ready. I'm dying." Sabu stared at the sky, eyes bloodshot.

Seti sat back on his heels, the image of the dead giant's empty eyes returning. "You're not dying, you fool." He looked away as he said it, his words ringing hollow even in his own ears.

"Then contact the healer gods. Sekhmet, Isis, Imhotep—anybody."

"No!"

"Well, do something!"

Seti's heart raced as he ran a hand through his hair at the panic in Sabu's voice. His friend had never sounded so weak or scared, not even in the cistern. Seti's priestly training again proved useless, emphasizing a wasted life.

Turning to the Cloud Pillar, he mustered a sliver of humility. "God of the Hebrews, tell me what to do. Save Sabu and these men who should have never had to fight to begin with." He tapped his forehead with a fist and clenched his eyes shut, biting back the next words on his tongue.

"Well, isn't that just like you to pray," Sabu scoffed. "Egyptian!"

A stout, old, bald man lying on his back a few paces away waved an arm while pressing the other hand to his side. He didn't appear to be a pyramid slave—too old—which meant the young and old alike had joined the fight. "Leave the arrow in his leg for now, or he'll bleed out. Get us back to the camp where the women can tend to us."

"You were saying?" Seti shot at Sabu, masking his surprise. Had God answered him through the old man, despite his anger-riddled prayer. "Can you ride?"

Sabu held his breath as he pushed himself into a sitting position.

Crouching behind Sabu, Seti grabbed him under the arms and heaved him to his feet.

Sabu moaned, eyes clenched, struggling to balance on his good leg. He held his cloak away from the arrow. "My sword." He nodded toward the weapon on the ground.

"Wait." Seti gently released him and hurried to Nimrod. He glanced at Moshe, who remained on the rock, his arms held high by Aharon and the other man. "God's controlling the fight through Moshe, or so I thought. But it doesn't make sense … there are so many wounded men …"

"He is, but when Moshe's arms drop, men are wounded, and when his arms go up, we're strengthened."

"Really?" Seti paused, staring at Moshe, pondering God's strategy.

"Are you waiting for him to drop his hands?" Sabu growled through clenched teeth. "Hurry up!" His arms flailed, and he stumbled backward, eyes rolling back.

"Sabu!" Seti rushed and caught him. He lowered him safely to the ground.

"I—I'll be fine," Sabu whispered, eyes wide and searching until landing on Seti's face.

Seti took a minute to catch his breath and stifle the pain in his ribs before calling Nimrod. "You have to stand, Sabu. Slower this time."

"It's not my fault you stood me up too fast." Sabu's voice was weak, his grip tight on Seti's cloak.

Doubt and hopelessness set in with potency, smothering Seti's faith. That old man was just an old man, not a spokesperson for God. He wiped the sweat from his brow. "Ready?"

"Hmmm."

Seti heaved, and pain erupted in his side. He pushed through it until Sabu stood on one leg, his arm slung around Seti's shoulder. After calling Nimrod closer, he boosted Sabu onto the horse's back. Sabu teetered, barely upright, as Seti fetched his sword.

"Me too." The old man inched toward them.

"And me!" another yelled.

Seti shook his head at the number of wounded crawling and hobbling his way. He ran a hand through his hair again and glanced at the Cloud Pillar. All these soldiers wanted saving, but Seti was but one.

He dashed to the old man and lifted him to his feet, whistling for Chewy. Grasping his side, the man stepped into Seti's cupped hands and climbed onto the horse. He flashed a careful smile.

With a hand in the air, Seti lifted his voice, halting the advancing wounded. "I can only take one more, but I'll come back for each of you."

He grabbed Nimrod's reins and led him to a middle-aged man with a belt around his upper arm as a tourniquet. Blood ran down his leg from a stab wound to his thigh. Seti helped him up, but the man's legs gave out, and he fell, bringing Seti down with him.

"Hold on." Seti gathered his strength, pulled the man to his feet again, and hoisted him onto Nimrod behind a trembling Sabu.

"I'll come back," he promised the others, suddenly invigorated to save them all. He handed Nimrod's reins to the man and mounted Chewy in front of him.

Turning toward the hills, Seti questioned how fast to ride, fearing Sabu might slip off.

"Go to Horeb." The old man pointed toward the mountain Moshe stood on. "Take that way, around the far side of the hills."

"Horeb? That's too far. Sabu—"

"Your friend won't make it unless we go to Horeb. They have water and skilled healers."

Avaris didn't have healers? Seti wanted to argue, worrying how Sabu would handle the long ride. Avaris was closer. But the state of the camp after the ambush, as well as their weakened health and lack of water, proved the old man right. Sabu would need that wound cleaned.

Keeping a close eye on Sabu, Seti led them in the direction the old man indicated. He shot the Cloud Pillar a silent plea. *Save him.*

Once over the last hill, the settlement at Horeb came into view. Thousands of tents filled the bustling valley below. Typically, Seti would've found it too congested for his liking, but now the scene lifted his exhausted, doubting spirit.

With a sigh, he guided the horses down the hill toward the nearest bend in the stream. Screaming erupted, and women came running to meet them. One pulled the old man from Chewy before Seti could get a word out.

"Don't tell me you're all that's left?" she cried.

"There's more," Seti said over the wailing. "But they're still fighting. I have to go back."

"Get that young man some help." The old man pointed at Sabu, who slumped on Nimrod.

"Can you help him?" Seti asked.

"We'll take him." An elderly woman grabbed Nimrod's reins. "Go back for more."

"I need help. I can't do it alone."

Wagons were emptied and hooked to oxen and cattle. Women climbed aboard, and Seti led the way back to the wounded.

It was late afternoon before the fighting waned and soldiers rested, sweaty and broken. Moshe, Aharon, and the third man had disappeared from the hilltop. It took three trips to collect the wounded. After every soldier was transported to Horeb, the people set out with carts to collect spoils from the dead. Seti, aching and exhausted, returned to Horeb. *Sabu better be alive.*

Chapter 23

Unable to find Sabu in the chaos, Seti collapsed in a shallow part of the stream and let the water rush over him. He tilted his head back and closed his eyes. It amazed him how the rejuvenating water from the Rock reached this far. It never ceased to flow. Every muscle in his body ached, and it hurt to breathe. The crackle of campfires and the aroma of warm manna stirred his senses, waking his stomach with a ferocity he hadn't felt since before the quail. He opened his eyes. It was time for the evening meal.

Children darted back and forth, filling buckets and rinsing bandages, while families gathered around tents to eat. Voices broke out in song nearby, accompanied by tambourines and clapping. Seti drank from his cupped hands, then unwrapped Eliza's headwrap from his forearm. His heart sank at the way he had left her. He craved her warmth, her drizzle-on-a-hot-day scent, and her calming presence. She was a jewel to be treasured, hidden in plain sight, beautiful beyond measure.

The clear, cool water rinsed the long, deep gash stretching from Seti's elbow to wrist. An odd sense of loneliness swept over him.

Sensing eyes on him, Seti lifted his head. Hoshea stood across the stream, arms crossed.

"What are you doing here?" Hoshea asked, squinting from the reflection against the sun's glare on the water.

Seti stood but stumbled forward as the pain flared in his side. He cleared his throat. "H-helping."

Hoshea leveled him with a measured look.

"Why wouldn't you let me fight?" Seti asked.

After a slow inhale through his nostrils, Hoshea waded across to Seti's side. "According to El Shaddai, a man must be twenty years of age to fight in a war. I'm sorry, but you are not old enough."

"War," Seti emphasized. "I was defending the camp, not going to war."

"You weren't defending the camp when we went to save Eliza's friend."

"So I'm not allowed to rescue anyone even if I know where they've been taken?"

Hoshea sighed. "Understand, Seti. You are not to fight unless physically attacked."

Was that a Hebrew law or did Hoshea just not want Seti to fight? Seti climbed up the stony embankment and grabbed his cloak from the ground near Chewy. He turned to face Hoshea. "Why did we even have to fight? Couldn't God have wiped them out before they reached us? He kept the Philistines away and killed off the Egyptian army."

"That's a question to ask Moshe. I know this: since the Red Sea, we've been through a series of tests. Not only that, but we now have proper food and water. Perhaps it was another test."

Seti frowned. "Tests?"

Hoshea held out a manna muffin. Seti eyed it, trying not to lick his lips.

"Take it. I have more." Hoshea pulled another from his cloak pocket. "You look famished. Let me elaborate—tests of our faith."

After devouring the muffin, Seti tossed his cloak over Chewy's back and followed Hoshea along the embankment.

Hoshea handed him another muffin, then pulled out a third. "The Amalekite giants are a bloodline that has reached its end, while the Egyptians and the Philistines aren't."

"Then teach me to fight, Hoshea. Like you," Seti said between bites.

"It appears you already know how."

"Not like you. By the time I'm twenty, I want to be skilled. How did you learn? Did you think you'd have to fight someday?"

"Nothing wrong with preparing." A hint of a smile appeared as he regarded Seti with a sparkle in his eyes. He handed Seti the third muffin, then stuffed both hands in his pockets. A ram's horn hung on a strap at his side.

"Exactly! So teach me."

Stopping in his tracks, Hoshea smiled, emphasizing that sparkle. "You remind me of myself when I was young."

Seti let out an exaggerated sigh and dropped his head. "Is that good or bad? I can't even tell if you like me. You were ready to kill me this morning."

"Who said anything about liking you?"

Shooting him a glare, Seti stomped ahead.

"I'm kidding." Hoshea caught up, his sandals scuffing against the hard sand. "How can I not jest with a man who fights in his undergarments?"

Looking down at his thin, tattered kilt, Seti's cheeks warmed, not sharing Hoshea's amusement. He checked the gazes of those around to see if he drew attention, but nobody paid him any heed.

With a tone laced with sarcasm, he hissed, "Next time we're attacked in the middle of the night, I'll make sure to get dressed first."

"Yet you brought your cloak."

"The cloak was given to me by Eliza's father, and I use it as a blanket, but you wouldn't know that. I also sleep outside. Need more fuel for your ridicule?"

Easily keeping pace with Seti's hastened steps, Hoshea continued undeterred. "Did I hit a sore spot? Seeing you in the daylight, you're covered in sore spots."

Seti spun around. "If you're not going to teach me to fight, then let me be."

"You're a likable young man, Seti. Though you're incredibly frustrating."

"*I'm* frustrating," Seti scoffed, rolling his eyes and marching on.

Silence ensued, and Seti pondered his defensiveness. Hoshea spoke with grace. He could have easily turned away and cast Seti off as a waste of time, yet he hadn't. And Seti didn't want him to, despite the jabs. He matched Hoshea's stride, searching for a way to break the silence. "Did you train your men, or was it somebody else?"

"A little of both."

How had a slave time to train for combat? "Then teach me, Hoshea. Yehoshua."

Hoshea smiled again and pulled on his beard. "I'll train you—if you teach me to read."

Seti's eyes widened, and his heart lifted at the wonder of having something Hoshea wanted. "Truly?"

"In Hebrew," Hoshea added. "You know Hebrew script, am I correct?"

Seti chuckled. At last, his training came in useful. Since priests accompanied the vizier, envoys, and generals on expeditions, they were required to learn the languages of the surrounding nations. Hebrew script, a prerequisite to the myriad Asiatic dialects, was an easy feat when surrounded by Hebrews on a daily basis. Unbeknownst to them, their ancestors from the pre-servitude era left property records, sufficient to learn their script, and as the years passed, few, if any, Hebrews ever learned it themselves.

"When do we start?" he asked.

Hoshea stared ahead, eyes unfocused. "Soon enough." He kicked a stone. "We must wait until my men return and get settled. I sent them to scout Elim in case of more abductions. If God so chooses, they are to finish off the Amalekites; otherwise, send word back to me. This battle may not be over."

"Why didn't you go with them?"

"Moshe wanted me here. And I trust my men. They fight with the hand of El Shaddai."

Hoshea proved to be more than a foreman of the Ameneten pyramid slaves and more than a commander of an army. He was a confidante of Moshe. Moshe called him Yehoshua. Seti studied the man beside him, who seemed wise beyond his years, who walked with nonchalance, as if he hadn't just conquered a tribe of monstrous men. The creases around his eyes and mouth contrasted his boyish face.

"Moshe has settled in his tent, and from the looks of it, he doesn't plan on moving again for a while." Hoshea shot a pensive glance toward the Pillar. "The great mountain, Sinai, where the Cloud Pillar now rests, is where God first spoke to him. From my understanding, God has something planned before moving us forward."

The thought of prolonging their arrival at the Promised Land drained Seti's momentary joy over teaching Hoshea to read. Sick of the desert and wandering with nothing to call his own, Seti yearned for greenery, acreage, and productivity. He yearned to consummate his marriage. Not wanting to show his disappointment, Seti steered the conversation back to the battle. "God directed the fighting through Moshe, didn't He?"

"Yes, in obedience to God, Moshe raised his arms, reminding us to rely on El Shaddai and not our own strength."

"Is that how we'll take Canaan?"

"Perhaps. According to Moshe, God will clear the land for us. Whether that's through fighting or some other way, I don't know. But I wouldn't be surprised if he does it in such a way to display His glory, as He did here."

Seti pressed his lips together and peered at the Cloud Pillar over the mountain. Mount Sinai. He dreamed of climbing a mountain one day. What would the Pillar do if he met it at the top? "Did anybody die?"

"Not that I'm aware of."

He let out an apprehensive breath, thinking of Sabu.

"After Moshe finished with the battle, he sent men to assist and assess for casualties where attacked, but most had already reached Horeb. It appears only the tail end of our people were attacked. Why did you all linger, anyway?"

"I don't know," Seti mumbled, distracted by the thought that Eliza might be in Horeb. He glanced around for anybody familiar but found none. "The Avaris group was the last to leave Goshen, being the southernmost town. Then the trek wore us down." He turned to Hoshea. "Do you know where Eliza might be?"

Sidestepping a running child, Hoshea said, "I'd presume on the outskirts of Horeb, toward the south, where you came from. They'd probably stop for water from the Rock before moving on."

The Rock stood atop a mound visible from all directions. Much of the multitude had moved further downstream toward the great mountain. If it were up to Seti, though, he'd set up camp as close to the Rock as possible, but he also wanted to stay near Hoshea and Moshe.

Yearning to see Eliza, Seti scanned the area again for a familiar face. Families ate around fires or tended to their animals. Children played with no concept that a battle had raged nearby. He'd have to find Sabu first, as there'd be no returning to Nala without her husband.

"Where are the wounded?" Seti didn't dare let Hoshea know Sabu had joined the fight.

"Just beyond these tents." Hoshea pointed after pinning Seti with a suspicious look. "Look for a cluster of white canopies. There may be more near the Rock since some returned that way."

Before parting, Seti asked, "Can I borrow your shofar?" He pointed to the ram's horn.

Furrowing his already furrowed brow, Hoshea asked, "What for?"

"Betrothal." The word alone made Seti grin.

Hoshea smiled, the look of suspicion obliterated. "Wow. I'm impressed. Her family agreed?"

The question stung, and Seti struggled to hide it, lowering his gaze. "Yes."

"You need a ram's horn?"

"To get everybody's attention."

Hoshea handed it over. "I'd like to come, if you don't mind. Then you can return it."

Seti's jaw dropped. "Of course. I don't know when it will be yet, but I'll let you know."

"Thank you." Hoshea pointed toward the tents. "Now you'd better check on Sabu before I find him first."

How did he know? But then again, who else would Seti have wanted to visit among wounded? Once again, Hoshea saw right through him. But he also saw promise in him.

Seti gave Hoshea a quick nod, avoiding his cutting gaze, and grabbed Chewy's reins.

After asking around, Seti located Sabu beneath a large canopy, reclining on a canvas chair. His sword lay on the ground beside him. A long table laden with alabaster jars, linen, medical tools of silver and copper, and buckets of water stood to one side. A strong scent of frankincense and cassia tickled Seti's nose. With the arrow removed, a clean white bandage encircled Sabu's thigh where the arrow had been. He, too, wore only his undergarment, something Seti took no notice of before, but now he couldn't help but smirk at. Except for the absence of scars on their backs, he and Sabu blended in with everybody else. Sabu's eyes were closed, hands folded over his chest, breathing steadily, but he remained as pale as ever.

Seti brushed past the other wounded and their hordes

of loved ones and hurried to Sabu's side. "Sabu."

Sabu's eyes fluttered open. His lop-sided smile sent a wave of relief through Seti. "Hello, my friend."

"How are you doing?"

Sabu's gaze went to the bandage on his leg. "No wine. No spirits. Just—just this stuff …"

"What stuff?"

"Nothing for pain but incense, which hel-helps but makes my head tired. Like wine, but not. I asked, but th-hey drank their wine long, long time ago. Cleaned it with hyss-ssop mixed with s-something else. People here are s-strange."

Despite Sabu's listlessness, he seemed stable. Still, having an arrow yanked from his leg with no wine would have been unbearable. "Are pieces left in your leg?"

"All out. Two beaut—pretty women with hands like bronze. N-no mercy. Yanked it out like I was a dead animal. I don't know if it's…" His eyes drifted shut, as his voice trailed off.

"Sabu." Seti nudged his arm.

Sabu blinked. "I d-don't know if it was 'cause I'm Egyptian, but they rough. Blood ev—everywhere. Th-they burned the bloo-bleeding channel shut with hot metal and sewed the outside. Made me bite on he-hemp sack with herbs so I—I wouldn't chip a tooth. My teeth still there?" He flashed an exaggerated grin.

Seti nodded, trying to piece together his friend's slurred narrative.

"Pu-put honey on top, then this." Sabu nodded toward a small alabaster jar on the ground near his sword.

"Can you ride?"

"They said I can go. Wa-waiting for you. Gave me those—" he pointed to a pair of acacia crutches. "And to keep it clean. Nimmmmmrod?"

After fetching Nimrod from a group of oxen and donkeys, Seti helped Sabu to his feet. He teetered and swayed, pointing his finger in the air and laughing. Somehow, with the crutches, he remained upright. Seti draped his cloak around Sabu's shoulders and helped him mount Nimrod.

A young woman rushed over. "Keep an eye on him. He needed more incense than planned, but it should wear off shortly. Keep his wound clean and use honey."

She handed Seti the alabaster jar and a long strip of linen to tie the sword and crutches together, which he then looped around his shoulders.

"You all right, Sabu?" Seti tapped Sabu's leg to get his attention after catching him staring off in a daze.

Sabu glanced down with a slight smile, then nodded toward the woman. "Yes, my lady."

Seti exchanged an uneasy glance with her before mounting Chewy, gritting his teeth against the pain in his side. Whatever Sabu had inhaled worked, and Seti wanted some.

Chapter 24

Eliza stood at the stream's edge and stared at the rushing waters. Seti had brought Sena here. She shivered, imagining them frolicking, splashing, and playing together. The water grew deep, and the current churned more violently the closer she ventured toward the mysterious water-spouting rock. No one swam here. It was too forceful. Instead, the multitude gathered further downstream.

She knelt to drink and fill her pouch, sensing Sena's eyes on her as she gazed at the foamy water, her face a mere handbreadth above it. Sena and her family had not let Eliza out of their sight. Conviction prickled at Eliza as she replayed the morning's skirmish in her head. Her rash actions not only marked Sena for life but made her own family a spectacle for all to see.

The current tugged at her hair. Mist cooled her face, and the low rumble muted the voices and bustle around her, soothing the headache she'd carried since hitting the ground earlier. She longed to let go of the rocks and let the rapids sweep her away to a new place. Nobody would see her beneath the bubbles and foam. If only she could swim.

"Hey." Adam pulled her from the ledge, and she landed on her backside, wincing. "We've been calling you. Time to eat. What are you doing, anyway? Do you want to drown?"

Eliza yanked her arm free, ignoring the pain. "I'm not hungry."

"Sure you are. You're being all emotional again. Come and eat before you starve."

She jumped to her feet with a snarl and shoved him. "Leave me alone!"

Adam laughed, barely budging. "Settle down. I know you well enough to know what's going on in that head of yours. Tents are up, and everyone's going to bed early for the big day tomorrow. I don't need you trying any stunts before that."

Unfortunately, he was right. Eliza scowled. "Big day?"

Adam nodded toward Sena's family. The girl and her sister huddled beside their fire, staring. When they weren't staring, her parents were. Even her giggly friends came by earlier to sit and stare with them, whispering and pointing.

She was about to give them something to stare at when Adam threw an arm around her shoulder and pulled her close, putting himself between her and her spectators. "Come on. You're already in enough trouble." He nudged her toward the tents.

As the sky darkened, the Fire Pillar bathed the mountains in a bright orange. Gazing upon it swept Eliza's angst away like the orange bubbles in the water. Seti would love the vibrant splash of colors. His face was swollen, and the cut in his arm was deep. How could he defend himself against giants? Would she ever see him again?

She searched the shadowy hills in the distance while her family talked quietly between bites of manna-muffins and milk. The weakness and dehydration of Sena's family proved beneficial for Eliza, buying her an extra day to sulk while they replenished their strength, not bothering to set up their tent. Animals brayed in the shadows, singing drifted in the air from the camps ahead, and Eliza's family joked and laughed like nothing was wrong and nobody was missing. But one person shared Eliza's despair.

Nala's tent sat alone in the dark, on the outskirts of the camp as usual, as if the Hebrews carried an inherent stench.

Only the flicker of firelight allowed Eliza to distinguish it from the surrounding blackness. Despite Nala's exhibited trepidation around Eliza's family, they welcomed her and Sabu, even transporting their belongings. Zechariah helped tear down and erect their tent. Miera had placed a plate of muffins near the flap, which still sat untouched. Eliza's heart ached for Nala. They had more in common than Nala probably cared to admit, and Eliza craved a friend to share her frustrations with, but Nala kept to herself, brushing off any effort from Eliza.

Adam shoved a muffin into her lap. "Eat, sister."

One thing separated Eliza from Nala—a doting family. Her heart swelled with pride at their attempts to include Nala, especially in Sabu's absence. And they'd defended Eliza that morning—against her wishes, sure, but they'd drop everything for her. Nobody had ever come to her defense, ever. Except Seti.

Her eyes moistened, but instead of giving in to the tears, she whipped the muffin at Adam, smacking him in the face.

"Hey!"

Laughter erupted, and Adam dove to fetch it.

Miera and the twins squealed as he pounced on Eliza, throwing her to the ground. She clamped her mouth shut and thrashed her head as he attempted to jam the muffin down her throat.

Sarah jumped to her feet. "Be careful with her, Adam. She's fragile."

He pried her mouth open and crammed the muffin in. "Seasoned with dirt. How's it taste?" He stood and brushed sand from his tunic.

Eliza sat up and spat out the gritty bread. Her head spun, and her arm throbbed, but she shot a look to her mother. "I'm not fragile."

"Tents are set up. You can go in and cry now," Adam teased.

Her neck burned red hot with fury, which only ramped up the pounding in her head. She seethed with clenched teeth. She'd give him a piece of her mind if it weren't for the dizziness. Miera stifled a laugh behind her hand while her mother huffed with arms crossed. Her father sat stoic, barely lifting a brow.

Adam's banter proved she wasn't so fragile after all, and Sena was sure to have witnessed it. Fragility came in handy sometimes, but most of the time it was a nuisance. Eliza hated it.

"Seti!" Miera shouted above the laughter.

Eliza's head snapped up. Everyone silenced. Seti arrived on Chewy with Sabu in tow. Time stopped, and the breath left her lungs as his glowing eyes found hers. Was she dreaming? Miera ran toward him.

Seti dismounted near Nala's tent. As he helped Sabu down, Eliza looked on in a daze before shuffling forward. Nala stumbled out of her tent in a blubbering mess.

"Careful," Sabu muttered, leaning on her. "Come on, get a hold of yourself, Nala. I'm alive."

"Nala." Seti pulled the strap off his shoulders and untied a pair of crutches. "He'll need these."

Eliza stopped short behind him, gaping at the deep purple bruise encompassing the left side of his back. Besides that and the open gash on his arm, he appeared unharmed. She slipped her hands around his bare chest, hugging him, and rested her forehead against his back, taking in his familiar scent and warmth. She whispered prayers of thanksgiving. His hand found both of hers as he continued speaking with Nala. Eliza hugged tighter, eliciting a catch in his voice. He spun and clenched her hands painfully tight in both of his.

His piercing eyes stilled her.

"Please," he said with quiet sternness. "Don't squeeze."

Eliza froze, unable to speak.

"Seti, you should've seen what happened this morning!" Miera bounded between them, and Seti's eyes softened.

"Careful." He held his breath as Miera hugged him, using one hand to keep her at bay and the other still grasping Eliza's. His face, still swollen but so beautiful, so perfect, held her captive.

The bruise wrapped around his chest. She longed to touch it.

"You should've seen what happened to Eliza!"

Eliza blinked and turned to her sister. "Miera! That's enough. Stay out of my affairs."

"What?" Seti asked, looking between them.

The concern in his voice melted Eliza's heart, but alarm set in. "What? What happened to you? To Sabu?" She nodded toward the hobbling Sabu, who paused and turned.

"What happened?" Adam barged in to help Sabu.

Their mother rushed over with a plate of muffins. "Sabu, Nala, why don't you sit with us and have something to eat?"

"Food," Sabu rasped. He inched toward her, face contorted with agony.

Nala left him in the capable hands of Adam and Zechariah and darted toward the tent.

Eliza's brothers lowered Sabu to the ground near the fire, propping him against a rock. Nala returned with his cloak and draped it over his shoulders.

"Now eat. All of you." Eliza's mother set a plate of muffins in Sabu's lap and handed another to Nala.

While Sabu devoured his muffins like a starving dog, Nala ignored hers. Instead, she slathered him with kisses on his neck and down his shoulder. Her fingers dug into his chest; her tears dribbled all over him. The endearing display of affection rooted Eliza where she stood. She was about to turn back to Seti when his arm encircled her waist and pulled her against his chest.

"I'm sorry," he whispered, his breath caressing her neck, raising every hair on her body. His bare chest warmed her back, and she started to turn, but he tightened his hold.

"I'm sorry," he whispered again. "We'll talk later—alone, but I'll tell your family everything. I owe it to them."

Before she could respond, her mother stepped in with a plate. "Eat, Seti. You must be starved."

"Thank you." He released Eliza and took the food, moving toward the fire as he ate.

Eliza didn't miss the suspecting look in her mother's eyes. Her parents may have accepted Seti's presence but not so much the affection growing between them. She huffed and sat beside him, wishing to cuddle him like Nala cuddled Sabu.

Seti offered the plate. She took a muffin but kept her eyes lowered. The orange glow from the embers danced with the twilight shadows, accentuating the contours of his chest and shoulders. What was wrong with her? For five years, she'd refrained from ogling him, afraid of anyone catching on, and she did well, considering how clueless he was. So why was she having so much trouble now? His presence—so close, so alluring—tried the lifetime of patience slavery had built. She hugged her knees and examined her muffin after each bite, trying to distract herself.

"Thought you weren't hungry," Adam needled from where he sat with Zechariah. He flicked his hand, dismissing her before she could answer.

She opened her mouth to fire back, but Seti touched her hand. When she lifted her eyes to meet his, all else faded.

"Now that we're all here." Her father stood, his sudden stir silencing the group. "It's time for a family meeting."

Chapter 25

"Family meeting? You people have those?" The words slipped out before Seti could stop them. He clapped a hand over his mouth and glanced around. Of course, they had family meetings. Every family did.

Jeremiah wrinkled his brow. "I spoke with my cousin, and tomorrow, upon waking, we—"

"Wait!" Eliza thrust out a hand as if to stop him from doing something inconceivable. "Wait. Seti has something to say. I'd rather he did it now before he backs out."

Backs out? Did she think him a coward? Not a man of his word? Why must this meeting wait on his confession? Seti squeezed her hand and raised a brow.

"Please, Seti."

He devoured the rest of his muffin and met Jeremiah's gaze, silently willing the man to continue. Instead, Jeremiah nodded, sat, and folded his hands in his lap. Great. Seti hadn't rehearsed anything. "I—I was planning to do this tomorrow, but I suppose I can now."

Sweat beaded on his forehead. The eyes of her entire family, as well as Sabu and Nala, rested on him with a mix of curiosity and expectation. Adam smirked.

Seti sucked in a breath. "I left the camp the other day."

"Of course you did." Jeremiah threw a hand into the air.

"Actually—" Seti winced. "I've left the Avaris camp

several times now. But the other day, before bringing you water, I left the presence of God. I know you didn't want us leaving, and I'm sorry. As you can see, I've paid a price, and I'm fortunate God allowed me back in." No use incriminating Sabu. It was Seti's idea, after all.

"Fortunately for you, God proved more merciful than I. I specifically told you, all of you—" Jeremiah pointed at each of them—"not to leave the camp. The Avaris camp. Especially after what happened to Eliza at the Red Sea."

Seti gulped.

Jeremiah stood, eyes aflame like a lion on the prowl. "Is it because you're not used to answering to anyone? Or you can't find it inside yourself to take instructions from a Hebrew? Maybe—"

"Please." Seti waved his hands frantically. "It's not that. I swear. The first time was to search for Moshe. Then, I got water from the Rock because Eliza was sick. You all needed it. And the other times, well, the other times, including when I left the Presence, were for good reason. I promise you."

Jeremiah crossed his arms, his slouched posture confirming an inner struggle. "You better have a good reason. I was beginning to like you—"

Zechariah shot to his feet, pointing at Seti. "You went to the Amalekites!"

"No—"

"You're a spy. Led them to us to make yourself look like a savior. You conspired—"

"No—" Seti sprang up.

"—against us because we devastated your land." Zechariah's eyes blazed with venom.

"He would never, Zechariah!" Eliza cut in, her voice sharp and shrill.

Sabu raised his hand. "I can confirm that's not what happened."

Silence descended on the family as glares flickered

around the circle. The only way out now was to admit the truth, but the circumstances worked against him. Circumstances of his own doing.

If Seti admitted his reason for leaving camp, he'd be forced to propose. But what father would accept a proposal after a confession of deliberate disobedience? Though Eliza's father held no authority over him, Seti needed the man's favor.

"Alright." Jeremiah sat and crossed his legs, his penetrating stare unmoving. "Let's hear what you have to say."

With a huff, Zechariah also sat. His disdain for Seti had surpassed even Adam's. And they had barely spoken. Why the animosity now?

After glancing at Eliza's desperate eyes, Seti scanned the group. No turning back now. Not if he was serious about Eliza. He squared his shoulders and met Jeremiah's eyes. "I want to marry Eliza. But I want to do it right. I came out here with nothing to offer but the gold cuffs for the dowry—I mean mohar. I have no money, and my jt's … er … abba's dead. So I found a merchant willing to se—"

"Merchant?" Adam cut in.

"Yes. A man traveling with us, selling his master's possessions. I saw him on the way to the Wilderness of Sin. He had the perfect mattan and some papyri for the contract … er … ketubah. But he'd only sell them to me if I found him water. This was before God provided it from the Rock. The closest place with water was Elim. Since I had Chewy, I figured it'd be an easy trek, though an enormous risk. But worth it."

Zechariah scowled. "Proves how little you regard our God."

"Eliza was sick!" Seti checked his tone and lowered his voice. Like the rest of Eliza's family, Zechariah wielded words like a double-edged sword, carving Seti's heart right out of his chest. "If it meant getting her water, so be it."

Yes, God would have provided eventually, but it had been urgent. The items were his goal, but he fully intended to bring water back for Eliza too. Didn't he?

Zechariah pressed his mouth into a thin line and leaned back against the wagon.

Seti filled his lungs, reclaiming himself. "But we were caught by the Amalekites in Elim and thrown in a cistern, hence the injuries. I never got the water, but after escaping I found a gold sword, which the merchant was willing to accept. By then, Moshe had reached Horeb. That's when I went to Horeb and brought water back for everyone."

Miera jutted her chin toward her brothers. "Seti told me when he got back. I knew before you."

"Then it's true." Adam sat forward, as if he'd given Seti the benefit of the doubt and now took it back. "You did lead them to us."

"No." Navigating the family's grievances was like paddling across the Nile. One misstep could prove fatal. "They'd already scouted our camp before I even left. Eliza and Miera spotted them the previous morning. They didn't get any information from either of us."

"I can confirm that," Sabu added.

"Wait." Sarah's eyes widened with alarm. "Eliza and Miera?"

"It's true," Eliza said quietly, eyes downcast. "The day before the attack, we caught one spying. I meant to tell you, Abba, but you were gone, and I didn't think they'd return."

Adam raised a brow, and Zechariah stilled, mouth agape. Jeremiah shifted, grimacing as he processed his daughter's words. The group waited for his response for what seemed an eternity of awkward silence. Miera flashed Seti a pleading look across the fire as if hoping he wouldn't elaborate on her part in it. She'd held her end of the deal, after all, and not blabbed, until now. He winked at her and turned to Jeremiah, who displayed such consternation that Seti sat.

Jeremiah cleared his throat and spoke with marked heaviness, eyes downcast. "And the mattan?"

Seti nodded at Nala. She rose, disappeared into her tent, then returned with a sack and handed it to him before returning to Sabu's side. She had hidden the items during the move and assured him of their safety upon his return with Sabu. He peeked inside. Everything was there except the lute. That would come later.

Seti silently rehearsed the most important words of his life.

The air thickened with anticipation as Seti lifted his countenance and faced Jeremiah, pulling out the golden arm cuffs his Father-of-Old had given him. He'd never removed them from his arms until he declared himself no longer an Egyptian, but a Hebrew, on that fateful day at Eliza's house.

"Now all I need is your approval, Jeremiah. If you so accept, I would like to marry your daughter." Was that how he was supposed to ask? Adam had said "in front of everybody."

Eliza gasped, her hand shooting to her mouth, and Miera let out a stifled squeal. But Jeremiah didn't move. Shivers rippled through Seti. He glanced toward Chewy, suppressing the sudden urge to jump on his steed and flee.

All eyes turned to Jeremiah, whose fingers steepled before his face. The waning embers in the hearth reflected in the piercing stare that pinned Seti in place, scrutinizing, ridiculing. But was he? The man was like a god-statue. Unreadable.

Seti swiped rivulets of sweat from his forehead. "Eliza will never be treated as a concubine. You have my word that I will provide for her, protect her, and give my life for her."

Nothing.

"With God as my witness,"—Seti gestured toward the Fire Pillar in the distance—"she will be second only to God."

If those words didn't move Jeremiah, nothing would. Seti kept his gaze hard, unflinching, silently challenging his potential father-in-law to respond. Everyone in his peripheral blurred, and seconds dragged into minutes.

Finally, Jeremiah stood. A collective gasp emanated from the group. He stepped toward the fire. Seti struggled to his feet, mouth dry, unsure of what to do. A gentle nudge from Eliza urged him forward. At the firepit, Seti met the man shoulder to shoulder.

Jeremiah's hand shot out in a welcoming gesture. "Consider yourself a Levite, my son."

The breath Seti had been holding came out in a whoosh as he grasped Jeremiah's arm. He let the man pull him into an embrace, reigniting the pain in his ribs. His body trembled from frazzled nerves until, with a deep sigh, tension oozed from his muscles.

When Jeremiah let go, he gazed at Seti with moist eyes and said with a cutting rawness, "Be the man I could never be for her."

Unable to speak, Seti nodded, and Jeremiah pulled him into another hug. This time, Jeremiah trembled. He whispered in Seti's ear, "But until then, she's still my daughter. You will keep your distance and listen to what I say tonight."

The words cut through Seti like a sudden chill. Was that a threat? Jeremiah let go, offered a quick smile, and turned away, leaving Seti dumbfounded. Miera covered her mouth with both hands, and the brothers sat with arms crossed, leveling Seti with a hard look. Seti gave a curt nod before sitting beside Eliza, though the urge to run still tugged at his every fiber.

"Seti," she whispered, taking his hand in hers. The sparkle in her brown eyes warmed his heart. He hadn't seen that shine since she played the lute weeks ago.

"Show her the rest, Seti." Miera jumped up, reaching for the sack, but Seti grabbed it first.

"Yes, show Eliza what I nearly died for," Sabu said.

With a wry smile, Seti opened the sack. The siblings

inched closer, Miera nearly falling over.

He pulled out the blue cotton bolt and handed it to Eliza. "For your dress."

Her eyes rounded, and her mouth fell open as she ran her hand down the light, silky cotton. After a lifetime of cheap flax, she deserved to know the feeling of true softness on her skin. Seti could only imagine. . .

"It's blue," she said on a gasp, making Seti laugh.

"Cotton." He pulled out the sandals next. "The mattan, my lady."

Gasps of wonder rippled around them as the others came closer. Eliza snatched the sandals from Seti with a squeal, measured them against her foot, then fingered the gems.

"They're real. Real turquoise!" She slipped one on and tied the straps around her ankle, the gems lying flat against her skin, transforming the foot of a slave into that of a dazzling queen. She laced on the other and stood, admiring her feet as quiet words murmured off her tongue like the ending of a lullaby. "Oh, Seti. How did you know my size? How did you know I love turquoise? How did you know? Oh, Seti."

Miera jumped beside her. "Look at us!" She danced, kicking her feet in Lumeri's old sandals, now dull from daily use. Eliza took Miera's hands and danced in a circle. The twins bounced over, giggling.

Seti leaned back and considered the gifts well worth his troubles. He hadn't seen Eliza dance in, well, never. But her boisterous laugh had returned. The lute would wait until the betrothal, though it would fit nicely with the moment.

"Perfect!" Sarah jumped to her feet. "Let's do this as soon as possible."

"Tomorrow!" Miera yelled.

"No, not tomorrow." Jeremiah stomped that suggestion.

"Then the next day!"

Sarah beamed. "Day after tomorrow it is!"

"Wait. What?" Seti straightened. "Day after tomorrow?"

"Too soon?" Adam grinned.

Eliza fell to her knees and bowed, face to the ground, hands folded in front of her. "The day after tomorrow, Seti. Please?"

Her prostration caught him off guard. Images of her in that very position back home in Egypt flooded his mind. It used to boost his ego, maybe elicit mockery. Not now. Not ever again. He shrank away, glancing at the others. Had they noticed?

"Please, Seti," Eliza whispered.

"Yes." Anything to get her off her knees. "Yes, the day after tomorrow."

Miera threw herself onto Eliza, hugging and squealing. The toddlers and Sarah joined in, obliterating the slave imagery.

Jeremiah gave a sharp nod, then stood. "That's settled. Now, back to the family meeting."

Chapter 26

While the girls and Sarah sat, Eliza flung her arms around Seti, making him wince. Her face reddened, and she let go, grabbing his hand. "Sorry. No squeeze." She gave his hand a gentle shake that sparked a nervous smile.

Her grin disappeared as she looked away, and Seti followed her gaze to her father's stern glare.

"I spoke with my cousin. Tomorrow at first light, we will meet him and Sena. Adam and I will go with you." Jeremiah paused, and Eliza gave a solemn nod. "I anticipate the line to Moshe will be long, so we need to get there early. After our return—hopefully by early afternoon—we'll move inward, closer to the mountain. Your mother and sister will gather the manna and pack our things."

His gaze then honed in on Seti, who sat confused. "Seti will remain here until we get back from Moshe."

Seti's stomach dropped at the gravity of Jeremiah's voice. He looked to Eliza for an explanation.

Eliza turned to him, eyes lowered, caressing his fingers. "I knocked out Sena's front teeth, and her abba came this morning to avenge her. Abba stopped him from hitting me. So now we're taking it to Moshe for a fair judgment."

"Wh—what does that mean?" Seti asked.

"Eye for an eye, tooth for a tooth," Adam said, "but I'm confident Moshe will take her injury into consideration."

Seti pulled his hand from hers and breathed deeply, the weight of Adam's words cutting through like a dull knife.

Everyone stared. Jeremiah stood and crossed his arms, as if waiting for Seti to erupt.

"So, Eliza must lose her teeth? No," Seti said, still not fully grasping the implications. "It's my fault. I should be the one. I took Sena out. It's my fault."

"Don't worry, Seti. Moshe knows me," Eliza said.

"Moshe's not going to be partial to you, Eliza." Adam leaned forward as if surprised by her words. "He'll be just, whether he knows you or not. That's the point."

"Each person faces the consequences of their own actions. Eliza hit Sena, so she must be the one to stand before Moshe," Zechariah added.

"But it's more complicated than that." Seti shook his head. "I provoked her. Let Sena knock my teeth out, not Eliza's. She's getting better. Do you see how happy she is? I won't let her suffer again."

"Seti, you can't." Sadness laced Eliza's voice.

"Yes, I can."

"Remember my words, Seti." Jeremiah narrowed his eyes. "You are to stay behind. We will not have you getting in the middle of it."

Seti shot to his feet. "I'm already in the middle of it!"

How could this be happening? He ran his fingers through his hair. It was just like the family meeting back home. A discussion over what to do with Eliza. Her temper had once again landed her in trouble, her fate in the hands of her accuser.

A tirade of accusations against her father threatened to spill from Seti's mouth. Jeremiah purposefully set the betrothal after her punishment, effectively excluding Seti from having any say.

Seti's whole being pulsed with anger. He clamped his mouth shut and stomped toward Sabu's tent, but catching sight of Chewy changed his direction. If he didn't get out of there now, the words would fly, and his blessing to marry Eliza would be retracted.

He should have made her his bride and skipped the whole betrothal process—the blessings, the gifts, the waiting, all of it. At least then, as a husband, he could stop this madness.

No. What was he thinking? That would make her a concubine. She deserved the best. The whole thing. If only he'd guarded his heart and never trifled with Sena, none of this would be happening.

"Seti!" Eliza's footsteps padded behind him. She caught his arm and spun him around.

"Why didn't you tell me?" he spat. "You purposefully waited until after I bared my soul, then let your abba ambush me!" Seti pointed toward her father. "You knew he wouldn't let me go. He planned it ahead of time to exclude me. You could've warned me, Eliza. You could've pulled me aside and told me what was happening, like an adult, so I wouldn't become a spectacle for everyone's amusement."

"No. I didn't mean it to be like that," she fired back. "I didn't know you were going to propose!"

"Then what did you mean? It's pretty clear you knew what your father would do and waited to tell me until after I made a fool of myself."

"Because, Seti. Because I deserve it, and I knew you wouldn't accept that."

Tears welled in her eyes, melting his defenses. Yelling at his bride over hurt pride when tomorrow she would take a beating far worse. What was he doing? He took a deep breath and gently gripped her arms. "You don't deserve it. I took Sena out. I played the game. You were right all along. I'm weak and wasn't guarding my heart."

"I shouldn't have hit her." Her voice quavered.

"You should've hit me."

"I should have, but hit her instead. I didn't even know I could hit that hard. Maybe a gap-toothed smile will improve her personality." Eliza sighed. "But I did what I did and must be punished."

"No. I'll speak with Moshe and tell him everything," he said, unable to take her crying because of him. He'd risk standing face-to-face with the man of God.

"I deserve it. It's only a couple of teeth." Her words hung in the dry air, pricking his heart.

He shook his head. "Do you hear yourself?"

"Don't worry." She touched his cheek so lightly it vaporized the last traces of anger. "She's a weakling. I can handle it. Moshe will make sure it's fair."

"No. Do you hear yourself, Eliza? You sound exactly like you did before you were whipped. You're underestimating it now, just like you did then. You couldn't handle it then, so what makes you think you can now?"

"Your ima had a whip. That was different."

"Eliza." Seti took a deep breath. "She's going to hit you. In the face. With her fist. You're still healing from a head injury, remember? And even if Sena's weak, she could still do serious damage. You're starting to get better. I need you to be better. None of this is your fault."

"Yes, it is."

"No, it's not!"

"You're upset because you're blaming yourself for when I fell."

"Because it was my fault."

"But it wasn't your fault."

"Yes, it was!" He sighed, realizing he was yelling again.

"Seti, stop. Just stop." She moved out of his grasp. "Just let me get it over with. Stay behind. Abba said that because he knows you'll step in."

"He's right I will!"

"Please, Seti, stay here. Don't meddle."

"Meddle?" His voice cracked in disbelief. "That's what you're calling it? If I remember correctly, when I saved you last time, you said it was your God not failing you, and you certainly deserved it then. But now it's meddling?"

"My God? He's your God too."

"You're missing the point!" He turned, ready to end this conversation but paused. After raking his fingers through his hair, he faced her again.

The Fire Pillar reflected in the tears streaking down her face. "I am not missing the point." Her voice trembled. "You are. And yes, God used you to save me, even when I deserved it. That doesn't mean this is the same. That was God. This is you trying to intervene."

Seti stared, caught by the fierceness in her eyes. "That was not all God."

"If God wants to save me again, He will. But you can't overstep Him. You might make it worse."

How could he possibly make it worse? God hadn't protected her from the Amalekites, and He wasn't protecting her now. "What if," he began, "what if Moshe decides it's my fault?"

"Then we'll come get you."

He wanted to both punch something and kiss her. Instead, he cupped her face with his hand and wiped away a tear with his thumb. "When you chose to be whipped instead of going to the bricks for Miera's sake, I couldn't help but admire your bravery. You didn't even try to get out of it. It was one of the reasons I fell in love with you."

Her determined expression softened into a demure gaze, rendering him helpless. "Promise me."

"I promise I won't meddle."

"And you will stay here," she said.

"I promise I'll keep my distance and won't meddle, but I can't promise I'll stay here."

Her shoulders slumped with a tired sigh. Leaving it at that, she ignored the watchful eyes of her family as she marched past them to her tent.

"Wow, that was beautiful," Adam said loudly.

Seti rolled his eyes and sulked toward Sabu's campsite. Unlike Eliza, he didn't have the luxury of a tent to hide in.

Chapter 27

Eliza opened her eyes to her mother nudging her shoulder. Pale morning light filtered into the tent.

"It's time to go, my dove," her mother said with a tentative smile.

Eliza lifted her head, surprised she'd even slept. Fearing another sleepless night, she had prayed for decent rest and mercy for both herself and Seti, and here she woke with readiness, feeling like she had slept at least a few hours. With an unusual vigor, she sat upright. No dizzy spell overcame her. Would Sena undo all that?

"Let's go. I don't want to be in line all day," her father called from outside.

Adam and Miera had already left the tent, leaving only Zechariah snoozing on the far side. A swath of blue fabric spread across Miera's sleeping mat.

Eliza stood to go outside, but her mother stopped her with a measuring rod. "I'll start on your dress this morning. I've already cut it down, and there's plenty of fabric left for tunics. I'll send word about the betrothal before we move. I'm thinking of inviting Dodo's family, the Hodiah family, Jodadiah and –"

"Whoever, Ima. Just please make sure you find Rahel. She can't miss this. And how will everyone know where to find us after we move?"

"I'm telling them we'll be along the river with your abba's work crew." Sarah measured Eliza's waist with a string. "Don't worry, we'll have all night after we arrive to spread word and prepare. Embiah has a whole flock of chickens. He said he'd even slaughter some and provide eggs. And Sheri has jam. I can make honey-manna and cinnamon-manna muffins. How does that sound?"

Did her mother even sleep? Whether she did or not, pure joy bathed her face. Unwilling to sap her mother's sudden sense of purpose, Eliza shrugged and headed toward the flap. She didn't look forward to being the center of attention, but the talk of food made her stomach rumble.

Miera peeked in, eyes wide with wonder. "The manna's forming!"

The sun barely skimmed the horizon, painting the sky in an array of oranges that chased the deep reds eastward, while a hazy blue stretched like a canopy over the camp. As Eliza stepped outside, she nearly collided with Seti.

"Hi," he said, stepping back.

She straightened with a quick inhale. His cheerful tone betrayed his tired eyes.

"Did you sleep?" he asked, his warm breath gusting her face.

She could ask him the same. His hair stuck out in all directions, evidence of a restless night. "Better than I thought."

"Let's go," her father barked from behind Seti, rubbing his hands together.

Seti glanced over his shoulder then back at Eliza, brow furrowed. "I have some manna for you." He held up a basket. "You might be there a while."

"Seti ..." Eliza took the basket and the small pouch of water he handed her.

"You should tie your hair back." He brandished a scrap of her blue cotton. "Don't want it getting in the way."

"How—"

"You have plenty. It'll match your dress tomorrow." He stepped behind her and gathered her hair.

His behavior, though charming, raised her suspicions. He remained uncharacteristically calm about staying behind while Moshe dealt with her and Sena.

"Remember your promise," she said as he tied the cloth around her head like a scarf.

"Of course." He turned her to face him and patted her cheek like an old father. His hands then rested on her shoulders, and he gazed into her eyes. "I'll be waiting."

Either he'd had a change of heart since last night, or it was all a façade for her sake. Or her father had spoken with him. Hopefully, it wasn't the latter. Chewy and Nimrod stirred near Sabu's tent, shaking the newly formed manna from their manes. Adam rose near the hearth, stretched, and yawned. Her father cleared his throat and shot a nod toward Eliza.

Something flickered in Seti's eyes, and his hands tightened on her shoulders for a split second before he forced a smile and kissed her forehead.

"I love you, Seti." If anybody needed reassurance, it was him.

Even when forced, his handsome smile melted her heart and sent flutters through her chest. "I love you too."

She looped the pouch strap over her shoulder and glanced at Sena, whose piercing blue eyes glared from beside her tent. Her hair hung loosely over her shoulders, and a pale pink scarf covered the bottom half of her face.

Eliza's father marched forward, mouth hard-set, and joined Sena and her father. Swallowing the knot rising in her throat, Eliza followed, while Adam trudged behind.

Miera waved from near the stream, the twins beside her, omer baskets in their hands. One of the toddlers blew a kiss. Eliza returned the kiss, but a wave of trepidation swept over her. Everyone went about their day as usual, but what if she didn't return the same way she left? Or worse, not at all? She had brushed off Seti's concerns as unfounded, but he could be right. She and her family might be underestimating Sena and Moshe. *Eye for an eye, tooth for a tooth*, Adam had said. But Moshe could charge her with more than just knocking out Sena's teeth. He could use her to make an example. How, she wasn't sure, but her mind raced with all kinds of possibilities.

Moshe stood on a rocky hill beneath a makeshift canopy, arms raised before a small group of onlookers. From there, a line of Hebrews stretched down the hill and wound through the city of tents below. Eliza would soon join that line.

"Look how long it is already," Adam groaned as they descended into the congested valley.

Eliza's father shielded his eyes as he looked toward Moshe. "From what I heard, this is nothing compared to midday. I wouldn't want to stand out here at noon."

But by noon, the line had only crept halfway up the slope. The closer they drew to Moshe, the denser the crowd. Eliza craned her neck for a glimpse of him, but spectators blocked her view. A cheer erupted from a group of men ahead—justice, presumably, had been served in their favor.

Eliza's shoulders burned under the sweltering heat, and the sun's brightness triggered a headache behind her squinting eyes. She turned to the forbearing Cloud Pillar, but its canopy offered little shade, as though those in need of judgment had lost favor in God's eyes.

The oppressive heat forced her father and Sena's father to drape their cloaks over their arms, tunics drenched with sweat. Sena pulled her scarf down, revealing her swollen face and cracked lips, her eyes fixed in a tired stare toward the horizon. Eliza shared her water and manna with her father and Adam, grateful for Seti's foresight. Neither of them had thought to bring any of their own.

As her father and Adam discussed possible places to relocate the family tents, Eliza scanned the horizon for Seti.

If he showed, she'd be livid. Yet a small part of her craved his comforting presence. Even a glimpse of him in the distance would ease her growing angst.

She turned to study the Cloud Pillar behind Moshe. Its light and dark vapors swirled upward in a mesmerizing dance, as if carried by the wind. But not even the faintest breeze stirred, at least where Eliza stood. Never had she been so close. The base of the Pillar covered the top of the Great Mountain, giving perspective on its ominous size. Her chest tightened. The immensity of it reduced the multitude to chaff on a threshing square on the verge of being blown away at the slightest wrong move. It bore no semblance of a personal God who heard the prayers of a mere slave girl.

She looked away, hugging herself tightly. Whatever Moshe deemed to be just must come from God, as He knows the hearts of men and reveals them to His prophet. What would God say about her heart?

One of two young men ahead sparked a conversation with Sena's father, though his gaze often wandered toward Sena. The scarf quickly went over her face again, and she coyly twisted a lock of hair near her puffed chest. When she slid one of her tunic straps off her shoulder, Eliza's mouth dropped. She stepped forward, tempted to yank the scarf down, but stopped at the sight of a dead goat at the man's feet. Beside him, another young man looked on, his own goat chewing a clump of brown grass.

Ahead, a middle-aged woman sat on a rock, her sweat-slicked face partially hidden behind a patch over one eye. The woman beside her stood with crossed arms near a man whose beard trailed nearly to his waist, sparking Eliza's curiosity. She followed the line toward Moshe. People sat on the grass or rocks, rising only when the line moved. Some hunched over with eyes closed, while others chatted idly. No one looked toward the Cloud Pillar.

"Hi, Eliza!" The voice belonged to little Calev, who had worked for Seti's neighbor in Egypt.

A spark of joy lifted inside Eliza at his familiar face. She knelt to meet his eyes. Several pouches of water hung from his shoulders, and a tray of baked manna slices bounced from leather straps looped around his neck.

"What brings you here?" he asked as cheerfully as she remembered him. "Frog juice?"

Eliza laughed. "Not this time. Looks like I'm a troublemaker lately, doesn't it?" She glanced at Sena, who continued to eye the young man. "Justice. Justice brings me here."

"Need some water? Manna?" His brown eyes displayed an innocence Eliza could no longer relate to.

"I do." Adam reached over Eliza's shoulder.

Calev handed him a pouch. "Drink, but give it back. Ima will have my hide if I return without her pouches." He looked to Eliza. "Ima says I have too much energy, so she sent me to replenish the naughty people. Says it will do me good. That was yesterday. I'm going to do it every day now. It's fun."

Adam guzzled from the pouch and handed it to Eliza. "Thanks."

"Yes, thank you." Eliza finished it.

After her father drained a pouch and grabbed a slice of manna, they trudged forward, and Calev moved to the next person, waking each from their sun-cooked stupor. Eliza studied him. His cheerful presence and small provisions revived those waiting, a hint of grace to the guilty.

What felt like eons later, the two women and the long-bearded man stepped up to Moshe, who sat on a rock, leaning on his knee with one hand, Aharon's staff in the other. Aharon was nowhere to be seen, though an unfamiliar older man with hair as white as wool stood behind Moshe. The midday sun blazed down, and Moshe wiped sweat from his brow. His gaze flickered toward Eliza before returning to the three before him.

A sweat-drenched crowd surrounded them, clearly there for the entertainment. Eliza tightened her lips and turned away. Once again, she'd be a spectacle. Did these people have nothing better to do? Murmurs and chatter rippled through the onlookers. Several pointed to the woman with the eyepatch, speculating aloud about what would happen next.

Moshe straightened. "State your purpose."

Both women launched into a torrent of accusations, pointing at each other while the man stood quietly to the side, looking away with unseeing eyes.

Moshe raised his staff to silence them. "You first." He pointed to the woman with the eyepatch.

"She took my eye!" She lifted her patch to expose the gaping hole beneath, then faced the crowd, intensifying their gasps and murmurs.

"Because she slept with my husband!" the other shouted, face flushed.

Moshe stood and raised his staff again to quiet the commotion. He chugged from a clay jar handed to him, then stepped forward. "Is this true?" He turned to the long-bearded man. The crowd fell silent.

"It is. But I am remorseful and pledge to be faithful to my wife."

Eliza's heart pounded. The case echoed her own. She leaned forward, holding her breath.

Turning to the wife, Moshe lowered his chin. "So, you took matters into your own hands, assuming the role of judge and enforcer. What inclined you to deem this act as just?" He gestured toward the woman with the eyepatch, who had thankfully replaced it.

"It was instinct, my lord. The first thing I could get my hands on. Besides, it's the lust of the eyes that stimulates the lust of the flesh."

"And what of the lust of your husband's?"

The husband and wife exchanged stunned glances.

"She clearly didn't force herself on him." Moshe turned to the one-eyed woman. "Do you have a husband?"

"I am a widow, my lord," she said matter-of-factly.

"Family?"

"Two grown daughters. Both married with children."

Moshe sighed and glanced around as if expecting her daughters to appear. The many lines on his face deepened. He pulled his sweat-soaked tunic away from his chest and motioned to two young men in loincloths. Their chiseled muscles glistened in the scorching sun, Amalekite swords in hand. Hoots and hollers erupted as they stepped forward, awaiting Moshe's command. The one-eyed woman smiled while the other woman shrank behind her husband, digging her fingers into his arm.

Eliza's heart thumped against her chest.

"Adultery is an abomination. Death be to the adulterous husband and the widow."

The crowd roared, and the wife threw herself on her stoic husband in sudden hysteria. One of the men grabbed the widow, whose smile vanished.

Eliza's knees buckled. The breath left her lungs. Would they really kill them—right in front of everyone? She stepped behind her father, a hand over her mouth, bile rising in her throat.

"Please, no! I beg you. Please spare my husband. I still love him," the wife wailed.

Moshe lifted his staff again, halting the young man from approaching the husband.

"Moshe, please." The sudden silence amplified the wife's desperate plea. "You're punishing me by making me a widow. It's not fair. Please don't take him from me. He's all I have."

Her appeal struck deep. Those could very well be Eliza's words. Family or not, she couldn't live without Seti. And this man was truly remorseful.

"Have mercy, Moshe. Beg God for mercy." The woman fell to her knees, and at once, Eliza did too, her stomach lurching.

Adam reached for her but stopped when Moshe spoke, his gaze toward the heavens. "Very well," Moshe said. "For his lust, the husband shall lose one eye. His other eye shall remain that he may continue to support his wife and also the widow now tied to him. But the widow will not live in his household. She shall lose her remaining eye—to prevent further harm and spare her life."

The onlookers again broke into cheers and shouts. Eliza covered her ears and closed her tear-filled eyes, shaking uncontrollably as justice was served. Despite the commotion, nothing could drown out the screams of the man and the widow.

Maybe this was why her father didn't want Seti to come—to protect him.

As the wife, her adulterous, one-eyed husband, and the now-blind widow stumbled away in wails and moans, the line moved forward. The two men, with one dead and one live goat, approached Moshe. But Eliza paid them no heed. She cowered behind her father, shaking. Adam and her father watched with quiet awe, no different from the gawking audience that had grown around them.

Sena stood strangely silent, hunched behind her father, arms crossed, eyes downcast. If Eliza had known it would come to this, she would never have hit her. She'd welcome Sena's punch—anything but this.

One of the two loinclothed men raised his Amalekite sword skyward at Moshe's command. The blade glinted in the sun. Eliza covered her eyes with her hands but peeked through her fingers. Her whole being pulsed with terror. The man's muscled arm brought the sword down, slicing through the neck of the living goat. Eliza's heart lurched into her throat, and she yelped at the clash of metal on stone. She turned to run, but her father grabbed her tunic.

Chapter 28

Cheers thundered in Eliza's ears and reverberated inside her. She fought against her father's tightening grip.

"No, Eliza. We're next." Her father's voice could barely be heard over the commotion. "You can do this. Hold it together."

"No. No, no, no, no, no."

Adam stepped forward, ready to grab her if she broke free. Tears poured down her cheeks as she squeezed her eyes shut. "Let me go! This was a mistake. Just let Sena hit me."

She swung at Adam, but he sidestepped her.

"I can't do this!" she cried.

"Nobody's leaving until Moshe decides," Sena's father growled.

Sobbing, Eliza collapsed to her knees.

Her father yanked her arm, cramping her shoulder. "Get up."

"Oh, you stupid, blubbering idiot. Nobody's going to die." Sena's searing voice was far from comforting. But it wasn't death Eliza was so afraid of.

It was God.

"I can't." Eliza clawed at the stony ground. "Please, I don't care about my head. Just let me go."

She grabbed Adam's ankles. "You wouldn't let Sena hit me the other day, but now you want her to?"

"I don't care if Sena hits you. She's weak, and you're

not." Adam bent and grabbed her wrists. "It was her father I was concerned about."

"Get up!" Her father ordered again, dragging her to her feet.

Her knees buckled, and she clung to his waist, not wanting to collapse only to be yanked up again. Her purposeful, deep breaths succumbed to hyperventilation. Her vision blurred. Seti was right, this was worse than the whipping pole.

"Eliza!" Moshe's commanding voice cut through the crowd, and everyone went silent. "Eliza, look at me at once."

She slowly turned. Moshe stood only a few paces away, while the white-haired man behind him leveled her with a curious but strained look.

Moshe's stern expression softened, and he lowered his voice. "What are you doing here, Eliza?"

He remembered her name. But then again, how could he not? She had humiliated him at the palace. Unable to form words, only a small whimper emerged from her raw throat.

Her father spoke. "We've come for fair judgment."

"On Eliza?"

"Eliza and Sena." He pointed to Sena.

The flicker of sadness in Moshe's eyes stung. Eliza looked away in shame.

He pressed his lips into a grimace. "What did you do now?" The disappointment in his tone crushed her.

When she didn't answer, her father nudged her.

She squeaked, "I hit her."

Moshe turned to Sena. "So, hit her back." Then back to Eliza. "Why come to me?"

Sena's father stepped forward. "We tried. Eliza knocked out my daughter's two front teeth. And since she suffered a head injury a few weeks ago, they won't let Sena hit her back. A tooth for a tooth. Teeth."

Sena pulled the scarf from her face, revealing her swollen chin, crooked black-and-blue nose, and gap-toothed smile.

Whistles and murmurs spread through the crowd, and Moshe's eyes widened. He faced Eliza. "Don't tell me this was over a boy."

How did he know? Both girls nodded.

"Truly?" Moshe's shoulders slumped. "A boy? What is it with you and getting into trouble over boys?"

"There's only been one," Eliza said quietly. She scanned the crowd for Seti. She needed him beside her. But the further away he was, the safer.

Moshe did a double-take. "Don't tell me—no. Not him."

He slowly lowered himself onto the rock, face pale. A spark of defensiveness rose inside Eliza. She studied Moshe, unsettled by his reaction. His grave expression confirmed her gratitude that her father had kept Seti away. Moshe clearly held something unspoken against him.

Moshe's face shifted from pale shock to red-hot fury. "You're a fool to mess with the likes of him!"

"I am no fool!" Eliza snapped, surprised by her own vehemence. Moshe's retort had strengthened her resolve and chased away any lingering dread. He misjudged her and Seti, and it didn't matter who he was, she wouldn't stand for it. But if he misjudged her so easily, how could he be just?

The horde of viewers quieted to a hush of gasps while Moshe straightened on the rock, brow raised, clearly not expecting her reaction. He regained his composure, and his face relaxed. What was happening? She stared him down, impressed by her own tenacity yet unwilling to show how it quickly wavered.

Her father cleared his throat. "If you'll pardon me for saying, my lord, I'm with her on this one. She has chosen well."

With a swift inhale, Eliza spun to her father. He liked Seti. She knew he did, but to hear it from his own mouth meant the world. He rested his hand on her shoulder and gave a curt nod.

"Well then," Moshe said, averting his eyes.

He stood with a huff and gazed toward the Cloud Pillar, his expression worn and tired, shattering the momentary joy Eliza had just held. She couldn't shake the image of the adulterous widow and the long-bearded, wayward husband.

"You're not going to kill us, or Seti, are you?" As the words escaped, Eliza's hands flew to her mouth, as if to stop them from reaching Moshe.

"What was that?" His forehead crinkled beneath bushy white brows.

"Nothing."

"Out with it, girl."

"Do we … does Seti deserve death?" she asked in a small voice, "or our eyes gouged?"

"What? No. What on earth would make you think that? Unless you two are married—"

"No. Not yet." She shook her head.

Moshe turned to Sena. "Did you and that boy have sexual relations?"

"By the gods, no!" Sena yelled in disgust. "I merely stole him away for a brief moment—tried to show him what he was missing. We swam. Talked. That was it."

Despite the gut-wrenching jab at Eliza, Sena's words were a relief, and Eliza should have known better. Seti might have wavered between girls, but he was diligent about remaining pure. At least in Egypt he had been, when becoming a priest meant the world to him. Even with Eliza, he limited himself to kissing and nothing more.

Moshe raised a brow at Sena, then shifted his unsettled gaze to her father. He pulled his sweaty tunic from his chest and turned to the mysterious man behind him. The two locked eyes. After what felt like eons, Moshe lifted his face to the Cloud Pillar.

Eliza inched back, more willing to endure the misjudgment of an old man than the dreaded word of a God who seemed distant and cold despite His nearness. With a huff of acknowledgment toward the Pillar, Moshe turned and thumped Aharon's staff on the ground. Eliza's stomach dropped. Sena leaned forward, eyes wide.

"You know I can't judge in partiality because of our acquaintance, Eliza," Moshe began, nodding toward her. "Considering the head injury, Sena must strike below the eyes with at most three punches. One tooth or three punches, whichever comes first."

Murmurs rippled through the growing audience.

"But she knocked out two teeth!" Sena pointed at Eliza, her voice a shrill. "I swallowed one."

Moshe took a deep breath through his nostrils and said in a monotone voice, "Considering the head injury."

"The head injury? Why should that matter?" Sena's father stammered. "That twit hurt her head before the incident. She should have thought about that before hitting my daughter."

Moshe squared his shoulders with a look of scorn, silencing the man.

Sena glared at Eliza and muttered something under her breath.

"So be it," Jeremiah said. He removed his hand from Eliza's shoulder.

Moshe stepped back. "Right here, right now. I will oversee. Any further incidents regarding this matter will be judged two-fold." He aimed his staff at Sena, then pointed it to the ground in front of him.

The onlookers moved back with a rumble of excited chatter, creating enough space for a fighting ring. Her father moved aside, leaving Eliza in the middle, sweating profusely.

Sena's father whispered something in his daughter's ear, then nudged her forward. She wrung her hands, eyes locked on Eliza like a lioness ready to pounce. "Three? I can do three."

Eliza's blood chilled as she braced for more debilitating headaches, lethargy, and tears. She'd pay, even for Seti's part in it. A quick glance around for him proved futile, the view blocked by spectators closing in on all sides. No Seti to the rescue this time. That would only make things worse. She clasped her hands behind her back and closed her eyes. "I'm ready."

"There you go, baby girl," Sena's father said. "Step forward and use your dominant hand like I taught you. Remember how to make a fist now—"

"I know, Abba!"

Eliza opened her eyes as Sena stepped forward, then back, then forward again, as if weighing each step. Her fists wavered at face level, and Eliza was half tempted to shove one of those fists back into Sena's face.

She was about to smirk when Sena's fist slammed into her mouth, sending her stumbling backward, arms flailing. The world spun, and cheers erupted. The crowd caught her before she fell and shoved her back toward Sena.

After she regained her balance, Eliza straightened and bared her teeth for all to see before planting her feet, the metallic taste of blood filling her mouth. She glanced at her father and Adam. Their blurred forms stood still amid the rambunctious, obnoxious onlookers, who hollered suggestions to Sena as if Eliza was nothing but a rabid dog awaiting its fate.

Sena repositioned herself, and the crowd's cheers morphed into rhythmic chants of her name.

Closing her eyes only made the spinning worse. Eliza opened them just as Sena's fist clipped her chin. She lost her balance, swaying into one of Moshe's musclemen. The chanting and shouting matched the throbbing in her head. As Eliza moved back into place, she glimpsed Moshe's stoic form on the rock, arms crossed. Thankfully, she couldn't make out his eyes. She'd never show her face to him again.

"One more, Eliza!" her father shouted over the din.

"You can do it."

The chanting grew hypnotic. Her vision narrowed. One more, then it would be over. With a deep breath, she clasped her hands tightly behind her, fingernails digging into her palms.

Sena's third punch nailed her in the mouth, sending Eliza into a spin. The crowd parted, letting her smack the ground face-first.

Pain exploded from her nose as it broke her fall. White lights flashed behind her eyelids. She rolled over and spat blood and dirt, blinking up at a sea of blurred faces staring down at her.

"Show us!" someone shouted, followed by a chorus of demands to expose her teeth.

Blood filled her mouth. She sat up, spat again, and wiped the dribble from her chin. She flashed her teeth for all to see. Boos whirled in echoing waves, muffled as if her ears were plugged with water. Better than the high-pitched ringing that plagued her when she first fell at the Red Sea. She ran her tongue along her teeth, glad they were all intact.

Two sets of hands pulled her to her feet.

"Congratulations, Eliza. You didn't fight back." Adam slapped her on the back, and the muffled sounds cleared with a pop in her ear. A cacophony of shouts demanded she get out of the way of the next in line.

She couldn't speak. Everything swirled in a mass of colors, and her pulsating head was too heavy to hold upright.

"Here." Adam pressed a rag to her face.

She flinched and stepped back, gagging, as pain shot up the side of her face. "Adam!" She pushed him away and snatched the rag. "I can do it myself. Get away." Her voice sounded nasally.

"I'm only trying to help. How's your head?"

Her nose stung with each dab. She may have all her teeth, but she'd be going to her betrothal with a face like Seti's.

After she didn't answer, Adam gently guided her out of the mob. "That last punch was impressive," he blurted, clearly masking his concern. "For a girl."

Not as impressive as mine.

The thought shamed her. Let Sena have her moment. Let Adam play it off like it was no big deal. She fought the urge to lean into his firm grip. He may have seen her a blubbering mess before, but never again.

"Let's get you home, Eliza." Her father's voice, uncharacteristically tight with apprehension, never sounded so comforting.

Before she could find Moshe in the blur of activity or see Sena's reaction, her father whisked her away, not letting her even gather her bearings.

She stumbled down the slope, barely able to keep pace with her father, his arm firm around her shoulders.

"How are you doing?" he asked once they reached the bottom of the hill, away from the noise.

"I'll make do." Maybe if she could sit. "I bit my tongue."

"I'm proud of you, sis. I was sure I was going to have to tie your hands." Adam gave her a teasing jab to the shoulder.

"Wouldn't you have liked to." Though her head pounded, the dizziness faded faster than expected, and she managed to keep moving. The thought of being carried by her father or Adam mortified her.

The chanting of Sena's name continued deep within Eliza's insides. She shook her head, focusing instead on the sound of her father's sandaled feet slapping the ground. Of course everyone cheered for Sena. She was the victim. And beautiful. Eliza—scar-faced frog girl—was nothing to them. Nothing to anybody.

Wait—how could she think that? But her emotions ran amok, heedless of truth. Her father's voice blurred with Adam's in a muddled ramble, something about hurrying to move the tents and wanting to beat Sena's father back to camp.

Eliza stumbled, knees weak. She slowed several paces behind, as the tears threatened to flow. If she could dry her eyes and push on, she'd return to Seti in no time and save her breakdown for the privacy of her tent.

The sadness in Moshe's eyes returned with vivid intensity. *"What did you do now?"* His grave words skewered her heart. He was God's representative. Did Moshe's reaction reflect God's? And did God harbor the same disdain for Seti that Moshe did?

Eliza lost the internal battle, and the tears poured out. She swiped at them in vain, unable to stop them or the snorts of her swollen nose. Her vision blurred, and her breathing came in ragged gasps. The dull throbbing in her nose and jaw, along with the sting of her tongue, were nothing compared to the barrage of relentless, negative thoughts suddenly consuming her.

Her father was bound to turn around at the sound of her blubbering. She sucked in a fortifying breath, turned her face to the side and said with as much calm as she could muster, "I see Rahel. You go ahead. I'll meet you back …"

Their footsteps faltered. "Don't be long. We'll be leaving soon."

"I won't," she replied, still facing away. As soon as their steps shuffled on, Eliza broke into a run. Where to? She didn't know, as long as she could hide.

Chapter 29

Seti sighed and stuffed the rolled papyrus into a side pouch dangling from the rope around his waist. He had searched all morning for Hoshea, hoping the man could find him some papyri. Hoshea had plenty, despite his illiteracy.

The blaring sun forced Seti to shield his eyes, and that's when he glimpsed Eliza. She staggered unknowingly in his direction, head ducked, with a hand covering her face. He stood atop a giant boulder piled on an old rockslide that trailed off the Great Mountain, forming a wall of boulders and rocks along one side of the valley. It provided an excellent vantage point. Barren mountains and hills encapsulated the valley of tents, animals, people, and wagons below, reminding Seti of a bowl of almonds. He licked his lips. The narrow river of miracle water wound near the far end, embellishing the browns and whites like a blue ribbon that matched the sky, before snaking toward the opposite side of the Great Mountain.

His plan had worked. Eliza's glimmering blue head wrap stood out among the drab grays and browns like a blueberry in his imaginary bowl of almonds. What these people did with their Egyptian treasures, he didn't know, but they didn't wear them. Maybe they saved them for special occasions. Whatever the case, it worked to Seti's advantage. From wherever he stood, he could spot Eliza in the long line of those seeking Moshe until she disappeared into the small crowd that surrounded Moshe on the hill in front of the Great Mountain. The malicious audience had been loud all afternoon, but when their cheers turned into a chant of Sena's name, Seti's heart twisted in an agonizing knot. He'd have marched up that hill and barged through the crowd if he didn't fear losing Jeremiah's blessing—or the honor of his word. He had to remind himself that her father loved her at least as much as he did. Thankfully, the chanting hadn't lasted long, and Eliza reappeared, herded down the hill by her father and Adam.

He had spent the previous night fretting over her and her father's words. The man had Seti in a precarious position, unable to weigh in on the punishment that should have been his, not Eliza's. And instead of opposing her father, she had opposed Seti. It was his fault all this had happened, but she insisted on taking the blame.

So let her. If it would make this go away, let her and the others have their way. It had taken all night to accept that. She would put on a strong face, but eventually she'd break. And when that happened, Seti would be there to pick up the pieces.

Her blue head veered away from Jeremiah and Adam, then bobbed through the meandering crowds, weaving between cookfires and tents, and around a small herd of cattle before arriving at the edge of the camp at the boulders. She was alone. Perfect. Seti moved across the top of the rockslide in her direction until she disappeared amid the lower boulders. Noting where he'd last seen her, he started down but stopped when she appeared again, climbing up.

He suppressed the urge to call to her, succumbing to his curiosity instead. Where was she going? He wiped sweat from his forehead and shielded his eyes. If he waited and followed, she'd lead him to a secluded spot, and they could finally be alone without him having to drag her from her family. The climb would tire her as well, making her less willing to protest his joining her. They'd have the honest conversation he'd been waiting for since returning from Elim.

Seti ducked behind a jagged boulder and watched, amazed at her agility while barefoot. He hadn't worn sandals since the Red Sea, and though the stony ground had toughened his soles, he still struggled for grip on the smooth limestone.

When Eliza reached the top of the rockslide, she paused and turned toward the valley, scanning the camp from one end to the other. Wild curls sprang from her headwrap, swaying in the breeze, begging Seti to tame them. They blocked his view of her face. As she turned his way, he ducked. He smiled, remembering a conversation with Sabu back in Egypt. His friend had been right—the perfect girl wouldn't be content merely hearing about Seti's adventures. She'd join him, no matter the danger.

Fearless Eliza would walk beside him in every moment of life, encouraging and uplifting him. Where he had wanted someone to respect his love for learning, she'd inspire him. Where he'd hope for a woman to share his devotion to the gods, she'd bolster his love for the one true God.

Seti peeked over the rock as she descended the other side. Abandoning his cover, he crept after her, thanking the Hebrew God again for everything. Back in Egypt, his aspirations had been foolish. God had a bigger purpose for him.

Tucked in a crevice beneath a large boulder on the ground, hidden in its shadow, Eliza buried her face in her knees. If Seti hadn't been looking, he'd never have found her. When his feet hit the ground, she snapped upright with a quick gasp. He straightened, meeting her tear-filled gaze in a moment of palpable anguish.

Before he could take another step, she bolted toward him. He braced himself for the impact. Instead, she stopped a handspan from him. Her breath caught as her gaze lifted to his. The sorrow in her eyes stole his voice.

"Seti," she whispered, trembling. Her bottom lip oozed blood, swollen and dark. Her nose bruised. A short whistle from it accompanied her staggered breaths.

Seti stifled the sudden well of emotion at the sight of her battered face. He'd imagined it all morning, but seeing her firsthand took his breath away. He reached to touch her cheek, but she barreled into him in a fit of sobs.

Her arms tightened around his torso, and he winced, holding his breath. Her shoulders shook as she wept against his chest, seemingly unconcerned about his sweat-soaked tunic.

"Eliza." His voice cracked.

She shook her head. He pressed his nose to the blue scarf on her head and breathed in her sweet scent. With trembling fingers, he brushed the curls from her damp cheek.

"Eliza," he murmured again.

When she didn't respond, he scooped her into his arms and carried her back to the crevice where she'd hidden.

"What are you doing?" she asked between sniffles.

"What happened?" he countered.

"It's okay. I'm okay." She carefully wiped her nose with her hand.

"Obviously not." He set her down in the shadow of the rocks and knelt beside her. Composing himself, he gently took her chin, assessing the damage. His beautiful, precious Eliza had taken a beating for him. Why had he let her? Because of him, she fell from the cliff and hurt her head. Because of him, she now sat here, battered and broken. Pain gripped his chest, sharper than the pain in his ribs.

"Well …" she muttered, flinching at his touch. Her bleeding lip quivered despite the swelling.

"Oh, Eliza." He'd wash her feet with his tears and beg for forgiveness. He held her face as gently as he could, though anger and despair raged in his veins. Her beauty shone beneath the swelling, stilling the storm of emotions within him. With a deep breath, he fought the tears threatening to flow and said with forced calmness, "Do you still have all your teeth?"

She peeled back her lips, revealing intact teeth, then pulled away and spat a wad of blood. "I bit my tongue. I told you she's weak. She didn't even know how to punch."

He cracked a grin at her change in demeanor. "Then what's wrong?" Stupid question, but he needed her to talk, open up to him.

"I—" She paused as tears filled her eyes again.

He swallowed and looked away, unable to hold back the emotion.

"I needed you." She collapsed into him, fingers digging into his biceps.

His mouth fell open as he pondered her words. He lifted her off and stared her square in the eyes. "You made me promise—"

"I know. And it's better you didn't come." She wiped her nose again, tears cutting lines through the dirt on her cheeks. "I just wanted you there. With me. I'm glad you weren't, but I wanted you there." She pulled her tunic up and blew her nose into it, grimacing.

Seti shook his head. He'd have been by her side if that's what she wanted, gone in her place. Would he ever understand her? With his thumb, he gently wiped the blood dribbling from her lip, only for more to ooze out in its place.

He had her alone, away from interruptions, open and unguarded. It was time to bare his heart. "Why do you hide?" Of all the questions, why this one? Yet it had haunted him since their first conversation.

"I'm scared." Her whisper stopped his heart.

"Of what?"

"Being seen as vulnerable."

"But you are vulnerable. Right now."

"I know, but I trust you."

The urge to passionately kiss her from head to toe and make her his wife right then set Seti's heart racing against his ribs. They were alone, after all. Everything about her called for his touch: her baby-smooth skin, wide brown eyes, even her bleeding lip. The way her tunic draped over her slender shoulders and hinted at the curves beneath. How completely unaware she seemed of all of this, and how she unraveled him with just a look.

With all the self-control he could muster, he cupped the back of her neck and brushed the gentlest, smallest kiss on that bottom lip, then drew back, taking a bead of blood with him.

Her eyes slid closed as her breath sighed out.

Seti sat on his hands, letting his gaze travel over her from head to toe, pausing briefly on her chest. "Rahel told me you overheard Sena. Why didn't you say anything?"

She opened her eyes and swallowed an audible lump. "I was afraid you'd confront her."

"That would've been better than what happened."

"I didn't think she'd go through with it. Besides, if you confronted her, you'd have to talk to her."

Seti smirked. "And you worried I'd fall for her?"

Eliza's fingers fidgeted in her lap. "Maybe. But more than that. I was afraid of what you'd think of me. I've never loved anyone like this before, and I'm scared of losing you. It still feels too good to be true." She gave a side-long glance. "Things never go right for me, and when they do, something bad is bound to happen. I've learned to expect it."

Was that the mentality of every slave? He crinkled his nose, unsure how one could think in such a way. "But you said yourself that you prayed for me and for my love. Do you really think God would answer your prayers only to take it all away?"

Eliza shrugged. "I think all kinds of things, Seti. I don't trust God as much as you think I do. I want to. I'm willing to. But there will always be that cynical part of me."

Cynical. The head scribe once told Seti he didn't have a cynical bone in his body. Eliza might match or even outshine him in some areas, but she complemented him where they differed.

"You're not—" He shifted on his hands, resisting the urge to take hold of her. "You're not a slave anymore."

Her gaze lifted, and a slight smile softened her reddened cheeks. "I know." Her voice was as gentle as a dove. "But leaving that behind will take time, as with you leaving Egypt."

Seti laughed. "I already have."

"It's still in your heart."

"No, it's not. You haven't noticed? I'm a changed man." He lifted his hands, presenting himself. "I seriously hope you've seen at least some change in me."

Her smile fell. "I don't want you to change. I fell in love with you for a reason."

Seti dropped his hands, mouth open. "You are incredibly conflicting, you know that? You're a conundrum."

Eliza touched his cheek, melting away his every defense. His restraint crumbled.

"Seti," she whispered, as gentle as ever. "Someday you'll understand. Someday I will too. You are—and always have been—the man of my dreams. Even more so now. And if God ever takes you away from me, for whatever reason, I will always cherish the moments I had with you. I'll pray for you and thank God for blessing me with our time together. But for now, I will try to trust God with all my heart, even with you."

He pulled her hand from his face and folded it in his. "You don't have to worry about that." Her shaken faith unsettled him. It was her devotion to her God that drew him in from the beginning. If she faltered, could Hoshea? Could Moshe?

Tears welled in her eyes again, and Seti scrambled for something to say. "S—so, where'd you learn to punch like that, anyway?"

She wiped her eyes. "My brothers."

"They beat you up? I hardly believe that." He held her hand in his lap. "You were mostly at my house."

"That's exactly it." She sniffled and wiped her eyes again. "I had to protect Miera. They made me tough when we worked together on the plantation. After that, no one else could protect her."

He had lived his whole life in his little world, completely oblivious to hers, and her mindset baffled him. His home had felt safe, and his family had provided the girls with more than most slaves could have dreamed of—an outhouse capable of withstanding a dust storm and food scraps from the table. After all, most slaves ate cow feed or stale bread. His mother had tolerated them while Kabelo hadn't gone beyond verbal insults. But the outhouse was small, hot, and full of bugs. Both girls had been thin and weak, and who knows what his mother or Kabelo had done while Seti wasn't home. The lifestyle may have seemed lavish for a slave, but now it was beneath Eliza.

"What could you possibly have to protect her from?" he asked, hoping not to learn of anything drastic done by his mother or Kabelo. "My family?"

"Everything. Your family, whippings, the brick farms. Being taken advantage of. Going anywhere without me. She's innocent."

Miera had an infectious, joyful air about her, and Seti cringed at the thought of it being snuffed out. "But that doesn't mean you aren't."

Something unidentifiable flashed in Eliza's eyes so quickly that Seti stared, second-guessing whether he'd seen it at all. But she looked away, letting the loose strands of hair fall forward, hiding her face and whatever she held beneath that tough exterior. Her hand trembled as she pulled grass blades from the ground, twisting them around her fingers.

If Seti could take that burden from her, would she let him? And if she let him, could she be free to be herself?

Suddenly, her words made sense. It was all she had ever known.

"That's her. Not me," she mumbled, strangling her fingers with the grass.

"What do you mean? Why does it have to be either/or? Who are you, Eliza? Besides the big sister, the slave. Who are you?"

Eliza crossed her arms and scowled. "You're turning this around on me."

"I'm turning it around on you? Then I'll answer for you. To me, you're innocent and vulnerable too. And there's nothing wrong with that. You're this girl—this girl—God listens to. Beautiful and mysterious. I'd search the ends of the earth in all your hiding places to find you. You love music and beautiful things like I do. You love your family and everyone around you, and you nourish that love. You reach for the stars and don't settle for anything less. But you're stubborn. You're complicated, and it drives me crazy in a way I can't explain, but I love it."

Eliza turned away, but Seti slipped his arms around her waist and pulled her into his lap. She resisted for a split second but relented and fell limp against his chest. Warmth and tingles pulsed through him. He inhaled her sweet scent and let the butterflies in his stomach settle.

"You don't believe me?" Seti challenged, struggling to stay focused. "Fine. Then who am I to you? Tell me."

"I have," she whispered.

"When? Say it again."

"I have, Seti. On the hill, when we talked about your future house. When I hit Sena. At the Red Sea."

Seti smoothed the hair from her face and nestled his arms around her. "And what if I didn't believe you?"

She shook her head.

Would Seti believe what God said about him?

"It's okay if you don't believe me, Eliza. You will, sooner or later. I understand now what you meant about leaving Egypt behind. And slavery. It will take time."

Eliza turned to face him, tears spilling onto her cheeks. "I'm sorry. I truly am. I want to believe you."

There was something precious about her. So pure and real. She held him in that disarming, mesmerizing gaze that had ensnared him from day one. Seti clung to that look, and to the feeling of her weight on his lap, wanting to embed the moment in history. That she trusted him with such vulnerability was enough for him to do whatever it took to keep her, to watch her grow into what God saw her as, and to believe it.

Chapter 30

A hint of sadness flickered in his serious eyes, tearing at Eliza's heart. She wanted to believe him and hated that she couldn't. She slumped back against his chest so he wouldn't see the tears.

As if reading her, he said, "I just want you to trust me."

"I do." The words were barely audible.

"No. I mean not just with your vulnerability, but with my words. I wouldn't lie."

"I know you wouldn't."

His arms tightened around her, and she pulled her knees up. She had longed for this moment earlier that day, and now here she sat—safe in the arms of her beloved. His hands folded over hers.

"When you want to hide, I'm right here," he whispered.

His breath on her neck erupted a flutter in her chest like a flock of gulls taking off. She gulped, focusing hard on their intertwined hands in her lap. His soft lips barely skimmed her shoulder, stilling her heart midbeat. Every hair on her body stood on end.

"By this time tomorrow," he whispered, his lips caressing her shoulder, "we'll be betrothed."

Tingles raced down her spine as he moved to her neck, his lips trailing up toward her ear. An unfamiliar vulnerability—different from before—stirred within, heating her face. Thrilling. Exhilarating. She melted into him, succumbing to his strength. With his teeth, he eased her tunic strap off her shoulder and let it drop before returning to the curve of her neck. Her eyes widened. She held her breath as his lips traced a line back down to her shoulder, stopping where the strap now hung. He hovered there, his hot breath penetrating her pores.

Then, with almost palpable restraint, he leaned back and released her, exhaling. "We should head back."

Her father's words flashed through her mind, and Eliza spun around. "Oh, no! My family's moving without us!"

Seti stared into the distance, eyes glazed.

Eliza sprang to her feet. "Seti, we must hurry, or we'll never find them." She steadied herself with a hand against a boulder as a dizzy spell ran its course.

The handsome young man who could magically obliterate her pain with the touch of his lips sat unaffected in the dirt, with one leg stretched out and the other bent, an arm resting on his knee.

"Seti!"

Finally, he straightened. "No worries. I left Chewy on the other side, not far from here. And they know you left them, right?"

"I told Abba I'd found Rahel and would catch up."

Seti shrugged. "Then what's the hurry?"

Locating her family in the massive throng would take forever. How long had she been away? Time with Seti either sped by or stopped completely—she could never tell. She glanced toward the foreboding desert spread from horizon to horizon. Rocks and boulders dotted the hilly terrain, which followed a short range of low mountains to the north. Seti had said he'd search the world for her, in every one of her hiding spots.

She faced him. "How did you find me?"

A mischievous grin lifted his swollen cheek. He shuffled to his feet and dusted sand from his tunic. Eliza instinctively stepped back as he approached, noting the hunger in his eyes, yet they held a gentleness she had dreamed of for years—gentleness that now belonged to her. She moved forward, hoping her retreat went unnoticed, suddenly craving the low thud of his heartbeat against her ear. The gulls inside her chest took flight again as his hand slid around her waist, warmth spreading from his fingertips through her tunic.

He swept a few curls from her face and tucked them under her headwrap. "The blue wrap on your head. I could see you from the top of the boulders. The only time I lost you was when you reached Moshe. I even saw you leave your abba."

Embarrassed and flattered, Eliza dropped her gaze. Heat warmed her cheeks. Of course he'd think of something clever like that. She should've expected it. It explained his odd behavior that morning.

"Oh, Seti." She leaned into him, wrapping her arms around him. He kissed the top of her head as she rested her ear against his chest and savored the beautiful thump of his heart. Time and again, he had proven that his heart beat for her and her only. Not Lumeri. Not Sena. Not even himself.

She inhaled his strong scent and held it, not wanting to let go. "I'm sorry." Her voice trembled.

"For what?" He held her at arm's length and lifted her chin.

She nearly melted into a puddle at his feet. How could God form such a gentle, compassionate soul? And who was she to deserve such a gift? Cynical, doubting, emotional Eliza. There were plenty of faithful Hebrews far more worthy. She proved to be rash and unpredictable, making a spectacle of her family, permanently marring a fellow child of God, and spitting vile words that should have shamed her. What a disgrace.

She stared into Seti's eyes and spoke from the depths of her quivering heart. "I'm sorry I've been so mean. I took everything out on you. And—" the shame spilled over like a broken dam—"I threw sand at you and called you a fool. I was awful." The tears came anew, streaming down her cheeks.

Seti smiled. "I deserved it."

"No, you didn't. And even after that, you still came for me. You came when I ran to save Rahel and then went to save her yourself. Yet I tried to keep you from saving Sabu. And—"

Seti put a finger to her swollen lip. "I could say the same for you, Eliza."

"Look at me," she cried, shaking her head. "I'm a broken soul. An emotional wreck. I don't deserve you."

With a chuckle, he held her face in his hands, gently guiding her eyes back to his. "If you're broken, I'm shattered beyond fixing." He grew intense. "I lost my family, my whole life, everything. I'm trying to earn your family's approval and doubting every step. For five years, I mistreated you, and you still came for me. Only because of your prayers did God save me."

He had a point. Eliza sniffled and nodded.

His arms encircled her, pulling her in. "We're broken together, and we'll heal together."

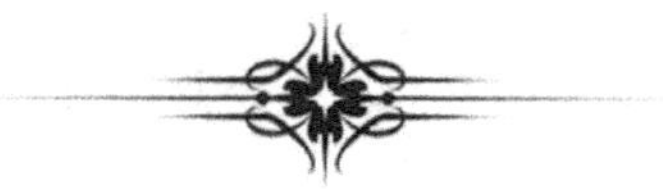

A smidge of anger pitted in Seti's stomach at the sight of the bare spot where Eliza's family's tents once sat. But then he softened. Her parents likely assumed she was with Rahel or him. Sabu's tent was gone as well.

"I knew it." She sighed and bumped her forehead against his back as he turned Chewy around. "Abba said he wanted to be close to the water and near Moshe. I guess just follow the river."

As Chewy followed the stream away from the Rock of Horeb into the multitude at the foot of the mountains, Eliza recounted the events of the morning. From how the manna and water pouch he had given her proved a lifesaver during a far longer wait than expected, to each blow received from Sena, she left out no detail. She delivered a gruesome account of Moshe's dealings with those ahead in line and the animalistic behavior of the surrounding crowd. Why Moshe tolerated such conduct was beyond Seti, but his attention snagged onto Moshe's reaction to him being involved with Eliza.

What did Moshe mean by "the likes of him"? Eliza's words only confirmed what Seti suspected, and it stung. While she rattled on, Moshe's words haunted him. Should he care what Moshe thinks? He was wrong about Seti, wasn't he? Though, Seti did accept the blame for throwing rocks at him at the palace. But surely something more fueled the man's continued disdain.

Seti cringed. Moshe's first encounter with him revolved around Seti's taunting words that night at the palace. He had spewed a slew of questions and sarcastic remarks at Moshe and Aharon, each laced with ridicule. As if they owed him answers.

He measured his breaths as shame pooled deeper in his chest. That behavior had spoken volumes about his character before the Hebrew God saved him. No wonder Moshe reacted to Eliza the way he did. Seti would have done the same. He could never show his face to Moshe or Aharon again.

But he had to. The yearning for a friendship with the man gnarled inside him like an unsatisfied stomach growl. If Seti wanted to know God on a deeper level, he'd have to get close to Moshe. If Hoshea looked up to Moshe, then Seti would even more so—if that were possible. Moshe emanated wisdom. Godly wisdom. The kind Seti had wanted for as long as he could remember—but sought from all the wrong gods.

Eliza's family came into view among a host of tightly packed tents lining the riverside. Ironically, the new site wasn't far from the rockslide, near where Seti and Eliza had started out on Chewy. It was evening when they arrived, and had they paid closer attention earlier, they might have saved a lot of time. Regardless, the delay had been worth the conversations they otherwise wouldn't have shared.

The congested sprawl of tents resembled the slums in Egypt. Wagons parked end to end behind them, some flipped into makeshift shelters, others used for storage, before another row of tents began. Tables and shelves piled with earthenware, clothing, and random items propped up canopies. Linen flapped in the light breeze on strings spanning the camp. Livestock rested in random places, unbothered by unattended children running along the narrow paths, hopping over animal dung. Seti couldn't tell where one family ended and the next began. People young and old sprawled out on the ground in groups, lounging in quiet chatter or sleeping, like basks of crocodiles.

Seti sighed. He'd have to find a new getaway spot to escape the madness.

Miera bounded over, squealing as Seti dismounted. She bounced like an excited puppy while he helped Eliza down. Her rambunctious greetings had grown on him, and if he ever arrived without such a welcome, there'd be cause for worry. Before Eliza could say a word, Miera bombarded her with questions and comments about her battered face, taking her hand and leading her away.

Sabu waved and nodded from where he sat near the campfire with Nala and the others. A warm sweetness wafted from the manna roasting over the fire, sending Seti's gut into a long rumble. The entire valley warmed in an invisible cloud of smoke from the rising manna on cookstoves, flavored with varying spices and oils, easing his misgivings about the otherwise unsightly place.

Evening mealtime had become a favorite of his. It unified the multitude as one, much like how the monthly ceremonies in Egypt momentarily halted daily life for a single purpose, though this gathering held a more intimate air. Perhaps it was God's presence hovering over His people, like a mother eagle sheltering her young beneath her wings amid the surrounding wilderness. The image lingered in Seti's heart as he joined Eliza's family.

Eager family members crowded around Eliza to hear the morning's details. She shrank with each question until she might as well disappear. Why hadn't her father or Adam filled them in and spared her the renewed humiliation? If that weren't embarrassing enough, her bruises would worsen by tomorrow when she'd once again be the center of attention.

"We saved you the honors of telling them." Adam gestured proudly toward his sisters as if Eliza should be grateful for the opportunity.

When she shook her head, he jumped at the chance. Taking center stage, he reenacted the morning's events and Moshe's judgments right down to the man's very words. His animated gestures and vibrant dialogue elicited laughter from the whole family. Even Nala cracked a smile. Eliza laughed, though she withered behind Seti. Adam's perception of the whole incident, and now that of her family, mirrored the reactions of the crowd surrounding Moshe. It was pure entertainment.

But he hadn't seen how the married couple and the widow struck a nerve inside Eliza that would forever haunt her, or that their tormented screams never seemed to cease. Neither did he capture how the sound of the sword hitting the rock still rang inside Eliza's head, or how the dull thud of the goat's head against the ground rose above the haughty cheers. And though he had mimicked Sena's stance perfectly, he forgot to mention how Sena's father called her *Baby Girl*, which sounded silly at the time but now lingered in the depths of Eliza's heart.

The laughter at Sena's expense unnerved Eliza, despite having done it herself.

Adam moved to Moshe's reaction, jolting Eliza from her thoughts. Unlike the rest of the crowd, Moshe expressed no joy in the spectacle. In fact, he held his head during the fight. He even covered his mouth with his hand when Eliza first hit the ground, before turning his face away completely.

Moshe's poignant words, *"Now, what did you do?"* ripped through her all over again. She dropped her eyes and bit her lip, recoiling inwardly. Seti's hand squeezed hers. His acknowledgment of her pain lifted the shame, if only for a moment.

Thankfully, her mother interrupted Adam's performance with trays of manna muffins drizzled with honey and a roasted desert snake, courtesy of Zechariah. The conversation quickly shifted to Zechariah's hunting skills, then to Jeremiah's connections with high-ranking Hebrews from the brick farms. They had set up camp along both sides of the river but allowed him in among them. Apparently, everybody wanted to camp near the water.

Chapter 31

Seti's feet sank into the cold water, and he shuddered before pressing forward. He waded until waist-deep, then took a breath and lifted his gaze to the glowing Pillar atop the Great Mountain. The Fire Pillar, wrapped in a swirl of reds, yellows, oranges, and blues, spiraled upward in mesmerizing silence. Only the sounds of night bugs and snores drifted on the light breeze.

Unlike the purification pools in the Menf temple, the title *Living Water* truly applied to the miraculous stream flowing from the Rock. It replenished him with more than hydration. He gained strength and clarity, maybe even purification.

The last time Seti consecrated himself was to help his father clean the temple pools after the frog infestation. He gulped and dropped his eyes to the Pillar's orange reflections on the stream. If his father had lived, he'd never have blessed this betrothal. Seti might not have even left Egypt. Leaving would bring lasting shame upon his family, ruining their priestly legacy. But he had already shattered the Ameneten priesthood when he inadvertently killed the Api bull. Perhaps it was a mercy that his father had perished in the final plague.

Seti scoffed at the thought.

His betrothal to Lumeri had been set for the wheat harvest, to be officiated by his father. With Eliza, he'd have to do it himself.

He looked again at the Fire Pillar. "Thank you for this."

The words came out forced, surprising him. He wouldn't trade this for the world, even with the pain that accompanied it. His circumcision had marked the beginning of a new life, and marrying Eliza would seal it—officially make him a Levite. Did his old life serve any purpose at all?

In just a few hours, Eliza would be his. No more struggle with her family, Sena, or even The Lank. They'd accept him. Respect him.

Seti ducked beneath the water. The cold enveloped him, first shocking his nerves, then soothing them. He surfaced with a whoosh and flung his hair back, letting out a soft chuckle. He peeked over his shoulder at the tents, hoping nobody stirred. There was something intimate about this moment that begged for privacy, as if it were between him and God only. With Sabu's blade in hand, Seti started with the hair on his head.

Two women Eliza had never met dragged a large bronze mirror into the tent, kicking aside linen to make space. Miera squealed beside her, spinning Eliza to face her reflection.

Eliza lightly touched the faded scar on her cheek, her swollen nose, and her fat lip. Excluding those blemishes, she'd become a woman, at least on the outside. Braids laced with blue ribbon crowned her head, and small curls framed her forehead. The leather sandals Seti had given her adorned her calloused feet. But it was the gown that transformed Eliza from a broken vessel into a beautiful flower.

She laughed. Never had she thought of herself as such. The sky-blue gown hugged her curves and fell to her ankles, its length an extravagance reserved for special occasions. The white braided hem and simple sash around her waist bore witness to her mother's resourcefulness with what little time they'd had. A neighbor had donated a sheer silver cape that draped over her shoulders, an embellishment that suggested royalty.

"Look at you!" her mother gushed, entering the tent after the women left. "The blue and silver shine against your olive skin!"

Eliza couldn't tell in the bronze mirror. She gave a tentative smile as her mother joined her and Miera in the reflection.

"We look like queens!" Miera twirled in her red gown trimmed with gold thread. A carnelian brooch and bronze clips pinned her braids, all courtesy of the Egyptians.

Her mother, wearing a pink beadnet gown, fastened a mother-of-pearl choker around Eliza's neck and dusted her cheeks with gold shimmer powder.

Eliza sneezed. "Too much."

"Nonsense. Now close your eyes." Her mother added a thin line of kohl to Eliza's eyelids. "There." She stood back proudly.

Miera gawked. "Now do me!"

Her mother held Eliza at arm's length. "My." She wiped a tear from her eye. "I never had the privilege of looking so beautiful at my betrothal."

Eliza smiled, unsure how to respond.

"Now," her mother said, turning her back to the bronze, "if you think this is too much, just wait until the ceremony."

The kohl made her eyes stand out, thankfully softening the bruised and swollen parts of her face. "That will be in the Promised Land, Ima. Maybe I'll wear something more native then."

Miera scrunched her eyes. "Like what?"

"I don't know. Maybe a dirty white tunic and a loincloth?" Eliza smiled.

"Be serious!" Miera put a hand on her hip.

Eliza shrugged. "Something earthy. Flowers in my hair? A wreath?"

"You don't like the gown?" her mother asked, spritzing a flowery perfume on herself before spraying Eliza.

"Oh, I love it. It's original. I'll probably wear it at the ceremony too, but maybe dress it up with something from the land. Something from our heritage."

Miera scrunched her eyes. "We have a heritage?"

Eliza smiled. "We do now."

"Don't be silly." Her mother straightened. "We've always had a heritage from our abbas. We just have to remember it."

The tent flap opened, and Eliza's father stuck his head in. His face lit up as he gazed at his wife and daughters. "Everyone's waiting."

Eliza's heart fluttered, and she covered her mouth with a shaky hand. This was it—the moment she'd desired since first laying eyes on Seti. She spun around, scanning the tent for his gift. Fabric, jewelry, and clothing piled on their mats beside a spilled sewing kit and empty water pouches, all scattered among a mess of manna crumbs.

"Don't worry about the mess. I'll get it." Her mother spritzed more perfume into the air, then flounced through the mist, sniffing.

Miera coughed, waving her hand.

"Rahel," Eliza gasped. "You told Rahel, right?"

Her mother faced her, mouth open.

How could she forget? "Ima!"

"You were with her yesterday, Eliza. Why didn't you tell her then?"

Rahel was going to miss her betrothal because of her lie. Eliza hung her head as the weight of another transgression settled on her shoulders.

"Eliza, let's go." Her father's head disappeared from the tent flap, and Miera shoved Eliza.

Upon stepping outside, Eliza halted, stunned at the sheer number of guests packed into the small area. Tents had been cleared to make space for tables, benches, and mats where large groups lounged and mingled. People resting on pillows lined both sides of the river, facing the campsite. Woven rugs of vibrant colors blanketed the nearby boulders, where families sat waiting. Children darted in every direction.

None of these people looked familiar—all decked in Egyptian formal wear. Bright colors and shimmering jewelry dazzled in the noon sun. The place resembled an Egyptian ceremony minus the elephants. Tiaras, ornate collars, beads of precious stones, and bangles adorned both men and women. Some even wore wigs. Eliza's mouth dropped open. Word of her betrothal had clearly spread, breaking the monotony of the tent life of a restless multitude waiting on an ever-silent God.

Hopefully, Rahel's family received the message.

"Go on, Eliza. Seti and the others are by the river." Her mother nudged her forward, and she tripped.

After steadying herself, she grabbed Miera's arm. "Get Seti's gift and be ready when I say."

With a squeal, Miera disappeared into the tent. Eliza took a breath, put on a brave face, and marched forward, though the crowd blocked her view of the river. It was like one of Moshe's gatherings in Avaris, but much more extravagant and condensed. Excited chatter and laughter filled her ears, and the air was thick with perfume, spices, and the scent of roasting meat. Two boys in leather kilts darted between her and her mother, nearly toppling her.

Eliza's head spun, and she slowed her pace. Ahead, several paneled tables formed a long row, laden with an array of manna treats. Decorative glassware and silver and ivory utensils surrounded a gold-rimmed bowl filled with water on one table. Men sauntered over from the fire, carrying silver trays of roasted chicken. They placed them on a large table beside porcelain bowls filled with eggs.

"Look who's here!" Her father's voice boomed over the crowd. He stood with Seti, Adam, and Zechariah at the head table.

Eliza froze. Seti turned toward her, his eyes wide and sparkling. Her heart skipped a beat.

He looked like he did when serving at the temple: bald, no thick dark eyebrows, no long lashes, no stubble. At least his tunic was clean. The grin plastered on his face attested to his blissful ignorance.

Eliza glanced at her father, who beamed with pride, unbothered. Adam stepped forward, offering his hand, a glint of amusement and satisfaction in his eyes.

"Ad—"

He pulled her close and whispered, "He cleans up nice, doesn't he?"

The blood drained from her face, and the air left her lungs. How could he do this to Seti? To her?

Zechariah patted her sore arm. "You look stunning, sis."

As her father called for everyone's attention, a wave of nausea ramped through Eliza's throat. The voices blurred into a cacophony. Her vision swam in a whirl of colors. She reached for the table to steady herself, but a pair of hands caught her shoulders.

"You all right, Eliza?" Seti's whisper cut through the noise. She drew in a deep breath.

No. Adam wasn't going to ruin this moment. This was *her* betrothal. She straightened, swallowed back the bile, and mustered her resolve. Everything inside her wanted to bolt with Seti in tow, but she planted her feet. Seti's firm grasp grounded the chaotic emotions within her.

"I announce the betrothal of my daughter Eliza to Seti, son of Amen-Amm—an Egyptian priest!"

Cheers and whistles erupted. Eliza dropped her gaze to the papyrus on the table. Seti had written a ketubah? How?

The table, made of cedar and varnished with a clear gloss embedded with dung beetles and stones shaped like Api bulls, would be hers and Seti's as a gift, according to Egyptian customs. Her mother's old beaded necklace, passed down through many generations, framed the edge, tied with blue cotton strips, lending an Israeli tone to the otherwise Egyptian decor.

But what constituted as Israeli? Apart from their improvised celebrations amid slavery, their only customs came from the Patriarchs, which likely came from the Canaanites.

Eliza lifted her eyes. Miera cheered, clutching a woven bag. The twins, dressed like Egyptian royalty, bounced around their mother. Adam and Zechariah had joined them, grinning. Sabu and Nala clapped from a mat near the fire. The rest were strangers, a mob of lost people dressed like their captors. The thought calmed Eliza. Seti didn't stand out after all. Adam's trickery had no effect.

A horn blast made Eliza jump, and she covered her ears before spinning around.

"Sorry. I tried to blow it away from your ears." Seti turned to blow again but paused as the cheering came to a screeching halt.

Why'd he bring a horn?

Clearly rattled, her father rubbed his temple. "Was that necessary?"

Seti furrowed his brow and gestured toward the now-silent crowd. "It worked."

The entire gathering stared, wide-eyed. Children froze mid step. A baby cried somewhere. Adam and Zechariah smothered their laughter with their hands. Eliza's heart pounded as she took in the stunned crowd.

Her father sighed and stepped back. "The rest is yours." He gave Seti a quick pat on the shoulder and joined the others, still rubbing his ear.

Seti's clammy hand grasped Eliza's and squeezed. "You ready?"

She gulped. "Ready?"

He set the shofar down and reached beneath the table for a woven sack—the one from Nala's tent that held the gifts. Eliza moved aside as he pulled out the gold cuffs and held them aloft.

"The mohar," he announced, then placed them on the table.

Her father gave an approving nod, arms crossed. The crowd murmured with awe then quieted again as Seti withdrew a lute. Eliza stepped back with a gasp. More *oohs* and ahhs filled the air.

Seti lifted the instrument high. "The mattan."

That was the mattan? Not the sandals? Eliza covered her mouth. The lute was enormous, with ivory inlays and more strings than the musicians' instruments. This was no Egyptian lute, or Hebrew. Seti had stolen it from the Amalekites. Eliza's throat went dry. Her breathing quickened.

With a trembling hand, Seti grabbed the ketubah and held it out. "And I present to you, as my witnesses … the ketubah!" He winked at Eliza and said in a low voice, "Your ima let me copy the writing on hers."

Eliza stared, mouth agape.

He plucked a string on the lute, then handed her the papyrus and played a dissonant melody—strangely beautiful. The murmuring crowd went silent and gazed with fascination and curiosity. Adam and Zechariah snickered, struggling to hide their faces.

A sinking feeling replaced the angst consuming her.

Seti had no clue what he was doing.

The last notes faded into the breeze, and Seti nodded at Eliza. She held out the ketubah, her gaze locked on the lute. She couldn't look at him—or anyone. She bit her lip and tried to steady her trembling hands so he could read the marriage covenant.

Seti strummed a new chord. "My Brave Little Kitten," he sang. "I have written this here ketubah and now sing it for all to witness my solemn oath to you. Even Yahweh stands as my witness." He nodded toward the Cloud Pillar in the distance.

This could not be happening. What had her brothers done to him? Blood trickled from her lip as she bit the wound open, fighting to hold herself together. If he hadn't already made a fool of himself with his appearance and the shofar, this would surely seal it.

His voice trembled but rang loud and clear as he sang:

"On this day of three months from the famed Passover, from the Great Exodus of Egypt, here at the foot of Mount Sinai, the Great Mountain, I take you as my bride. I will work for you, honor, provide for, and protect you in accordance with Hebrew tradition. I set aside the golden cuffs from my Father-of-Old as the mohar. They now belong to you as insurance in the dreaded event I should die before you—but not for divorce, because that will never happen. These items I present as a remembrance of me and this betrothal: the blue cotton fabric, the sandals, and the lute, as the mattan. I only request you devotion and respect. Do you, Eliza, daughter of Jeremiah, agree with the terms written in this here ketubah?"

When Seti muted the lute strings, the resulting silence amplified the trickle of water from the river behind him. His ever-present smile faltered, and his eyes begged her to respond. Eliza wiped the blood from her mouth and met his gaze. He wouldn't be the only fool at this betrothal.

She reached out and plucked a string on the lute. After a steadying breath, she sang with a whistling nasal tone, "I agree with all that is written in the ketubah and attest in front of these witnesses to be your loving wife—to honor and respect you. And trust you."

Seti beamed and let out a long-held breath. The crowd burst into cheers and applause so loud it drowned out the nervous laughter escaping Eliza's lips. Tambourines sounded from somewhere she couldn't see, and fists pumped in the air.

After setting down the ketubah, Eliza grabbed the shofar and sucked in the biggest breath she could manage. Giggles escaped as she blew, weakening the blast, but it was enough to hush the crowd to murmurs.

"Wait, there's more," she sang, then motioned for Miera to come forward.

Seti looked on in surprise as Miera squealed and skipped over with the bag. Eliza wiped her clammy palms on her dress, a thrill shooting through her in anticipation of his reaction. She took the bag, and Miera returned to her parents' side.

"I, too, have a gift in remembrance of our relationship and how we came to be." Her screechy voice had no ill effect on Seti or the audience. Still gazing into his eyes, she pulled out the mesh head net he had given her at the whipping pole.

Seti's smile brightened his swollen face. His dimples deepened, and his eyes glistened with emotion.

Holding his gaze, she rose on her toes and placed the net on his head.

"I love you, Seti," she sang, her voice cracking. She wrapped her good arm around his waist and sank into the warm solidity of his chest. His pounding heart matched hers.

His arms encircled her, holding her tight, but the only sound from his mouth was the catch of his breath.

After a moment, he removed the head net and kissed her forehead. "You saved it."

"It's all I have from your house. I know it's ugly, but it means a lot to me."

Seti chuckled, twirling one of her curls around his finger. "It's perfect."

His eyes shone as he gazed into hers, vaporizing any remaining angst in her heart. The world faded, leaving only Seti and Eliza, holding each other in a dream. Everything inside her calmed.

"Saving you from my mwt was the best thing I ever did."

"God didn't fail me," she said, remembering her first prayer and how the very moment Seti placed the head-net on her head had solidified God's providence.

Her father rushed between them, bumping into Eliza and shattering the moment. The melee of cheers and chatter crashed back into her awareness with a pop in her ears. He signed a single letter on the ketubah, then handed the reed pen to Eliza. She stared at the papyrus, unsure what to do, never having written anything in her life. She left a squiggly line then quickly passed the reed to Seti, who signed what appeared to be his full name.

After Sabu added an Egyptian mark, her father held the ketubah up for all to see. "And now we eat!"

Chapter 32

After Jeremiah thanked God for a smooth betrothal and the delicious food, Seti filled his porcelain plate with chicken and eggs. Only enough food for Eliza's family, Sabu, and Nala spread across the serving table. Thankfully, everyone else had brought their own dishes of manna, sharing the myriad of different renditions with each other.

Seti joined Eliza at the front table on two wooden chairs topped with cushions and draped with yellow lace, while her family, Sabu, and Nala sat on stools at the other tables.

Seti inhaled her overpowering floral scent and leaned in, resting his hand on her thigh, and smiled. Her head shot up in alarm.

"Thank goodness for tables." He stuffed his mouth full of meat. "I don't think I told you how amazing you look. I doubt I can wait until we get to Canaan to bed you. If I had a tent, I'd take you as my bride and consummate this thing right now. Food can wait."

Her mouth dropped open, and her face turned as red as a sunset. No amount of swelling or bruising could mar the beauty she radiated. Even at her angriest or sickest, she was a sight to behold.

Her mother had worked that fabric into a masterpiece that accentuated Eliza's curves. The breeze played with the loose curls around her eyes, deepening their already entrancing draw. No need for kohl. Both stunning and reserved, she probably had no idea of the sensations she stirred within him.

A battle raged behind her eyes as they met his. She swallowed what remained in her mouth and spoke in a measured tone. "Please don't say such things, Seti. I'd like to be a proper woman for once. Innocent, if you will."

Seti dropped his gaze as his appetite succumbed to guilt. He removed his hand from her thigh. If anyone deserved to feel proper and innocent, it was her. He wouldn't take that away. Her words deepened his already fathomless love for her.

Eliza's hand slid into his, and the sensations returned with a vengeance. She flashed him a reassuring smile, as if to retract her words but not really. He wouldn't let her. He'd at least kiss her if it weren't for the massive audience before them.

A shadow fell across his plate, and a husky voice broke the moment. "Don't think for a second you're keeping this table."

Seti lifted his face to an unfamiliar man standing before them with a beautiful woman draped on each arm. Copper beads clicked in his thick beard like a wind chime.

"This is mine. I'm only letting you borrow it because of her." The man nodded toward Eliza. "Afterward, I'm taking it back."

Seti gave a slight nod, still caught off guard.

One of the women leaned in. "You put on a stunning show. Let me know when you have the ceremony. I wouldn't miss it for the world."

The two women giggled as the man led them away, and an older woman approached. "Great betrothal. You might even start a new tradition." She pinched Seti's cheek before moving on.

Seti glanced at Eliza, hoping she'd elaborate, but she sat silent, her face pale.

A little girl with a wreath on her head ran up and handed Eliza a reed flower, then dashed off, leaving Eliza smiling.

As the guests finished their meal, they came forward one by one.

"Next time, find some wine," an elderly man spat.

"Who gets married in the desert?" a woman hollered.

Somebody followed up with, "Only Egyptians who bed their slaves."

Laughter ensued. Rage and defensiveness surged in Seti's throat, threatening a tirade of retorts, but he suppressed them, determined not to make a scene.

An older couple approached, arm in arm. The man scowled. "I know you. You're that kid who terrorized the streets of On with his obnoxious horse."

"Congratulations on the betrothal." The woman glared at Eliza. "Consider it a betrayal of your heritage."

The pink shade of timidity on Eliza's face deepened into a fiery red. Seti squeezed her hand, and she flashed him a look so intense he didn't know whether to cower or kiss her.

"You could at least try to look like a Hebrew!" somebody shouted from the crowd.

"Traitor!"

Murmurs picked up among those nearest them. Seti contemplated whisking Eliza away. His chest heaved with trepidation as the mob seemed to turn against them.

"Nice touch with the shofar," a young man asserted with genuine kindness. "Usually, one blow is a summons to battle. Don't worry though. You'll catch on."

Somebody blew a *toot* behind him, followed by laughter.

An elderly couple approached with kindness in their eyes. They set a gold goblet on the table. "We offer sincere condolences for the behavior of our people and a joyous welcome to our tribe. Most of us are glad to have you join us."

The alarm pounding in Seti's chest eased. He let out a soft sigh, his smile returning.

"Yes," a young woman added from behind the couple. "The lute and the singing enthralled us."

"It's nice to have a change in tradition now and then," said another young woman with three children hanging on her. "Maybe my children can add their own touch to theirs. It makes it more personal."

"Not so boring," one child said.

A queasiness settled inside Seti as he feigned a proper response to each comment, regardless of tone and subtext. But seeing Eliza's face in her hands, a pit formed in his stomach, churning the small amount of chicken he'd managed to eat. How much of the betrothal had been real? He abruptly straightened as The Lank approached with a younger boy in tow.

"You look lovely, Eliza." The Lank's cheeks flushed, and so did Eliza's, fanning the embers of jealousy that had only begun to die within Seti.

Eliza's countenance brightened, and she spoke for the first time since admonishing Seti. "Yuval! Where have you been? I haven't heard you play in weeks, since the manna came. Your whole family disappeared."

So, Yuval's his name. Seti sat back and crossed his arms. *'The Lank' sounded better.*

The Lank's eyes rested on Eliza with warmth and tenderness, clearly flattered by her words and oblivious to Seti's leveled glare. "We left in devastation. Somebody tainted our instruments with spoiled manna, and we were forced to burn them. Everything but the three harps that weren't in the tent."

Eliza gasped, a hand flying to her mouth.

A sharp guilt cut through Seti's insides. He sat forward. "Burned them?"

"Everything was covered in maggots." The Lank folded his hands in front of him and dropped his gaze. "Nothing was salvageable. It was a loss too much to bear for my parents. My abba vowed to find the culprit and kill him."

Seti gulped. His mind raced back to the incident weeks ago. How was he to know it was the instrument tent? He swore it was The Lank's after he had left his cloak inside.

"Kill him? What if it was an accident?" Seti winced at the tremor in his voice.

"That was no accident." A vein bulged in The Lank's neck, and his face hardened. "We will find who did it, and we'll burn him at the stake."

Fear and disbelief boiled beneath Seti's calm façade. He hid his sweaty hands under the table. The day's oppressive heat seemed to seep into everything, including Seti's resolve. He blinked, assessing The Lank's words. "That technically means you'd burn him before he confesses. Why not bring him to Moshe? The truth would come out then."

Eliza leveled The Lank with a look Seti couldn't interpret. "I don't think God would allow that kind of vengeance out here. Or anywhere."

"Then we'll curse him." The Lank searched Seti's face, pinning him to his chair. "Music was my family's heritage. We cared for those instruments with reverence from before the days of servitude. It was how we worshiped El Shaddai. My abba delighted to serve Him that way. Not just my abba—all of us. We were born to play for the Lord."

"You served God with your music?" Eliza clasped Seti's arm with both hands, eyes wide in wonder. "I want to serve God like that! I'll play for Him with all my heart." She looked at The Lank. "Yuval, will you teach me to play my lute?"

The Lank's face softened, and he relaxed. "I'd be honored to. Perhaps it's how our legacy can live on."

Seti's heart dropped, his sins pummeling him tenfold.

"Oh, Seti! Thank you so much for the lute!" Eliza beamed, shaking Seti's arm. "Oh, I can't wait. When do we start?"

"We're camped on the other side." The Lank pointed across the river. "With the rest of the Levites. Why aren't you there?"

Eliza glanced toward the river. "Because Moshe's here. My abba wanted to camp near him and near the water."

"Understandable. I'll come by tomorrow or the next day, now that I know where to find you." The Lank's face split with a smile that brought a blush to Eliza's cheeks and inflamed Seti's.

A squeal interrupted the moment as Sena barged between The Lank and his friend. She grabbed The Lank's arm. "Oh, Yuval, I've missed you so much!"

Seti met Eliza's surprised gaze, and he reached for her hand again, hoping the antics between her and Sena were over.

"I've missed all of you," The Lank replied. He tousled the hair of the boy beside him. "It feels like I've been away forever. But really, we haven't been far. Only up the river."

"Me too! My abba moved us there yesterday." Sena pressed herself against him, her carnelian and lapis lazuli-studded tiara slipping askew over her sleek blonde hair. She pecked The Lank on the cheek and flashed Seti a sultry grin, no longer embarrassed by her gap-toothed smile.

Seti regarded her with a polite nod, surprised she'd show her face at his betrothal.

She regained her composure and smoothed her silky pink gown. Her fingers came to a rest on the carnelian bauble that dangled strategically on her chest from a simple gold chain. "Fabulous betrothal, Eliza. Seti truly is one of a kind.

And Seti, you stand out no matter what you do with your hair. But the dark waves really did bring out your eyes.”

“Sena.” Eliza straightened. She removed her hand from Seti’s. Her mouth hung open as if to keep speaking, but nothing came out.

“Yes, Eliza?”

Eliza folded her hands on the table and lifted her chin. “I want to apologize for my actions against you. They were unwarranted, and I’m mortified.”

The Lank stepped back, his mouth agape. “You did that to her? Wait—” He looked between the two, eyes narrowing as he assessed their faces. “I didn’t want to say anything …”

Eliza nodded, lowering her gaze.

“Oh, don’t think you had any effect on my life, Eliza. You only revealed your true nature. I am a survivor. And when anybody asks, I tell them exactly who did it.” She fanned herself with a pink and gold fan. “Everyone loves the story. Seti, being the compassionate man that he is, saved my life with Living Water. Then you overreacted and laid into me with that innate rage of yours. But with Moshe’s sound judgment, you got your due.” She leaned over the table at eye level with Eliza, grinning. “It’s a great conversation starter.”

Seti stood abruptly, his chair clattering to the ground behind him. “Why are you here, Sena?”

“We’re family.”

“Time to go.” Seti rounded the table and seized her arm, spinning her in the opposite direction. “Go home.”

Sena yanked her arm free and straightened her gown. “Seti, I mean no ill will to either of you. I only speak the truth.”

“Don’t we all?” Seti muttered, yet his own words cut him to the core. Ignoring the sting, he stepped closer, towering over her, and she inched back.

“Come on, Yuval.” She looped her arm around The Lank’s. “Show me where you’re staying.”

The Lank waved at Eliza before turning away with Sena. Seti turned back to the table, ready to end this meal and whisk Eliza somewhere private, when Hoshea approached.

Eliza jumped from her chair to embrace him. "Hoshea! You saved Rahel. Thank you so much." She hugged him, and he whispered something in her ear before pulling away. She glanced at Seti, then back at Hoshea, and nodded. Seti paused, unsettled by the odd exchange.

"Anything for the sister of an old friend." Hoshea squeezed her shoulder.

"You left your men for her—for me." Eliza's voice cracked, and she wiped a tear from her eye.

A gentleness softened Hoshea's otherwise rugged features. He threw an arm around her shoulders and faced Seti. "Yes, but it worked in everyone's favor. Everyone but the Amalekites', that is. Thanks to you, we reached her before he could do any real harm, and thanks to Seti, we drove them from their camp and raided the place, killing most of them in the process."

Seti's muscles untensed.

Hoshea eyed him with an inquisitive look before shifting his stance and glancing at the table. He grabbed the shofar and stuffed it in his cloak pocket. "You two finished eating?"

"Yes. We're about to leave," Seti said.

Hoshea's gaze drifted to Eliza's family and then to Sabu and Nala. "Good. Come with me to Sabu. Bring that goblet too. I must have words with you."

Chapter 33

Hoshea headed toward Sabu, and Eliza moved to follow but paused at the amused look on Adam's face as he rose from his stool, eying Seti. Hoshea had wisely advised her to break the news to Seti before someone else did.

"Seti!" She reached for his hand.

He turned. "What?" He glanced over his shoulder, clearly eager to catch up to Hoshea.

She shook her head, searching for the right words.

"What is it?" Seti raised a hairless eyebrow.

"You didn't—"

"Eliza?"

Rahel stood alone near the head table.

Relief poured from Eliza's heart in a gasp. She ran and embraced her.

"Rahel, you came!" She hugged her tight. "I'm so sorry for what happened. I didn't even get to speak with you after you returned. It was my fault, all of it. If I hadn't led you out to the spy, he wouldn't have come after you. If I hadn't fought with Seti, you wouldn't have been in my tent when they came. If I'd paid more attention, he wouldn't have gotten away—"

"Relax, Eliza. I'm fine." Rahel pulled away, scrutinizing Eliza's face. "It's not your fault. It's nobody's fault."

The scent of rosemary clung to Rahel, tickling Eliza's nose. A burgundy ribbon laced Rahel's single braid, matching the gown that flowed over her tall, slender frame. Onyx and gold beads dangled from the fringed hem at her ankles, highlighting the black leather sandals on her tan feet. Silver bangles jingled on her wrists as she stepped back and took Eliza's hands.

"You look beautiful, Eliza. I've never seen you dressed up." Her gaze flickered beyond Eliza for a split second.

"So do you." Eliza glanced over her shoulder for what caught Rahel's attention. Seti stood behind her, waiting with arms crossed. She faced Rahel again, torn between breaking the truth to her husband-to-be and giving her best friend her undivided attention. "Rahel, I have so much to tell you. And I want to hear everything. How did you find out about the betrothal? Did you just get here? Where'd your family go after you left us?"

"I was late." Again, Rahel's gaze flickered behind Eliza. "I overslept, then couldn't find you. Zechariah came by yesterday with your lamb and told me about it. We arrived when you were signing the ketubah, but my parents wouldn't let me leave them until after we ate. They've been hovering over me a lot since … you know …" Her voice faded, but she quickly straightened and squeezed Eliza's hands with a slight smile. She took a deep breath, then exhaled a minty scent. "I want to speak some more with you, but first I must have words with Hoshea."

The joy drained from Eliza like wine from a burst wineskin. She dropped her shoulders. The rosemary, minty breath, and beautiful gown—none of it was for her betrothal, but for Hoshea instead. Did Rahel even notice her face? Did she even want to see her?

Nonsense. Of course Rahel wanted to see her. But she'd pined for Hoshea since childhood. His saving her must have rekindled that spark. But never had she dared to speak with him. Coherently, that is.

Rahel must have read her dejection. "I just want to thank him. Then we can talk."

"You're welcome," Seti said from behind Eliza.

"Thank you, Seti, for helping me. But I must also thank Hoshea." Rahel gave him a polite nod and dashed off, leaving Eliza open-mouthed.

Seti slid his warm hands down her arms and pulled her back against his chest. "That was odd."

Though Rahel normally exuded confidence and boldness, being near Hoshea usually reduced her to bashful giggles. This time, though, Rahel boldly walked up behind Hoshea and tapped his shoulder. When he turned, her smile gleamed, and what appeared to be a rehearsed speech gushed out in one long breath.

"She looks happy." Eliza sighed. Her dramatic outburst several nights ago had led to Rahel's abduction and possibly altered their friendship for good. Rahel didn't owe her a thing. Eliza would swallow her pride and wait, as hard as it might be, for Rahel to come to her. Who was she to expect anything more? Let her friend have this moment with the man of her dreams.

Hoshea's brow wrinkled as Rahel went on. He put a hand on his hip, then shifted his weight from one foot to the other. Eliza inched forward, straining to hear what had him so perplexed. He ran a hand down his beard before gently guiding Rahel away from the curious ears of those around him.

"What did you want to tell me?" Seti's voice broke into Eliza's runaway thoughts.

After one last glance at Rahel, who now stared intently into Hoshea's eyes while he quietly spoke to her, Eliza turned to Seti. "It was Adam, wasn't it?"

"What was?"

"He told you to sing the ketubah and to blow the horn and shave all your hair off, didn't he?"

Seti's eyes narrowed. A scowl crossed his bruised face. "It made sense. To consecrate myself—"

"You don't have to do that for a betrothal. Not even for the wedding ceremony. Only the bride consecrates herself beforehand, not you. And the singing …"

Seti shook his head, as if battling something deep inside. "But … but you sang too."

"Seti." She wrapped her arms around his waist. If only she could ease the humiliation clouding his handsome face. "I couldn't let you do that alone."

The comments at the table had already sparked Seti's suspicions that he'd blundered the betrothal, but Eliza's confirmation tipped the pot simmering inside him. She could have told him earlier, yet what good would that have done? They had an audience then. Now that the betrothal was over, and he had her father's blessing, what was left to restrain him? He marched toward Adam, his face hot.

"Why mourn at your own betrothal, Seti?" Zechariah smirked as Seti passed.

Seti shoved him aside without even a glance and continued on. Adam stood near the fire, curiously watching Hoshea.

"Seti!" Eliza ran after him. She grabbed his arm, but he shook her off.

Catching Adam off guard, Seti grabbed him by the tunic. "You said you didn't want to embarrass your sister, but that's exactly what you did. You made us look like fools!"

Adam struggled against his grip.

"What did I do to deserve this?" Seti pushed Adam back. "Is this what I should expect from a Hebrew?"

Sabu quickly stood, fumbled with his crutches, lost his balance, and fell against Nala.

"Seti, stop!" Eliza reached for him again, but he plowed forward until Adam fell on his rear.

"I saved her from my family!" Seti pointed to his own chest. "I set her and Miera free. I did what Pharaoh couldn't do. And this is what I get in return?"

Adam crab-crawled away, but Seti put a foot on Adam's chest and leaned in. The lack of fight the coward put up only stoked Seti's fury. He pressed harder, ignoring the shouts and cries around him.

"You call yourself a brother? It wasn't enough that she was beat up in front of the world and bore the effects at her betrothal, but you made her out to be a fool. Not only her, but your whole family. I hope it makes you happy, Adam, because it makes a mockery of you too."

Adam rolled out from under Seti's foot and leaped to his feet. He met Seti eye-to-eye, chest heaving, nostrils flaring. Every muscle in Seti's body tensed, waiting for Adam to make a move. To run his mouth. The slightest twitch on Adam's part was all Seti needed. Then nobody would mess with him again.

A sharp slap cracked through the air.

"How dare you!" Rahel's vicious scream snapped Seti out of his moment. She leaned forward, her red cheeks shaking as she railed, "How dare you speak of me in such terms, you foul-mouthed man-dog. I am not a tool for your gain!"

With a sob, she spun so fast her braid hit Hoshea's stunned face. She disappeared into the silenced crowd.

"Rahel!" Eliza shot Hoshea a deathly glare and dashed after Rahel.

Seti instinctively started after her but paused, processing what had just happened. The commander of Moshe's army had been reduced to a piece of meat by a girl in front of everyone, while Seti was about to pummel his brother-in-law and ruin his betrothal. He had compared himself to Pharaoh loud enough for all to hear. Any recollection of his betrothal would be this heightened moment. Not the song. Not the horn. If he hadn't looked Egyptian earlier, he did now. A dark shadow befell him as he realized he had surpassed Adam in fault. The betrothal was ruined.

Seti exchanged an awkward glance with Adam, rubbing the back of his neck.

Zechariah charged Hoshea and shoved him back. "What did you say to her?"

Hoshea put his hands up. "Zech—"

"What did you say? She finally left her parents after days, and now look what you've done!" Zechariah lunged again, but Hoshea caught his arm, spun him, and twisted it behind his back.

With the boy unable to move, Hoshea lifted his heated gaze toward Seti and Adam. "What is wrong with everybody?"

Zechariah's odd behavior suddenly made sense—he had fallen for Rahel. The eavesdropping, volunteering to rescue her, inviting her to the betrothal, and now this. If Zechariah's accusations against Seti had been true, and her abduction his fault, then Zechariah's animosity toward him would have been justified. But they weren't. He'd let the boy off the hook. This time.

Bystanders whispered and pointed. Jeremiah's jaw twitched as he restrained Sarah from rushing to their son. Seti turned his back toward them, unable to face them after his idiotic behavior.

"I came to speak with Seti and Sabu, but by the looks of it, you all need a word." Hoshea's stern voice held the weight of a father's scolding, and Seti squirmed under his piercing gaze.

After releasing Zechariah and briefly touching the handprint on his cheek, Hoshea continued, "You people—

everyone out here—are acting like heathens. I'm ashamed. God set us apart to be different. Distinct. Yet you behave like animals."

Rubbing his arm, Zechariah backed away.

Hoshea shook his head. "Moshe was right. Humanity can't handle freedom. We gravitate toward servitude, no matter who or what it's to. We *need* to be reined in. We *need* a purpose greater than ourselves."

He met each of their eyes in turn. "And unlike the rest of the world, we have that. He's right there." He pointed to the Cloud Pillar. "He chose us when we didn't deserve it, and we still don't deserve it. We are the portion of El Shaddai that will lead the world back to Him. It's time we act like it."

Guilt and shame twisted Seti's heart. He had dedicated himself to the Hebrew God and failed yet again.

"Enough of my rant. Now, why the high emotions? I heard Eliza got in a fight? A literal fight?" He threw his hands in the air. "How? And all of you went to battle. How many of you killed somebody?"

No one answered.

"Come on, let's hear it."

Seti took a deep breath. "One or two."

"One," Adam mumbled.

"Something like that," Zechariah added, studying his feet.

"Not sure," Sabu said proudly. "But at least two."

Seti cringed, knowing what was coming.

"You should know God forbids males under twenty to go to war—"

"We didn't go to war—" Zechariah started.

Hoshea silenced him with a raised finger. "You all need something to do. Something besides sabotaging one another."

Leaning on his crutches, Sabu stood and asked the question Seti didn't dare ask. "Like what? We're not going anywhere. We're stuck out here in the middle of the desert."

After a long sigh, Hoshea turned to Zechariah. "My men and I train and spar every morning. I think it would benefit all of you to join us. It'll prepare you for when you come of age."

"Really?" Zechariah lifted his face, hope lighting his eyes.

"Yes." Hoshea looked at Seti. "And Moshe needs messengers on horseback to spread his word among the multitude, since there seems to be a lack of communication among tribes." He nodded toward Sabu, whose lopsided, toothy grin lit up his face. "Moshe is in the process of appointing tribal leaders, but even so, we're too many and too spread out for effective communication."

Sabu's shining eyes met Seti's, who returned the smile. The lack of purpose had dampened Sabu's spirit, but he'd have to wait until his leg could bear weight.

"Adam." Hoshea turned, and Adam jerked his head up as if ready for a scolding. "I need someone to teach me to read and write. But after sparring."

The breath left Seti like a blow to the gut.

Adam jumped on the offer. "Yes, of course, but I'm not fluent."

"Anything you can offer helps."

Betrayal knifed Seti's heart. The honor of teaching this great man to read had been stripped away and handed to his nemesis. Yes, he'd get to train with Hoshea, but that was beside the point. Was it the fight with Adam or his involvement in the battle that turned Hoshea away? Defeat washed over Seti. He fought to keep his composure, to mask his pain. No one knew about Hoshea's broken promise to Seti, not even Adam. So, they couldn't possibly sense his impending eruption, could they?

Seti's gaze darted, seeking an escape before succumbing to his overwhelming emotions. Again. Hoshea could read him like a hawk. So could Sabu. He stepped back with trembling nerves, wanting to run.

"Seti."

"Yes?" He inclined his head as if listening all along.

"Don't go anywhere. I'm not done with you."

Adam smirked. Seti pressed his lips together and choked back the burning lump in his throat. He gave a slight nod, then dropped his head, heart pounding. *God, please provide me an escape.*

"Where's the goblet?" Hoshea asked.

The goblet? Seti had left it on the table. The world fell silent, even his own footsteps, as he walked in a trance toward the table.

He stopped and stared at the gold goblet, fighting the urge to keep walking. The table's owner had yet to claim his property, but his words echoed in Seti's head. He had lent it for Eliza, not the Egyptian who bedded his slaves, mourned at his betrothal, sang his vows, and summoned warriors with a ram's horn. The Egyptian idiot who joined the Levites but then compared himself to Pharaoh.

A powerful hand landed on Seti's shoulder, startling him back to reality.

Hoshea grabbed the goblet and held it up. "Don't look so dejected, Seti. I didn't forget you." He handed over the cup, then brandished a small wineskin from his cloak and poured a measure into it.

Unfazed, Seti stood with the goblet in hand, unable to speak.

"The Amalekite camp in Elim had all kinds of aged wine," Hoshea went on. "It's more potent than any I've ever tasted. But we can't let word get out, or it will be gone in days. I want to save it for medicinal purposes. And special occasions … like today."

Seti stared into the red liquid, swirling it around, avoiding Hoshea's eyes. The last he'd drunk wine had been to numb his pain during the gnat infestation on his trip to Giza. He couldn't care less about the stuff now. Sabu might want it.

"You don't want it?" Hoshea asked.

Seti shrugged.

Hoshea glanced at those around the firepit, then lowered his voice and leaned in. "I didn't want to say this in front of Adam, but Moshe needs a scribe, and I'm sending you."

Seti lifted his face. Had he heard correctly?

"You're the only one I know who's fluent in Hebrew script. Moshe knows very little. God has instructed him to write everything down, and it's too much for him."

"I—I'm pretty sure Moshe hates me."

"You'll grow on him. I know it. No one can not like you, Seti. He just hasn't given you a chance yet. The thing is, he doesn't have a choice."

Seti stared, mouth open, as another swell of emotion thickened in his throat. Now was his chance to get close to Moshe. To get close to God. He would sit with Moshe, one-on-one, speaking, conversing, writing. He'd be recording the very words of the Hebrew God.

"I knew you'd like that better than teaching me," Hoshea said with a smirk. "Now, have a sip of wine and share some with Eliza. It's a blessing on your betrothal. But don't tell anyone else about the wine. I told Moshe I'd bring his new scribe to meet him at sunrise, so you'll miss training in the morning. He's planning to speak with God, so I want this handled before he ends up on that mountain all day. Do you know where his tent is?"

"He doesn't know it's me?"

"No, not yet. Don't worry, I have it under control. But do you know where his tent is?"

Seti glanced around, heart pounding in his throat. Trying to look casual, he sipped the wine. "No."

"Fine. I'll come get you. Actually, I'll get all of you— show you where we spar, then take you to Moshe. At sunrise." Hoshea peered over his shoulder at the others, then lightly touched his pink cheek where Rahel had slapped him.

Seti wrinkled his brow. "What was that about?"

"Rahel? I don't know. She's a little traumatized or something." Hoshea swigged a mouthful from his wineskin and swished it around before swallowing. "She's stronger than she looks. I have to go. See you at sunrise."

Seti nodded, the goblet shaking in his hand. Moments ago, he'd been on the verge of fleeing to avoid making yet another scene. He had ruined his betrothal. Now, he struggled to keep from dancing. If Adam or Zechariah found out about his new assignment, they might hate him even more. The thrill of it threatened to roll off his tongue. Unable to contain it, he scanned the dispersing crowd for Eliza.

After pouring the wine into an empty pouch and filling another with water, he mustered his courage and sought out Jeremiah. He had to get alone with Eliza. Now that they were betrothed, and her family had pitched their tents amid the rest of the multitude, he no longer knew what constituted as "the camp" or if leaving it still mattered.

Jeremiah sat at a table, deep in conversation with Sarah and two men whose scraggly beards and bushy eyebrows masked their weathered faces. Adam and Zechariah, along with several young men, hauled away the other tables and stools, signaling the end of the celebration.

Shame at his childish behavior with Adam sent Seti's heart racing as he approached his father-in-law. He cleared his throat.

To his surprise, Jeremiah turned to him with kind eyes, making Seti stumble for words. "Jere … um … sir, if you don't mind, I'd … like permission to take Eliza to the edge of the camp." He stopped short of adding "to be alone with her".

Without hesitation, Jeremiah nodded. "Go find her before she gets into trouble."

"Thank you, Abb—sir." Seti backed away before Jeremiah could change his mind.

Unsure of the meaning behind Jeremiah's words, Seti hurried to Chewy. Even though Eliza seemed more herself each day, she could easily succumb to the day's heat and stress, especially after enduring Sena's punches. Could that be what Jeremiah had meant? The hostility they'd faced at lunch returned to his mind, and he hastened his step.

Chapter 34

A sharp cramp shot through Eliza's side, and she pressed it with her hand, coming to a halt. Since hitting her head, she had lost her endurance. What had she been thinking, running after Rahel? Rahel had always been faster. Panting, Eliza searched for a place to sit among the seemingly thousands of tents surrounding her. Her head spun, and the tents blended together. People and animals jostled past as they dispersed from the betrothal, returning to their camps.

Heat radiated from her throbbing head. She grabbed hold of a clothesline pole in the ground to steady herself. The farther she wandered from the river, the more everything looked the same. Her only point of reference was the Cloud Pillar atop the Great Mountain. She suppressed a bout of nausea and sank onto a rock. Her throat burned with thirst, but if she drank, it might come back up.

"El Roi," she whispered toward the Pillar. "I'm lost."

Her eyes started to roll back when a male voice startled her.

"It's the bride!"

"Get off my campsite, traitor!"

A shove knocked her off the rock, and she crumpled to the ground.

Eliza stared up at the three people laughing at her: a woman, a man, and a child.

"Did your new husband do that to your face?" the woman asked.

Eliza bit her lip, having forgotten her battered face. "No …"

Another man joined the young family. "And her abba blessed the union. Can you believe that?"

"The whole family's traitors for accepting him." The first man spat near Eliza and cursed. "He had no shame flaunting his heritage."

It took a moment to process their words. She crab-crawled backward. "That's not true."

A group of teenagers walked by, laughing and pointing.

"Get off our campsite!" the child yelled.

The woman marched forward and snatched the hem of Eliza's gown. "This isn't even Egyptian. Where'd you get this?"

Heart pounding, Eliza yanked it back and struggled to her feet. All she wanted was to be alone, to breathe, to drink some water. As they laughed at her loss of balance, she turned and staggered away.

"Is she heavy on drink?"

"Her family must be hoarding it …"

The taunts followed her as she rounded a tent and grabbed onto an ox for balance. Her eyes stung, and she buried her face against the animal's flank. The heat blurred her vision.

"Leave her alone. Her husband saved us in the battle," an unfamiliar male voice said.

"But that man had hair."

Eliza stumbled between several oxen, eager to put as many animals and tents as possible between herself and the scoffers. She'd find Rahel later. This place was worse than the slums in Egypt. Here, her own people rejected her.

Once the world stopped spinning, shelves of earthenware came into focus, with no owner in sight. She made her way toward them, glancing at the empty tent near the cookstove for the owner, but saw no one. A large vessel of water sat beneath a table. Eliza grabbed a cup, dipped it in, and then ducked behind the tent. The cool water soothed her scratchy throat. After wiping the tears from her eyes, she returned the empty cup and pressed on in what she hoped was the right direction.

There was no memory of what she had passed on the walk here. Her muddled thoughts refused to focus. The river would lead her back to her family, if she could find it.

Her foot sank into something soft. A sharp sob caught in her throat as she lifted it—warm, fresh manure caked her new sandal. "No."

All motivation vanished. She slumped to the ground, every muscle limp under the weight of defeat. She buried her face between her knees, and for once in her life, willed herself to cry, to release the tension, to burst the dam inside her. But the tears wouldn't come.

What a waste. She had barely seen Rahel, once again missing the opportunity to comfort her. Now, on the so-called happiest day of her life—ruined by Adam's scheming and Seti's behavior—she sat lost amid a congested maze of tents and people who had rejected her.

As she mumbled another prayer, the cramp in her side and the lurching in her stomach subsided.

"Is that her?" a child's voice asked.

"Yes, thank you." Seti's voice replied.

A horse whinnied, feet thudded to the ground, and before Eliza could lift her head, a hand touched her shoulder. "Eliza?"

As if a gust of cool air had hit, energy surged through her at the sight of Seti's face. She jumped to her feet and flung her arms around his neck. "Seti? How'd you find me?"

He gently pulled her arms free. "Are you all right? You didn't find Rahel, did you?"

She stood back and shielded her eyes, glimpsing Chewy nearby. "I … I prayed, and you came." She straightened, wiped her sweaty palms on her gown, then took a deep breath. His warm hands on her waist calmed her nerves. "You came for me. Again."

"Yes." Seti's eyes assessed her before settling on her face again. He tucked her loose curls behind her ear. "I asked your abba if it'd be all right to take you to the edge of camp. I have some things to tell you. And I had a feeling you wouldn't catch up with Rahel."

Eliza choked back the emotion threatening to pour out. Like a pendulum, the day's highs and lows swung to the extreme, exhausting her more than the blistering sun or the sprint after Rahel. "Please, let's get out of here."

Seti nodded and helped her onto Chewy. Two water pouches dangled from the horse's neck, making her mouth water. He climbed up in front and took the reins, steering Chewy around. From her perch, she realized just how lost she'd been as she gazed upon the hundreds of tents in every direction. She mouthed a *thank you* toward the Cloud Pillar, then rested her face against Seti's back.

God, El Roi, made Himself visible from the depths of despair, a constant reminder of not just His presence, but of His awareness of those lost beyond finding.

After leaving Chewy near the rock wall, Eliza followed Seti to the other side, where she had hidden the day before. Ashamed of her soiled sandal, she ducked into a rock-crevice, slipped it off, and scraped the manure against the limestone. He must have smelled it the whole ride. She rubbed dirt on her foot and the sandal, hoping to stifle the stench. Her moment of beauty had lapsed, and the dirty slave beneath had returned.

"Come and sit," Seti called. "You can wash them later."

He knew? And wasn't upset? She sighed and joined him where he sat, cross-legged in the shadow of a boulder, the pouches in his lap.

"I brought something for you."

Eliza tucked her legs to the side, delicately dusting the dirt from her gown as Lumeri used to do after a chariot race through town.

With his brow knitted, Seti waited for her to settle before handing over one of the pouches. "Hoshea found wine at the Amalekite camp. He brought some for us, said it's a blessing, and he wanted me to share it with you."

Eliza gasped, taking the pouch, self-consciousness obliterated. God had prevailed. "Seti! Do you know what this means?" She opened it and breathed in the strong aroma.

"No."

"This seals the covenant we made with the ketubah. Wine symbolizes blood, making it a blood covenant in the eyes of God—between you and me. We drink from the same cup today and again at the wedding feast. Then, with the consummation, we truly become one."

Seti smiled. "If it's a blood covenant, why didn't we just use blood?"

"Because we drink it, silly. Together. It's an abomination to drink blood. It represents life." She gripped the pouch, emotion welling in her chest. *God is good. Very good.* "Well, we could have sealed the ketubah with a blood offering, but for a betrothal and a wedding, it's more intimate to ingest it. Oh, Seti. The day was ruined, but now it's truly blessed!"

Seeing the joy on Eliza's face settled the angst growing in Seti all day. He'd gladly make a fool of himself in front of everyone every day if it meant arriving at such a moment as this. Seti's bride, the love of his life, sat before him, as beautiful as ever. Her face shone with a joy that eclipsed even her elation at the proposal.

Adam hadn't mentioned anything about wine earlier, perhaps because none was available. Would the betrothal have been negated if Hoshea hadn't shown up with it? Did Adam know this and keep silent, hoping to humiliate him further? Yet, Jeremiah blessed the betrothal without a word about the wine.

"Did you have some already?" she asked.

"Just a few sips. It's strong."

Eliza lifted the pouch to her smiling lips. "Ready to seal this?"

With a nod, Seti leaned in and covered her hand on the pouch with his. He gazed into her sparkling eyes. "Remember, it's strong enough for a giant."

She sipped first. Her face puckered, her hand flailed, and she sputtered out a cough. Seti laughed and sipped next.

"Should we save the rest for the ceremony?" she asked after composing herself.

"No, there's plenty for later. Besides, we'll have a vineyard by then." He downed three gulps before pulling the pouch away, his throat burning. Despite the fruity smell, there was no sweetness. "Don't worry. I brought water too."

Eliza wiped her brow and held the pouch as if preparing for another sip. She barely swallowed before handing it back. Her hands went to her mouth, eyes wide and watery.

Though the wine might ease her jaw pain, Seti set the pouch aside, concerned how it might affect her head. He handed her the water. "Maybe we should stop."

Eliza nodded, taking the water. She stifled a small belch behind her hand.

After soothing the fire in his throat, Seti leaned against a boulder and gazed at the desert hills, letting the wine warm his insides. "I'm sorry about the fight with Adam."

When she didn't answer, Seti sat up, bracing for a scolding. But Eliza reclined, eyes closed. He should've saved the wine for last.

"Eliza."

She neither moved nor opened her eyes. "I know, Seti. I forgive you."

"And Hoshea wants me to be Moshe's scribe."

He waited.

It took a moment for her to sit up and gaze at him with a look of both confusion and wonder. "What?"

"Moshe needs a scribe fluent in Hebrew script. Hoshea recruited me."

"Moshe approves'?"

"He doesn't know yet. Hoshea says he won't have a choice. He's taking me to Moshe's tent tomorrow."

Eliza's shoulders slumped. "I don't think he'll accept you. He thinks you're a troublemaker."

"Well." Seti shrugged. "I kind of am. But Hoshea seems confident, and I really want this. I think we should pray about it. Both of us."

A smile lit up her swollen face. "Of course."

She crawled into his lap with a hunger in her eyes that could only be the effects of the wine. With a seductive boldness he hadn't seen before, she drew her knees up and wrapped her arms around his shoulders, pinning him with her gaze. "Hold me."

Her gown bunched around her exposed thighs as she nestled into him, the scent of manure muffling the flowery aroma that had overwhelmed him earlier. Seti smiled. Even Sena's sultry moves at the river couldn't match the way Eliza's awkward grace and innocence unraveled him. He cradled her, his heart fluttering with desire, ready to surrender to both the wine and her advances.

She closed her eyes and lifted her parted lips. He leaned in with his own—when she suddenly spoke.

"Oh, Lord God, You've heard my prayers. You are El Roi, the wonderful God who sees even the lowliest of the low. You've blessed our betrothal more than I could have asked. But now I implore You for one more thing. Please shine Your face upon this wonderful man You have blessed me with and bring him into the council of Moshe. Let him be of good use and let Moshe show acceptance toward Seti. Thank you, my Lord. Amen."

Seti stared in disbelief as she opened her eyes, her grin lighting her face.

"I thought you wanted me to kiss you," he muttered, afraid his physical desires and current position might hinder God's willingness to hear. Though sensuality aroused the Egyptian gods, Seti couldn't imagine the Hebrew God responding to such things. The prayer— elegant, impassioned, pouring from the lips of this beautiful girl— shook him more than any kiss ever could.

"I do. Kiss me, my husband, scribe of Moshe." She closed her eyes again.

Seti shook his head. The yearning to honor her request warred with the weight of her prayer and his longing to please God. He took a breath, pulled her close, and placed a hand behind her neck. The softness of her lips awakened stifled desires. Electricity coursed through his every nerve, and he drew her in tighter, desperate to absorb her very being, from her smooth skin to her enigmatic soul.

Then, with all the effort he could summon, he pulled away, releasing her. She sat back, wiped her lips with her hand, and pouted her bottom lip. "Marry me."

The wine was a bad idea. He chuckled, unable to look at those eyes. But his eyes grazed her body until he forced them away. "You're clearly drunk."

"I'm serious," she cried. "I don't want to stay with my family anymore. I love them, but I hate where Abba pitched the tents. There are too many people, and they act awful. I was scared until you came. We can find a place by ourselves on the edge of the valley, close enough to God but far from everyone else."

The pain in her voice pierced him. "Did—did somebody hurt you?"

"No, Seti. Because you came. But they all hate us. They mock us." She buried her face against his chest, her fingers digging into his shoulders. "They said you did this to my face. And someone grabbed my dress, and I thought they were going to tear it. They belittled my abba for accepting you. I can't bear it. Everyone knows where my family is camped. What if they come after us? I just want to get away. Please, Seti."

He wasn't thrilled with the new campsite either, yet it couldn't be that bad, could it? The taunts from earlier resurfaced, bringing with them a gnawing unease.

He had longed to consummate their betrothal—had dreamed of it—but not like this. Not driven by fear and heavy wine. Yet, what was he waiting for? He had no tent of his own, and besides that, was there a required betrothal period?

As her tears dampened his tunic, he stroked her back, unsure how to respond. When her grip loosened, he asked, "Don't you want a big ceremony?"

"No."

After that morning's spectacle, he didn't want one either. He guided her back so he could see her face. The kohl had streaked down her cheeks. The exhaustion and sadness in her eyes seared Seti's heart like a hot iron. He bit back the emotion building up, again unable to hold her gaze.

"Give me some time. Let me find out what happens with Moshe tomorrow, acquire a tent, and set things right. Ceremony or not, I want to do this properly." He smoothed the hair from her forehead. "Zechariah knows where to find Rahel. He can take you there. In the meantime, if you feel unsafe, stay close to your family and me. Does that sound feasible?"

With a sniffle, she nodded.

Chapter 35

The swollen orange glow of the sunset met Eliza's tired eyes as she stirred. She had dreamed of waking in the outhouse back in Egypt, as if her freedom and betrothal had only been a dream.

She inhaled the cool, crisp breeze, such a contrast to the stifling outhouse. Nothing like a little reminder of where one came from. "Thank you, God. I'm free. So free. All because of You."

The young man beside her twitched in his sleep, yet another reminder of how her life had taken a drastic turn for the impossible. His warm chest, which had served as a pillow for her head, rose and fell at a gentle rhythm. A string of drool stretched from his open mouth to a small puddle in the sand. His temple rested against a boulder. Only he could make a rock look comfortable.

"Seti?" She nudged him gently. "Seti, wake up."

He moaned, turning slightly but not waking. She'd stay there beside him all night if she could, but her abba would have her head.

"Seti, we must go back. We fell asleep. We left Chewy all alone too."

His eyelids cracked open.

Seti pushed himself up and rubbed his eyes. "We fell asleep?"

She nodded, reaching to smooth the marks on his cheek.

He took her hand and sighed, his gaze lost in the sunset behind her. "I slept hard. Haven't slept much at all lately."

He hadn't, and she hated having to wake him.

The memory of Eliza's drunken pleading with Seti earlier that day returned on their ride back to camp. Her heart sank. Their betrothal had barely begun, and already she'd burdened him with complaints and demands. It reminded her of his mother. Since gaining her freedom, she'd done nothing but hurt those she loved, her maturity waning when it should be growing.

"I'm sorry about earlier," she mumbled.

"What?" He turned his head.

She cleared her throat and stretched to speak near his ear. "I'm sorry."

"What are you apologizing for now?"

Was that irritation in his voice? She shrank behind him. "For pushing you to consummate our marriage just so I could move away with you. I don't want to be like that. Pushy like your ima— I mean, I—"

"If you were anything like my ima, I wouldn't be here with you. So, what's to be sorry about?"

She cringed at her careless comparison, regardless of his gentle reaction. With all the years guarding her tongue, this shouldn't be a problem. "And for crying all the time. I just—" She slid her hands from his waist to his sturdy shoulders, which mirrored his character and demeanor. While he resembled a beacon in the storm, she personified the storm, complete with lightning. "I—I don't know how to be free. I'm doing things and saying things I never would have dared as a slave. I begged God for something I cannot handle, and now I'm struggling with it. Servitude suited me."

"Don't forget you hit your head. Give yourself time. I've been free all my life, and I still do things I regret. You saw how I handled Adam, just cementing the opinions people already had of me." Seti steered around two toddlers sitting in the path. "And don't worry about being demanding. What my family did to you—what you endured—is far worse. You should never have to work again. I'll make sure of it. When we get our land, I'll build a house exactly how you want it. And you won't have to keep it up or cook or tend the livestock. You can do whatever you like. Find hobbies. Make friends. Practice your lute."

"But…but who will take care of things? You can't do everything."

"Easy, we'll get servants. You—" His voice trailed off, and his shoulders slumped.

Eliza smiled at his naïveté and consideration, but she wouldn't allow herself an easy life at the expense of others. She massaged his tense shoulders. "I don't mind working, Seti. In fact, I'd love to keep house and cook. It'd be my house. Our house."

The gentle clopping of Chewy's hooves, and the soft rocking on his back, calmed her senses amid the camp's bustling activity.

"See," Seti murmured, voice riddled with shame. "Eighteen years of freedom, and I still slip up."

Maybe Seti was right. Maybe she should be easier on herself. Rahel hit a man. Adam proved to be a conniving weasel. Miera had befriended a stranger to the detriment of the entire congregation. Yuval sought vengeance to the point of murder. And the people found entertainment in the judgment of their brethren. Not to mention Sena—who had no shame whatsoever. Like her, they all had much to learn.

She leaned her forehead gently against Seti's back and hugged his waist, careful not to squeeze his injured ribs. An ugly yellow bordered the faded purple bruising that peeked from beneath his tunic, proof of Seti's carelessness with his own freedom.

"I don't think people give much thought to what they do with their freedom," Seti continued. "Especially if they're born into it."

"Well, I will." Eliza straightened, determination reviving her aching muscles. She gazed at the Fire Pillar as darkness descended. "I'll make sure God doesn't regret freeing me."

Seti chuckled. "I don't think humanity knows how to be free … we all serve someone or something." He turned Chewy toward her father's tent. "But it depends on how one defines freedom. Even I was a slave to the Egyptian gods, though, at the time, I didn't know it."

He spoke with the experience of a hundred-year-old man, and indeed, he'd lived a lifetime in a few short months. Likewise, she'd gone through more than her people had in the past four hundred years. From this moment on, she'd make the most of it. No more jumping to conclusions, acting on emotions, or embarrassing her family. Every day of freedom would be given back to God. Whatever that entailed.

Seti woke the following morning to Hoshea shaking his shoulder. He lifted his head and leaned on his elbow, blinking moisture into his eyes. Today, he'd find out if Moshe would accept him. He glanced at Adam and Zechariah, who continued to snore beside the firepit.

Hoshea paced nearby, hands on his hips. "Let's go, you three. Being men requires work."

Untouched manna blanketed the brothers, the tents, and even the ashes in the firepit. The sun breached the horizon, casting pink and gold across the hazy morning. The Pillar on the mountain had already transformed into a spinning white cloud, a canopy slowly ballooning above. By noon, it would stretch over the entire valley.

"Don't worry, I'll wake them." Seti stood and brushed manna from his cloak. He grabbed a clay basin near the tent, filled it with water, and then splashed Adam and Zechariah with it. They sprang up with gasps and shouts.

"Wake up!" Seti towered over them. "Hoshea's waiting."

"I'd expected you all to be up before I arrived, judging from your reactions yesterday," Hoshea said dryly.

Seti laughed. "Unless you two rise before me, I'll drown you every morning."

Hoshea shot him a look.

Adam had it coming, and if Zechariah happened to be near, he'd get the same. Neither would get away with their part in humiliating him during the betrothal. Not until Adam felt the same humiliation and pain.

Rising to his feet, Adam glared at Seti and brushed soggy manna from his cloak. "I didn't sleep well."

Seti hadn't either. Besides being forced to sleep by the cook fire with Adam and Zechariah for lack of space, the domestic dispute nearby that lasted all night and woke seemingly every baby in the vicinity, and a cat in heat somewhere, Seti couldn't shake Eliza's haunting words from his thoughts. She cherished her freedom enough to shape her life around it and glorify God, while he'd taken his independence for granted. The realization admonished him and filled him with awe and admiration for her. Her faith may falter at times, but her love for God stood firm.

Yet he couldn't curb his desire for retribution on Adam.

Hoshea led them along the river to the south edge of the valley, near the hills where Seti had dragged the injured after the battle.

At the top, Hoshea paused and gestured broadly across the view. "Every morning at sun up, we meet here."

What had once been an empty valley now stretched from one barren ridge to another with sheep, cattle, and hundreds of men. Unfinished wooden fences corralled the livestock, and disassembled carts dotted the area.

"Why are they putting up fences?" Zechariah asked with a yawn.

"We won't be moving for a while." Hoshea nodded toward the Cloud Pillar. "At least, that's what Moshe said. He's been up that mountain a few times already, and I suspect there'll be many more ascensions." He put a hand on his hip, turning toward the men gathering below. "We take turns leading. You three, and Sabu when he's able, will meet at the rear. Don't get in the way."

When no one responded, Hoshea motioned to Adam and Zechariah. "Go on now. I'll meet you there after I show Seti where he's going."

Adam raised an eyebrow, and Seti met his gaze.

"Seti will be there later," Hoshea said as he turned to leave.

Seti winked at Adam, then jogged to catch up with Hoshea's long strides. "Moshe's not judging today?"

"He's in the process of appointing tribal leaders to judge the simpler cases. He'll still handle the difficult ones."

They plodded onto a narrow footpath, weaving between tents near the healers' canopies. More people had moved in since Seti last set foot in this part of the valley.

"Eliza dodged an arrow with that one. Moshe appointed Hannaniah over the Levites, and he's in league with Sena's family. These men may be considered honorable and reputable, but when it comes to integrity, I don't trust anybody but Moshe."

"You know about Eliza and Sena?"

Hoshea halted. "Everyone knows about Eliza and Sena. It didn't help that Eliza already had a reputation as a troublemaker with the frog incident and for rescuing an Egyptian. And Sena doesn't exactly blend in either."

Seti winced at the "rescuing an Egyptian" part. How many people knew? Hoshea's words from earlier echoed in his mind—that the Hebrews would one day regard Seti as a hero for rescuing Eliza, a slave at the time. It hadn't happened yet. Probably never would.

Hoshea started down the path again. "We're entering the Levite camp."

The Lank had mentioned the division of camps according to tribe. The area appeared no different from the rest of the valley, teeming with people, tents, and wagons. Women and children carried baskets and basins to collect their manna. Sleepy-eyed men stirred ashes or milked cows and goats.

A knot worked its way into Seti's stomach the farther they walked. "Wh-where are you camped?"

Hoshea cast a side-long glance at Seti. "Here."

"You're not a Levite."

"No, but I need to be near Moshe."

"Why did he choose you?"

The question came out before Seti could stop it, but Hoshea chuckled and slowed his pace. "That's a good question, Seti. You'll have to ask him. I give God the credit for that one."

"But don't you have family? What tribe are you again?"

"I am of Ephraim, son of Yoseph, the savior of Egypt. Remember? And he married an Egyptian, which makes me part Egyptian."

Seti stopped. Why hadn't Hoshea mentioned this earlier? "So, your entire tribe is part Egyptian?"

"More than that. Two entire tribes. And who knows how many Hebrews married their masters over the years?"

That meant a significant portion of the Hebrews carried Egyptian blood. Yet, God still included them. All of them.

Hoshea nudged Seti forward. "Moshe's tent is right ahead."

The knot tightened in Seti's gut, and he swiftly inhaled. Moshe would see him for the first time since that day in the palace. A white canvas tent stood out against the valley's various shades of brown, taller than the others with wooden beams. Besides that, there was remarkably little difference between Moshe's tent and the others. But then what did Seti expect? A portable palace? Moshe hardly seemed the type.

"After the battle, God instructed Moshe to build an altar to Him on the battlefield," Hoshea said. "He named it *The Lord is my Banner*."

Seti had just seen the battlefield—filled with sheep and men. There was no altar. But what did a Hebrew altar consist of?

"Then He commanded Moshe to record what happened with the Amalekites as a reminder of God's plans for them since a remnant still lives. It will be recited for future generations."

A chill slowed Seti's steps. "What will He do to them?"

"He'll wipe them off the face of the earth. Blot out the memory of Amalek from under the heavens as a warning for the rest of the world."

Apparently, what happened in Egypt wasn't the wrath of God. There was a side of Him Seti had not seen and didn't care to see. But what, besides attacking the Hebrews, had the Amalekites done to warrant His wrath? Their bloodline, like Homan suggested? And what exactly did that wrath entail? "Why—"

"You'll have to ask Moshe. But listen, this is just the beginning. He's going up the mountain tonight for something important. If he only needed the events with the Amalekites written, he'd have written it himself. He's anticipating a lot more writing." Hoshea paused outside the tent, holding out a hand to stop Seti. "Wait here for my summons." He lifted the lightly tanned flap, and a string of trinkets jingled. The flap closed behind him.

Seti ran a hand over his shorn head, rubbed the back of his neck, then clasped his hands behind his back, unable to keep still. He leaned toward the canvas, straining to discern the hushed voices inside above the clucking chickens at his feet. Giving up, he turned toward the Cloud Pillar in the east. Moshe would either accept or send him away, and Seti would be ready for either.

But please let him accept me. I promise to dedicate the rest of my life to you. Please, Lord God. Yahweh.

Upon leaving Egypt, Seti had promised to dedicate the rest of his life to God and had failed repeatedly. He'd hoarded manna and tossed it into The Lank's tent, been angry and frustrated at God over Eliza's condition, and defied God's word about being too young to fight. Though Seti barely knew Him, he trusted Him. Still, his promises had proven shallow.

The flap opened, and Aharon plowed out but stopped short at the sight of Seti. His mouth opened, then closed, and he lifted a finger but let it drop. Seti had no words. Aharon's gaze flitted between Seti and the tent before giving a slight nod and marching away.

What was that? Seti let out the breath stuck in his throat, heart hammering against his aching ribs. Suddenly, the morning sun was unbearable, and every ache from the past few days returned anew. Sweat beaded on his forehead. He checked his tunic for wet spots, hoping Moshe wouldn't see the terror radiating from him. Their past encounters had been humiliating enough.

Hoshea flung open the flap, the trinkets ringing like a windchime. He nodded toward Seti with his mouth pressed into a thin line and a solemn look in his eyes. "I am anticipating a certain reaction from Moshe and will explain later."

This was a bad idea. A dream meant for someone else. A Hebrew. Seti cast one last plea toward the Cloud Pillar, fighting the instinct to run. Then, with a deep breath, he entered.

Moshe jumped from his cushioned chair, his knee bumping the small table before him. With eyes wide, he pointed a finger at Seti. "You!"

Chapter 36

The breath left Seti's lungs at Moshe's obvious displeasure. He looked to Hoshea for help.

"What is he doing here?" Moshe demanded of Hoshea. He then glared at Seti. "Why are you here?"

Hoshea stepped forward. "He's been with us since we left Egypt. He's one of us—"

"Clearly not!" Moshe shot a hand toward Seti. "Look at him!"

Shame coated Seti from his bald head to his dust-covered feet. He swallowed the words at the edge of his tongue and clasped his hands behind him.

"Then you have no scribe," Hoshea said.

"Get someone else." Moshe pointed toward the tent flap and hissed at Seti. "Get out of here." He faced Hoshea. "You of all people, Yehoshua. How could you bring him here?"

Seti stepped forward. "I came of my own accord."

Unfazed by Moshe's rebuke, Hoshea nodded toward Seti. "He's the only scribe we have who is fluent in both Hebrew and Egyptian. He can write as fast as you speak."

"Preposterous! There must be somebody else."

"Moshe," Hoshea said calmly. "What do you think we've been doing all these years? Nobody knows the script any better than you—and even you can't do it alone."

Moshe speared Seti with a look of death. "Why would *you,* of all people, be fluent?"

Seti took a breath, refusing to shrink back. "I'm the firstborn of Ameneten the Third, who served the Ptah temple and Pharaoh himself. I've been in training to become a priest myself. We're required to learn Asiatic languages for trade and diplomacy."

Moshe lowered his chin but kept his gaze locked on Seti. He paced the large pelt that covered the floor. "Did you come out to taunt me? To report to your people my comings and goings?"

"What?" Seti shook his head. "No. I told you, I came of my own accord. God chose me and led me out here."

"He speaks the truth," Hoshea said.

Moshe halted, mouth agape at Hoshea. "You two—" He pointed between them. "How long have you known him?"

A lump formed in Seti's throat.

After a moment, Hoshea said, "I will let you two get acquainted." Without another look at either of them, he marched out of the tent, flinging the flap closed with such force that the trinkets tangled.

His abrupt exit beckoned Seti to follow, but he stopped short when Moshe sidled after Hoshea as if afraid to be left alone with an Egyptian. Moshe stared out of the flap in awkward silence, like a child watching his parent leave.

The moment of timidity gave rise to Moshe's humanity, and Seti relaxed his stance.

Then, with a huff, Moshe turned back to him, regaining the fury that had momentarily left. "You lie. God doesn't use the enemy for His work."

Every muscle tensed as Seti struggled to maintain respect for the man. "I am not the enemy. And He used Pharaoh. Regardless, God chose me and stirred Eliza's heart to pray for me. He—"

"Stop!" Moshe flicked his hand and resumed pacing. "Why would El Shaddai choose you of all people?"

Seti's mouth dropped open. He had wanted to ask Moshe that very question, but apparently, Moshe didn't know any more than he did. "Why would God choose you?"

Moshe paused, taken aback.

No longer intimidated, Seti laughed. "I know your story. God chose you before you were born. He spared you, placed you beside Pharaoh, and gave you the right connections for this very purpose. He stirred your heart for your people, and when you killed the foreman, He sent you away to learn His ways and humble you."

Moshe blared, "You know nothing about me!"

"I only know because God did the same with me. He chose me before I was born. Placed me in the priesthood for His purpose and stirred my heart for Him. He led me to Hoshea. You said yourself at the palace that God wants everyone to know He is the one true God. That includes me." Seti took a breath. "And He spared me during the last plague. I'm the firstborn of my family. I should be dead."

He met Moshe's fierce glare, unwilling to shrink.

Moshe crossed the pelt to the cushioned chairs but halted and spun around, his finger in the air. "You're not worthy of this position! Nor are you worthy to travel with us."

Shattered, Seti dropped his shoulders. What more did this man want? He turned toward the flap. "You're right, I'm not." He opened the flap and let the last words hang. "And neither are you." He winced at his own boldness.

"Sit down!"

Seti startled, dropping the flap closed.

"I didn't say you could leave. Sit!" Moshe pointed to a red velvet cushion—the kind once found in Egyptian high courts.

Trembling, Seti sat cross-legged on the pillow. Several stacks of pressed papyri leaned against the canvas wall. A single sheet lay open on the polished cedar table, covered in a blend of Hebrew and Egyptian scribbles—Moshe's failed attempt at doing it himself.

Seti looked up as Moshe's shadow fell over him. "If you count yourself one of us, why shave?"

"It was a prank, my lord, to make me look like a fool. Someone led me to believe consecrating myself like an Egyptian priest was necessary for my betrothal with Eliza. I plan to grow it back. I also underwent circumcision, according to the Hebrew way, as proof of my loyalty."

"You are betrothed to Eliza?" Moshe made no effort to hide his shock. "She told me you weren't."

"It happened yesterday. She didn't lie. Otherwise, I'd have at least a shadow of growth by now." Seti ran a hand down his chin.

Moshe tilted his head back, as if calling down the heavens. "And your face—is that because of the other girl?"

"No. The Amalekites did this." No need to elaborate on which encounter with the giants resulted in his battered face. Seti picked up the reed pen near the parchment, eager to change the subject. "What do you want me to write?"

With an exasperated sigh, Moshe stopped pacing and rubbed the lines in his forehead as if thinking long and hard. He closed his eyes, muttering something about Hoshea under his breath, then paced again. He shook his head, muttered something else, and ran his fingers through his beard.

"These are the words of God." Moshe glared at Seti. "Too precious—"

"Then God will decide, won't He. Yahweh. Let Him decide if I may utter His name and write His words." Seti stopped short of spewing more hasty words and dropped his gaze to the papyri. He treaded dangerous ground here, testing the Hebrew God. What would God do to him if He rejected him? Strike him down?

"Very well." Moshe straightened, satisfied. "Let's have it. Start with the Amalekites. Write the exact words I tell you. Do not add or take anything away. It must be in Hebrew. You must give me your word. If you change anything, you will answer to God. I may not be able to read every word you write, but God will hold you accountable. Do you understand?"

"Yes, my lord." Seti dared to look at the man.

Moshe leaned his head back and closed his eyes. After cracking his back, he slumped forward. "The Lord is humbling me."

But the Lord is humbling me. Seti stared at the old man, astonished. How could Moshe, of all people, need humbling?

Pacing again, Moshe clasped his hands behind his back. "What I tell you is what God tells me but with my words. He has commanded that these things be written for future generations. We are to conquer Canaan and call the land Israel. Priests will recite these writings each sabbath as long as God allows our nation to exist. This is not to be taken lightly. Do you understand?"

"Yes, my lord."

"We will see whether God permits your appointment. If so, I will dictate each evening. You will come to my tent after the evening meal. Yehoshua has requested your mornings."

He paused. "And what did he call you?"

"Call me?"

"Your name."

After all this time, Moshe had never heard his name? "Seti, son of Ameneten."

"You're named after an Egyptian god? And God chose you?" Moshe scoffed. "That will not be acceptable in His presence, nor mine, for that matter. From now on, you will be called Seth."

Seti lifted a finger. "That's still the name of the Egyptian god, my lord."

"You think I don't know that? In case you didn't know,

'Seth' in Hebrew means 'appointed'. You will be appointed my scribe, and it's a Hebrew name. Seth it will be." Moshe motioned with his finger. "That's if God allows … Stay out of trouble. Don't drag Eliza into trouble either. She need not suffer any more because of you. She has suffered enough. Do you understand?"

Seti gulped, feeling the sting. "Yes, my lord."

"Right. I will head up the mountain after this and leave you in God's hands. If I'm not back by evening, you have the night off. But don't go far. God has a proposal for us."

"A pro—"

"Now I will start. When I say 'begin', write every word I say after that. If I go too fast or you have a question, raise your finger to get my attention. When I say 'stop', you put down your pen. Understand?"

"Yes, my lord."

With a loud sigh, Moshe sat in his chair and rested both hands on his knees. He pierced Seti with a sidelong stare before leaning back and crossing one leg over the other. "Start a new parchment."

Seti reached for a fresh sheet and shifted on the cushion.

"We will begin with the Amalekites. Hopefully that'll put the fear of God in you."

Seti nodded. He already feared God. Should he fear Him more? Did Moshe wish God to strike him?

"Begin. Long ago, a man named Amalek was begotten, son of Eliphaz, son of Esau, a bloodline tainted with the blood of the Watchers through his mother, and he grew into a nation." Moshe stopped and shook his head. "No. No, scratch that. Stop. Start over."

Seti grabbed a new parchment.

"Begin. The Amalekites, from Amalek, son of Eliphaz, ruled the wilderness through which the new nation of Israel traversed. In the middle of the night, they raided the Israelites—no. Stop." Moshe waved his hands. "New parchment."

Did Moshe even know about the spy?

"Now begin. The new nation, Israel, escaped slavery in Egypt by the mighty hand of Yahweh. In the wilderness, they were tested by God. One of the tests consisted of the battle with the Amalekites, the desert wanderers. The … No. Stop."

Straightening, Seti studied the old man who ran a hand down his beard.

Frustration clouded Moshe's worn face. "Not this morning. I was prepared until you came. Maybe tonight or tomorrow night." His joints cracked as he stood, stretched, and moaned. "Toss those." He pointed to the parchment scraps.

Toss them? They were barely used. "My lord, if it pleases you, may I keep them instead? I have none of my own."

Moshe waved a hand. He finished his water and nodded toward the flap. "The meals here are communal, and you're welcome to them. I'm going to have a bite to eat before speaking with Yahweh. I expect you back here tonight when I return while things are still fresh on my mind, that's if He accepts you as my appointed scribe. Otherwise, come every evening after the meal."

Seti bowed his head. "Yes, my lord."

"And none of that bowing, either. I am not a pharaoh or king that I shall be bowed before. Call me 'Moshe'. I am merely a shepherd, not a lord."

"Yes—" Seti stopped mid-bow. "Yes, Moshe."

After straightening his robe, Moshe moved to the flap and opened it, letting the sunlight illuminate the dust particles floating inside the tent. He held the flap and gestured at Seti with a tilt of his head.

Taking the hint, Seti quickly gathered the parchments and rolled them in his hand, then hurried past Moshe with his head down.

Moshe shook his head at Seti, making clear his disappointment, and turned away.

As Moshe strolled toward a large gathering in an open area ahead, children darted past him with full baskets and jars, followed by mothers struggling to keep up. Seti released a long-held breath and relaxed his muscles, wishing he had a staff to lean on. He wiped his brow and let his eyes adjust to the early sun. Neither Hoshea nor Aharon was in sight. Everybody seemed to be heading toward the breakfast gathering. Seti's stomach growled as the sweet smell of toasted manna wafted toward him.

He glanced at the Cloud Pillar. A wave of weakness washed over him, and he grabbed a tent post for support.

"Thank you, Yahweh," he whispered, despite the difficulty of conjuring gratefulness amid his warring emotions.

Instead of the god-like figure Seti had conflated Moshe to be, he was forced to defend himself against what appeared to be nothing but an egotistical, tired old man. The realization was both comforting and disappointing. God's choice of such a complicated, emotionally driven leader said more about God's grace than about Moshe. But God hadn't informed Moshe of anything about Seti, leaving Seti needing to prove himself. Was that how God appointed men, or was Seti forcing his own will upon Him?

It appeared Moshe didn't know about the spies or Seti's involvement with them. Moshe assumed Seti was a spy. What *did* Moshe know? He could barely dictate the events of the Amalekites. Or was this God's way of showing His disapproval of him? Apparently, this man of God only knew what God chose to reveal to him, which didn't seem like much. That is what a 'Man of God' constituted—at least, that's what Seti was brought up to believe: one whom God spoke through. Moshe was merely a messenger. A shepherd for this wayward flock.

But he had to be more than that.

Chapter 37

Eliza had waited all afternoon for Seti to return from his meeting with Moshe. A weight lifted when her brothers mentioned he hadn't joined them for training. That had to mean Moshe had accepted Seti as his scribe. Thankfully, Zechariah jumped at the opportunity to show her where he'd found Rahel before the betrothal. While he led the lamb on a leash, Eliza hauled her oversized lute.

The afternoon sun baked her skin, and sweat trickled down her back on the hike to the Yehudite camp. The lute grew heavier with each step. When she lagged, Zechariah carried the instrument while she took the lamb.

"There." Zechariah pointed to a ram-skin canopy ahead, propped up by a giant boulder.

Beneath the canopy, Eliza inhaled the sweet incense wafting from a low table. The shade revived her exhausted body after the long walk. Zechariah paused and raised an eyebrow, urging her to keep moving. She rounded the boulder and stopped short at the sleeping beauty on the other side.

Rahel dozed on a thin mat, still in the gown she'd worn to the betrothal. Her head rested in the crook of her arm. Eliza smiled, not wanting to wake her friend, but she had come all this way and couldn't go another day without speaking with her.

"Rahel." Eliza crouched and nudged her shoulder.

Zechariah held out the lute. "Wake her with a song."

All morning, Eliza had practiced a made-up tune while watching the twins for her ima. With a nervous smile, she took the lute and positioned it on her lap. Unlike Yuval's, this lute created a sweet resonance with a unique reverberation at the end of each note. It would add a new sound to his family's ensemble. Her heart warmed at the thought while she played.

Zechariah's hand went to Rahel's cheek but sprang back when she stirred.

"Give us a moment," Eliza hissed.

He took the lamb's leash and stood, gaze lingering on Rahel. As he moved away, alarm shot through Eliza, and she spun around to him. "But don't go far!"

His face contorted, and she shrank back. He'd barely stepped beyond the canopy's shade, yet she called after him like a scared child.

"I mean, just for a few moments. I don't know the way back." That was a lie. She had internalized every turn, every structure along the way, determined never to lose her friend again. But the prospect of making the daunting return without him petrified her.

"Eliza?" Rahel sat up, brushing sand from her gown. "What are you doing here?"

"Rahel!" Eliza gasped, spinning toward her. "Listen." She strummed her little tune, while Rahel leaned against the boulder and rubbed her eyes.

"How do you like it?" Eliza asked when the last notes faded on the breeze. "Now I can play for you when you're down, just like you sing for me."

Rahel nodded, blinking the tiredness away.

After setting the lute aside, Eliza moved beside her, the coolness of the boulder against her back. "I'm worried about you."

Rahel rested her forehead in her hands. "I can't sleep at night."

That was hard to believe. Besides Rahel's long legs, Eliza coveted her friend's ability to sleep through anything. Rahel had once confided how she managed naps in various hiding places on the plantation in Egypt. Eliza gave a sheepish grin. "Now we can stay up late together and talk about everything."

"Hardly," Rahel mumbled. She pulled her knees to her chest and smoothed her gown over them. "You at least fall asleep before morning."

Eliza mirrored Rahel's position. She rested her cheek on her knees and faced Rahel. "Because they abducted you at night? Do you even remember it?"

"No. That's what I don't understand. I fell asleep in your tent, and the next thing I know, I'm in the middle of the desert. My first memory is hitting the ground, Seti running by. Hoshea's fighting the giant, yelling at Seti. I was in a daze." Her forehead wrinkled, and her eyes grew distant. "How did I sleep through all that? And if I was asleep most of the time, why does it affect me so much?"

"He put something over your mouth when he took you. Something in his hand. Maybe it kept you asleep. And it's only been a few days."

"True. Maybe it'll get better." Rahel offered a hopeful smile.

Questions weighed on Eliza's heart, but she hesitated, not wanting to prod. But with their friendship teetering on a blade's edge and the events at the betrothal, curiosity got the better of her. "What happened yesterday? With Hoshea."

"He's not what I thought…"

Eliza raised an eyebrow. "I've never seen you approach him so boldly. Tell me—"

"That's because my thirst for revenge outweighed my feelings for him." Rahel turned away, cheeks flushing. "I'd hoped Hoshea had put that man in chains or maimed him so I could finish him off."

"The one who abducted you?"

"Yes." Rahel faced her, fire in her eyes. "I wanted to behead him. It would end my misery. But Hoshea had already killed him. His men killed most of them at the camp and chased off the rest. I anticipated that, so I had a backup plan. I asked him to teach me to fight." She bit her lip and looked away.

"You asked him to teach you to fight?" The request would have been absurd in any other circumstance, but not now, not with Rahel. Compassion cut through Eliza's heart. She couldn't let Rahel sink to her level of emotional hardness, never allowing her vulnerability to be seen.

"I'll teach you." Zechariah peered down from atop the boulder.

"No." The word flew out before Eliza could stop it. She covered her mouth. How could she make Rahel understand?

"No?" Rahel asked.

"It won't make you feel better." God, Seti, and everyone else saw Eliza's true nature. Her ima had said she was fragile. Is that what God wanted? Had He let her hit her head so she'd be forced to depend on others and Him?

Rahel nudged her. "Eliza."

"Please." She met Rahel's gaze. "Please don't let what happened change you."

"I won't." Annoyance riddled Rahel's reply. "I just want to defend myself. Why does everybody act like I want to join the army?"

Zechariah shifted on the rock, dropping dirt onto Eliza's head. "Let me teach you."

"Zechariah." Eliza swatted at the soil on her head. "Leave us alone!"

"Don't you have something better to do?" Rahel asked him. "We're having a private conversation."

Relieved Rahel hadn't accepted his offer, Eliza used the interruption to move to the next subject. "You told Hoshea that he was treating you like a tool?"

Rahel scoffed. "Yes. That was the last straw. I will

never look at him the same. I should've known he was an insensitive man-jerk. No wonder he's forty and still unmarried."

"What did he say?"

"He said it was a good thing the Amalekites abducted me. Otherwise, he and his men wouldn't have found the camp in Elim."

Insensitive, yes, but it was true. Hoshea had said something similar when Eliza thanked him for saving Rahel, but it hadn't struck her at the time. "Maybe he was trying to cheer you up."

"He was more grateful for the booty. All for his benefit." Rahel stared straight ahead, her next words sharp. "I was nothing but bait in his eyes."

"No." Eliza shook her head, a flicker of defensiveness for Hoshea rising inside her. But she couldn't dismiss Rahel's pain. "No. He was trying to cheer you up. He just doesn't know how to talk to women. He's worked on the pyramid most of his life and has no sisters."

"That's no excuse. Other men figure it out."

"Or maybe …" Realization suddenly dawned. "Maybe, his heart belongs so fully to God that he's reluctant to share it with a woman. What if he meant to cheer you up and push you away at the same time?"

Rahel narrowed her eyes. "Well, it worked. The pushing away part, anyway. But that's what I want: a man with a heart for God. What woman doesn't? Plus, he's so … so manly."

Manly and devoted to God. That summed up Seti pretty well. Plus, the way he loved her. How did she get so blessed?

"Most women want the entirety of a man's heart, more than God's," Zechariah added, still atop the boulder.

"Zechariah!" both girls yelled at once.

His head slowly disappeared from view, and Eliza exchanged an eye roll with Rahel. The hint of a smile on her friend's freckled face melted her heart.

She took Rahel's hand. "I'm sorry for all this. It happened because of me. You're not bait or a tool. If not for my antics, that beast would never have laid eyes on you. Please, don't let it come between us. You're my best friend."

"I'm your only friend."

"You came to my betrothal for Hoshea. Not for me." The words spilled out before Eliza could stop them. "Whether you admit it or not, something's come between us, and it started with what happened." Was it all in her head? Was Eliza so desperate for friendship that she couldn't accept the damage she had caused? "Tell me the truth."

Rahel straightened at Eliza's tone, pulling her hand away.

"The truth, Rahel." Could Eliza even handle the truth? "Have you grown tired of me? Of my behavior since hitting my head? Do you think all your counseling has amounted to nothing but your abduction? Maybe—"

"Eliza." Rahel shook her head. "Don't be silly. Being there for you is not a burden. It gives me purpose, especially out here. I don't do it to receive something in return. I do it because I want to help you. That's what matters."

"Then let me do that for you!" The tears broke free.

"You are." Rahel opened her arms, and Eliza threw herself into them.

"Nobody should hurt you, Rahel. Nobody should change you." Eliza cried into Rahel's shoulder until shame tightened her chest, and she pulled back, wiping her cheeks. Not a single day passed without her dissolving into tears.

"I'm not going to change," Rahel said. "I did want to see your betrothal, but revenge was my focus and Hoshea my means to it. Plus, there was a lot happening. Last I saw you, you and Seti weren't getting along." She smoothed her gown over her legs, avoiding Eliza's eyes. "I meant to catch up on everything—especially after seeing your face—but it wasn't a priority then, and I'm sorry for that."

Eliza sniffled. "You don't have to be sorry for anything."

"But I do." Rahel finally met her gaze. "Obviously, it hurt you. Otherwise, you wouldn't be a blubbery mess."

"I'm always a blubbery mess."

Rahel smiled and reached for Eliza's hand. "Then maybe we should accept each other's apologies and move on."

The weight lifted from Eliza's shoulders, and she took a deep breath and nodded, smiling.

Rahel wiped a tear from her eye. "You're my only friend too, you know."

Eliza giggled. "I know."

While the lamb grazed on patches of brush, its leash dragging in the dirt, Eliza filled Rahel in on the events since they last parted. Though it had been only a few days since they last spoke, it felt like weeks.

Afterward, a sense of accomplishment, plus the anticipation of hearing about Seti's day, carried Eliza with a skip in her step all the way back to her tent. But Seti wasn't there, and neither was her family.

Zechariah peeked inside one of the tents. "Where is everybody?"

Nala stumbled out of her tent as if waking from a nap. "Moshe wants everyone to meet him at the foot of the mountain, and Sabu's sending me in his place."

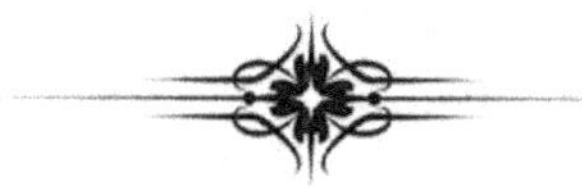

From the valley, the Great Mountain, the tallest of the peaks, appeared to tower over the assembly. But that was an illusion. In truth, a considerable distance separated it from the main valley and surrounding hills.

Seti wiped his brow and paused on a rock ledge to

gauge the multitude making their way over the hills and onto the flat plain that circled the mountains. He hadn't returned to Eliza's family after his meeting for fear of missing Moshe's descent. Instead, Seti had joined the communal breakfast, then followed Moshe at a distance to the edge of the valley, determined to observe every aspect of the man.

Who was this conundrum of a Hebrew leader with an Egyptian name? And what were the day-to-day mannerisms of a man of God? Moshe hadn't grown up among his people, yet he led and mediated for them. Nothing special set him apart during breakfast. He conversed and laughed with others on a swath of cushions spread across the rocky terrain rather than separating himself or eating at a table. He nuzzled his wife, making her blush, and played with his manna to entertain the little ones. But when he rose and took hold of his staff, his countenance sobered, and his posture straightened. He marched down a narrow path with an agility and speed that belied his years.

A voice calling Seti's name startled him from his thoughts. He turned and sighed, relieved to see a familiar face.

Hoshea paused beside him and shielded his eyes as dust billowed over the advancing multitude. "You're not with Eliza's family?"

"I was hoping to find you and get up close to Moshe. I don't want to miss what he has to say."

"Good." Hoshea nodded toward the mountain and started forward. "He'd like that. You never know what he'll want you to write, anyway."

Seti followed him off the ledge toward the plain. "Where did you go after leaving Moshe's tent?"

"Did my plan work?" Hoshea asked over his shoulder.

"What plan? You didn't do anything. You left us, and Moshe yelled at me. A lot. But he eventually accepted me, so I don't know."

Hoshea chuckled. "Did Moshe think I was upset with

him?"

"What? I don't know. He looked surprised when you left. Maybe disappointed."

"I've never been upset around Moshe, so him questioning my judgment for choosing you as his scribe was the perfect fuel. He knows I trust in God, so he trusts me. I knew choosing you wouldn't sit well with him. My offense at his questioning me would remind him that this was God's doing."

"As soon as you left, he laid into me. Said I didn't belong. That I wasn't worthy. I don't think anyone's ever made me feel so low. Well, except Pharaoh."

Hoshea raised a brow. "Really? And what did you say?"

Heat rose up Seti's neck as he recalled the moment. "I told him straight out that God chose him before he was born and orchestrated everything leading to this point. He's no more worthy than I am. Everyone knows his story."

"Everyone knows his story? And what did you believe about him before you met him?"

Why was Hoshea questioning him? The morning's complicated emotions surfaced again. Seti measured his tone. "He was pulled from the Nile by Pharaoh's daughter after his ima placed him there in an attempt to save him from the royal decree that all male Hebrew newborns were to be drowned. He became a prince of Egypt. But he defended a slave and killed an Egyptian foreman, then fled."

It all came back—Seti's attitude toward Moshe the first day they met. He'd held the view of most Egyptians: that Moshe had been fortunate to gain his position but had squandered it when he killed the Egyptian and fled like a coward. That it was the gods' doing, to prevent him from freeing his people when he would have risen to power.

"You're not so different from everyone else. Plus, it didn't help that when Moshe asked how you could read and write Hebrew, you answered by stating your status in

Egypt." Hoshea's words, though sharp, were gentle.

Shame engulfed Seti. He still flaunted his status, even in the middle of the desert. At the betrothal—and now to Moshe.

"Moshe was testing you."

"I understand now," Seti muttered. His words confirmed Moshe's initial reaction to him. And it didn't help that Seti looked every bit the haughty Egyptian he was. Eliza's words about leaving Egypt behind came to mind. She had seen it before he did. Yet, she hadn't wanted him to change? If only he could change. Seti was no different now than the night he taunted Moshe at the palace.

"He accepted you, right?" Hoshea gave him a playful nudge. "You must have passed the test."

"I don't know if he did or not." Unable to look at Hoshea, Seti focused on kicking a stone.

"It took at least forty years to prepare Moshe's heart for his calling," Hoshea continued. "That's a lot of humbling. If anybody knows about humility and testing, it's him. Maybe God wants your heart in the right place for tonight."

Shaming his heritage, forsaking his family, and emerging from it all with nothing but a cloak, only to be seen as a laughingstock, wasn't humbling enough? How much testing and struggle would it take to shape Seti into the man God wanted him to be?

Seti gazed at the Cloud Pillar spinning ominously above the mountain. What God of gods, King of kings had a proposal for mere humanity? Whatever lay ahead tonight was the very reason they had detoured to this mountain.

Chapter 38

Eliza, Zechariah, and Nala halted on the last hill as the dense crowd packed the plain as far as the eye could see. Crying babies, shouts, and laughter interwove with the low rumble of voices reverberating off the hillsides like the roar of an earthquake. The daunting expanse of heads and shoulders moved forward in waves but stopped abruptly before a small hill at the base of the mountain, circling around the sides like a living hedge. The river divided the people like a fissure.

Nausea crept up Eliza's throat, and her vision blurred. Despite the shade from the canopy above, the late afternoon sun heated her skin, and her knees weakened.

"I'm not going down there," she muttered.

"Should've brought some water," Nala said, resting her hands on her knees to catch her breath.

Eliza shielded her eyes and scanned the plain for Seti. If he was with Hoshea or Moshe, he'd be near the front. If only he had Chewy with him, then he'd be easy to find. Though everyone faced the small hill at the foot of the mountain, fronted by a platform of giant boulders, no one stood on it. She sighed and dropped her arm. Zechariah started toward the scads of children dotting the rockslide on the far end of the plain.

"How will we even hear him from back here?" Eliza asked as she followed.

Her brother thumped his walking stick into the hard ground as he led the way. "What if it's God who speaks? Like the thunder on the night of the quail. Everyone said it was God talking from the Cloud Pillar."

Eliza glanced at the Pillar. The closer they approached, the more ominous it appeared. It covered the summit like a vertical asp poised to swallow the mountain whole. "Maybe God will speak through Moshe loud enough for all to hear."

"I'd rather it be the thunder," Nala said. "Like what Sabu described. I want to feel what he felt." She kicked a stone. "I want this God to speak to my soul."

The wonder in Zechariah's eyes when he peered over his shoulder exemplified what Eliza felt. She had only heard the thunder from a distance, and while Seti had witnessed it, he'd barely spoken of it. Her head injury had been at its worst then. Not once had she heard God's audible voice, and the anticipation of it hastened her steps.

The three settled atop the rockslide, far enough away to move freely. If God wanted them to hear Him, He'd make a way.

At the sight of Moshe, Seti and Hoshea rose from where they rested against a boulder. The crowd parted as Moshe marched forward, Aharon and another man at his heels. The three climbed between several boulders before emerging on the rock ledge overlooking the massive audience.

Seti's heart quickened when Moshe's gaze locked onto his for the briefest moment. Nothing could have prepared him for the awe and authority Moshe emanated as he turned to face the people, arms raised. This was it—the moment Seti had been waiting for. And here he stood, behind the man of

God, witnessing everything firsthand. He glanced at the enormous Cloud Pillar behind them, expecting it to move.

Aharon raised his staff, and a hush fell over the millions of onlookers, as though a wind had swept their breath away.

"I have spoken with Yahweh on the mountain." Moshe's commanding voice carried on the light breeze, and Seti leaned forward. "This is what He says: 'You have seen what I did to the Egyptians, and how I bore you on eagles' wings and brought you unto Myself. Therefore, if you obey my covenant, you shall be a peculiar treasure unto me above all people. All the earth is mine. You shall be unto me a kingdom of priests and a holy nation.'"

Covenant? What covenant? Nobody moved. Seti held his breath, heart pulsating in his ears.

"Yahweh has spoken," Moshe said, as if concluding already.

Eliza had come to know God as El Roi, the God who sees, after He heard her prayer. Hoshea often referred to Him as El Shaddai, the great God Almighty, while El Elyon and Adonai graced the lips of the Hebrews in casual conversation. But to Moshe, He was Yahweh—the mysterious I Am—spoken with reverence and endearment. The Hebrew God would be Yahweh to Seti too.

Moshe's chin lifted, his expression like granite before he gave a solemn nod toward a dozen elderly men in long robes standing just below the boulders. As if on cue, they huddled together in quiet conversation while a myriad eyes watched from every direction in a vacuum of silence. Not a cough nor a baby's cry broke it—only the pounding of Seti's heart in his ears as he glanced between the elders, Moshe, and the Pillar.

Moments later, the men broke their huddle and stood upright. Moshe knelt on the ledge as they spoke to him, steadying himself with a hand on his bony knee peeking from his robe.

One with a beard of white curls stepped forward, face lifted toward Moshe. "All that He has spoken, we will do."

"Will do what?" Seti blurted, then slapped a palm over his mouth and bowed his head.

Moshe rose, unfazed by Seti's interruption, and held his hands up as he addressed the audience. "The tribal leaders have agreed to the covenant. I will relay the message to Yahweh."

Murmurs rippled across the plain, some in affirmation, others in confusion. Seti glanced again at the Pillar, waiting for a sign. God had proposed a covenant, and the elders agreed to it, apparently on behalf of the entire congregation. The twelve clasped hands with affirming nods, then raised their hands skyward.

Moshe took the staff from Aharon, exchanging silent words with him and the other man at his side. He turned to Seti. "Tomorrow."

A tirade of questions threatened to spill out, but Seti held his tongue and nodded, too stunned to move. Hoshea rushed forward with a water pouch and a hemp sack and looped them over Moshe's shoulders. He gave Moshe a pat on the back and whispered into his ear.

Laden like a man on a journey, Moshe set off toward the trail with the same determination as that morning, followed by his brother and the unfamiliar man.

The murmuring swelled through the multitude, split by the occasional question shouted in the air. Movement stirred among the people, creating a ripple effect in the most condensed areas.

Hoshea started after Moshe, but Seti grabbed his arm. "Where are they going? What's happening? What covenant?"

Waving him off, Hoshea motioned for the elders to come up the ledge before he turned back to Seti. "Moshe's going to tell God that we are in agreement. Aharon, Hurr, and I will follow him until he begins his ascent. Then, we wait."

Seti shifted his weight and eyed the mountain. "Can't God hear us? Why does Moshe have to relay it? He's going up the mountain again? How long will he be gone?" He scanned the crowd. "What are we supposed to do? That could take all night."

"Precisely. Go home, Seti. You look tired. Many will return to their camps; others will wait. Either way, Moshe will relay the message upon his return."

"What?" Seti shook his head, frustration mounting. "What did we agree to?"

"To be God's people, of course." Hoshea slapped him on the shoulder and turned to descend the boulders.

Seti followed at his heels. "But we're already God's people. A covenant goes both ways. Why does Moshe have to go up the mountain to tell Him?" He stepped aside to let the elders pass in the narrow space between the rocks. "How will I know when he comes back?"

Hoshea paused, face fixed on Moshe's back. "I don't know. We'll figure it out when it happens. Moshe said to meet him tomorrow, right?"

"Yes."

"Then go to your tent, eat something, and rest. If no word reaches you beforehand, assume you'll meet Moshe at your appointed time."

The message was clear: Seti wasn't to follow. He resisted the urge to defiantly hound him some more. Instead, he slumped against a rock with a heavy heart. The day had turned out to be an utter waste. Nothing was written or gained between him and Moshe, and his expectations at the foot of the mountain had proved futile. The elders had agreed to submit to a God they'd already submitted to. Not only did the people have no say, but not a single question was answered.

Why summon the entire congregation to the mountain if only the elders were to speak? Maybe Hoshea was right.

Maybe Seti would feel better after a nap.

No aroma of baked manna permeated the camp that evening when Seti returned. The place remained empty but for a few young families and those injured in the battle. Seti's growling stomach deflated at the sight of the empty cookstove.

He peeked inside Sabu's tent only to find him asleep. With a heavy sigh, Seti straightened and shuffled to the firepit.

"Seti," Sarah peered around her tent flap. He perked up, hoping she knew where Eliza was. "Everyone's still waiting for Moshe. I brought the girls back to sleep. No supper. It's a fend-for-yourself day."

He pressed his lips together to keep from saying something stupid and nodded. Hoshea's words from that morning rang in his ears: "*Maybe God's preparing your heart for tonight.*" He smirked. Though his heart felt ready for God's proposal earlier, it had relapsed. No matter how hard he tried to shake off the frustration, it only deepened. He slumped beside the cookstove and scooped a handful of raw manna from the clay jar.

With both hands, he pressed it on all sides until forming a lopsided orb.

"Mold my heart the way You want it, Yahweh."

God could soften even hard hearts, couldn't He? "*When is a heart susceptible to change, Seti?*" His father's words resonated loud and clear: "*When it's in pain.*"

Does humbling only happen during suffering? Seti gently smoothed his fingerprints out of the manna, shaping it into a perfect ball. It took forty years to prepare Moshe's heart, and Seti was only three months in. He studied his handiwork and sighed, then took a large bite.

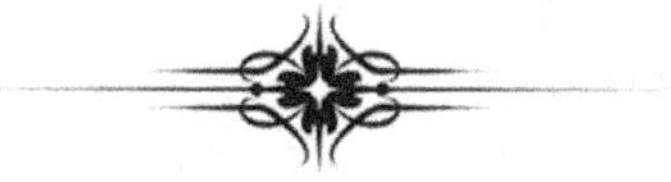

"I think you're confusing stubbornness with frustration," Eliza said gently. "You're being hard on yourself." She took Seti's hand.

Across from them, Nala cuddled Sabu, who lounged with his injured leg stretched to the side. A small oil lamp flickered, illuminating their faces in the darkness of Sabu's tent. After hours of waiting in the sun, Eliza and Nala had left the mountain, leaving Zechariah to search for their parents. Despite a satisfying afternoon with Rahel, a knot of disappointment formed deep in Eliza's chest. Moshe had walked away, creating a sense of anticipation. Though her presence at the mountain hadn't been required, she wanted answers. It seemed like all they did was wait.

Eliza gazed into Seti's downcast eyes, his disillusionment stirring emotions deep within her. The orange glow from the flame sharpened the lines of his jaw and the contours of his shoulders and arms. A sensual compassion fluttered in her heart, begging her to smooth the hardened edges of his soul. Not only had he made leaving his family and the Egyptian gods look effortless, adapting to foreign customs and journeying with strangers appeared as child's play. His easy demeanor in the chaotic environment modeled resilience and levelheadedness. But when it came to God, Seti was just as undone as the next person.

She smiled, hoping to encourage him. "One can also be humbled by the grandeur of God's greatness, like when He spoke to you in thunder. Or when you're made small beneath the stars. But I think one of the greatest tests is long-suffering."

"Sounds horrible." Sabu scoffed.

Nala rubbed his shoulder. "I'm still waiting on that

thunder."

"I have a feeling you'll get it, and soon." Seti leveled her with a somber look. "If you ever want to know the state of your heart, it'll be apparent when He speaks. Even someone as strong as Moshe must crumble before Him."

As if regretting her words, Nala shrank back.

Sabu shifted on his elbow. "What about when Moshe spoke today? What did he sound like?"

Seti tilted his head. "Like usual."

His response froze Eliza mid-stroke of his forearm. Not once did it cross her mind while at the foot of the mountain that she had heard Moshe speak as if face-to-face. "That's strange," she murmured, pressing a finger to her lips. "He sounded normal. I could hear everything, even from the very back."

"Yes," Nala added. "It was clear, and he wasn't even yelling."

"Maybe the rocks and hills carried his voice," Seti suggested. "Or maybe God amplified Moshe's voice so no one could claim ignorance."

Sabu readjusted his leg. "That's kind of scary. You mean ignorance of the covenant? I didn't actively take part. I don't belong to a tribe the elders represent. How can He hold me accountable?"

Did God include those outside of the Hebrew lineage in His plan? The betrothal couldn't have come at a better time. Seti was safe, grafted into the Levite line, officially belonging to God.

"What are you saying, Sabu? That you would have answered differently?" Seti retorted.

"I don't know this God's ways." Sabu fixed his dark eyes on his friend. "But I'm not going anywhere, Seti, if that's what you're wondering. The Hebrew God had me locked in that morning He spoke in thunder. If I have to agree to a covenant to follow Him, then fine. I'll represent myself." He nodded toward Nala. "And Nala."

"Then do it!" Eliza blurted, then shrank into the shadows when all three faces snapped her way. Her stomach churned at the sudden attention, but she forced it still and softened her tone. "Tell God."

Sabu blinked. "How?"

Never had Sabu addressed Eliza directly, and the realization stole her breath and dried her mouth. A gentle squeeze of her hand snagged her attention, and she met Seti's encouraging gaze. His expression softened, and his eyes swam with joy, catching her soul. Let him have the honor of officially leading his friend to the Hebrew God. His desire to do so would forever remain tucked in the depths of her heart. With a squeak of delight, she returned the hand-squeeze.

Seti inhaled a deep breath, then turned to Sabu. "Pray. He will hear you."

Sabu's brow pinched, though his face remained serious. "Here? Now?"

"Yes. You witnessed my prayer on the battlefield. Set your heart on Yahweh, and tell Him how you feel."

"But—" Sabu glanced at Nala, who squeezed his arm. "You're a priest. You're appointed. I ... I—"

"I'm no priest." Seti dropped his eyes to his hands, brows furrowed. "Never was. God called you out of Egypt as He did me. He placed you in those fields with Hoshea, softened your heart. If only I'd not been so consumed with myself and had listened when you tried to tell me—" He stopped when his voice wavered, then lifted his face. "And God heard all of it. If it helps, look toward the Pillar. Just pray."

The air stilled as Seti and Sabu locked eyes. A wordless language passed between them—one only lifelong friends would understand. The buzz of insects and the occasional shuffle of livestock outside dispelled the silence.

At last, Sabu flung an arm around Nala and squeezed her shoulder. "Are you ready?"

A smile of admiration lit her face in the warm glow of

the lamp. "If you are, my husband."

"Help me up."

Seti sprang to Sabu's opposite side, and together with Nala helped him to his feet. With a hand pressed to her heart, Eliza held the tent flap open as the three hobbled out into the cool night.

The sky sparkled with an array of stars even the Fire Pillar couldn't dim. Only a God as this could create such a masterpiece. Eliza couldn't take her eyes from the orange pillar hovering in the distance, casting the Great Mountain in an ominous orange glow with pockets of shadows all about it.

Seti left Sabu with Nala at the river's edge and bounded back to where Eliza stood, gaping at the mountain. He wrapped an arm around her waist and swept her into the air, twirling her around. She gasped and clung to his shoulders, stifling her giggles so as not to wake the camp.

"I love you," Seti whispered, setting her on her feet. He kissed her forehead.

Eliza filled her lungs with his scent, taken aback by his strength and vigor as if it were the first time he'd swept her off her feet. She leaned into the warmth radiating from his chest.

Emotion rose in her throat. "Oh, Seti …" He may not be a priest, but the delight he found in sharing such fellowship with others was a new step for him that he didn't seem to recognize. God didn't stop answering her prayer.

With his arm around her shoulders, Seti led her to join Sabu and Nala, their faces glowing from the orange reflection on the water.

"Here I am, God of the Hebrews." The breeze caught Sabu's voice, and Eliza leaned in to hear.

Sabu pulled Nala closer. "Here *we* are, I mean. You are the only God for us. We will follow whatever covenant You propose. You have my word." A man of few words, Sabu dipped his head in a slight bow.

"As will we," Seti added.
Eliza's heart swelled with pride.

Chapter 39

Slumbering piles of sheep dotted the lifeless valley like tufts of white wool. The early morning sky, a deep navy above the pale brown desert, held a quiet and unique beauty. No progress had been made on the fences, understandable, considering yesterday's events. Not a man stirred. The absence of fighters could only mean one thing: Moshe had returned, and plans had changed.

Seti rubbed his hands together, a satisfied grin splitting his face. He turned toward Adam and Zechariah, both soaking wet from another rude awakening.

"Now what?" Adam muttered, arms crossed and shivering in the morning breeze.

"We go find Moshe." Seti started down the slope toward Moshe's tent, a thrill of anticipation rushing through his veins.

"You know where his tent is?"

"Of course I do." No point in hiding it now. If Moshe accepted Seti, maybe Adam would too.

Adam huffed behind him as Seti weaved through the tents.

Hoshea jogged over from a group of sleepy-eyed young men, intercepting the three outside Moshe's towering tent. "No training today."

"So we saw," Seti said, side-stepping him.

"Moshe's speaking with the elders. He's not taking visitors."

Seti raised his chin in defiance, eager to prove his connection to Moshe to Adam, but Hoshea's stern look sobered him. No sense in letting pride run amok so early in the morning, especially in front of Hoshea.

Zechariah whined in protest. "You mean we got up this early for nothing?"

"What's the word?" Adam asked, nodding toward the tent.

Two men several camps down hollered at Hoshea, who responded with a wave. The camp bustled with activity far earlier than usual. Over the mountain, the Cloud Pillar hovered in place, its canopy slowly unfurling as if in a race to beat the debilitating sun rays. Once fully formed, the manna would appear.

Seti turned to Hoshea with a brow raised. "When did Moshe return? Nobody alerted me."

"No need." Hoshea shrugged. "He's sending word through the elders as we speak. He returned in the middle of the night and went straight to sleep. I found out this morning when he told me to call off the training. We're to spend today and tomorrow consecrating the entire camp. God will speak to us from the mountain, and we must be cleansed and ready to meet Him."

Seti's eyes went wide. "Wha—"

"He's coming out of the Cloud?" Zechariah asked.

"From what I understand." A pensive undercurrent laced Hoshea's voice as he looked past them toward the mountain. "And no one is to set foot on the mountain lest they die."

That last word—die—reverberated in Seti's bones, freezing him solid.

Zechariah let out a low whistle. A voice called Hoshea's name.

"No training today!" he yelled.

"So, this is it," Adam breathed, gaping at the mountain. "God brought us here to speak with us."

That was why the Cloud Pillar had kept its distance—holiness. Every encounter Seti had ever had with the mysterious God flashed through his mind in stark clarity. Holiness was not to be trifled with. It was deadly when approached carelessly.

An awareness shuddered through him from head to foot, not from awe, but from fear. A deep, primal fear. When Yahweh had spoken in thunder, the Pillar had drawn so close, Seti was sure he teetered on the brink of death. Everything carnal about him protested against the very thought of being near again. And now, the great God Almighty was coming down? Face-to-face? Hadn't Seti and Sabu naïvely longed for this just last night?

The far-off look Hoshea had moments ago made sense now.

"Seti!" Hoshea's voice jostled him from his thoughts. "Are you listening?"

When Seti nodded, Hoshea gestured at Adam and Zechariah. "You woke them up with a bucket of water again, didn't you?"

Adam gave Seti a shove on the shoulder.

"Unfortunately, that's not enough," Hoshea said. "You must immerse yourselves in the water to be cleansed." He leveled the boys with a somber look. "On your own accord. Nobody can do it for you."

While Adam muttered something under his breath, and Zechariah cracked a joke, Seti's mind reeled. "Will we see Him? God, I mean?"

"I don't know."

"But we will definitely hear him, right?"

"I don't know, Seti."

"But why would we die?" Zechariah asked.

Hoshea shifted his weight and squinted at the Cloud

Pillar as if contemplating. His serious expression silenced Adam and Zechariah. "Think of God's holiness like the sun. Not like Ra—" He shot Seti a knowing glance—"but for what it is. Without it, there's no life. We need it but can't go near it lest we die. No amount of cleansing changes the fact that we are flesh. Fallible."

"But if God could do anything," Zechariah pressed, eyes on the mountain, "couldn't He make it possible for us to approach Him?"

"Perhaps." Hoshea ran a hand through his dark waves and turned to face them. "But that would mean He'd have to reverse the curse of Adam."

The words struck a spark in Seti's core, pulling him a step forward. "What?"

A muffled chuckle escaped Zechariah's covered mouth, but Seti ignored it. Eliza had mentioned the first man, Adam, and how his choice separated all mankind from God. It was God's mission to win the love of humanity. The story had seemed ludicrous then but altogether fascinating now.

Hoshea folded his arms and held a finger to his chin, eyes glazing as if losing himself in a different world. "God created man to walk in fellowship with Him. But He wanted man to do so by his own free will. So, He gave Adam, the first man, the option to walk with God or not, by placing the tree of knowledge of good and evil in the garden. When Adam chose the tree, he chose his own will, which, of course, was limited only to the knowledge of good and evil. We can't follow both our will and God's. A great chasm then separated the physical and spirit worlds—one we can never cross as long as we inhabit our mortal bodies. Unless God bridges that rift, there's no way we can approach Him."

Eliza had said nothing of a special tree, chasm, or a divide between spiritual and physical worlds. She had focused solely on God's love. But then, that was what Seti had asked of her and probably all he could handle at the time. No, he couldn't even handle that.

"But *He* can cross it," Adam interjected. "He spoke with Avraham and Yacov. He speaks to Moshe."

"That's true. But only by changing His form."

"Then did Adam have a mortal body before he sinned?" Zechariah asked.

"Yes. But—" Hoshea pulled at his beard. "Think of it like this: He wore some sort of spiritual covering over his flesh that was stripped away when he chose his will over God's. He became naked and exposed to the elements. Actually, he'd been naked, but he'd become exposed, as well as ashamed. Shame, insecurity, and vulnerability were not known until then. And ever since, humanity has used its knowledge of good and evil to cover itself as well, as to reach God. But it's impossible."

This fascinating conversation had just turned into utter nonsense. "That's ridiculous," Seti laughed before he could stop himself.

"Not as ridiculous as worshipping gods that act like humans," Adam shot.

"Ha," Seti huffed. "Says the one named after the man who sent humanity spiraling away from their creator—naked."

Adam barked a laugh. "Adam means 'man', you idiot. That wasn't his name. Still better than being named after the enemy fake god." He jabbed a finger into Seti's chest. "What was your abba thinking when he named you? Not to mention with the intent of making you a priest to Osiris! Talk about irony!"

Seti's spark of hope flared into a raging flame, searing any sense that remained. He slapped Adam's hand away, stepping forward, but Adam continued.

"I mean, with all due respect, Osiris—" Adam faked an ominous voice "—I know your brother drowned you in the Nile in your own coffin, but I thought it might be sweet to name my son after him and train him to mediate between you and humanity. Or maybe your abba did that out of spite for Set. Make him serve Osiris."

Seti's jaw dropped. He clenched his hands into fists.

"And you think our legends are ridiculous?" Adam scoffed and crossed his arms. "There's no regard for holiness in Egyptian lore. Only servitude. No wonder you struggle out here."

All resolve snapped. Adam's jabbering jaw needed to be taught a lesson. Seti hurled his fist, but Hoshea caught it before Seti made contact, using the momentum to spin him away from Adam. Seti stumbled but righted himself. He tried to turn back, but Hoshea's firm grip held him fast. He growled against Hoshea's strength, seething with rage.

"Boys," Hoshea's cool tone subdued the roaring fire within Seti just enough to regain a sliver of self-control.

Adam roared with laughter, taunting him to fight like an Egyptian. Let Adam laugh now. It would be his last.

"You two are so much alike, yet you squabble," Hoshea said.

"We are nothing alike," Adam hissed.

The hair on the back of Seti's neck stood on end, and his skin prickled at the venom in Adam's voice. He drew a slow breath. Something sinister brewed inside that boy, and Seti would find out what. Whatever Seti had done to cause such animosity, he'd take back—but not before putting Adam in his place.

Hoshea pulled Adam close and draped an arm around his shoulders. "Neither of you are ready to meet God."

The raging flame reignited. Seti ducked out of Hoshea's hold and spun away from his reach. "I did nothing wrong! God is my witness."

His own words stung. He may have done nothing to Adam—as far as he knew—but he certainly wasn't sinless. The Lank's pulsating neck vein flashed before his eyes. There was no atoning for that. No living water nor cleansing pool.

He walked backward, facing Hoshea. "The living

water is not to cleanse us, Hoshea. You know that. It's nothing but a symbol, to show our allegiance to Him. A mark of before and after. Nothing can cleanse me of what I've done."

"That's not what I meant, Seti!" Surprise rang in Hoshea's voice, and Zechariah gaped beside him. Even Adam's eyes widened at Seti's uncharacteristic outburst. Or was he just surprised Seti reacted to Hoshea more strongly than to him?

A tinge of guilt prickled in Seti's chest, but he ignored it and hurried away. After rounding a tent, out of their sight, he bolted, torment propelling him. *What just happened back there? Was it Adam's words or Hoshea's? Both?* Something snapped inside Seti, something unidentifiable.

Chewy's hooves hitting the hard ground echoed off the stony cliffs. Long overdue for a run, Seti gave him the freedom to lose himself in speed through the empty valleys surrounding the camp. Seti leaned low, reveling in the power of Chewy's fierce gallop and the snap of wind in his ears. His lungs screamed, unable to draw a full breath.

He gripped the reins, every muscle straining. They burst free from the cloud of manna that Chewy kicked up and fled the presence of the all-seeing God.

Once again, Seti turned his back to the Cloud Pillar, but for different reasons this time.

A mound of rocks broke the monotony of the flat desert ahead, and Seti straightened, blinking in the blinding sun. He slowed Chewy to a trot.

"Chewy, my old friend." Seti collapsed onto his horse's neck, breathless. "You always get to see the worst of me, don't you?" His throat burned.

Chewy snorted, his coat lathered with sweat.

"I'm sorry it took so long to let you out. I haven't been minding you much lately, have I?"

No response this time. At the rocks, Seti dismounted. His legs buckled, and he crumpled to the ground. Just like old times.

All four limbs trembled, unable to straighten after straining for so long. He eased out a long breath and pressed a hand to his ribs. Everything hurt—but in a satisfactory way that dulled the storm inside. He scooted up against a rock, leaned his head back, and closed his eyes.

What had unraveled him? Though Adam's relentless mocking riled the simmering unease of Seti's hopeless position against God's holiness, Hoshea's confirmation tipped him over the edge. It was the truth. Seti knew it, but hearing it from Hoshea's mouth sealed it. His problems with Adam were minuscule compared to his fallibility.

The humiliation heaped on Seti at his betrothal obviously wasn't enough to settle whatever boiled inside that scoundrel's soul. Adam would have to face God with that. Maybe Hoshea was right about that too—they were more alike than either wanted to admit.

Seti could never face God. Nothing could erase what he had done, especially to The Lank's family. They would never recover from their loss. If mortality alone was enough to kill a man in God's proximity, harboring sin would incinerate him even from a distance.

God wouldn't be satisfied with worship from afar or concealing his majesty just to come near. The way this God pursued humanity exemplified that. If the love between God and man should surpass that of man to man, then Seti should be closer to Him than to Eliza. But it wasn't possible, not in his current state. God would have to do more than unite the spiritual world with the physical. He'd have to fix Seti's heart once and for all.

Seti sighed and sat up to peer around the rock toward the mountain range in the distance. Only the top of the Pillar could be seen above the peaks.

He belonged out here in the Desert of Sin.

He slouched in defeat. What was he thinking? Chewy didn't belong out here, and Eliza needed him.

"Yahweh," he whispered, staring at the hoof prints in the sand. "I'm spiraling into an abyss of self-loathing. I need your daily reassurance again. I'm sorry for my weakness."

Exhaustion set in. He drew his knees to his chest, resting his head on his arms.

It was one thing to run before pummeling Adam to the ground, or even to raise his voice at Hoshea. But to leave the presence of God? That was suicide. Yet, if God had heard him in Elim, He would hear him out here.

Chewy's snort startled Seti awake. He sat up against the rock, his tunic soaked in sweat. How long had he slept? The sun hovered directly overhead. Osiris, halfway through his daily ride. Seti shook the instinctive reference from his head and sighed. His once-favorite god was finite, splitting his time between surveying his homeland and that of the *Duat*, the realm of the divine. How silly.

Seti had to return to camp, but what would he say when asked where he'd gone? A lie would only add to the mound of sin already piled high. He stood, brushed sand from his tunic, then grabbed onto Chewy to dispel a sudden lightheadedness. He blinked away the spots in his vision and focused on the lathered face of his horse.

"I'm sorry," he said once his head cleared. "Next time we run, we'll stay near the mountains." He smoothed Chewy's windblown mane. "It sure felt good though, didn't it?"

As they set out on a fast trot, the irony of Seti's actions hit him raw in the face. He had run from God, afraid of rejection, yet knew full well he'd be welcomed back.

Chapter 40

A freshly baked almond manna pie with raw manna cream filling awaited Seti. Though it smelled delicious, his appreciation for such food had waned. He essentially ate dessert for every meal. He'd give anything for a plate of gazelle or fish and stewed vegetables. At some point, there'd be nothing left to mix with the manna.

While the girls had gone with Sarah somewhere, and Adam worked with Hoshea on the alphabet, those who remained at the camp, thankfully, asked nothing of Seti's whereabouts that morning. Neighbors gathered around the cookfire with Jeremiah, joined by Sabu and Nala, to discuss the latest word from Moshe. Apparently, nobody knew any more than Seti regarding the details of the covenant they had impulsively agreed to, though many had opinions.

"It's a vassal covenant," a young man wearing a turban said. He cradled a toddler in one arm. "The conqueror makes a covenant with the conquered, offering protection and care as long as they obey the covenant stipulations."

"You're saying the God of our fathers conquered us?" Jeremiah asked.

"It appears so. Or He conquered Egypt and took us as the prize."

"Just to be clear," an older man said, holding up a finger, "it's not always about conquest. Elohim's covenant with Father Avraham was a vassal covenant as well."

"Right," the young man agreed. "But it requires the undying loyalty of the lesser to the greater."

"But He didn't list stipulations," a bald man with a braided white beard said beside him.

The man with the turban chased down a large bite of pie with a gulp of water. He capped his pouch and eyed each of them. "Oh, He will. I'm sure of it."

Vassal—or suzerain—covenants, according to Seti's studies, were common, with Egypt often acting as suzerain to the surrounding regions. Its vast military and monopoly with grain during famines had given it the upper hand.

But that didn't match what Seti had witnessed from the first plague. These men tossed around theories, missing the whole point of the ten plagues. Then again, they hadn't seen Moshe speak the word of God to Pharaoh.

God could have easily wiped out Egypt in one fell swoop. Instead, He chose to send a message to both His people and the Egyptians. The entire world. Not to mention the covenant with Avraham was more than just a pledge of loyalty, according to what Eliza had told him, anyway. These men knew the story. So why didn't they see it? Why would God promise to make Avraham a nation, a kingdom of priests to the world, but then treat them like mere subjects?

No. There had to be something more to all this. Something personal.

Seti kept his mouth shut, all too aware of his place— an Egyptian surrounded by Hebrews. The men spoke freely, but their sideways glances toward him and Sabu said more than enough.

"Maybe you should ask Moshe tonight about it," Sabu whispered.

Moshe! Seti jumped to his feet. "I'm late!"

Seti sprinted toward Moshe's tent, heart pounding at the prospect of disappointing him on only their second meeting. The arsenal of questions plaguing Seti's mind left no room to invent a decent excuse for his tardiness. If Moshe caught him in a lie, he'd be done for. The truth would have to suffice—that a discussion with a group of clueless Hebrews had captivated him more than meeting with the man of God.

He skidded to a halt outside Moshe's tent, lost his footing, and fell. The tent flap hung open, a scent of frankincense curling out into the air. Panting, he clutched his ribs and peered inside.

No Moshe. But he couldn't have gone far, for the incense had barely burned. Seti forced back a swell of negative thoughts. Moshe had said *"tomorrow"*—after supper. How long did he wait before giving up?

"Looking for Moshe?" a man asked, shaking a rug outside his tent.

Seti nodded, catching his breath.

"He just left with the twelve toward the mountain. You'll see a big group—"

Before the man could finish, Seti was gone.

Having spied on Moshe the morning before, he easily found the path Moshe had taken to the mountain—only a brisk walk from the communal area. A gathering of onlookers standing on the trail, facing away from the camp, suggested Moshe was near. When Seti broke through the group, the entourage came into view. Aharon walked ahead, staff in hand, followed by Moshe, then the tribal leaders.

Seti quickly fell in step at the rear of the group on the narrow trail as if he'd been with them all along. They walked in haste, thumping their staffs into the dirt, each wearing dyed robes with muddied hems that brushed their ankles. Despite the speed, it didn't match Moshe's stride from the morning before, and they kept an easy conversation.

Were they really going up the mountain? But it was holy ground. Hesitation slowed Seti's steps. Mt Sinai, as Hoshea called it, towered over the other peaks. The Cloud

Pillar loomed on top, unmoving. A deep orange glow emanated from within the spiraling swirl of white and gray.

A sudden flash of lightning from the Pillar stopped Seti in his tracks. Every hair on his body stood on end, and his heart thundered in his chest. He hadn't cleansed himself in the river yet. Had the others? The men continued, unfazed or unaware.

Suppressing the terror roiling inside, Seti hurried after them. Sooner or later, someone, God Himself perhaps, would call him out. Maybe even strike him down. No thunder followed. No more lightning. Seti questioned his sanity. But there was no denying the tingling sensation it left behind.

As twilight approached, the flame within the Pillar seemed to devour the cloud. Or had it only become more prominent in the dark? Either way, the process mesmerized him. A sense of surrender enveloped Seti. He couldn't take his eyes from it. The men's conversation, thumping of their staffs, and shuffling of their feet faded to oblivion.

Every question consuming Seti's heart melted away, every doubt from that morning demolished. His pulse normalized as the motion of the flames held captive his full attention—until he plowed into the back of the last tribal leader.

"Seth!" Moshe's voice and the collision snapped him to the present.

Fourteen pairs of eyes landed on him as he composed himself.

"Don't think I didn't notice you sneak up back there. You're late."

Seti dropped his gaze and gripped his tunic to still his trembling hands. "I'm sorry, my lord … Moshe."

"You are appointed, are you not?"

"Yes." It was barely a whisper.

"And we had an appointed time you agreed to." Disappointment riddled Moshe's voice.

The unease returned, heavy in Seti's heart. He glanced at the Pillar again, urging whatever consumed him moments ago to return. "Yes."

Moshe huffed a loud sigh, as if yelling at Seti tired him, and leaned on his staff. "Men, this is my scribe, Seth."

Murmurs and nods of acknowledgement followed, some with light dips of their heads. Seti returned the gestures.

After their introductions, Moshe motioned toward the mountain with his staff. "We'll make two lines from the south side to the far hills. I will lead the official boundary, while Aharon follows ten paces outward. The outside boundary will guard the sanctity of the inner one. Whoever crosses mine—man or animal—will be shot by arrow or stoned."

The men watched in revered silence as Moshe stepped off the trail and dragged his staff through the dirt, carving a line. "Six of you and Seth, follow me. Deepen the boundary with your staffs. The rest of you and Hurr follow Aharon. I want deep gashes along this entire side of the mountain, as far as the camp reaches, to ensure no mistaking the boundary between holy and unholy."

Moshe took a swig from his water pouch and passed it to the next man. "Seth, it's a good thing I anticipated your late arrival." He marched through the elders until he stood face-to-face with Seti. His eyes softened, though he maintained his imposing tone. "You missed our meeting in the tent. You're to draw warnings on the rocks, images showing the consequences of crossing. Add words if you like. Can you draw as well as you write?"

Seti rubbed the back of his neck, avoiding Moshe's gaze. "I believe so."

"Good." Moshe grabbed Seti's hand and slapped a piece of charcoal into it. "Since you don't have a staff, this will put you to good use. Anyone else not have a staff?" He looked at the others.

Each man held up a walking stick fashioned from various materials from Egypt.

Moshe dropped a heavy hand on Seti's shoulder. "Looks like you're the only artist. Try to keep up."

There was nothing discreet about it. The spectacle of old men tracing lines around the mountain drew crowds and curious children into the late hours. But as they reached the farthest edges, where the slope met the surrounding hills, not a soul followed. Seti pushed on, etching pictures of flying arrows and crossed swords onto nearby rocks, then running to catch up. Moshe's stamina proved as unnerving as his tenacity. Only at the periodic prompting of an elder did he stop and rest.

The men kept a cheery demeanor throughout the night, telling stories of old and singing uplifting tunes, reminding Seti of the pyramid slaves in the fields. One would have been hard-pressed to deem an elderly Hebrew inadequate of anything. Their energy and jovial spirit defied their lifetime of servitude. And neither a trace of bitterness edged their words nor a smug remark came Seti's way.

Contrary to the treatment he'd received at the betrothal, muffins and water pouches filled his lap at rest stops, despite him denying his exhaustion. Whether it was God's doing or Moshe's quiet acceptance of him, something had shifted in the attitudes toward him.

Between weaving around rocks, sheer cliffs, and loose gravel, the trek persisted into the wee hours. Then, while Moshe's beautiful wife welcomed him to a feathered mat in his tent, Seti collapsed behind the tent on the hard ground. No cloak, no pillow. Seti the artist—not the scribe—curled into a ball, harboring the questions he'd dare not ask yet another night. He would wake when Moshe woke and follow the man everywhere, determined never to be late again.

Seti squinted at the Cloud Pillar in the growing dawn

light. Swirling black clouds, pierced by lightning, morphed into a translucent face of the Angel of Death looming as large as the mountain itself. Flaming eyes leered down at him, and he crumpled face-first to the rocky ground in terror.

"After all I did for you ..."

"No. Please," Seti begged into the dirt.

He raised his gaze, desperate for a response, but the face exploded into a ball of fire, setting him ablaze—

A splash of cold water shocked Seti out of his dream.

"Your turn." Zechariah stood over him, holding an empty clay basin. Adam laughed beside him.

Seti sat up and wiped the drips from his eyes. Though thankful they'd wrenched him from the nightmare, he'd never let them know.

"We actually woke before you." Zechariah laughed.

"How does it feel? Too bad you don't have any dry clothes." Adam jeered. "What are you doing out here anyway? Eliza was looking for you last night. The Levites are consecrating themselves today. Wait until I tell her this!" The two keeled over, laughing.

Moshe rounded the rear of his tent and stopped short behind the brothers. With arms crossed, he fixed his gaze on Seti, who sat on the ground, covered in wet manna. "What's the meaning of this?"

The boys jumped, eyes as round as Sarah's manna cakes. Adam slowly turned, while Zechariah froze in place.

Cheeks aflame, Seti rose to his feet. His joints cracked and ached. "All is well, Moshe. I had it coming."

Moshe studied his wet scribe with such intensity that Seti stepped back. Whatever reeled behind his assessing eyes chilled him more than the cold water. The twitch in Moshe's jaw was unmistakable, even beneath his thick, white beard.

He motioned with his head and advised the brothers to scat before stepping forward. Once they had gone, he asked,

"What are you doing sleeping outside my tent?" His tone held more accusation than curiosity. "Were you listening—?"

"No … no, my lord, uh, Moshe." Seti inched back again, avoiding Moshe's gaze. "We returned late last night. I was exhausted and didn't want to walk back to Eliza's—"

"You're sleeping with Eliza?"

"No!" Seti's head shot up. Instead of climbing out of the pit of Moshe's contempt, he dug his hole deeper. "We're betrothed, not married."

"Exactly."

"I usually sleep outside her family's tent, by the fire. I stayed here last night because I didn't want to be late again. As God is my witness, I've never slept with her."

Moshe's face softened. "You don't have a tent?"

Could Seti look more pitiful? The absurdity of it struck him—cowering, soaked and muddy, confessing his poverty to this man. He gulped and hung his head.

"Where are your parents?"

"The Angel of Death killed my abba, and I left my ima and brother to follow your God. I came only with my horse, the clothes I'm wearing, and my golden cuffs, which I used for the dowry."

Moshe's lips parted, but no sound came out. He dipped his head, letting the silence stretch between them. Seti took a deep breath, filling his lungs to capacity as the tension slowly dissipated.

With renewed clarity, Moshe straightened. "You are Seth, my appointed scribe," he said with pride. "No scribe works without pay. You will be provided a tent, bedding, and clothing. Pitch it near mine. You will no longer sleep near Eliza or her family until you consummate your marriage. Have you a witnessed covenant contract with her?"

"A ketubah? Yes, my lord."

"Good."

Moshe's inquisitive look pinned Seti in place,

dimming the spark of joy the good news had kindled. The question about the betrothal felt off—as if the ketubah mattered more than following Hebrew customs or holding true to Eliza.

With a clap of his hands, Moshe lifted his chin. "I want you to sup with us in the evenings to ensure you're not late again. I'll have Aharon arrange your things."

Seti stopped himself from bowing. "Thank you, my lor—Moshe."

"I will call an assembly later this evening." Moshe turned to leave. "My scribe shall always be in attendance with the elders."

"Yes. Th-thank you, Moshe."

As soon as Moshe disappeared around the tent, Seti let out a breath. A weight lifted from his shoulders and lightened his steps. At last, he would own a tent! And a mat and a pillow, and blankets! Never had basic essentials meant so much. Eliza would be thrilled. He suppressed the urge to run and wake her but lingered instead. Aharon would be looking for him.

"Oh, Yahweh." He faced the Cloud Pillar, his knees weakening. Rays of sunlight poked through the growing canopy like hope breaking forth. Like favor or grace shining down on him. Adoration flooded him, and he nearly dropped to his knees in worship when footsteps approached.

"Ahh, yes, the boy who tried to stone us."

Seti spun at Aharon's voice. He nodded and grinned, unable to form words.

A hint of a smile lifted Aharon's cheeks. "Come and eat breakfast. Then we'll gather your tent and supplies."

Chapter 41

The next day, Eliza sat on a flat-topped rock, dipping her toe into the cool water. The Levites had poured into the stream, packing it full for an afternoon of consecration. Only the deepest parts remained untouched.

"Make room!" Zechariah dashed past her.

She ducked just as his splash drenched her tunic. It might be midday, but she was too tired for play. What should have been a sacred act of worship had become a noisy party. Upstream, an old couple provided a delightful tune with their windpipes. Miera's squeals and giggles at Adam's playful antics blended with the joyful laughter of other children. Mothers dipped their infants into the water as they inched forward, while fathers either tossed children off their shoulders or gathered in deep conversation, untouched by the surrounding chaos.

The overstimulation ached Eliza's already heavy head. She had woken late after another sleepless night. Yawning, she glanced downstream toward the Yehudites, looking for Rahel. Since both clans consecrated themselves that afternoon, couldn't Rahel join her here? The Danites and those of Naphtali had occupied the river that morning, while the tribes of Simeon and Reuben would follow that evening. Per the tribal leaders, the clans took over the stream in reverse order of their birth, the first six having gone in the day before.

"Come on, Eliza. Hurry!" Miera stood on Adam's shoulders, water sluicing down her thin frame.

Where was Seti? He had yet to return from his appointment with Moshe last night.

"I'll get her." Adam tossed Miera, then sloshed toward Eliza.

"No!" Eliza inched forward. "I'm going. Don't touch me."

The mischievous gleam in his eyes urged her on.

"Get her!" Zechariah called from where he stood, shoulder-deep.

"No!"

When Adam reached the rocks, Eliza slipped off the ledge with a soft squeal and plunged into the river. The cold shocked her senses as she went under. Water filled her nose and throat, seizing her lungs. She pushed off the muddy bottom and broke the surface, only to receive a face full of water from Adam jumping in beside her.

The air sliced her burning throat, coursing into her lungs like fire. Coughing racked her chest. Everything blurred in an array of moving colors and noises.

"Eliza." Adam's voice broke through her gasps and coughs. "Eliza." He grabbed her shoulders.

Her vision stabilized in time to see his sardonic grin soften to match the concern in his eyes.

"You're not supposed to inhale it." His grip tightened.

Tears stung her eyes, but she wiped them away in defiance. Of course she wasn't supposed to inhale the water. She tried to scoff at him, but instead broke into another coughing fit. There was a time when she enjoyed Adam's shenanigans, but they had lost their allure. Adam was nothing but annoying now, especially after he humiliated Seti at the betrothal. Eliza wouldn't have it, and she wouldn't give him the pleasure of retaliation.

"I'm sorry, Eliza ..." Adam began.

She twisted free from his grip. His rueful tone pulled

at her heart, but she wouldn't cater to that side of him, either. After regaining herself, she turned her back to him. "Leave me alone."

"I'm sorry," Adam said again. "I didn't think you'd drown!"

Eliza rolled her eyes and moved away, dodging a flying manna-muffin from a group of boys nearby.

"Wash that face!" one of them yelled, and they burst into laughter.

"She'll never wipe off that mark of shame."

She froze. Their remarks were directed toward her. Barely recovered from the shock of nearly drowning, a renewed alarm stilled her breaths as she turned to face them.

"She's the one who hit Sena," one of them spat.

Another laughed. "Maybe we should knock her teeth out."

Eliza gasped. All she had for defense were the vile words now edging her tongue. In the water, she was powerless. Plus, there were four of them, all a head taller than her. Smirks lined their faces as they pointed and laughed. Eliza bit back a smart retort, remembering her promise to God.

"You'd have to get past us first." Zechariah and Adam glided between her and the boys.

Laughter ensued at the expense of her brothers. They retaliated with insults, stoking the embers of an underlying tension. Various outcomes cycled through Eliza's mind. She winced at the thought of a physical confrontation. Near the stream's bank, her father played with the twins, oblivious to his sons. Eliza backed away, hoping not only to separate herself from the drama, but to draw her brothers away as well.

Why couldn't people just leave her alone? The scar on her face made her easy to identify, and thanks to her antics with Sena, she'd forever be targeted.

Miera climbed onto the bank and started toward the

boys.

"Miera, stop! Don't go near them!" Eliza scrambled after her. If any of them laid a hand on Miera, the war of words would explode into a scuffle of flying fists.

"What are they doing? What's happening?" Miera asked.

"Let Adam and Zechariah handle it."

Eliza peered over her shoulder as Zechariah edged toward his scoffers, hurling threats like a dog fending off a pack of wolves. No one she loved should suffer any more because of her. She climbed up the embankment and snatched Miera's hand before the girl could take another step toward them.

Eliza sat in the sand, pulling Miera down with her. She glanced around for Seti. Downstream, Sabu and Nala strolled, hand in hand, back toward their tent, soaking wet, blissfully unaware. But no sign of Seti.

"El Roi, my God," Eliza prayed, squeezing her sister's hand in her lap. "I'm sorry I put frog guts in Huya's soup. Please wipe the scar off my face. I want it gone. I'm sorry. Please make me clean again. Make me clean from that, and what I did to Sena, and remove any stain I've put on my family—"

"Zechariah!" Her father's shout split the air. The music stopped. All eyes turned toward him. He ran along the embankment toward the scuffle near the rock ledge. One of the youths held Zechariah's head beneath the water, while the other three restrained Adam, laughing.

Eliza jumped to her feet. "No!" She broke into a mad dash, beating her father to the rock ledge, and lunged off into the midst of them. She surfaced, coughing and hacking again, and grabbed the assailant's shoulders. "Let him go! It's my fault!"

Zechariah's feet kicked desperately.

"Stop it!" Eliza cried, struggling to pull the teenager off her brother. "He can't breathe!"

He wouldn't budge.

One of the others, with a slew of braids and beads hanging from his head, yanked Eliza backward. "I've got Scarface!"

Before she uttered another word, her father plunged from the rock ledge and barreled into the one who held Zechariah, driving him beneath the surface. Everyone stilled, watching where the two had gone under. Zechariah came up, gasping. When her father resurfaced, he pulled up the stunned teenager by his hair.

"Who's next?" her father snarled, shaking the perpetrator and eyeing each of the others.

The braided one let go of Eliza. "She started it!"

Ignoring him, Eliza reached her wheezing younger brother and grasped his arm. She brushed his bangs back to look into his dazed eyes. He wasn't one to back down from a fight—especially when defending his family, even when outnumbered.

"She didn't do anything," Adam fired back, now free of his captors.

"She looked at us," one said.

"She started it when she hit Sena," another piped in. "And it won't be over until she's worse off."

"Nobody touches Sena and gets away with it."

The world rushed to defend Sena regardless of fault or justice served.

"The whole family could use a lesson," the one with braids hissed.

Eliza spun toward him with a wad of spit in her mouth ready to plaster his face, but she swallowed it. "You provoked us." She hit the water with her hand. "The only reason you side with Sena is because she shows you things other girls wouldn't. You spineless boys think that makes you men, but you're far from it!"

Gasps rippled through the growing crowd, and Eliza's stomach dropped.

"Eliza," her father growled. "That's enough out of you. Get away from them. Adam—go. And if the rest of you don't move as I speak, I will have your necks as with this one." He shook the grimacing teen by his hair. The boy flopped beneath her father's grasp like a dirty rag.

"Sena's right," the braided one muttered as he waded by Eliza. "It doesn't take much to unleash the dragon within."

"Did you talk to your master with that mouth?" somebody behind her sneered.

The one with braids turned and walked backward, flashing Eliza a derisive grin. "Obviously. One look at her face says it all."

"She must've run out of flesh on her back."

Laughter filled her ears.

Eliza clamped her mouth shut. She wouldn't give them the satisfaction of knowing the sting of their words. And no one else would see it either—not Seti, not her brothers, and especially not her father.

Adam joined her and took Zechariah's other arm. He cut Eliza a look. "Let's go, Eliza. Now."

She glanced at her father, afraid he'd overheard the taunts, but he hauled his detainee away toward a group of men. He moved like a soldier—unyielding, strong, heroic. At his age, he'd definitely feel the ache later. One of the men came forward, face red. Her father pulled the boy to his feet and shoved him into the man's arms. The teen, who moments ago held fast to Zechariah, now cowered like a sullen fool.

Though pride for her father stirred Eliza's heart, it couldn't offset the shame pressing in from yet another outburst. Tears welled in her eyes. She had proven both Sena and these mockers correct. No matter how much she cherished her freedom, she'd always revert to her old self.

Once safe on the embankment, Adam left them to fetch the now crying Miera, while Zechariah dropped to the ground. Eliza joined his side.

"I'm going to kill every last one of them." Zechariah snarled.

He shook his long bangs from his forehead, and Eliza glimpsed the fierceness in his eyes. It resembled what she knew all too well. She loosened her grip on his arm and stared at the crescent marks from her fingernails. Her knuckles had seized. It was all she could do not to flee in a fit of tears. Indignation and despair surged through her in tremors, urging the tears to break loose and her legs to run. No, she wasn't that girl anymore, despite her rash retort about Sena.

"Please don't," she whispered.

Zechariah turned toward her, nostrils flaring.

"Not for me. Not even for what they did to you. We're better than that." Eliza sighed. When he didn't budge, she added, "Plus, we're meeting God tomorrow."

His hands clenched into fists. "Afterward."

"No." She locked eyes with his. "You cannot go near God with that in your heart." She shook his arm. "I mean it."

He swallowed audibly and stared ahead, his silence chilling.

"Let God handle it," she pleaded. "He knows our hearts—and theirs. He's just."

"And merciful." He pressed his lips into a hard line.

"Right. Give it to God, and let it go. Please. For your sake. For my sake."

God would deal with them as He saw fit, even if that meant mercy. But demanding Zechariah forgive his enemies meant she must do the same.

She leaned her head on his shoulder and wrapped an arm around his waist. It was a foreign gesture, showing endearment to her brother, but strangely comforting. He didn't flinch or pull away. Instead, something about him relaxed in resignation. She would be his comforter, the strong one.

A heavy blanket dropped over their shoulders, and she

looked up to see Seti standing behind them. The concern in his eyes unraveled her, evaporating whatever strength she clung to. She looked away, blinking back tears. He had interrupted her moment of triumph. Everything inside her begged to throw herself onto him and sob into his chest.

"Eliza?" His voice, thick with concern, choked her up.

"P-please, Seti." She struggled to stifle her trembling. "I'm fine."

When he didn't respond, her heart plummeted. She turned to see if he had left.

Confusion and worry clouded his face. His brown eyes deepened beneath a furrowed brow. Eliza's chest heaved as she swallowed against the lump in her throat.

"Well," he said after she hid her face. "I will be with Sabu if you need me."

As his steps faded, she pulled the blanket tight around her shoulders, cowering in humiliation. As if God wanted her to break down and cry, He compounded the reasons to do so until she could no longer hold back. She rested her head on Zechariah's shoulder and let the tears fall. He wrapped an arm around her.

Chapter 42

"These people never cease to amaze me." Sabu smirked after updating Seti on the latest drama. "You'd think after being slaves for so long, they'd have some sort of sense of unity or something."

Seti regarded his friend. It was an interesting point he hadn't truly pondered, maybe because, unlike Sabu, who watched from the sidelines, Seti often found himself knee deep in every debacle on this side of the mountain—except this one. "I guess when there's nothing to do, humanity is bound to entertain themselves, even at another's expense."

Indeed, if Seti had been there, he'd no doubt would've inserted himself right into the fight. Zechariah wouldn't have been attacked, and Jeremiah wouldn't have had to intervene. But would the scoundrels have left Eliza alone in the first place if Seti were there, or would his presence have triggered more taunting? He bit back the anger rising in his throat. He had spent the morning helping Aharon set up his tent when he should've been by Eliza's side.

Sabu leaned back on his hands, his legs sprawled, as the two sat outside his tent, waiting for Nala to change into a dry tunic. "And they hold on to grievances they wouldn't otherwise hold on to."

"They?"

"Humanity. Us. These people." Sabu swiped a hand through the air. "Whoever."

Seti twirled a piece of fleece he had pulled from a

thorny bush. Around the bend of the river, Eliza still sat beside Zechariah. She had to be freezing by now. The blanket he'd given her came from a pile of linen Sarah had tossed from their tent. He fought the urge to run to her, to comfort her, to apologize for not being there.

"I have a tent now, but don't tell Eliza," he muttered, not wanting word to spread before he shared it with her himself. He had pictured it all day, intending to break the news to her at the stream while teaching her to swim. It would be a sweet, rather romantic moment.

The ensuing drama had ruined that. Plan B was to use the new information to cheer her up after the fiasco, but she rejected his comfort and shooed him away like he was one of her brothers. Wait—

"How?" Sabu asked.

Seti blinked, having been lost in his thoughts. "Moshe gave me one for being his scribe … And a bed too. We set it up after breakfast near his tent."

"So that's where you were." Sabu let out a low whistle. "How ironic. You go from walking alongside Egyptian demigods to doing the same out here. Will you ever be a commoner?"

Sabu had a way of pointing out the obvious and keeping Seti grounded. Though once annoying, Seti had grown to appreciate it. "I sense a hint of jealousy."

"I kind of hoped I'd get to be the prominent one for once, and you'd be my poor tag-along." Sabu flashed his lopsided grin.

"Three months, Sabu, I slept outside your tent like a scavenger. Did you not notice?"

"Oh, I noticed. And I savored it."

Seti smiled, letting the words hang between them. Even as a poor nobody, he couldn't stay out of trouble. Everyone had their eye on him, especially out here surrounded by ex-slaves. How many had known of him in Egypt and now enjoyed watching him struggle? "Sometimes

I wish we could trade places."

"Nah." Sabu stared toward the Great Mountain. "I rather enjoy the benefits of knowing you while staying obscure."

"Thanks." The aroma of baked manna alerted Seti to the late hour. "I have to get back. Moshe wants me there for evening meals to ensure I won't be late again. He has another announcement tonight." He turned to leave but halted. "I want to tell Eliza about my tent, so don't mention anything."

Nala emerged and tossed Sabu a dry tunic.

It hit him in the face. He pulled it off, unfazed. "When you see Hoshea, tell him I'm ready to do whatever he wants. I'm sick of sitting around. I'll take Nimrod for a test ride, catch Moshe's speech, and see how my leg handles it."

"I'll tell him tonight."

Seti took a quick dip in the stream before he'd forget. Meeting God on the mountain after failing to consecrate himself would be more disastrous than everything he'd done up to this point—tenfold.

A strong whiff of cassia assailed Eliza's nose as she opened the flap to her tent. She paused at the entrance, fanning off the incense and a sneeze. Her mother looked up from where she perched on Miera's mat, folding linen.

"Look at all this!" her mother gushed, gesturing toward several piles of fabric. "Rivka brought the wagon back filled to the brim."

Eliza, Miera, and her mother had delivered the cart the day before so the women could gather items for her to sew. Eliza stepped inside, amazed at the slew of colors and materials. After taking it all in, she asked, "Where's my mat?"

"Beneath the wool. Hobad's family wants me to make them cloaks. He'll give us eggs in return." Her mother flapped a hand in the air. "Don't worry, I'll make room before nightfall."

"But why use our tent? We barely have enough room for our own things." A long table covered with beads, thread, needles, and various other items replaced the chests and dish crates.

"I'm having your abba put up a canopy for our belongings. I don't want what doesn't belong to us left out for the world to see. Somebody could steal everything in the night. These are all highly regarded materials." Her mother lifted a bolt of red cotton from her lap. "Real cotton. Beautiful, isn't it?"

Eliza sighed. Her mother deserved recognition for her talent as well as the renewed sense of purpose. The light in her eyes spoke volumes.

"Your tunics are outside. Tonight, I'd like you to stick around and help me sort all this out."

"Eliza!" Miera's voice squealed from outside. "Yuval's here looking for you."

Heart leaping, Eliza rushed outside. Yuval tuned his harp near the river, Miera and the twins danced before him, but sitting delicately on a nearby rock was Sena.

The sight of her nemesis stopped Eliza cold. God seemed intent on testing her limits today. She scanned the campsite for Seti but, thankfully, didn't see him. Though he had handled Sena quite well at the betrothal, she didn't feel like watching the girl bat her eyes at him. Reluctance slowed Eliza as she grabbed her lute from near the wagon.

Even Yuval's tuning was beautiful. It had been weeks since hearing such lovely sounds, and they penetrated her heart. They might even make Sena's presence tolerable.

"Here she is." Miera bowed dramatically before Eliza as if presenting her as a gift to the famous Yuval.

When he looked up, his face lit up, and he stopped

tuning. "Frog Girl," he said, as if surprised. "I told you I'd come by to help you with your lute."

The nickname shattered the beauty of the moment and brought back the afternoon's events. Frog Girl and Scarface went hand in hand. Eliza glanced toward Sena, who watched her with a raised brow. Amazingly, her gap-toothed smile only embellished her exotic look. The dark tones of her flawless skin enhanced the yellow of her tunic, which barely reached mid-thigh. Crossing her shapely legs made the hem ride up even more. Eliza paused. If she were that pretty, would she wear such things?

Though her earlier retort about Sena making the boys feel like men had no basis, the provocative pose and alluring dress validated such assumptions. The boys certainly hadn't denied it. Still, guilt churned Eliza's empty stomach. If she were wrong, she'd have slandered Sena's reputation. If she were right, it wasn't her business to tell.

She straightened and held her tone. "You know what my name is, Yuval."

He'd called her Frog Girl before, but after the incident in the river, the blinders had lifted from her eyes. He was no different than the teens who'd mocked her.

He smirked. "Sorry, Eliza. Let me have your lute. I'll tune it for you."

Yuval—the vengeful, Sena-doting, smirking musician who once boasted of how many lashes he'd received.

"No."

Miera and the twins stopped dancing. Sena's brow raised higher.

"No." Eliza dropped her arm, lute still in hand. "Seti knows how to tune it. Thank you, Yuval, but he can teach me."

She turned to leave.

"Wait. What did I say?"

"Careful, Yuval," Sena said. "You don't want to anger her. Next thing you know, she or her abba will drag you to

Moshe."

Pressing her lips tight and inhaling deeply through her nostrils, Eliza suppressed the all-too-familiar storm that brewed inside her. She refused to turn and let Sena see her unravel. Without a backward glance, she marched back to her tent, ignoring Miera's calls.

Trembling with fury, she dropped onto the mat before her mother. Why did she let things affect her so? Why did she care? She probably would have let it slide if the afternoon's events hadn't still been fresh in her mind. But every insult, every snide remark, compounded inside her. She stitched a red cotton lining to a fringed tunic with such ferocity, she barely noticed her shredded fingertips.

Chapter 43

The shofar blew twice, summoning the men of Israel to the foot of the mountain. Moshe had sent messengers throughout the camp during the evening meal to warn them in advance.

Hoshea pocketed the horn and scrambled down the slope of loose stones and jagged rocks until he reached the ledge overlooking the sea of men. After exchanging nods with him, Moshe joined Aharon and the man he called Hurr, who had been waiting for him on the ledge. He raised his staff, and the crowd fell silent before he stepped forward.

Unwilling to remain below with the elders, Seti climbed up between the boulders and darted behind Hoshea to where he had previously perched. He wiped his brow, then dried his sweaty palms on his new tunic.

"You move like a mountain goat," Seti whispered when Hoshea joined him.

Hoshea gulped water from a jar, then flashed a sly grin. "And you can't stay put."

"I'm the scribe. I have to be where I can see everything and write it all down."

"Ha! You don't even have your parchment."

"Papyri, Hoshea. And no. I'll be up here with you every time." As long as Moshe didn't object.

Aharon and Hurr stepped back, leaving Moshe alone at the edge, staff raised high. Hoshea shushed Seti with a flap of his hand.

"This will be short and to the point." Moshe's voice carried across the rocky terrain. Even behind him, his words rang loud and clear. "By now, all but two tribes should be consecrated by the Living Water. Once they finish tonight, all work shall cease until further notice. As instructed earlier, you should already have tomorrow's manna collected—just like for a sabbath. In the morning, after two blasts from the shofar, you may come forth."

Moshe paused and assessed the crowd. No one spoke. Seti squinted, scanning the edges of the multitude for Sabu. He'd said he would be near the back, on Nimrod. But the shadows from the setting sun behind the mountain obscured the rear half of the multitude.

"We have set a boundary so you know where not to go. The Lord will descend upon the entire mountain, making it holy. Any flesh that crosses onto holy ground will be shot or stoned, according to Yahweh's command. My men warned you earlier, and I warn you again now. Pen your livestock. Inform your loved ones, because after this announcement, you will be held accountable."

The weight of his words settled on the assembly like a shroud. If one were to touch the mountain while Yahweh's presence encompassed it, they'd become holy themselves. But what was wrong with that? Or would they instead defile God's holiness? Would they burn and melt as if coming too close to the sun, like Hoshea had implied, by a fire too pure to withstand? But Moshe said they'd be shot or stoned. So, unless one were witnessed crossing the boundary, how would anybody know?

Moshe continued. "My men and I have clearly marked the boundary and added signs. A claim of ignorance will not be accepted. Please do not bring shame upon me or your families by disobeying. And do not go near a woman."

His gaze swept the crowd, as if searching each soul one by one.

"That is all." He clasped his hands behind him and retreated to where Hoshea and Seti stood.

As Aharon and Hurr dismissed the assembly, Moshe drank from the water jar and leveled Seti with a look of expectancy. "We have writing to do."

Upon returning from Moshe's speech that evening, Eliza's father reiterated all Moshe had to say, emphasizing the boundary line and the consequences of crossing it.

Eliza huddled under a blanket with Miera at the campfire, regretting not having snuck out to the meeting. She'd been too upset at the time. If she'd gone, she might have seen Seti. He had run off earlier to meet with Moshe and hadn't returned. Would he be gone all night again? She'd barely laid eyes on him today and hadn't given him the chance to tell her about the night before. Instead, she had rebuffed him, choosing to wallow in self-pity.

Sabu and Nala hadn't returned either after taking his horse to the foot of the mountain with the others—albeit very slowly.

Standing with his hands on his hips, Eliza's father sobered his voice. "I want to have a word about earlier." The seriousness of his tone silenced the mumblings of her siblings.

Eliza stifled a sigh. It would be unreasonable to expect the night to pass without a lecture regarding the afternoon's episode. Every time she tried to forget it, someone brought it up. Zechariah sat across from her, his chin resting in his palm, eyes downcast. Adam sat beside him with a raised eyebrow.

"From now on, no more fights." Her father eyed each of them. "I don't care who started it. It nearly cost my son his life. Keep your tongues bridled."

"They were going after Eliza," Adam pointed. "What were we supposed to do?"

"Move away. Run, if you must. But whatever you do, don't escalate it."

"That's ridiculous," Zechariah spat. "That would pin us as cowards and entice them all the more. They needed to know we're not to be messed with."

Her father heaved in a breath. "We are priests. It's time we act like it. You heard Hoshea's words at the betrothal. We are not to be like the world but of a higher order. I want my family to model that, to show others what it means to be children of God."

"Have you forgotten that you just clobbered one of them in front of everyone?" Adam jeered. "Yet you lecture us?"

Sarah dropped the linen she had been stitching into her lap and pointed at Adam with the bone needle. "Heaven forbid my husband walk away while his son is on the brink of death!"

"What's a priest to do then, Abba?" Adam demanded.

Fighting words ruled Adam's tongue as much as Eliza's. She pressed her eyes shut, bracing for her father's fury to unleash. When nobody spoke, she peeked through.

Her father's posture had softened. "I speak for myself as well. We have much to learn in this new life we've been given." His tone sounded surprisingly even. He lowered himself onto a cushion, dark creases etching his forehead. "It was you, Adam, who opened my eyes."

Adam blinked, stunned to silence for once.

The firelight reflected in her father's eyes as they met Adam's. "At Rephidim, when I fought with my cousin, you demonstrated what I aspire to be: levelheaded while appealing to the Word of God. Since then, I've reminded myself of that every moment of every day." He tapped his own chest. "I reacted purely out of instinct there, but you showed self-control. Neither of us let him lay a hand on Eliza. There's more than one way to defend a loved one."

His gaze shifted to Zechariah, whose eyes shone beneath his bangs. "The boy at the river needed to be stopped. I had it in me to send him to Sheol—all of them. But my children were watching. My girls."

Eliza struggled to suppress the emotion welling in her throat at the raw honesty of her father's words.

His hands fumbled in his lap as he continued. "In the brick fields, I didn't give my words or behavior a second thought. I've barely been a father to any of you. But the Lord has given me a fresh start. I want to embody what a Godly man should be." He looked at Zechariah again. "So, yes, I clobbered him in front of everyone. The threat had to be removed, the situation averted. Zechariah is safe, the others dispersed, and judgment rests in God's hands."

Her father's exposed vulnerability didn't weaken him. It displayed strength and wisdom. A heaviness slumped his posture, as if emotionally and physically spent, yet he maintained his honor and dignity. Pride swelled in Eliza's heart upon viewing him in this new light.

He straightened, lifting his chin. "And so, in like manner, we are priests. Priests to the world, which is always watching. Through us, they will know who God is."

Something about his openness made Eliza sorry for every hurt and wrong she had caused him. Every careless word, every eye roll. She wanted nothing more than to please him. Not to earn his love, but because of it.

Her actions that afternoon had been no different than any other day. Though she'd shown some restraint, it wasn't enough to avoid marring her father's name. Worse, she had slandered Sena's. From now on, if Sena's fame were ever to be tarnished, it would be because of Sena, not her.

Seti's absence gnawed at her. He needed to witness this softer, endearing side of her father rather than the usual gruff head of the household, to participate in this rare tender moment with her family. She longed to gush her love for them all and pull them in for an emotional embrace. But no. She couldn't do that. Instead, she bit the edge of the blanket to keep herself in check.

"I love you, Abba," Miera cried, bounding to her father and throwing herself into his lap.

Seti settled at the table in Moshe's tent, papyrus spread flat before him. He watched the man scurry about, lighting several candles with one he had snagged from outside. Questions about the covenant, consecration, and God's holiness begged to spill out, but Seti bit his lip and waited.

Moshe finished by lighting the oil lamp on the table beside Seti. "That enough light?"

With the sun fully set, only the candlelight and lamp illuminated the tent. The orange glow dancing on Moshe's face gave him an ominous appearance, reminding Seti of the blazing mountain-face from last night's nightmare.

"I…I'm sorry I was late last night. And thank you for the tent and…and everything…"

"No matter." Moshe waved it off and plopped into his high-backed chair. He set the candle aside, pulled a blanket over his legs, and rested his hands on his knees. "We will begin with the psalm of the crossing."

Submitting to Moshe's direction, Seti suppressed his questions and picked up the reed pen. He'd love to hear Moshe's take on crossing the sea, but that would have to wait. Moshe instead began with a psalm.

His vivid depiction of Seti's people perishing in the sea brought back the devastation they had suffered, as well as how his entire worldview had been swallowed into the abyss of the waters. The perceived slight against him and the

Egyptians quickly transformed into words of revered devotion, formatted like a prophecy. The all-powerful God, through conquering and seizing, would dwell on the earth—with His people, His inheritance, in a sanctuary.

Was this the song Moshe had sung after the waters engulfed the Egyptian army? Seti hadn't been able to discern the words then. Though eloquent, the poem roiled his insides.

Moshe named the small oasis with the bitter water 'Marah'. It was the first of many tests of the people's faith, confirming Hoshea's words. Hearing it from Moshe's perspective brought a wave of shame on Seti over the bitterness and confusion he harbored. The journey from Egypt to the Rock of Horeb had tried Seti's newfound faith. His mouth watered and his stomach growled at the vivid memories from a time not so long ago. Yahweh's faithfulness never wavered, yet the people, including himself, continued to cater to their carnal needs. But Eliza had suffered from her head injury. And what had Moshe experienced during that time? Did he hunger and thirst? Moshe didn't elaborate on his personal trials but rather kept the focus on God.

Leaning back in his chair, Moshe closed his eyes and breathed in a long breath through his nose as if savoring something sweet. "Then they came to Elim, where there were twelve springs of water and seventy palm trees, and they camped there by the waters. Stop."

Seti dropped the reed pen and flexed his cramped hand. "Moshe. I don't doubt you know what you're talking about, but there weren't that many springs, and there were hundreds of trees. Only a few were palms. It was literally a forest." A forest one could get lost in.

Without moving, Moshe opened his eyes a slit, peering at Seti. "It's symbolic. The numbers." He sat up. "I will use numbers symbolically—but not always. When future generations hear this, God wants them to understand the

Edenic symbolism as they look forward to His end goal."

Seti turned the words over in his mind, then wrinkled his brow. "I don't understand."

The waning lamplight softened Moshe's angular features but shadowed his eyes, making it hard to discern if Seti had overstepped his bounds. When Moshe leaned forward, the flame illuminated his piercing gaze as if Yahweh himself stared Seti down. Seti gulped, resisting the urge to back away.

"Crossing the sea wasn't just leaving Egypt, Seth. As an Egyptian priest's son, you should know that."

The Red Sea divided the realm of the living from that of the spirits, the Duat. Light from darkness. Order from chaos. No one left the safety of Egypt without the personal blessing of Ra. But this God they followed proved to be not only the God of the Hebrews but the God of all realms.

Moshe raised an eyebrow. "After enduring that and the threats to your flesh in the wilderness, Elim offered a temporary rest. A precursor to Yahweh's ultimate rest: the new Eden."

When Seti didn't respond, Moshe sat back, eyes once again shadowed. "But the new Eden will not only offer rest for Israel, but for the nations—hence the 'seventy'. Those who accept Yahweh's offer will live with Him there forever."

Nothing made sense but the awe and reverence tempting Seti to drop to his knees before this man of God. Why? The words exceeded his understanding. Or was it Moshe's intimidating presence? Sitting there in that chair as if it were a throne. Moshe wouldn't allow anyone to prostrate before him. That would be blasphemous. Seti had vowed to only bow to the Hebrew God. He stilled his breath as silence enveloped them.

Moshe stood and stretched his back with a crack. Once again, he appeared as the eighty-year-old man he was, weary from a long day. "Leave the papyrus as it is."

Seti stood and took a deep breath. "Thank you, Moshe. Thank you …"

After gesturing toward the tent flap and mumbling something indistinct, Moshe turned away with a loud sigh, letting his arm drop.

Seti paused. "Something amiss? Did I do something? I'm sorry."

Moshe shook his head. "No apologies. That's not it." He blew out a candle.

Would such a powerful, God-fearing man indulge Seti with his inner musings? "Please … what is it?"

Seti met Moshe's gaze, and for a fleeting moment, a sense of brotherhood passed between them, until Moshe looked away. "Tomorrow, the people will meet God."

The weight of Hoshea's words returned, clenching Seti's stomach. "You don't think they're ready?"

Moshe rubbed the back of his neck, avoiding Seti's eyes. Days ago, Seti had witnessed the sensitive eighty-year-old, who impulsively spewed defensive words. Most of the time, Moshe exuded a confident leader, impressive and commanding. But now, a man of the flock stood before Seti. A true shepherd, concerned for the safety and character of his sheep.

He exhaled a slow, long breath. "I don't know."

Compassion swept over Seti. Pride at witnessing Moshe's vulnerability dissipated, as did the countless questions that had built up. This was the man God had chosen—a hero who'd defended his comrade at the cost of exile, a mediator for an undeserving people who were but strangers to him, a tender heart attuned to not just the pains of these people, but to the very sentiments of God.

"Moshe," Seti choked. "I'm ready." He winced. Why would Moshe care whether Seti was ready or not?

Moshe lifted the last candle and met Seti's eyes. "Are you?" He blew out the flame.

Chapter 44

Eliza plucked a string on the lute. It didn't sound right. It had been perfect at Rahel's camp, but now it needed tuning. Maybe something had bumped it during her mother's reorganizing.

She sighed and looked at the Fire Pillar. Once her eyes adjusted to it, she could differentiate it from the top of the mountain. The rocky apex glowed a brilliant bronze against the black backdrop. The Fire Pillar hovered above it, never touching. During the day, its cloudy form swathed an entire quarter of the mountain. However it appeared, it struck her in spellbinding awe. If only she could add a beautiful ambient melody to accompany the visual masterpiece.

She plucked another string and winced as the note rang flat. It wasn't horrible, just off. Yuval could probably tune the lute in seconds. Maybe rebuffing him had been a mistake. A melodramatic moment stemming from the incident in the river. She'd tolerated him calling her Frog Girl before, so why the offense now?

"I'm sorry, Lord." Eliza stood and veered toward the bank of the stream. Here, several paces from her family's campsite, the water ran shallow enough to wade through but deep enough to submerge. After confirming her family slept soundly, she'd slipped away for a true consecration. One uninterrupted, sacred, and special.

The cool water and wet sand welcomed her bare feet

after suffering abuse from the hot gravel. When she stood knee-deep, she lifted her gaze to the Pillar once again. "Oh, Lord, I've tarnished Your holy name. You heard my prayer in Avaris and witnessed my plight. I'll never forget that. I've tried to live in remembrance, but I keep failing."

"You continue to bless me, regardless of my failings. You have given me this lute to glorify Your name. To worship You."

She closed her eyes and strummed the first chord of the only song she knew—the one she'd composed for Rahel. The melody buzzed dissonant in her ears, but surely effort pleased God, not perfection. He deserved His own song, but this moment had taken her by surprise. After things settle down, she'd compose something unique for Him.

The light breeze snatched the notes away as if God claimed them for Himself. Eliza smiled, enamored with the thought. Music had a way of transforming everything it touched, like the same image reflected on different surfaces.

"You put a love of music in my heart, and I want to honor that." Even her voice soared to the heavens.

She replayed the short tune, hoping her offering pleased God. As the final chord faded, she lifted her tear-filled eyes. "I consecrate myself to You."

After setting the lute on dry ground, she waded deeper until the water reached her waist. The cold shuddered up her chest. She paused to adjust her footing, then held her nose and dipped beneath the gleaming surface.

The song ceased, and the musician vanished below the water. Seti blinked. Did he see what he thought he saw? After leaving Eliza's camp, the faint tune lured him along the stream until the shadowy figure in the river materialized.

He bolted to the edge. Ripples fanned out in concentric circles where the person had gone under. Then, as if in slow motion, a girl surfaced, gripping her nose. Moonlight sparkled off her languid silhouette, hair matted against her head and down her back. Her tunic clung to a delicate, womanly figure.

He gasped. "Eliza."

She spun. "Seti!"

A rock dropped in his stomach as memories of his own betrothal consecration flashed before his eyes. Of course. The God of the Hebrews meant to make His people His bride. Yahweh, who wooed them out of Egypt with his unrivaled strength and power, who lavished them with gifts and proved Himself faithful to protect and provide, this God of all gods desired a relationship. Seti knew this, but seeing Eliza like this solidified it. This was a betrothal.

The men were wrong. This was no suzerain treaty where the ruler demanded allegiance from his subjects but cared nothing for them. This God concerned Himself with each individual heart.

A sovereign fear shivered through Seti as he looked at the blade in his hand. What had he done?

"What are you doing here?" Eliza demanded, breaking through his thoughts. "Seti!"

He wetted his parched mouth and eyed her stunning figure as he searched for an answer. The physical sensations begging him to take hold of her couldn't compete with the dread encompassing his insides.

"Seti?" Her voice, raw and pleading, begged for an answer.

He straightened and pocketed the blade. "I was looking for you." A partial truth. "What are *you* doing here?"

Her shoulders slumped, and she muttered something under her breath before saying, "I was having a moment with God. A personal one. Me and Him."

The sharpness in her reply clawed at Seti's heart. He

treasured his own private moments with Yahweh, yet intruded on hers. Seti measured his tone to hide the emotion in his voice. "I will leave you be." He started to turn but paused. "It's not safe in there by yourself. Who would save you if you got swept away or stepped in a hole?"

As her future husband, he could insist she return to her tent, but demanding anything of her didn't sit right anymore. Though the current was weak, he hesitated to leave.

She lifted her arms, assessing the flow, then gazed at Seti. A glint of moonlight hit her eyes. "What's wrong?" She saw right through him. Even in the dark.

"Come out of there." Seti lifted a hand toward her, his heart in his throat at the concern in her voice.

"No!" She slapped a fist on the water's surface, startling him. "I came here to make up for my ruined consecration. I want to show God I'm serious. Now please, Seti, leave me be."

So much for that concern. Seti gave a curt nod and turned away. He had barely taken two steps when she called after him.

"Where are you going?" The longing in her voice tugged at him.

He pressed his eyelids shut. This wasn't how he wanted to break the news. "You told me to leave you be."

"Yes, but where are you going?"

"I have a tent now, across from Moshe. He gave it to me."

Even in the dark, the shock on her face was evident. His words hung between them with a stark heaviness. His knees weakened as he fought the urge to join her in the water, but he'd lose himself in her beauty and risk God's displeasure.

Her head dropped. "I see."

"I meant to tell you earlier, but—"

"I know. And I pushed you away—"

"But I'm not bothered. You needed that."

"I needed what?"

She didn't see it? "You needed the moment with your brother."

Eliza stepped forward, eyes shining. "It was ruined anyway. I cried. I tried not to, but when you came, and you were so thoughtful, I couldn't help it."

"But that's you, Eliza." Seti moved closer. "That's who you are. Otherwise, you wouldn't be out here right now playing your lute for God. And you allowed yourself to be vulnerable in the open, for Zechariah. That's why I didn't prod."

Eliza looked away, a hand pressed to her heart, and it was all Seti could do to keep from leaping into the river. If only she could see what a wonder she was—a constant tension of passion and timidity, of sensitivity and boldness. Yet before the Great Almighty, it all harmonized.

With a hand outstretched, she waded toward him. "Come to me." Her voice wavered.

"No."

She halted as if slapped in the face.

"If …" He had to tread carefully. "If I came to you, I'd for sure lose myself in you, and we'd both be defiled. God said not to go near a woman."

When she didn't respond, he added, "And anyone could see us."

The light breeze stilled between them. Only Seti's soft but staggered breaths and the whirring night bugs remained. They could do this—right here, right now—and then reconsecrate themselves afterward. Yahweh would understand. After all, it was He who had set Seti's heart toward her and He who orchestrated this very moment.

Seti traced her edges with his eyes against the contrast of the glowing water. God might be testing him, and if he touched her, that would be the end. All self-preservation would vanish, but so would sorrow, angst, and every nagging question about everything. Their souls would touch.

The thought set his body aflame.

"To … tomorrow …" He withdrew, unable to say more. His breath caught as he waved goodbye like a fool, every step toward the shadows of nearby tents twisting the knots into tight loops in his stomach.

He collapsed behind the first tent, his heart shattering like a vase on marble. Everything inside him screamed to run back. The passion and ecstasy would surpass his wildest dreams, but he couldn't flagrantly disobey God. His fingers dug into the dirt as he tried to stifle his breathing.

How fitting for the God of the Hebrews to prohibit sexual acts in His presence. It was He who planted the uneasiness in Seti's heart with the Egyptian worship system. Seti had been mocked in Egypt for it, but God was preparing him all along. And now, when Seti was willing to give in to desire, he had to wait. God came first, even before Eliza. Seti would prove to Eliza he loved her by presenting her to God undefiled, perfect.

But Adam was a different story. Seti had set him up to fail, and now they both would pay.

Eliza stared at the ceiling of her tent, counting tattered threads, unable to sleep as Seti's words reeled through her mind. Besides him acquiring a tent, which in itself roused a night's worth of pondering, his claim that God instructed him not to go near a woman didn't make sense.

But he wouldn't lie.

Despite him interrupting her one private moment with God, something about him stirred her heart. Something lost and vulnerable. His poor attempt to pass it off as some sort of animalistic sexual desire did nothing to hide it either.

What was he not telling her?

She had barely seen him the last couple of days, and the one chance she had, she'd given to Zechariah. Any other man might have become offended or possessive, but not Seti. He truly wanted the best for her.

Eliza wrapped her arms around herself, longing for his touch. He had been looking for her. Maybe to tell her, maybe to invite her to see his tent. No, he couldn't go near a woman, apparently, which would explain why her father slept by the firepit with the boys. That meant Seti had come for a different reason.

The stacks of linen blocked what little moonlight filtered through the thick canvas. Eliza sighed. The darkness offered comfort; no one could see her struggle. Yet, it also brought unease. Miera slept on the far side, her soft, rhythmic breaths the only indication she was still there.

If only Rahel were closer. She could use her company and her counsel. Maybe a sweet song to help her sleep.

"Moshe?" Seti reached for the flap of Moshe's tent but hesitated. Moshe would be livid to be awakened in the middle of the night for his petty problems.

He let his hand drop and choked back the knot in his throat. Let the old man sleep. He had a multitude to worry about. Seti shuffled to his own tent across the path and opened the flap to darkness. He paused. There would be no joy in crawling onto his new sleeping mat. He would not slumber tonight. Hoshea's dreaded words pitted in his stomach, as true as the burning pillar on the mountaintop. He wasn't ready to meet God.

The jingle of trinkets jolted Seti around. Moshe stood in the opening of his tent like a god silhouetted by clouds. The dark skin of his bare chest accentuated the whiteness of his beard.

"I—I'm sorry to wake you." Seti looked away, preparing for a reprimand.

"I wasn't asleep."

Seti shifted his stance, at a loss for words. He had sulked back to camp, his mind a whirlwind of questions and shame. He desperately wanted Moshe's reassurance, but not at the cost of disturbing him.

"Out with it, boy."

"I'm not ready to meet God." The words rushed out. "I thought I was, but I'm not. Hoshea's right. I've done terrible things. I left God's presence and went to Elim for water. I killed two Amalekites in the battle. I saved manna overnight and contaminated The Lank's family's—"

Moshe raised a hand. "Stop."

With a swift inhale, Seti dared lift his gaze to meet Moshe's, but the man had already retreated into the blackness of his tent. The flap hung open.

"Come in and sit."

Seti shook his head. "But your wife … my lord."

"She's with her sisters. Come in."

Moshe had been up all night? Alone? A single candle on the writing table where Seti had left his work barely emitted light. Moshe closed a robe over himself as he sat on his usual chair.

"Sit." He gestured toward the stool, only his outline visible.

The gentleness in Moshe's voice caught Seti off guard. Maybe he was bored. Seti sat and stuffed his sweaty palms between his legs. He kept his eyes lowered, sorting through his thoughts.

"Don't list your grievances to me, son. Those are between you and God." Moshe leaned forward but still out of reach of the meager candlelight. "What's really on your mind?"

"But that's it, my lord." Seti searched for words to

make Moshe understand. "I cannot face God like this. I have blood on my hands and fought in battle at eighteen. I ruined The Lank's heritage, and nobody knows it was me … I will die in the presence of God." *And so will Adam.*

Moshe stroked his beard. "Who said you would die?"

"Moshe." Seti straightened, as if to school the man of God. "If a good person cannot approach God, then one harboring sin will surely die. Even you worry that your people aren't ready. Well, I'm not, and I don't know how to be."

Moshe sat back with a long, drawn-out sigh that unsettled Seti's already frazzled nerves. "Well, that would be a problem, wouldn't it?"

"My lord?" This was Moshe sitting before him, right? Seti snatched the candle and lifted it to make sure, illuminating Moshe's familiar face. He set the candle down, embarrassed. "So … so what happens if one isn't ready?"

"If one does not consecrate himself as commanded and enters the Lord's presence, I'd suppose he'd die." The apathy in Moshe's tone belied the fact that he had clearly been awake all night, likely worrying for his people. Either he was more unstable than Pharaoh, could compartmentalize on command, or he put Seti to the test once again.

He definitely wasn't unstable.

Seti cocked his head, determined to corner him. "You're an honest man. What if I were your son, Moshe? What would you tell me then?"

Though Moshe wore his emotions as openly as Seti, he could easily lie under the cover of darkness. But would he?

Except for uncrossing his legs, there was little shift in Moshe's demeanor. Not even in his tone. "I'd tell him to obey the Lord and examine his heart. He's a grown man. Nothing more I could do."

"Examine his heart?"

"For whatever sins you may be harboring—pride, bitterness, unforgiveness."

"Right. I already said I have evil in my heart. My flesh. So now what? If I were your son, what would you tell me to do with it?"

"I would instruct you to repent before God."

"I've done that. Now what? It's still there." He had repented, right? Unless that involved making amends. It'd be impossible to make amends to the Lank's family and too late to make it right with Adam.

"You must refrain from sinful acts."

Seti balled his hand into a fist, inhaling hard through his nose. "But that doesn't erase what I've already done."

"I guess we'll find out if it's really still there or not."

This man was impossible. "By dying?"

"Indeed."

"Moshe!" Seti stopped his fist from slamming on the table. "That's what you would tell your son?"

"It's the truth. I'd hope I raised him right." Was it the talking in circles or Moshe's nonchalant tone that irked Seti so much?

Seti dropped his head to his arm on the table, no longer caring how pathetic he looked to the man of God sitting before him. He might as well die right there. "You're willing to lose your only scribe?" he mumbled into his arm. "Can't you consult God? Ask Him what I am to do?" He lifted his head. "God answers you."

"It doesn't work that way, son." Moshe sat stoic, but a hint of compassion wavered in his voice. "God speaks only when He chooses. Time has run out. You'll have your answer in the morning."

Swallowing the hard knot in his throat, Seti rested his forehead in his palm. Did Moshe even care? He called him 'son'. That was hope, wasn't it? Hope for his relationship with Moshe, but not for Seti's life. Not for his relationship with Yahweh.

Maybe Hoshea would tell him what to do. He was an honest man and had no problem telling Seti flat-out what he thought. Seti would see him in the morning, before going to the foot of the mountain. Time had not run out.

With nothing more to gain from the conversation, Seti stood and composed himself. "Thank you for your time and wisdom."

"I expect you to join me and my men at the foot of the mountain."

He couldn't have placed Seti in a worse position—as close to God's presence as one could get, as if Moshe rubbed it in to torture Seti all the more.

"Yes, Moshe." Seti inclined his head and opened the flap. He glanced back, willing Moshe to stop him and confess it was all a test, and then reassure him. Maybe embrace him. Call him 'son' again.

But for a slight nod, Moshe remained unmoved.

Unable to appreciate the softness of his new layered mat and pillow, Seti clenched his woven blanket with both hands and curled on his side. Perhaps God mocked him by furnishing these comforts for his final night this side of death, like the bountiful nourishment the two farmers had provided him the day before the last plague. Bile burned his throat.

The dream from the other morning haunted the night, the Angel of Death's deep voice clear as day. *"After all I did for you."*

Chapter 45

Eliza bolted upright at Adam's screams and met Miera's wide-eyed gaze. She tore through the tent flap, Miera on her heels. A flying sandal narrowly missed her head. Adam thrashed about the campsite, hurling rocks, dishes—anything within reach. He kicked the wagon, a slew of curse words pouring from his mouth in a violent tirade.

He turned to Eliza, eyes wild beneath missing eyebrows. Patches of dark hair splotched his otherwise bald head. "You!" He pointed at her. "You had to marry that scoundrel! That worthless Egyptian scum-rat!"

Curses filled the air until her father jumped to his feet at the firepit. "That's enough, Adam. Tame your tongue."

Adam stormed toward Eliza, stopping a hand's breadth from her face. "We were a family before he came." His hot breath pushed her a step back. "Where's your dignity? You had to fall in love with him. With your Egyptian master. What kind of sick person does that?" His whole body trembled. "I'm going to kill him."

"Wha—" Eliza stepped back, stunned.

"Adam!" Sarah peeked from her tent.

He speared Eliza with a look of pure venom, his smooth face smoldering red. Only a small patch of curls remained near his neck. With a snarl, he spun around and snatched his cloak from the ground.

Eliza froze, mouth agape. Miera stood beside her, hand

covering her mouth.

"It will grow back." Her mother rushed toward him, but Adam threw out a hand to stop her.

He flung the hood of his cloak over his head and pocketed a dagger.

"Where do you think you're going?" her father demanded. "Did you not hear a word I said last night?"

But Adam flicked his hand dismissively and stormed off, his cloak billowing behind him.

"We're leaving to the foot of the mountain soon," her mother called, but he continued on, refusing to acknowledge her. She turned back toward the tent, a look of defeat on her face.

Miera grabbed her mother's tunic. "We can't leave without him."

Heart hammering against her chest, Eliza stepped back as her mother brushed past, avoiding eye contact. Her father threw up a hand and trudged toward the wagon, while Zechariah stood slack-jawed.

Did they all share Adam's sentiments? No one moved to stop him. The murderous look in his eyes told her all she needed to know.

"Adam, wait!" Eliza bolted after him.

Seti pulled on a clean tunic and stepped into the morning sun. Without manna blanketing the ground, the morning resembled a sabbath, except Levites crowded the paths toward the mountain. While most were decked in fancy Egyptian gowns or kilts, gold rings in every orifice, jeweled collars, and beads in their hair, others donned long robes of faded colors like those of Moshe and Aharon. Not a single Hebrew bared the everyday loincloth. The sight reminded

Seti of his betrothal. Despite dressing for the occasion, there was no evidence they knew God's intent.

Yet, unlike the betrothal, a solemnness hung thick in the morning air. No aroma of baked manna wafted on the breeze. No music, no excited chatter. Only quiet murmurs and the occasional baby's cry.

Seti glanced toward Moshe's tent, wetting his mouth in preparation to speak, but Moshe didn't emerge. Had he already gone?

A sudden crack of thunder shattered the moment, rippling through Seti's chest and vibrating the ground. He stumbled back, catching himself before falling into his tent. Cries arose, and children wailed. The Hebrews crouched, sheltering the little ones, and gazed at the sky before pressing forward in hesitation. Before Seti could rise, another thunderclap boomed with the same intensity as the previous.

After finding his feet, Seti put a hand on his chest to feel his palpitations. The clear blue sky gave no trace of storm clouds. But as Seti rounded a few tents, the source became apparent. His stomach dropped. The Cloud Pillar engulfed the entire mountain. Black smoke billowed and rolled in waves. Orange flames twisted into a vortex to the heavens.

The sky above contrasted with the black, broiling mountain in some exotic way that took Seti's breath away. Why would God manifest in such a ferocious form? The haunting words from his nightmare returned. Seti ran a hand down his face, scanning the reaction of those nearby, hoping it was just another dream, and he'd wake up in his tent.

"Seth, this way." Aharon waved Seti over to where he stood with two elders arrayed in fine robes. Gold sashes cinched their waists, and shimmering beads hung in the beard of one of them.

It wasn't a dream. Dread pooled in the pit of Seti's stomach. He took a deep breath and hurried to join them.

"Moshe and the others have gone ahead." Not a hint of

anxiety laced Aharon's voice.

Seti locked eyes with him and opened his mouth to speak, but nothing came out. Something inside of him hoped Aharon would ask if he was ready. If he slept well. Hoshea must have gone with Moshe, leaving Aharon the only one who might have answers. Yet, a sudden fear of what those answers might be stole Seti's voice.

He glanced around, guilt cutting his insides at the spectacle Adam and Eliza would wake up to. If only he'd awakened earlier, he might have had more time. This day, meant to be sacred and holy, would be anything but for them. He couldn't face God with this on his heart. They might still be at their campsite. If Seti ran, he could reach them before they left. But for what? To make amends? The entire family would be livid. He had exacted vengeance on Adam with no thought of the consequences. Satisfaction for the ultimate revenge had driven him, along with the hilarity of it. He had timed it for the night of consecration to mirror that of his betrothal to Eliza. But the sight of her in the water last night had exposed the foolishness of his actions.

"Let's go." Aharon turned toward the mountain, his staff pointing forward.

Sharp pangs stabbed Seti's chest. *God, please, give me more time. Let me fix this.*

But like Moshe said, it was too late.

"Seti!" Eliza's scream spun him around.

Something sliced past his face, and he flinched. He stumbled backward, catching himself against a wooden beam. His eyes widened at the dagger in Adam's hand. He ducked another swipe as the blade cut through the air with a hiss.

Adam snarled as he lunged forward, eyes ablaze. Seti sidestepped, grabbed Adam's wrist, and used his momentum to throw him to the ground. As Eliza screamed in the background, Seti pounced on Adam as he rolled onto his back and pinned his hands down near his head.

"Adam, stop!" *Think clearly. Don't retaliate.*

A wad of spit struck Seti's face, and he gasped. He released Adam's wrists and slammed his fist into his chin. An upward swing from below caught Seti's cheek, snapping his head to the side. Blood flew from his mouth. He pinned one of Adam's arms with his knee and fought for the other, but Adam's fist slammed into his throat. Choking, Seti keeled over. Adam shoved him the rest of the way off and grabbed the dagger.

"Seti, watch out!" Eliza screamed.

As Adam dove, Eliza barreled into him. They tumbled in a tangle of limbs against a tent, toppling a corner post. Seti clutched his throat and righted himself, gasping. Out of the corner of his eye, Aharon bounded toward them, staff raised.

Seti shot out a hand to stop him. "Please. I have it under control." He coughed at the burn in his throat. "I'll be there short—"

"Seti!" Eliza grabbed her brother's leg as he pulled away from her.

He yanked it free and stumbled. Seti caught him, flipped him onto the dirt, and drove his knee into Adam's chest. "Adam, listen to me—"

"I hate you! You ruined my family! You ruined my life!" Adam spat at him again, but Seti dodged it.

"Adam, I'm sorry."

"I got the dagger!" Eliza yelled behind them.

"Adam—"

"Look what you did. You humiliated my family. You ruined us!" Adam's face contorted. "I have to meet God like this. Do you realize—"

"I do, and I'm sorry." A deep compassion in Seti's soul held him together.

Kicking beneath Seti's weight, Adam's thin frame struggled. He jerked his head forward, forcing Seti back enough to free his arms. His fist slammed into Seti's eye.

Seti countered with an elbow to Adam's eye, slamming

his head into the dirt. Instant regret flooded him.

"You need to stop this, now!" Seti yelled, spittle flying. "We're going to meet Yahweh, and you need to right yourself."

"We're leaving." Aharon cut in.

Seti took a breath. His vision spun as he looked at the men. Others walked by, staring, but none stopped. An explosion of thunder shook the earth, and everyone ducked. Eliza yelped, falling back into the collapsed tent.

After its vibrations dispelled, Seti locked eyes with Adam. "You're coming with me." He stood, let the dizziness pass, then yanked Adam to his feet by the tunic. "We're going to the foot of the mountain, and we're going to repent."

Adam's glassy stare worried Seti. Had he hit him too hard? He shouldn't have struck him at all.

"Me too," Eliza said.

Seti turned and motioned her closer. Her brown eyes roved over his face, widening.

"Oh, Seti." She reached out to touch him, but he grabbed her hand before it made contact with his stinging eye and jaw. Thankfully, Adam had hit his bad eye.

Aharon and his men had left, leaving no time to examine each other's bruises. Seti dipped his head and kissed her knuckles. She had followed her brother to stop his attack when she easily could have done nothing. Yet now, Seti had pitted her between him and her family, something he never dreamed of doing. He swallowed his shame and turned from her. Keeping a firm grip on Adam's arm, he ushered them ahead to catch up.

As they plowed down the dusty path toward the plain, Seti kept his eye on the turbulent mountain. He led them at a steady pace to keep Aharon within sight. Adam stumbled occasionally, forcing them to pause and putting them further behind.

The absurdity of Seti's selfishness mortified him. All

that mattered was Adam and Eliza's standing before God. He owed them that much.

They stopped to rest on the flat-topped rock where Seti had stood days before and gazed at the vast open plain before them. Instead of the typical browns and whites of a valley packed with people in their mundane tunics, cloaks, and head-coverings, the plain now filled with an array of brilliant colors and glistening jewels as the multitude approached, ready to present themselves as a bride to the Great Adonai. The astonishing splash of every color imaginable against a drab backdrop reminded Seti of Egypt's many festivals and processions—but without the hypnotic drums, incense, and bejeweled animals that embodied Egyptian worship.

A quiet breeze lifted Eliza's wild curls. She had neither dressed up nor pinned her hair. Dirt caked her bare feet. She must have chased after Adam upon waking. Seti's heart sank. She'd appear as a disgrace on the most important day of her life.

Seti cleared the guilt-ridden knot from his throat and turned toward Adam. "I'm…I'm sorry about—" He gestured to Adam's head. "I realize now how foolish it was."

"I don't think you do," Adam growled, his good eye narrowing. "You're used to shaving your head. It's nothing for an Egyptian. But for an Israelite—we shave our heads only in mourning, in an open display of humiliation and despair, a loss of honor."

Seti averted his gaze as Adam's words compounded his shame.

"You've ruined everything," Adam spat. "I finally had my family back, and then you came and took over. I barely had a chance."

"Chance?" Seti choked, unable to look up.

Adam scoffed.

Thunder roared across the plain, and the people cowered. Below, a shockwave tore through the crowd from front to back. Seti glanced at the roiling Cloud Pillar as if it had reprimanded him. He must keep Adam talking. Let it all come out now before the mountain, even if every word from his mouth would feel like a kick in the gut. Maybe Adam would cool off, perhaps even forgive him.

"My sisters looked up to me." Adam slid on the gravel but caught himself. "It was the one thing I still had. I barely saw them. Then, when Moshe freed us, it was like God gave back all those missing years. My family was together, and I got to be the big brother I'd always wanted to be. A presence in their lives, leading them, protecting them."

Eliza's grip on Seti's arm tightened.

"But you, like every entitled Egyptian, barged in and took that away from me." He pinned Seti with a look before continuing. "And the sick part is, you already had that. You had your whole life being the big brother, the firstborn. Probably your father's favorite. But you had to take that from me too, didn't you?"

"Adam—" Eliza tried.

"Don't 'Adam' me, Eliza," he snapped. "My words used to mean something to you. You were opening up to me. Now, when he's around, you don't come to me for anything. Neither does Miera. Admit it. You know it."

"So, all this is about jealousy?" The words slipped out before Seti could stop them.

Adam raised a swollen brow. "Mock me all you want. You can't possibly relate."

"I'm not mocking," Seti corrected. He stuffed his hands into his pockets and picked up the pace. "But it sounds like jealousy. What else would you call it?"

"So what if I'm jealous?" Adam flung his hands up. "What do I have left?"

"Adam," Eliza said again. "You're still the firstborn."

Let her say what Seti wished he could say. He had no words of wisdom, no defense.

"And what does that mean, Eliza? What inheritance do I get? For seventeen years, that meant nothing. All I ever wanted was my family—my siblings' admiration, Abba's respect."

Adam let out a drawn-out sigh and dropped his head. His long legs had no trouble keeping pace as he shuffled along. Eliza kept quiet, letting go of Seti to swing her arms as she hastened to keep at his side.

How was Seti to respond? He couldn't begin to empathize. Though he had lost his own heritage and inheritance, that was mostly by choice. To grow up believing he'd never receive it at all—despite being the first from his father's loins—would have altered his entire life as well as his view of the gods. Everything Seti had going for him hinged on that position, including how he related to his family.

His relatively minuscule relationship with his brother depended entirely on Seti's lead. Though they clashed often, Kabelo looked up to him. They'd probably have been closer if Seti hadn't thrown himself into his academics.

Sabu used to say Seti commanded the room whether he tried to or not. It became a running joke for a while, and Seti would make a show of it at times. But the truth of those words hadn't sunk in until now. And it was so natural he never gave it a second thought.

Again, Eliza's words rang true—he couldn't leave Egypt behind if he tried. Little by little, an acute awareness arose of what life entailed for those growing up alongside him, those he had long considered unworthy as so much as a passing thought. And the more he learned, the more his old worldview shrank. The luxurious lifestyle he once took for granted resembled nothing of reality.

Chapter 46

Eliza stepped out from between two towering boulders onto the ledge, gripping Seti's hand. Viewing the multitude from above and in front sent a panic spiraling up her throat. From as far as the hills on the horizon, innumerable faces stared her way in quiet anticipation. The crowd shifted like rippling water, reminding her of the dense carpet of locusts in Egypt. The howl of the wind on the ledge drowned out all conversation below.

Could her parents see her? She had intended to rejoin her family, not follow Seti to the brink of insanity. Her heart hammered, and her head spun.

Adam plowed ahead, mouth agape, eyes wide.

Seti chased after him. "Adam, listen. I'm sorry. Please. I didn't mean to do any of that. I have my own tent now and won't stay with your family anymore. They're all yours. Well, except for Eliza. Please, you have to forgive me."

When Adam waved him off, Seti grabbed his arm and spun him around. "Look, I understand why you're angry. But now's not the time. You have—"

"Get away from me." Adam shoved him aside and surveyed the mountain overhead.

"You're late!" Hoshea shouted over the wind.

Seti grasped Eliza's hand and guided her across the rock platform toward Hoshea, who huddled with Aharon and another man against a rock wall, their robes whipping against their legs. Moshe knelt at the edge and spoke with several elders below. His cloak billowed upward like a cape, revealing a long tunic plastered against a firm body. He appeared poised, as if he did this every day. The gale-force winds beat his beard around his neck toward the tight bun tied at his nape.

Eliza faced Hoshea with a tinge of relief at his familiarity. Behind him, Aharon struggled to pin his whipping robes in place with his hands. The unfamiliar man beside him knelt in prayer, face buried in his folded hands.

Hoshea's gaze drifted past Eliza, and she turned to find Adam frozen behind Moshe, facing the multitude, holding his hood in place. Seti hurried out to him and grabbed his arm, startling him. The hood flew off, exposing his humiliation to the world. Adam threw it back on and shot Eliza a terrified look.

Hoshea pulled him from Seti and pinned him against the rock wall. "Stay here."

Eliza hurried to her brother's side as he slid to his knees, his trembling hands grasping at the gravel.

"Why'd you bring them?" Hoshea demanded.

Moving between Eliza and Adam, Seti nudged her behind him, sandwiching her between himself and the rock wall. "They came to me. I was already late."

Unspoken words passed between Seti, Hoshea, and Aharon, rousing Eliza's defenses. She held her tongue, unwilling to embarrass Seti. Sending her back wouldn't be such a bad idea, anyway. Though standing before the nation of Israel stirred a sense of honor, she couldn't ignore the intensifying urge to run—not only from their watchful eyes, but from the mounting dread churning in her gut.

Though Hoshea's disapproval was evident, Aharon's expression was unreadable. What had Seti been thinking, bringing her and Adam here?

Seti knelt beside her brother. "Adam, listen to me. You must repent. And forgive. Yes, it's my fault, but you tried to kill me. God's coming down. Release your anger and forgive me. Repent so you stand blameless before Him."

It was no use. Adam stared off into nothingness, eyes wide and glazed.

"Check your heart, Adam!"

Eliza touched Seti's shoulder and gestured toward Moshe, who had leveled his gaze on them with an indecipherable expression. He then turned to Hoshea and gave a curt nod.

Hoshea raised his shofar and drew in a deep breath when a sudden, deafening blast from above rocked the earth, knocking the multitude to the ground. Eliza cowered behind Seti, hands over her ears, but the earsplitting sound pierced through, no matter the pressure she applied. The blast continued unbroken, intensifying in magnitude.

When Hoshea's shofar rolled against her, she dared crack open her eyes. He lay prostrate on the platform, face hidden beneath his arms. Moshe stood upright like a war general, eyes lifted to the mountain behind them, robe flailing violently against his legs. His face—emanating a peace and belonging—reflected a man fulfilling his destiny, standing before God's imposing glory. Beyond him, the entire multitude plastered against the ground, burying their faces.

Though Eliza screamed for Seti, her voice muted in the ongoing blast that resembled a heavenly shofar. He gripped her wrist and crouched over her, hiding his face in the crook of his other arm. When the intensity of the blast faded, Eliza caught Adam's terrorized gaze. Another clap of thunder sent their faces to the ground.

She saw herself from above—standing in the river the previous night—accompanied by an overwhelming sense of adoration. More images from her past flooded in, good and bad, with feelings of compassion and terror. Then, a burst of white light. She curled her body into a ball to become as small as possible, as if to contain the light but fearing she'd burst if she did so.

Lightning spiderwebbed through the sky. Thunderclaps followed in a series of violent rumbles. Shockwaves sent stones tumbling from above and vibrated the gravel beneath. Everything inside Eliza reverberated to the point her bones might shatter. *God, stop. Please stop!*

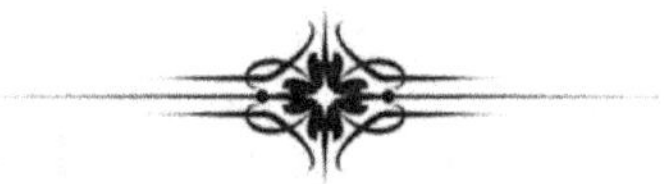

Seti pounced on top of Adam. "Yahweh, spare him!"

The wind tore the words from his mouth. He pressed his face against Adam's shoulder—not trying to squeeze him, but the fear surging through him tensed every muscle in his body.

"Yahweh," Seti prayed. "You are my God. Take me. Spare him. Spare Eliza."

Thunder cracked across the sky in response, startling Seti. Would the very firmament splinter? A chill shot through him. Not daring to open his eyes, he filled his lungs to capacity. Only the snuffing out of his breath would keep him from confessing.

"Moshe said to take my transgressions to You. I provoked Adam, Lord. It's all my fault." Everything poured out like the water from the Rock of Horeb. "I provoked Eliza too. She'd be truly innocent if not for me. Forgive them. I left the camp in defiance, stole from the enemy, and went to battle. Oh, God, I ruined The Lank and his family. Have mercy on them. Overlook Sabu's part in it, too. It was my idea, not his. I was selfish and vengeful."

He couldn't stop. "I left my mother and brother in ruins, abandoned them, Yahweh. I disgraced the Ameneten legacy. I betrayed my father. Oh, Lord, forgive me. I couldn't save him. I tried and couldn't. If I hadn't been hard-hearted, I might have had more time."

The air left his lungs. "I've failed you. Take me. Take everything—even my scribal duties with Moshe—but spare these others. Spare them from—"

"I AM YAHWEH, YOUR GOD, WHO BROUGHT YOU OUT OF THE LAND OF EGYPT, OUT OF THE HOUSE OF SLAVERY. YOU SHALL HAVE NO OTHER GODS BEFORE ME."

Seti's eyes shot open. His heart froze midbeat.

The ominous voice continued. "YOU SHALL NOT MAKE FOR YOURSELF AN IDOL IN THE FORM OF ANYTHING IN THE HEAVENS ABOVE, ON THE EARTH BELOW, OR IN THE WATERS BENEATH. YOU SHALL NOT BOW DOWN TO THEM OR WORSHIP THEM. I, YAHWEH, AM A JEALOUS GOD, VISITING THE INIQUITY OF THE FATHERS ON THEIR CHILDREN TO THE THIRD AND FOURTH GENERATIONS OF THOSE WHO HATE ME, BUT SHOWING LOVING DEVOTION TO A THOUSAND GENERATIONS OF THOSE WHO LOVE ME AND KEEP MY WORDS."

Except for the deep voice booming across the sky and off the limestone surfaces, nothing else could be heard. No howl of wind, no crack of thunder, not even a rumble from the earth, as if nature itself bowed in reverence to the Great I Am.

"YOU SHALL NOT TAKE THE NAME OF YOUR GOD IN VAIN. THOSE WHO DO SO WILL NOT GO UNPUNISHED."

As God continued, Seti slipped from the trembling Adam to the ground in a heap, clenching his eyes shut as if to block out God's words. The words penetrated deep into his soul, yet all comprehension slipped through his grasp as if life itself were leaving his body.

Stop!

It was the only coherent thought he could muster in the swirl of squeezing pressure and sound consuming his mind.

With an intensity that surpassed even the moment God had spoken in thunder, Seti's spirit strained to split from his flesh—the two warring in an unrelenting battle to the death. Every fiber of his being screamed with burning waves of pins and needles shooting in all directions.

When Seti's last will to live quavered, God ceased His message, as if suddenly aware how perilous His voice was to humanity. Or perhaps, that was His intent—to bring them to the brink of death, then halt in an act of mercy. The resulting silence popped Seti's ears, followed by the all-too-familiar thud of his pulse against his skull. One by one, the sounds of life returned, including a crack of thunder which now felt minuscule and weak.

He blinked moisture into his eyes. A low rumble continued beneath the black smoke on the mountain. Flames shot from it sporadically. The wind had settled to a light breeze, cooling his sweat-soaked tunic stuck against his skin. He was alive.

His throat burned as if the air itself had scorched it, eliciting spasms with each gasp and preventing his chest from fully expanding. Every breath was torture. If he could move, he'd recoil in pain.

The withdrawal of God's voice left him hollow, as if his insides had vibrated into nothingness. Or was the resulting emptiness due to the purging of his sins?

Seti peered back at Eliza. Her head had lifted from its prostrate position, her eyes wide on an ashen face, fixed on Moshe straight ahead. She appeared frozen solid, reminding Seti of a temple figurine. He waited for a blink, a breath, anything to quell the fear that God had struck her dead.

"Eli—" He winced at the pain in his throat. "Eliza?"

Her gaze blinked his way, then back to Moshe. Relief washed over him, unlocking his muscles, and he collapsed. God had spared them. All of them. They had heard God's voice and lived. *You showed me my heart, Yahweh. Now show me Yours.*

Moshe raised his arms over the stunned assembly, who still buried their faces in the dirt. Before he spoke a word, Adam lurched to his feet and dashed into the open, jostling Seti from his stupor.

Adam's eyes darted in all directions. Holding his hood in place, he veered toward the path off the platform and disappeared. Moshe turned toward Seti with a raised brow.

Hoshea stepped into Seti's line of vision, face contorted and hair windblown flat against his scalp. He jutted his chin in the direction Adam had run.

Bringing Adam here was a mistake.

Determination revived Seti's muscles, and he shot to his feet. "Stay here." He pointed at Eliza. "Stay with Hoshea." He sent Moshe a curt nod. "I'll be back."

When? It didn't matter. Nothing mattered but Adam's restoration and forgiveness. Seti would miss Moshe's next move. Even if Moshe terminated his scribal duties and stripped him of his tent, so long as Eliza and her family stood blameless before God, Seti's purpose would be fulfilled. By not smiting them, God had given him a second chance.

Seti peered between the rocks where the path descended the hill and outcropping boulders. Instead of following the course into the plain, Adam had deviated toward the open desert.

Seti's stomach sank. "Yahweh, please help me." He skidded down the stony slope and broke into a run.

Chapter 47

Seti had gone. Adam had gone. Eliza backed up against the rock wall, as if that would conceal her from the great multitude below staring her way. She'd been in a stupor when Adam raced off, until Seti's first command as a husband—to stay put. That alone shook her from her God-induced trance. The usual instinct to resist such a mandate failed to surface. Instead, she cowered against the rock surface.

God's words had pummeled her with such authority and gravity, vaporizing all pride and self that when Seti pointed at her, it was all she could do to not disintegrate into the dust from which she was formed.

Her head spun, and she trembled, gripping her knees to her chest. Moshe's words to the multitude, his departure, all blurred in motion and sound. Nothing registered but the fear surging through Eliza's body until Hoshea barreled toward her, making her flinch. He crouched before her, blocking her view of the dizzying world like a privacy curtain dropping down.

"Eliza." He snapped his fingers near her face. "Come out of it."

She blinked.

"It's time to go."

"How—" Her throat constricted. She swallowed hard and forced the words out. "How long has it been?"

Hoshea's brow knitted. "Has what been? Moshe's going up the mountain to speak with God. You can return to your tent now. He won't be back until tonight."

Return to her tent? Not without Seti. She shook her head. "Seti?"

"He went after Adam. Come on." He held out a hand. "You?"

"I'll stay and wait for Moshe."

She let him help her up, but her legs gave out, and she collapsed to her knees. Tears rimmed her eyes as she gazed past him at the chaos below. There was no way she'd navigate that bedlam. Even if she did, she still had no idea how to find the river leading to her father's tent. The thought of being lost in that valley, pressed against thousands of hostile strangers, rekindled the panic and hopelessness from the day she'd searched for Rahel. Her chest tightened. She clutched it, trying to breathe, trying to force the panic down and recompose herself. But all her strength had vanished at the sound of God's voice, leaving nothing to glean from. The tears she'd struggled to contain poured down her cheeks. She shook violently, crouching at Hoshea's feet like a blubbering fool.

"What's the matter?" Hoshea lifted her to her feet and held her steady.

Hoshea and the entire world had witnessed her break, her feeble, emotional meltdown. God had left her undone—exposed, vulnerable. A deep urge to unload all her misgivings and shameful thoughts onto Hoshea edged her lips, as if God summoned her last shred of dignity, ripping her from the inside out for all to see. She pressed her lips together, refusing to let them out. A sliver of anger renewed her resolve, and she glared toward the smoking mountain. Though her very essence had been laid bare, only God would witness the innermost confessions of her soul.

Yet, the sight of the mountain—pure majesty among the mundane—calmed her a small measure. God had heard her pleas when lost before, He wouldn't pit her against the wolves, regardless of what her fleeting emotions suggested.

Seti's parting words returned with clarity.

Eliza straightened and faced Hoshea. "Seti told me to stay with you."

Releasing her, Hoshea huffed, looked away, then returned his gaze with a look of resignation. "Yes, I remember now. It may be a while."

A hint of defensiveness rose in Eliza's chest, catching her off guard since her pride had been so thoroughly stripped away. She shook it aside, reminded of her meltdown and how it must have looked to him. She would not be a burden. "Before Seti returns or Moshe?"

"Both."

The all-too-familiar desert appeared stark opposite of a safe haven. Out from under the security of God's presence, Adam would be ripe for the picking by whatever lurked out there. Though certain death awaited him, alone and exposed, his broken spirit would be the first to go. Away from God's presence, one's soul was a free-for-all in the world of evil.

His stumbling form, small against the sandy backdrop of vast nothingness, dropped to his knees. He glanced behind, gasping for air, and pointed at Seti, shouting into the silence. "Leave me be!"

Seti slowed to a walk. He pressed a hand against his cramping side, wishing he had Chewy. His muscles burned as if he'd never run before. With the back of his hand, he wiped sweat from his good eye to get a better look at his nemesis floundering in the sand before him. "Where are you going?"

"Why'd you bring me before God, you dog?" Adam

leaned back on his hands, chest heaving.

A deep purple had spread from his swollen eye to his chin. It reminded Seti of his injuries from Elim. The swelling had just begun to subside when Adam tore them open again. The two likely mirrored each other—from their lack of hair to the array of colors and swelling covering their faces. Add to that their bruised knuckles, hoarse voices, and labored breathing. Their similarities didn't stop at their outward appearance either. At the feet of God, both proved broken, unprepared, and unworthy.

Seti stopped a few paces away. Leaning with his hands on his knees, he heaved in a breath to speak. "I couldn't let you stand before God with hatred in your heart."

"Too late!" The emotion quavering in Adam's voice pierced Seti's heart.

Adam edged backward like an injured animal facing his predator just before the kill. He had no defense but vile words. The sight of him—pathetic, defeated—cast a new light on the morning's events on the mountain. God hadn't spared them due to Seti's begging on the rock ledge. No, the same compassion stirring Seti now had also moved God to mercy then.

The realization brought Seti to his knees in a broken reverence before the All-Loving God.

Nothing could atone for Seti's sins. It was a lesson on sacred space and the human condition. Even while consecrated and wholly repentant, one could not see God and live. And yet, God's all-encompassing love for a profane people had shone through—a steadfast love rich in mercy and grace.

"What's wrong with you?" Adam's condescending voice snapped Seti from his thoughts.

Seti turned to his brother-in-law, who had inched away and covered his head once again with his hood. Seti licked his crusted lips, searching for a reply. Something not too soft. "Ironic." He straightened. "You think I put you in danger, yet here you sit." He swept a hand across the stretch of desert but couldn't help gazing with yearning toward the Great Mountain, its storm still broiling overhead, an enigma among the range of peaceful peaks. Suppressing the pull of his soul toward God's presence, Seti moved closer to Adam.

"Get away from me." Adam jumped to his feet, flicking a hand at Seti. He brushed the dirt from his cloak and took several backward steps toward the camp. "Quit following me. Stay out of my life."

"Adam." Seti stood. "You ran from God and tried to kill me. Now you're out here, guilt-ridden, in the worst place you could be, especially in your condition. I'm not leaving you alone."

Adam shook his head with vehemence, as if Seti's words tortured him. "My condition?"

"You're shaken. Bitter. And the sun is burning you to a crisp."

"You know nothing about me. I wasn't going to kill you. Just teach you a lesson. And I'm not bitter, either …" He looked away as he said it.

Seti moved closer, and Adam backtracked. If the boy wouldn't repent, then maybe Seti could at least get him out of the desert. "But you did teach me a lesson. You showed me a lot. That I've changed little since leaving Egypt. That I'm full of pride, and I have more to repent than I thought. And you're still teaching me." Adam continued to move away as Seti pressed in. "Last night, I was so scared, I couldn't bring myself to God. But then you came this morning, and it gave me perspective. Only you and Eliza mattered. More than me."

"Quit following me!" Adam turned toward the camp, picking up his stride.

"Listen. You have every right to be jealous—even angry with me. But you must rein in that hostility before it consumes you, before you lose what you've gained. If you think Eliza doesn't look up to you now, it will get worse if you continue to hate me. Believe me. God is merciful."

As Adam gained headway, Seti slowed, exhaustion weighing heavy on his muscles. But giving up wasn't an option. He'd made this mess, and he would clean it up if it took the rest of his life.

"I couldn't let you approach God like that," he called after Adam's ever-shrinking form. "But I also can't make you repent." It was no use. He stopped and wiped his brow. No words or apologies could soften Adam's heart. Who was Seti to talk, anyway? He'd harbored revenge right up until last night. And jealousy.

"Yahweh, please. Only You can soften hearts. Please soften his."

This praying—speaking to Yahweh from whatever distance he'd run to—had not only proved a source of comfort, but had grown more natural the more he did it. He marveled at the simplicity of it.

He dropped his shoulders in resignation, watching Adam plod toward the camp. Though he hadn't ventured too far into the open, everything from the scuffle that morning to nearly dying at the foot of the mountain compounded with the heat of the blaring noon sun. Add to that the lack of sleep the previous night.

God meant Elim to represent a future rest, and Seti craved it.

Much of the congregation had left the valley only to return laden with food baskets, water pouches, cushions, and mats, ready to wait it out for Moshe.

Eliza perched on a boulder beneath the protruding flat rock that formed the ledge from which Moshe had addressed the multitude. The enormity of the rock outcropping offered a sense of security from the encroaching crowd. Hoshea and Aharon conversed in low tones with the elders and tribal leaders, each recounting his experience of God's approach that morning. Though the intense fear of dying, coupled with God's sovereignty, had rendered everyone incapacitated at the time, each person had something unique to add, as if God had spoken to them personally.

The images that had flashed through Eliza's mind during the encounter now returned as she tried to grapple with her own version of it. God had shown her His perspective on specific moments from her life. Many of them seemed insignificant except for the consecration in the river. But a sweetness had permeated each scene, giving the impression of a proud parent. No overwhelming emotions accompanied them, but rather a sense of solidarity, a confirmation of what she'd always known: God had created her as she was—smart mouth, fiery passion and all. He would rein in those traits if she so let Him, and He'd soften her hardened edges, sanctifying her into His prize fit for a future kingdom.

Eliza winced. How'd she get all that out of her chaotic experience? Hoshea approached with a tray of manna-cakes, lifting it to her perch.

"What did *you* hear God say?" she asked.

His brow lifted, then furrowed as he processed her question. He gazed at the tray, rubbing his beard for what felt like forever. "With my ears, I heard God give explicit instructions. With my heart … well, that's personal."

"Instructions?"

"Didn't you hear?"

Eliza piled three cakes onto her lap and thought back. God had spoken, but the visions and the overwhelming sense of death had drowned out His audible words. "I did but didn't understand."

"He gave instructions on how to love Him," Hoshea said, his eyes sparkling. "It's easy for God to love us, but we don't know how to love Him."

Even as God revealed His personal love for her, He simultaneously made known how to return that love. Butterflies erupted in Eliza's chest. How beautiful. "What … what words do you remember?"

A sweet smile lifted Hoshea's well-groomed beard, crinkles appearing on his otherwise youthful face. He gazed toward the mountain with the far-off look of a man in love. "I honestly don't remember much of it myself. Not word-for-word, anyway. I'm sure Moshe will have it written down."

That look alone had swept Rahel off her feet for him. His strength and valor came second, but the love in his eyes when he spoke of God could enslave a woman. The same spellbound gaze had graced Seti's handsome face when he'd spoken of his gods in Egypt, captivating Eliza. And now, by some miracle, the Hebrew God had replaced them in Seti's heart.

As she concentrated on what she'd heard amid God's presence, Seti's heart-wrenching confessions returned with clarity. Stricken, she slid from the boulder and crumpled in the dirt, muffins scattering, as his cries to God cycled through her mind. Unlike her, Seti had freely exposed the depths of his soul before God and everyone present.

Her adoration and respect for him exceeded what seemed possible. She scanned the vicinity, hoping to catch sight of him—but to no avail. How she longed to hold him, to reassure him, to become one with him.

Then, with matching intensity, the gravity of his words slammed her in the gut. "Hoshea?"

Hoshea turned and did a double-take at the sight of her on all fours in the dirt.

The world spun and blurred as she lifted her face to his. "Did you hear Seti while God was speaking?"

"No." He knelt before her.

The concern on his face did nothing to dispel the bile

rising in her throat. Though an intense suspicion coiled her insides, she asked the question anyway. "Who's The Lank?"

Chapter 48

The contrast in temperature between the desert sun and the shade beneath the cloud canopy never ceased to amaze Seti. Yahweh was everywhere, but the canopy signified His nearness, as did the Pillar. Yet, His sovereignty over both the world of the living and the world of the dead was evident—even the far edges of the earth bowed in obedience. Souls far and wide would know Him as the one true God.

Seti unstuck his sweat-soaked tunic from his chest and sighed.

As he rounded the last bramble-filled hill near Moshe's well-worn path, his breath caught. The rock-ledge ahead stood empty. Where had Moshe gone? Eliza? The plain bustled with life, though less crowded than that morning. Elders and leaders lounged below the ledge in quiet conversation. Voices from hundreds of small groups carried on the air, bouncing off the bordering rocks and hillsides in a low cacophony. No wonder Moshe's voice carried so far. Though the storm cloud and smoke continued as they had all day, the thunder and lightning had ceased, and the wind had diminished to a gentle breeze.

Hoshea's boisterous laughter announced his whereabouts in a group of upbeat men dispersing nearby. He waved them off and ascended the narrow path up the rock outcropping. Behind him, in the shadows, sat Eliza, alone and hugging her knees. She locked eyes with Seti for a brief second before rising, relief brightening her pale face.

The tightness in Seti's chest lifted. He hurried toward her with a slew of confessions and apologies on the edge of his tongue.

"Eliza," he breathed out, opening his arms for the embrace he longed for, but she stuck out a hand and stepped back.

"Where's Adam?" An air of caution dispelled the relief on her face.

Seti flinched at her sudden change in demeanor, then blinked it away as mere concern for her brother. "I was hoping he'd come back here. I followed him into the desert, but he returned ahead of me."

"The desert?" Her voice raised a notch, eyes widening.

"We didn't stay out there long. It was just a carnal reaction to being overwhelmed by God's nearness. He must have gone home. He'll be fine." Hopefully.

"What did he say?"

Her concern for Adam, though understandable, frayed Seti's pride. "He's still angry with me. But like I said, he was a little overwhelmed. He'll recover."

Eliza stood stark straight, putting Seti on edge. She set her jaw and looked away as if contemplating her next words.

Seti gulped, preparing for a lashing. "You're upset with me, aren't you?"

The burden of his sins returned, heavier, sharper. He had mistaken her concern during Adam's attack as forgiveness for his idiotic prank when it was nothing but obligatory wifely behavior. "I'm sorry, Eliza. I've brought dishonor on your family. I've pitted you between your brother and me without realizing it. I'm sorry."

Her unmoving stance and watery eyes confirmed an inner struggle. It was all he could do to keep from gathering her in his arms.

"Seti ..." She paused at the wavering in her voice. Her

hand shot to her mouth.

"Eliza …" He reached for her, but she turned away. A stone dropped in his stomach.

"Who …" She cleared her throat, regaining her composure. "Who's The Lank?"

That stone in his stomach grew into a boulder, knocking him off balance. He braced a hand against a protruding rock. Who else had heard his anguished confessions? God would hold him accountable, and Seti was willing to submit and apologize to The Lank, but now the very thought of it made him ill. "Yuval."

Eliza's mouth dropped with a gasp so loud that heads turned.

"I didn't think of the consequences. Otherwise, I wouldn't have done it."

"You threw spoiled manna into his tent?" The horror in her eyes reflected his heart. "How … How could you? And you never told me? All that time I was looking for him—"

"He called you Frog Girl. And you should see the way he looks at you."

"That's no reason to … to destroy his family's heritage!"

Seti winced at the words as if learning of it for the first time. He glanced at the curious eyes roving his way.

"All that time and …" Her breaths broke in staggered gasps. "And you kept it a secret."

"I didn't know they'd burn everything. I thought it would just dirty his tent a little. I didn't know the instruments were in there. You have to believe me. I'm sorry, Eliza." There was no coming back from this. He had offered everything to God in exchange for the pardon of her family, and now God would hold him to it. He should be sorry he did it at all, regardless of the outcome.

Eliza shook her head in disgust, the disappointment in her eyes enough to kill him right then and there.

A horn blast blew a shock wave through Seti's chest, jostling his heart into a staccato of painful beats. He grasped at his sternum and glanced toward the rock ledge. Moshe stood with his hands on his hips, like a god on a mountaintop surveying the people below. Beside him, Hoshea blared another breath through his horn.

Seti sucked in a breath. "Eli—" but she was gone.

He spun around in time to catch her barreling through the assembling elders.

"Eliza, wait!" He darted after her.

She skidded to a halt at his call, nearly tripping over a basin of water jugs. "No!" Tears streaked her reddened cheeks. "Go away. Leave me alone."

"Where are you going?" He reached for her, but she veered away and broke into a powerful sprint she couldn't possibly maintain for long. "Eliza!"

Another horn blast startled Seti, and he stumbled forward. How many stupid blasts did it take to summon the people? Rage rising, he turned toward Hoshea, ready to release a torrent of derogatory words, but Hoshea's gaze pinned him in place with a look of warning. He dropped the shofar on a string around his neck and motioned with his finger for Seti to join him.

Moshe shot Seti an expectant look as he continued his speech, but Seti glanced back at Eliza's retreating form. She'd never make it back to her family in her condition.

"God …no …" The words burned in his throat.

Then, with renewed vigor born of desperation, he tore through the congested mob of men coming forth, toward the ascending path of the outcropping.

He broke into the open on the platform and plowed into Hoshea, shoving him behind Moshe until slamming him against the rock wall.

Hoshea's eyes went wide with surprise. "Seti—"

"Go after her, Hoshea. She won't let me. You have to do it."

"What's the matter with you?"

"You saw her take off. I know you did. Make sure she gets to her camp safe. She's upset with me, and it will set off her head injury again, and she'll get lost and collapse or something. I'll never find her then."

Hoshea extricated his tunic from Seti's clutches and straightened it. "Are you serious?"

"Yes! You can have my tent. My mat. Adam's gone, and I'm afraid of losing her too. It's my fault."

Hoshea looked past Seti as if thinking about it.

"You're going to lose her!"

"Get yourself together, Seti. You're acting like a madman."

"Hoshea!" Seti shoved him against the wall again.

In one swift move, Hoshea swung Seti around and pinned him to the wall with an arm against Seti's throat. "Calm yourself."

Unfazed, Seti croaked, "Please."

Hoshea let up, and Seti slumped forward. "You owe me." He stepped back, assessed Seti long and hard, then turned toward the descending path.

As Hoshea set out, Seti pressed against the wall for support, having unleashed his last bit of energy. He gazed over the convergence of men in the plain. "God, please lead him to her."

Moshe dropped his arms, finishing the speech Seti had completely missed. How many people heard his pleading to Hoshea? How many had heard his confessions when God spoke to them? He craned his neck toward the broiling mountain behind them. Its grandiosity sobered his pounding heart. His legs gave out, and he slid to the ground, letting the air leave his lungs in a long, heavy sigh.

"They're all Yours, Yahweh." The breeze whisked his whisper away. Defeat washed over him, rendering him a pathetic mess. He couldn't save Adam or Eliza, having ruined them. Ruined his marriage.

Exhaustion dulled Seti's mind. The elders and those nearby pumped their fists into the air with a resounding, "All that He has spoken, we will do."

Moshe clapped his hands together in affirmation and stood after he had been kneeling on the ledge. "Tomorrow morning, at the sound of the shofar."

Acknowledgments reverberated from below. Moshe turned to Seti and raised an eyebrow. "Now if only I had a shofar. Where'd Yehoshua go?"

No words came. Not even enough strength to meet Moshe's gaze. Seti barely shook his head, no longer caring how he looked to the man of God.

"What did I say about getting into trouble?"

Here it comes—the loss of his position with Moshe. It mattered nothing if exchanged for Adam's redemption, and though Seti couldn't bear another loss, it would be worth it. He closed his eyes and exhaled, bracing for the sting.

"We have much work to do tonight. I need you at your best. Gather yourself. I want to get some sleep before tomorrow."

Chapter 49

Confusion, torment, and regret propelled Eliza into the crowded plain, but exhaustion quickly overtook her. Since her encounter with God, what little strength she had garnered had long gone. Her lungs screamed for air, and her pulse pounded in her temples. She paused, bracing her hands on her knees, trying to slow her ragged breaths.

To her relief, Seti had not followed. She'd nearly slapped him at the foot of the mountain. The look he'd given her shattered her heart. Unwilling to add to the bruises on his precious face or spew inflammatory words in haste, she had fled. The sprint had fulfilled its purpose, leaving her too fatigued to make a scene, but it left her amid a mob of staring strangers in a valley she had never set foot in. The great fiery mountain at her back remained her only sense of direction.

She had raced through the deafening cheer from the crowd, raced through whatever agreement they had made with Moshe after his speech. The last time she peered back at the outcropping, Moshe had turned away, and Hoshea was gone. Disappointed at what little ground she had gained, she pressed forward, pacing her breaths. This wasn't the way Seti had led her and Adam. They'd come from the hills along the side. She shook her head at her foolishness. The camp would be upon her soon, but as to where to go from there, she was at a loss.

The stares and wagging heads of women obviously

disapproving of her unkempt appearance curled her insides with dread. She ducked her face from the distinct undercurrent of ridicule surrounding her. Aside from the dark gray storm cloud overhead, it felt no different than the last time she'd gotten lost. Only this time, Seti wasn't around to save her.

The crowd retrieved their belongings scattered throughout the plain and headed toward their camps, arms laden with baskets, cushions, and blankets. Thankfully, the area wasn't as bottlenecked as that morning, but it still proved a challenge to navigate. Too much for her senses. If she waited for the plain to empty, she'd be left alone, which would make the journey easier, yet no shorter.

Pain shot through her foot as she stubbed her toe on a rock, and a wave of discouragement washed over her. Her fragile will crumbled, and pent-up tears burst forth, unbidden.

"Hey, it's Scarface." A familiar voice rose above the chatter of the crowd.

Two of the young men from yesterday bustled up beside her, meeting her slow stride.

"What's the matter? Why are you crying?" the one with the braids asked with feigned concern. He walked ahead, then turned to face her, walking backwards.

"She wore her sleeping clothes to the mountain," the other one jeered.

"Doesn't think too much of God, does she."

"Sorry excuse for a Hebrew."

"Married an Egyptian, beat up her own kin, and disgraced the God Almighty. Why didn't you just stay in Egypt, Scarface?"

Her head lulled as their voices swirled with the amassing sensory overload. No smart retort formed, no defense. It was all she could do to not collapse in front of them.

"Where are your brothers? Couldn't make it out? Too

dejected from yesterday? Pathetic excuses for men, they are. Couldn't even defend their own sister."

"Do you speak of Zechariah?" Hoshea's voice cut in from behind.

It couldn't be. Eliza lifted her eyes and slowly turned.

Hoshea's jovial face smiled down at her. He held out a hemp sack of manna and a water pouch. If she'd forbidden Seti from rescuing her, he'd simply send someone in his place. The storm in her head returned to order at once.

"Hoshea!" Her hecklers' faces lit up.

He acknowledged them with a nod, then said to Eliza, "Zechariah's made significant strides on the field even in the short time I've worked with him. His unconventional moves haven't gone unnoticed. And if Adam can make me, the least of intellectuals, feel smart after just one session in script writing, he has a great future ahead of him."

Renewed hope energized Eliza's limbs as she watched this great man pulverize her mockers with mere friendly words.

"Can we join your field training?" the braided one asked, unfazed.

After Eliza grabbed the water pouch, Hoshea let his hemp sack hang, pocketed his hands, and strolled ahead. "I've set forth plans to form training sessions for underage fighters, with Zechariah at the helm. He will decide who joins. At this rate, he'll be commander of thousands." He looked from one stunned face to the next. "Until then, I advise you to tread carefully. Now leave us." He flicked his hand.

Speechless, the defeated teens slunk away.

Hoshea slowed and turned to Eliza. "You look lost. Famished. A wreck."

Eliza laughed, wiping away the tears. "Please take me home."

"Gladly." He steered her aside by the elbow. "But that's this way."

With Hoshea at her side, the head wagging stopped. Staring, judgmental eyes lit up with friendly greetings. Some even offered treats, which Hoshea graciously accepted and shared with Eliza. Women, young and old flitted about him with exaggerated giggles and fluttering lashes, even blatantly in front of their husbands. Yet the men themselves congregated around in cheerful banter as if he were some prince visiting from far away. His polite disposition only encouraged the behavior. He never tired of it, nor exposed their hypocrisy, a skill Eliza aspired to master. Instead, Hoshea made it a point to mention he was merely escorting her, elevating her above the others in a gentle, roundabout way.

He led her to the edge of the plain, around the side, and over a low hill littered with goats and sheep grazing about. Beyond that stretched the valley of a nation. Eliza stopped at the sight, never having seen it from such a vantage point. Campfires dazzled against twilight's shadows, glittering across the darkened valley as if the night sky had settled upon the earth. The aromas of smoke, baked manna, and spices clung to the air. Bursts of laughter broke the low rumble of cheery conversation in an oasis of life and celebration amid the surrounding desert of darkness.

Hoshea interrupted Eliza's marveling. "Seti said you hurt your head?"

"A while ago, at the Red Sea."

After she indulged him with that humiliating story, he said, "Seti was mighty upset when you took off. Never seen him like that."

Her thoughts sobered against the exquisite backdrop of the valley.

Hoshea had purposefully waited until her spirit lifted before broaching the subject. "And the last time I saw you that upset was when I tried to stop you from saving him."

His wisely chosen words convicted her. The terror of losing Seti struck her as if it were yesterday. Saving him, against the advice of all who loved her, even her own better judgment, had been worth it. She'd do it again in a heartbeat, even after learning what he did to Yuval.

Leaving her to chew on the thought, Hoshea started down the slope. She hurried after him.

He spun around. "What did Seti say when God spoke? You asked me if I heard him."

Eliza huffed at the question as she caught up to him, unsure whether to reveal Seti's secrets.

"That's what upset you, isn't it? Whatever he said." Hoshea raised his eyebrows. "You asked me if I knew who The Lank was, then you said nothing until Seti arrived. What could he possibly have said to God that upset you so much?"

For denying hearing Seti's confession, Hoshea seemed to have a pretty good idea. But what else would spill from one's mouth in the presence of God? Praise and worship, perhaps. Eliza dropped her head in shame, shuffling alongside his pounding gait down the slope. Seti had clearly regretted his actions against Yuval. "He was repenting."

Hoshea shot her a knowing smile. "That boy's got a heart of gold. Yes, he does stupid things, almost daily, but finding a heart like his in a young man these days is like finding a pearl in the desert. His impulsiveness will wane over time, leaving a cache of wisdom."

Only hours ago, God had whispered something similar to Eliza's heart. Like her, Seti was a raw gemstone plucked from the dust of the earth. A little refining and polishing would make him fit for a crown.

"Did Seti send you after me, or did God?"

Hoshea barked a laugh so contagious, that Eliza couldn't help but laugh with him. "Perhaps both."

Smiling, she followed him out of the peaceful hills and into the lively festivities of a celebrating people. Gatherings as large as entire communities or as small as single families danced around fires to tambourines, reed pipes, and clapping. Laughter and song filled the air with renewed vigor that Eliza hadn't experienced since before the Red Sea.

The infectious joy fought against the ever-churning turmoil in her gut. She couldn't possibly let herself relax, not after leaving Seti the way she had. Forcing her thoughts away from the warring emotions, Eliza chalked up the question weighing on her mind since early morning.

"Hoshea." She quickened her pace to match his long strides. "Seti told me God said he couldn't go near a woman. Is that true?"

"Yes." He paused to adjust the strap of his bag and the shofar hanging from his neck, allowing Eliza to shake a cramp from her leg. "That was a command to all men to avoid defiling their consecration."

"How would that defile them?"

"Well, you see … How do I say this…" His furrowed gaze lingered on the smoky mountain behind them as if looking to God for answers. "Proximity with God requires a degree of consecration." He started down the path again. "He plans to dwell with us—here and in the Promised Land."

"He does?"

"His manifestation on the mountain was a test of our readiness." Hoshea's face lit up at his own words, and he shook his head with a soft chuckle. "He truly is amazing."

Eliza plowed ahead, then turned to walk backward in front of him. "But that doesn't answer my question."

"I know. I'm still thinking." He rubbed his beard, concentration wrinkling his brow. "Basically, it's like this: once consecrated, we're made holy to a certain degree. We become defiled when we lose something that conveys life or when we gain something associated with death. When that happens, we aren't fit to be in God's presence until restored and reconsecrated."

If that were the case, they'd forever have to remain consecrated, unless they left God's presence. Relations with a man would be defiling, as well as a woman's monthly visitation, a loss of a source of life. Hoshea's explanation made sense but stood in stark contrast to Egypt and its sexualized worship.

Hoshea chortled. "I didn't explain that well at all, did I?"

"You did." Eliza returned to his side. "I was just thinking."

His words gave new meaning to the idea of lifeblood. Not only did it carry God's breath of life, but to spill it during a sacrifice—in the presence of God—would defile the sacrifice itself. Eliza paused. What if the blood of a sacrifice were placed on a person? Would it purify them?

She started after Hoshea again, not willing to slow him. But the more she pondered, the more questions abounded. "But covenants are sealed with blood."

"That is correct," he confirmed. "And our covenant with God will be sealed tomorrow morning with many offerings. That's why I suggest a good night's rest. Tomorrow will be even more important than today."

Her heart leaped at the second chance to rightly present herself before God. She'd approach Him with her family, wearing her bridal gown as originally planned. It would be perfect—celebrate such a pivotal moment in history with the ones she loved. And though Seti would not be with her, a warmth spread from head to toe in gratitude for having had him by her side through the most painful, challenging part of the two-day event.

Chapter 50

As the sun dipped below the horizon, an unfamiliar, flowery aroma of incense greeted Seti when he stepped inside Moshe's tent. Oil lamps cast shifting shadows. He paused to let his eyes adjust to the dim light. Moshe placed a ceramic bowl on the table before him, filled with various manna preparations. A delicate Egyptian hieroglyph bordered the outside rim in blue, suggesting it came from a family of wealth.

Seti sighed, weariness pervading what little energy remained. Still, an underlying curiosity for what Moshe had to say won out, as well as the need to perform at his utmost for the man who could have so easily dismissed him.

Moshe set two clay cups brimming with goat's milk on the table, then slid his high-backed chair closer and sat with a long, satisfied sigh. "You're alive."

The comment had a sarcastic ring to it, eliciting a scoff from Seti. But that's all Moshe would get from him. If Moshe knew the depths of trouble Seti had caused, he might reconsider letting him continue to scribe.

"And unusually quiet." Moshe lifted his cup to his lips and made a show of savoring the warm milk. "When's the last time you ate or drank?"

Seti shrugged, eyes downcast. Come to think of it, he hadn't eaten or drunk anything since the day before.

"We have a lot to write, and I need your full attention."

Giving in, Seti sipped his milk. It soothed his raspy throat and coated his hollow, aching stomach. He lifted his gaze to meet Moshe's for the first time that day. Tenderness sparkled in the older man's expression, tempting Seti to unburden the contents of his heart. But he looked away, not willing to ruin yet another relationship.

"Very well," Moshe said. "Write legibly. What we record tonight will be read and reread for days to come, starting tomorrow." He sat back in his chair after draining his own cup and folded his hands in his lap. "Begin. I am Yahweh, your God, who brought you out of the land of Egypt, out of the land of slavery."

Seti winced at the abrupt transition into God's words.

"You shall not make for yourself an idol in the form of anything …" Moshe recited verbatim the very words that had interrupted Seti's confession at the foot of the mountain, minus the ominous voice. In comparison, Moshe's otherwise authoritative tone sounded mundane, ordinary. Yet it still carried a heaviness that stirred Seti's heart from its catatonic state. "… not bow down to them or worship them, for I, Yahweh, your God, am a jealous God, visiting—"

"Jealous?" Seti interrupted. "A jealous God?"

Moshe's head snapped up at Seti's first words since the mountain. The shadows failed to hide the softening of his countenance. He leaned forward into the light. "Righteous jealousy, son. God is protective and possessive toward His people. He is jealous for us, not of us. To give allegiance or worship other gods would be to our detriment."

As Moshe resumed, Eliza's fuming words from the day Seti took Sena to the Rock of Horeb resurfaced, piercing his heart anew. She wanted the best for him, and no other woman would strive to give him that. To give himself to another would be blasphemous to their relationship. Like casting pearls to the pigs—something precious trampled underfoot, never to return to its original state. His stomach churned with guilt. The milk rose in his throat. No god would love these people the way the God of the Hebrews did.

Seti bit his lip, fighting to keep up with Moshe's speedy dictation. Everything flitted in one ear and out the other, though somehow accurately made it to the papyrus. His marriage now hung by a thread, and he clung to it with all he had. He'd run to Eliza's camp this very moment and apologize left and right to all of them for everything he had done from day one. But he had already been late to Moshe on the second day, left Moshe's side mid-meeting on the rock, and had now interrupted him. How much more grace would Moshe extend to Seti if he were to leave now?

Moshe continued the list of commands— "Words," he called them—transitioning from those regarding man's relationship with God to those on man's relationship with man. He stopped after ten, then raised an eyebrow. "This is where you left."

Seti bit his lip and returned his gaze to the papyrus, taking note of Moshe's tone. No more mishaps.

"The heads of the tribes and elders approached me then, and said, "'Behold, Yahweh has shown us His glory and greatness, and we have heard His voice out of the fire. We have seen that a man can live even if God speaks with him. But now, why should we die if we hear the voice of God any longer? For who among flesh has heard the voice of the living God speaking out of the fire, as we have, and survived? Go near and listen to all that Yahweh says, then tell us everything He tells you, and we will listen and obey.'"

The many lines on Moshe's face deepened in the shadows, and he uttered his next words with care. "I told the people: 'Do not be afraid. God has come to test you so that the fear of Him may be before you, to keep you from—'"

"A test?" Seti blurted, dropping his pen. "This was all a test? You knew I wouldn't die and didn't tell me?"

As if anticipating Seti's reaction, Moshe leaned forward and pinned Seti with a look of a tender-hearted father. "A teacher is most silent during a test."

Seti leaned in and locked eyes with him. "I went there expecting to die. Expecting Adam to die. And Eliza. I poured my heart out to God to spare them. And now you're saying all that was for nothing? A stupid test? Why all these tests? Doesn't He already know the outcomes?" He caught his rising tone and forced himself to stop before getting carried away.

All this could have been avoided. He wouldn't have taken Eliza and Adam with him, and he wouldn't have confessed everything aloud. Eliza would never have learned about The Lank.

Moshe straightened with a lengthy inhale through his nose, suggesting Seti had overstepped his bounds. "First and foremost, you were not wrong."

Seti held his tongue, measuring his breaths.

"Nobody can come near God and live, as you know. That was the very lesson He meant to teach. He came as close as our consecration allowed without killing us. God wanted to instill the fear He demands, the severity of the human condition, and His sovereignty before dwelling in the midst of our camp. And what happened, Seth? What did you do?"

Seti set his jaw, heat rising to his face.

"Would you have approached the mountain the way you did if you knew it was only a test? When God tests us, Seth, it is for our sake, not His. It reveals what's truly in our hearts."

Seti's hands curled into fists. Pressure mounted in his chest like a volcano ready to explode. He knew this all along from Moshe's previous dictation and from hearing God in the thunder. How many more tests would it take to finally understand? Without the fear of God, Seti may have otherwise minimized or justified his transgressions. He would not have met Adam's vehement hostility with compassion. And he would've kept silent about The Lank.

"As for your fears of dying today, God only indicated

one cause, which I made very clear. More than once."

"Don't cross the boundary." Seti dropped his gaze. He'd been too caught up in Hoshea's words about not being ready to meet God. Yet they were no less true, and the test served its purpose. Better to stand clean before God and honest with Eliza than to hold guilt and chase the fleeting approval of those who are no more worthy than he.

Lifting his face, he asked, "Did you see Him? God, I mean, on the mountain?"

"No." Moshe's eyes glowed with a far-off look as if recalling a special memory.

"Not even you? But you're…you're Moshe."

A slight smile lifted Moshe's beard. "Indeed, I am." He paused to reflect before sitting forward. "Again, no one can see God and live—not even me—unless God so desires it. Then he'd have to change either us or Himself. And He will, by the seed of the woman. And we will once again walk with Him as intimately as in the Garden."

The wonder on his face pulled Seti in.

"I alone am permitted to summit the mountain. The elders will advance partway tomorrow for a celebratory meal." Moshe grabbed a manna bun and turned it over in his hand. "In the heavenly throne room, as well as on the mountain and anywhere God shows His presence, there are certain tiers of holiness to which those of His choosing may approach. But even then, one must still be in right standing." He looked Seti dead in the eyes. "One day, there will be no such thing. Anyone anywhere will be able to approach Him."

This God blew all other gods away.

Seti cleared his throat. "What's taking Him so long?"

"For the seed of the woman?" Moshe took a bite, chewing it slowly. "Yahweh's building a kingdom, a new Eden, with people from every nation and every era. But winning their love takes time, and He will use us to do it." He took another bite, making ravenous sounds like he hadn't eaten all day. "God is patient. He will win the love of many without violating man's free will."

He leaned forward, capturing Seti with a look of utter adoration. "There's something about glorifying God in our fallen condition that is precious to Him. Only now, in the flesh, can we prove our love for Him in a way that is costly and rare. Not even the angels can do that. Once we're in His Kingdom, that's it. It will be natural."

Seti's mouth dropped. Moshe's words ran deeper than a sky full of stars, deeper than a rainbow and sunset in the same view. The kind of love God sought transcended that of mere feelings or instinct. It was a sacrificial, genuine love born of free will and tested by fire.

A conviction washed over Seti, along with gratefulness for God's test. Like Eliza, who pledged to honor the freedom God had granted her, Seti would live every day in light of that moment in God's presence.

"I—I want—"

"To love Him the best you can? Good. He made it plain how to do so." Moshe straightened and took another bite, his gaze now assessing his muffin. "His ten Words, which I have recited, will guide you. They are designed to honor both the sovereignty of God and the dignity of man." He sat back, still eyeing his muffin in the dim light, then lifted an eyebrow toward Seti. "It would be insincere to say you love Him while hating those He loves."

That made sense. The animosity between Seti and Adam would rend Eliza to bits over time. Because he loved her, he'd do all he could to prevent that. How much more so if he claimed to love God?

"To love others is to love God." Moshe's summation of his thoughts solidified Seti's determination to make amends—not just with Adam and Eliza, but their entire family. Maybe even The Lank.

Moshe swallowed the last of his muffin and pinned Seti with an expectant gaze. "It'd be wise for you to internalize those words. He orated them for all to hear, but the rest, He will speak through me." He dabbed his mouth with a tattered cloth. "Now we shall finish with what Yahweh spoke after I ascended the mountain."

At last, Moshe would reveal what God had spoken to him in the cusp of the storm. Seti grabbed the reed pen and readied himself.

"Begin." Moshe sat back, refolding his hands in his lap. "Then Yahweh said to Moshe, 'This is what you are to tell the Israelites: You have seen for yourselves that I have spoken to you from heaven. You are not to make any gods alongside me—gods of silver or gold. You are to make for Me an altar of earth and sacrifice on it your burnt offerings and peace offerings, your sheep, goats, and cattle. In every place where I cause My name to be remembered, I will come to you and bless you.'"

Though the God of the Hebrews required much of the same type of sacrifices as many other gods, He had a peculiar element to each. An altar of unhewn stone would reserve all glory for God rather than the craftsmanship of man. Even if constructed with a heart full of devotion, its splendor would detract from its purpose. It was a brilliant taunt in the faces of all other gods. Now anyone could construct an altar, whether a lowly commoner or a renowned sculptor. Power, wealth, and skill would have no part. Temples wouldn't compete in grandeur.

Images or attempts to recreate His presence were prohibited. No wonder He cloaked Himself in nature—elements so common they couldn't possibly represent Him, even if man managed to replicate them. This God was wholly other—holy, separate. He demanded reverence for His peculiarity, refusing to be likened to or shared with any other religious system.

Seti's mind whirled as he wrote, struggling to absorb Moshe's words while not falling behind. The man's every utterance required a depth of concentration and understanding, which Seti vowed to dedicate when time permitted. He'd compile the papyri into a book and study them until memorized and cemented forever in his heart.

The elaboration of the Ten Words continued in due order. An unprecedented amount of time was spent detailing day-to-day examples of how to thrive as a society meant to stand apart from the nations. From the treatment of the servant of debt and the proper care of women, to the righteous judgment in cases of negligence or malice, God's attention to human relationships distinguished Him from every other deity.

The notion that a god would emphasize love among his subjects would've been preposterous to Seti only months ago. Then again, what god even desired to be loved by his followers, let alone to the point of crafting a covenant that resembled a marriage of all things?

Moshe concluded with God's declaration that He would send an angel to lead the people to the Promised Land, one that bore the very essence of Yahweh's name, granting him the power to forgive. But rebellion would not be tolerated. Loving-loyalty and exclusive honor would bring blessings beyond measure.

"Stop."

The moment Moshe said it, Seti's first question leaked out. "Angel?"

The dim light caught in Moshe's eyes as he lifted his head. "Another manifestation of God. If His name is in him, rest assured, it's God."

"In human form? Have you seen Him?"

"Once. At the Red Sea before crossing it. He led us then and will continue to do so."

"I thought He was in the Fire Pillar."

Moshe's patient endurance of Seti's constant questions defied the weariness slumping his posture. "God is everywhere and also here. It's beyond our ability to comprehend in our limited existence." He stood and stretched, his back cracking in its usual protest. The oil lamp burned low, and the incense had long turned to ash, indicating the late hour. "We must rest. Tomorrow's another big day."

Seti cleared the conundrum of thoughts from his head. "Tomorrow?"

"The covenant remains to be sealed."

"Moshe." Seti shook the cramp from his hand. "It's a betrothal, isn't it? Between God and us? Not just a vassal covenant. The consecration … our freedom and the loot from Egypt, the mattan. The Ten Words are the ketubah, and tomorrow we seal it with blood. Am I right?"

Moshe paused mid-stretch. The imposing silence that resulted caused Seti to stand, grab the lamp, and view Moshe's pleasant expression.

"Never mind." He set the lamp down, cheeks warm with embarrassment.

"No, you are quite correct, Seth. I have pondered it, but to hear it from the lips of another confirms my thoughts."

"So … what's the dowry?"

A smile creased Moshe's shining eyes. "Now, why would we need a dowry?"

The heat in Seti's cheeks increased. Gods don't die. But they don't marry either, or so he thought. "Good point."

Moshe held up a finger. "Yet there is a bride-price to be paid at some point before the marriage supper."

Seti straightened. Last he knew, they already belonged to God. "What … Why?"

"That's where the seed of the woman comes in." Moshe's face took on a mysterious glow as he faced Seti. "And that's what will reverse the effects of man's fall."

"Which is far in the future," Seti added.

The disappointment deflated his resolve, and the exhaustion from the overwhelming events of the day returned tenfold. He stifled a long yawn with his hand and started toward the flap, but stopped. "Why would the God of the universe propose a relationship with man in the form of a man-made tradition?"

"Who said marriage is man-made?"

"It's not?"

"Marriage is rather patterned after a God-made relationship. When done right, it illustrates the roles and responsibilities of each participant. I'll let you ponder that on your own, Seth. I need to rest now."

How could that be if every culture had a different definition of marriage? But then again, most were actually quite similar, as if they unknowingly modeled God's design. Seti stepped into the quiet night and gazed at the stars. Just as every culture conjured a story for the *Mazzaroth*, they all modeled one true meaning. Eliza phrased it as, "God's grand plan for redemption."

"Seth?" Moshe's head peeked out from his tent.

Seti turned at the friendly use of his name rolling off Moshe's tongue. As if two friends lived across from each other, bonded by their love for God.

"As usual, you are to accompany the elders to the foot of the mountain in the morning, but do not follow them over the boundary. They will have a celebratory meal on the mountain, representing the entire nation. Not you."

"Yes, Moshe." Seti sighed. One day, maybe, Moshe would regard him as he did Hoshea.

Moshe's words kept sleep at bay for yet another night. The Hebrew God never ceased to stun Seti to the core with one revelation after another, forcing him to repeatedly question everything he'd learned about his existence. The idea that such a God loved each individual was a slow-growing reality, but the thought God desired an intimate relationship with them struck him even harder. Maybe it was because he was so freshly betrothed to Eliza or so new to the Hebrew faith. Either way, it awakened in Seti a new purpose that far surpassed becoming an Egyptian priest.

In most marriages, the husband bore the weight as the head of the household from providing and protecting, to cherishing and leading his wife in every facet of life. He'd be her rock, exhibiting self-control and wisdom. She'd be his prize, but not a prize that sat in a safe, hidden and out of sight. No, a wife was a prize meant to be shown to the world. In turn, she'd respect and adore him. She'd pledge allegiance to him and him only, trusting him with her life. All in a perfect world. This peculiar relationship called marriage could only have been designed before the fall of man.

Chapter 51

Laughter startled Seti from his slumber. He opened his eyes to the blinding white of the canvas above him. The loudness of the chatter and laughing outside suggested it was late morning, which meant he was late to the foot of the mountain. He tossed on a clean tunic, thanked God for the unexpected rest, and darted outside.

A stampede of children, tailed by a toddler and a goat, forced him a step back. Somewhere in the distance, a woman belted out an upbeat song, accompanied by tambourines. Men congregated in the path in light-hearted conversation. Everyone dazzled in Egyptian formal wear, and thick perfumes mingled with the sweet scent of roasted cinnamon and honey manna, masking the usual livestock musk. The atmosphere pulsed with renewed life, a complete contrast to the day before. Their energy was mind-boggling, contagious even, but Seti stifled the chuckle begging to erupt, refusing to display any sign of joy. He may have repented to God, but the mess he'd made remained untouched, if anything, worse. Just that thought sapped his renewed energy. That gut-wrenching look in Eliza's eyes the last time he saw her tore him asunder all over again.

He shoved the angst down and glanced around for Moshe and the elders. With this many people still lingering in camp, he couldn't have missed much.

"Moshe?" Seti jingled the trinkets hanging from the

flap of Moshe's tent. No response. He peeked inside. The main room appeared as he had left it last night. The only difference being the missing papyrus. A canvas curtain separated the area from the sleeping quarters. Moshe couldn't still be sleeping, could he?

"Moshe?"

"He's at the foot of the mountain, building an altar."

Seti turned to a man, his wife, and several small children assembling outside the neighboring tent. "An altar?"

The man pointed toward the mountain, then corralled his children and disappeared into the strong current of moving people congesting the main thoroughfares.

Of course. To seal the covenant with blood, an altar would be needed. There was still time. Seti exhaled a breath of relief and joined the procession of merry families.

Only a few paces in, he stopped short at the sight ahead, causing those behind him to stumble. Adam stood in the exact spot he'd attacked Seti the day before, only now there was a peaceful countenance about him as he scanned the passing crowds. He stood tall in a clean gray robe. A white turban hid his shame, and a gold necklace with a tarnished gold pendant hung down to his folded hands. His dark eyes caught Seti's, and he squared his shoulders.

Alarm tensed Seti's muscles. Composing himself, he closed the distance between them. "Nice pendant."

A soft smile lit Adam's shaven face, easing Seti's racing heart. "It's an heirloom, passed down from firstborn to firstborn."

Seti pressed his lips together and nodded, stifling a snarky reply. "Did Eliza make it home last night?"

Adam's brow crinkled. "She was already asleep when I returned, and I left before she woke this morning. You didn't bring her back?"

"No." Knowing Eliza was safe would suffice for now. Adam didn't need to know the extent of Seti's troubles. If he didn't bring up Seti's confession from yesterday, Seti wouldn't either. It was humiliating enough.

The shofar blasted twice in the distance, interrupting the awkward moment. Children jumped with squeals, heads peeked out from tents, and the procession of Hebrews picked up pace. A jolt of urgency ripped through Seti's chest. Though he desperately wanted to hear what Adam had to say, he wouldn't dare be late again.

Adam rocked back on his heels, eyes darting everywhere but forward. "Look." His voice went somber. "You lost your family. I gained mine."

Shock and relief froze Seti mid-breath. Was that an apology? What happened to Adam overnight that he now sought amends? It should be Seti making amends. The few words spoke volumes, solidifying a mutual understanding between them. Seti struggled to hide the sudden emotion washing over him. He looked away. Adam's roundabout apology would forever remain in his heart.

"Well." Adam cleared his throat. "I welcome you to call my family yours." He extended a hand the way Jeremiah had when he accepted Seti's proposal.

Seti grinned, masking his shock. He had been willing to do whatever it took to clean up the disaster he'd created, but God did it for him—in one night. He clasped Adam's forearm and pulled him into a clumsy embrace.

"Now," Adam said shyly when he pulled away. "I was hoping you'd take me to the foot of the mountain."

Twelve pillars of rocks stacked two men high encircled an altar of unhewn stone below Moshe's platform. The sight halted Seti mid-step, still a considerable distance away. Moshe must have risen in the wee hours to prepare it, likely with an army of men to lift those rocks. Then again, the Hebrews had proven their strength and abilities in Egypt. These makeshift pillars appeared as child's play compared to Pharaoh's monuments.

The multitude settled into the plain, filling the barren desert to capacity and spilling into the hills in an array of colors and movement. Behind the platform, the morning sun glinted off moisture in the black clouds still rolling up the surface of Mount Sinai. Flames shot out, and smoke and cloud mingled as one, engulfing the mountain and leaving Seti to wonder if there'd be anything left of it when God's manifestation lifted. Except for the low rumble of vibrations roiling down into the valleys, one would be completely unaware of the impressive display unless one sets eyes on it.

Adam pushed ahead, breaking Seti's trance. Gratitude engulfed Seti's heart as if it were the mountain itself. He took one last look and whispered, "Yahweh, thank you for Adam's change of heart. But if you'd find it within yourself to offer a little more mercy, please reconcile Eliza and me too. I know that's asking for a lot, but nothing's too much for you."

Eliza dropped the family blanket and slumped to her knees to catch her breath, while her mother and sisters spread it on the stony hillside along with the baskets of manna and eggs. Taking her head injury into consideration, her father had followed the advice of his friends and settled on the hills skirting the rear of the plain. Though crowded, it was nothing like the shoulder-to-shoulder congestion below.

She held her lute firmly in her lap as she studied her family with new appreciation. All were present but Adam, whom Zechariah said had left before sunrise. The girls had donned Egyptian gowns and pinned their hair up in braids, while Zechariah proudly flaunted a newly stitched robe over his bland tunic. Her mother had finished both his and

Adam's garments the night before, but at the neglect of her own, which now billowed loosely in the breeze. Blushing, she pressed the fabric beneath her and sat to hold it in place.

Her father gave an affirming grunt as he scanned the front of the crowd, standing with hands on his hips and eyes squinting. His dirty old goat-skin coat, aged and rotted, hung stiff over a linen-white tunic. He wore it with pride, though it probably wouldn't survive the day. A fine rope woven with silver fibers from Egypt looped his waist, clashing with the coat. Eliza smiled as she gazed upon him in wonder. If he had a staff, he'd resemble the perfect shepherd—proven by how he shepherded his family, though he'd flatly disagree.

Eliza ran a hand over the smooth cotton of her betrothal dress. Nothing could be more appropriate for a Godly covenant than something made with the careful hands of an Israelite. Though she had washed her feet, she left the sandals behind. They'd be suitable for any other occasion, but not this. Let others wear what their hearts desired, but Eliza made sure even her outward appearance made a statement.

Now, if only Seti and Adam were here, the family would be complete.

Unlike the previous meetings, which only able-bodied Hebrews attended, cattle heaved carts filled with the old and maimed over the uneven, rocky terrain. Women with babies on their backs, children with arms full of food, and men hauling cushions jammed against mules carrying water pouches, chairs, and crates packed with manna treats. The overabundance of bodies and goods spilled outward into the hills and around the sides of the mountain.

"Can anybody make out Adam and Seti?" Zechariah pointed toward the outcropping of boulders across the plain.

Eliza's throat tightened at Seti's name. She shielded her eyes despite God's canopy blocking the glaring sun, looming over the vicinity like a low storm cloud. There was no way anybody could distinguish the tiny figures from so far. She dropped her hand and sighed, an ache settling firm in her belly. Just a day ago, she had huddled on that very platform, overwhelmed and terrified, on the brink of death.

That morning, when Zechariah had said Adam had gone to find Seti, an urgency to stop him propelled her out of her tent and nearly set her off in another desperate mission to save Seti, but her father put a stop to that. She would have gone anyway, but things were different this time. Hoshea's words from last night, as well as her severe humbling by God, held her firm. And she still belonged to her father. She must trust God with Seti and Adam. Besides, she couldn't face the intense fear of God's imminence again. Her family had chosen the perfect perch, as far from that rock ledge as possible.

"I miss Seti," Miera whined, plopping down beside her after dancing with the twins to a made-up tune.

Her mother wrapped an arm around Miera's waist but met Eliza's gaze, her kohl-rimmed eyes sparkling. "He'll come around. He's a busy man now, with his new duties." The pride in her words panged Eliza.

Despite Seti's scandalous actions, her family still spoke of him with favor. How would they respond, though, if they knew what he'd done to Yuval? He had clearly underestimated the gravity of his actions at the time. Yuval's calling her Frog Girl was no excuse. She had dismissed any affection in Yuval's eyes as mere friendliness. No one spared her a second glance anyway, unless gawking at her face. Regardless, Seti's worries were unfounded, for Yuval preferred the pretty girls, like Sena.

Funny, that used to be Seti's preference as well. Never once had he displayed even a hint of insecurity or jealousy in his past relationships, at least that Eliza had seen. The thought erupted a single butterfly in her knotted belly. She scoffed, then chuckled to herself. Of all the things to be flattered by. Apparently, she wasn't the only jealous lover.

"Look!" Zechariah pointed toward the river, its sparkly

blue ribbon no longer standing out in a plain of browns, but blending with the rich colors of a festive people.

"Oh, my!" her mother gushed.

Curious, Eliza stood, Miera following suit.

A procession of brown and black bulls, led by several men, pressed through the chaotic throng. Like a curtain slowly parting, the crowd split before them. A ram's horn sounded from that direction, announcing their arrival. Cheers rang out, alerting those further away. Waves of people jumping to their feet rippled outward into the hills.

At last, after weeks of squabbles and skirmishes, the people moved and cheered as one. A sense of pride, unity, and awe saturated the air. The gravity of the moment sobered Eliza. How could she have been so blessed to witness not only a once-in-a-lifetime moment, but a once-in-all-creation moment? She hadn't been cursed to die a slave like past generations. Nor was she born a wanderer with the fathers, or one lost among the Nephilim.

Her fingers dug into the arms of one of her twin sisters. Rahel had been right when bartering with the wayward farmer for his black bulls. They would not survive out here. Yet, to die for the God of all creation might be a greater honor than to be worshipped until death at an old age.

Unlike yesterday, no thunder or wind overwhelmed Eliza's senses. No ominous voice boomed from the heavens. A tinge of regret for not joining Adam and Seti up front swelled within her chest. She wouldn't have made it anyway. But, oh, to see the sacrifice, the grandeur of such an act of worship up close. The absolute capstone would be to witness this pivotal moment in history while resting in Seti's arms and playing her lute.

Eliza snatched up the lute. She faced the glorified mountain and strummed the notes of her consecration.

Chapter 52

The metallic scent of freshly spilled blood wafting upward assaulted Seti's nostrils. He pressed his back against the rock-wall to avoid the searing heat and smoke. Moshe stood on the ledge, seemingly unaffected by the smoke peeling upward from the altar below, calmly overseeing the slaughter. The crowd had screamed and cheered until the last bovine life was snuffed, at which point Moshe silenced them with his raised staff. He opened a scroll and straightened. With the authority of a king, he read from the papyrus Seti had written on the night before, his voice surging through the multitude as if amplified by God. A solemn hush settled over the valley as the weight of his words penetrated every soul. Only the crackle of flames on burning flesh could be heard against Moshe's commanding voice.

Plastered against the rocks, Seti slowed his breaths. Besides Moshe, only Adam had joined him on the outcropping, face-planted against the limestone in a jumble of prayers before Moshe had even begun. Seti gazed across the valley at millions of awestruck faces. The sight mesmerized him. He sank to his knees and bowed his head. Praise for the Hebrew God welled up inside him until it spilled out in broken whispers.

When Moshe finished, a chorus of agreement resounded from the multitude, sealing the people as one bride. Seti rose, recalling his own betrothal and the look in

Eliza's eyes as she agreed to his ketubah. The joy welling in his heart at the time surely paled in comparison to what God must be feeling now. Not long ago, Seti had laughed at Eliza when she described her God's desire to be cherished again after losing his people, and how He would pursue their love even while they hated Him. The idea seemed absurd at the time, made her God look weak. But He had the last laugh. He won. The joke was on Seti, for here he sat, won over by the God of the Hebrews.

Moshe handed the scroll to Seti and descended the trail off the platform to join Aharon, Hoshea, and the elders who stood by while several men prepared the offerings. Once he had gone, Adam crept toward the ledge, leaving Seti on his knees, staring at the rolled papyrus. Though he had known his work would be read before the nation for generations to come, seeing it done before his eyes cemented the immense honor of his position before the Lord. His earlier dreams of contributing to the ancient Egyptian hieroglyphs couldn't come close.

As the air took on the savory aroma of roasted beef, Seti's mouth watered, and he edged forward to join his brother-in-law. Adam watched the unfolding scene below with his mouth agape, as if he'd never seen raw bovine flesh or copious amounts of blood. His entrancement brought back memories of Kabelo, always fascinated by the gruesome. A crocodile could eat a child, and Kabelo would stand by in amazement.

Seti had witnessed more than enough offerings that it had lost its allure. Though Egyptian priests had designed a system to keep the mess to a minimum, he loathed the gore, especially of such perfectly healthy young animals. Of course, those feelings vanished once a juicy morsel of meat slid down his throat.

Yet here he sat, inwardly squirming as several men placed a quartered carcass on the altar. And to think he had desired to be a priest. Still, it was better than human gore.

He scoffed at himself and turned away, pausing on his awestruck brother-in-law. "You're a completely different person than yesterday."

"I'm free," Adam said proudly. He hunkered on his knees, bending over the edge. "Why don't we go down there?"

"You can." The platform provided a perfect view, safe from blood splatter.

Adam remained, though antsy to the point of annoyance. His crouching form bounced on his toes, gaze darting in all directions, taking in every action, every word, every slice of flesh.

The heat of the smoke forced Seti back. No need to sear his already damaged face. He turned to inhale unsinged air, only to break into a fit of coughs. Once recovered, he sat back and studied Adam, the question he'd been suppressing all morning on the verge of bursting forth. He rolled a smooth stone between his fingers, gathered his courage, and let it out. "So … what changed your mind? About me, I mean."

Adam peered over his shoulder, then forward again. "You."

"What—"

"I was so consumed with God speaking in all that thunder and stuff. The guilt was too much." He paused, and Seti leaned closer to hear him above the ruckus below. "It wasn't till later, when my mind cleared, that I remembered what you asked of God."

A boulder dropped in Seti's stomach. Adam had heard. He knew about The Lank. "What … what about?"

Adam's brow knitted as he studied Seti. "To forgive you. About your family. Your father."

"You heard?" Seti choked.

"You were practically screaming it in my ear." He returned his gaze to the commotion below.

Repulsed, Seti drew in his knees and buried his face in

them. He had screamed it? Or maybe it felt that way to Adam at the time. He had said many things that day and since, but strangely, it was his pathetic confession that moved Adam to repentance.

If only Eliza could hear this, could see them now, together on this ledge, getting along like old friends. He'd make it up to her first, then to The Lank. He'd reassure her of his undying love, his sincere repentance, and love her like God loves His people. The thought renewed a sense of hope, and Seti straightened. How perfect. How impossible. Yet, he'd die trying.

He scanned the multitude, hoping against all odds to spot Eliza. He searched the hills beyond and the cliffs along the horizon. God's new nation saturated every facet of the valley.

Adam's eyes lit up as he pointed. "The pillars symbolize the twelve tribes."

Curious, Seti scuttled toward the ledge. As the men continued adding carcasses and parts to the flames, those in front crammed together in unified fascination as Moshe approached a stone pillar with a basin of thick, red blood. He dipped his hand into it and sprinkled the pillar red.

"Reuben," he announced. Then, stepping toward another, he repeated the act. "Yehudah." Wasting no time, he moved to the next.

"He's covering the whole nation." Adam gasped, completely engrossed. "Everyone."

Not Sabu. Seti smirked. "Only your people."

When Moshe finished with the pillars, he flicked the remaining blood at the nearest onlookers. Squeals and cries of surprise erupted, eliciting a quick smile on Moshe's otherwise solemn face. While some pulled back in revulsion, others spilled forward, yelling for Moshe to sprinkle some their way.

"Over here, Moshe!" Adam waved his hands, rising to his feet.

"Seriously, Adam?" Seti scoffed. "You're covered by the Levite Pillar."

Moshe turned, lifting his nearly empty basin for all to see. He ran his hand along the sides, soaking his fingers, then flung droplets toward Adam, spiderwebbing red across his chest.

"Him too." Adam pointed at Seti. "For the foreigners!"

"No, Ad—" Blood sprayed Seti's face. He gasped, spitting the metallic tang from his tongue. He clenched his eyes shut and stifled the vile words working their way up. *Sabu. Think about Sabu.* He opened his eyes and inhaled a slow, deep breath, silently counting to ten.

Adam jumped to his feet, punching the air. "Yes!"

Mortified, Seti wiped his face with his tunic and scuttled back against the wall.

The late afternoon sun burst through the cloud canopy in shafts of light, flooding the valley of celebrating people. A nation, birthed from the womb of Egypt. Though they had suffered at the hands of the Egyptians, they were no less protected from the perils of the world until ready to follow a God who had planned their beginnings from long ago. Music and laughter filled the air as the new people, called Israel, danced and celebrated.

Laden with baskets of charred meat, manna treats, and jars of water dangling from their necks, the tribal leaders filed in behind Moshe on his well-trodden trail toward the mountain. But these were more than just the twelve. Elders and judges also followed. Hoshea brought up the rear, bookending the group with Moshe, preventing others from joining.

A sudden realization snapped Seti from his thoughts. He jumped to his feet after having rested against the rock wall for the remainder of the ceremony. "Hoshea!" He dashed between the boulders leading off the rock ledge.

"Hoshea, wait!"

Hoshea turned, his shofar clanging against two clay jars dangling from his neck.

Seti skidded in the gravel, Adam at his heels. "You're not supposed to go—only the elders."

Of course, Hoshea wouldn't be so foolish as to cross the boundary without the blessing of God, and a tinge of jealousy stirred in Seti's core, but he had to catch him before it was too late. Once the man crossed over, Seti would be left to wait for his return, and he couldn't bear to wait.

"I've been summoned to go with the elders," Hoshea said, assessing the blood on Seti's tunic. He acknowledged Adam with a nod, then turned back to Seti. "I see Moshe got you both."

"Yes." Seti smiled. Though repulsed at the time, a gratefulness for his inclusion in the rites had taken over. He'd save his tunic as a relic, at least until it rotted. He nodded toward Adam but wished the boy wasn't there to hear the real reason he stopped Hoshea. "Do you have any more wine?"

"You have wine?" Adam blurted.

Hoshea glared at Seti. He had become a blessing to Seti since their meeting on the Ameneten pyramid—saving him from one fiasco after another, and indulging him in countless favors, the last one costing him the witnessing of Moshe's speech. Yet, Seti needed one more favor. "Adam won't say a thing. I just need one cup."

A moment of hesitancy passed during which Hoshea watched the elders march further away, hands on his hips and expression tightened in contemplation. Only when Seti stepped back in resignation did he finally speak. "Aharon is staying behind. He knows where it is. Tell him I said you may have a small pouch."

Seti opened his mouth to thank him, but Hoshea held up a finger. "You owe me." He smiled and shook his head. "You're fortunate I like you." He slapped a hand on Seti's shoulder, then looked at Adam. "The wine is a secret, reserved for later. It came from the Amalekite camp in Elim."

Adam nodded. "Why's Aharon staying behind? Isn't he accepted?"

"Sure he is. Aharon holds a special place in God's plans. But nearly every leader is coming with us, and somebody needs to tend the flock. The people have no qualms listening to him. We won't be gone long." Hoshea nodded toward the mountain.

The look in his eyes belied that claim, stirring Seti's jealousy even more. Seti followed his gaze toward the mountain. How far would God allow them to ascend? Moshe couldn't set eyes on the mysterious God, yet these men would somehow dine with Him? Or perhaps it was in the midst of Him, or below Him.

"Hoshea." Seti wetted his lips, eyes still on the rumbling inferno. "Don't—don't you think it would be wise for me to follow and record everything? It seems rather important, for future generations, I mean."

Hoshea swung an arm around his shoulder. "That's not up to me. God wants you down here with Aharon. If anything happens, record it, and Moshe will decide whether to use it upon his return." A knowing smile creased his eyes. "Besides, you need to reconcile with *your bride*." He winked.

With that, he hurried after the elders, leaving Seti standing with Adam silently in the wake of his wise reply.

His choice of words suggested he'd be up there longer than for a simple meal. Seti squelched his envy and turned away from the mesmerizing presence of God. Instead, he cast his eyes on his brother-in-law, hoping to redirect his focus to the next most important aspect of his life: Eliza.

Chapter 53

The long day of noise and activity, though joyous, had exhausted Eliza's senses and heavy heart. A nap would help, but upon returning to camp, that prospect evaporated. A slew of friends and relatives had gathered in the narrow spaces between tents, continuing the celebration. People frolicked in the shallow parts of the river, singing and laughing. Others lounged in relaxed repartee. Tables laden with meat platters and various manna treats lined the main thoroughfare. Apparently, such an occasion warranted personal offerings in addition to the corporate ones at the foot of the mountain.

Between bursts of laughter and excited conversation, a chorus of harps, lutes, and stringed instruments floated on the warm breeze. Eliza scanned the gathering for Yuval's family. Not only would seeing him be as awkward as ever, but Sena was sure to be with him. Dread knotted Eliza's stomach, ruining her appetite. She'd rather spend the rest of the day hiding in her tent.

"Adam's back!" Miera broke into a run toward their camp, jolting Eliza to attention.

Adam emerged from a group of men, laughing, arms open as if to welcome his family back from a weeklong trip. Miera skidded in the dirt just shy of his embrace and recoiled at the blood on his tunic. As her mother cried out and ran toward him, Eliza halted at the ghastly sight. Seti's name squeaked from her throat in a gasp.

"Ahh, don't worry. All is well." Adam ruffled Miera's hair. "It's from the bulls Moshe sacrificed." He stretched his tunic flat for all to see.

That blood could have very well been Seti's. Eliza took a deep breath, resting her hand on her pounding chest. His actions the morning before testified to his ability to take a life, but the young man now embracing his family with hugs and laughter bore no resemblance. This was the Adam she knew.

The peace lighting his face outshone the marks Seti had left on him. Jubilant energy infused every gesture and word as he answered his family's questions. Eliza hung back, unwilling to dim his newfound joy with questions about Seti. The pain Adam had voiced on the way to the mountain the day before still rang in her memory. Confidence and purpose radiated from him, qualities she only now realized had been missing. He must have reconciled with Seti.

Adam mentioned very little of him, only that they were together, and that Seti had responsibilities with Aharon that prevented him from leaving. Eliza sighed and turned away. A defeating sadness eclipsed the anxiety over running into Yuval and Sena. She trudged toward her tent, leaving her family to bask in their happiness.

"Nice dress." Rahel stood near Eliza's tent.

Heart leaping, Eliza skipped a step and bounced into Rahel's arms. "Rahel!"

"I've been waiting here for hours. My parents already went back." After a long, tight embrace, Rahel stepped back and beamed a toothy grin that highlighted her freckles and sparkling eyes.

"I'm sorry." Eliza wiped her eyes dry, surprised at the bubbling emotion. "I've missed you."

"And I you. We have much to catch up on."

As Sabu and Nala arrived on Nimrod, Adam waved the girls over. He rubbed his hands together and wiggled his eyebrows before gesturing broadly at the group settling around the firepit. "And you'll want to hear this."

Eliza exchanged a glance with Rahel and found a spot near Zechariah.

Adam basked in the attention with his elaborate and gory reenactments of the events at the mountain's base. He included Moshe's speech, what had to be an exaggeration of the crowd's reactions to the slaughter, and the twelve pillars encircling an altar of stones bigger than he was tall. His dramatic retelling ended with Moshe sprinkling blood on him and Seti, thus including the sojourners newly embedded into the Hebrew society. Sabu lifted his chin with pride, squeezing Nala's hand.

Adam conveniently skipped over his mysterious disappearance the night before and how his face came to be so colorful and swollen. And to Eliza's surprise, no one asked. Let him shine. She'd hound him for answers later.

When Yuval arrived with his band of brothers and their instruments, Eliza grasped Rahel's hand and jumped to her feet. "Let's go to my tent."

"Care to join us, Eliza?" Yuval plopped onto a large rock and positioned his giant harp. Thankfully, Sena was nowhere in sight.

Eliza hesitated, throat instantly dry. Yuval had winked at his use of her name, a twinkle in his eyes. Seti's words echoed in her mind, loud and clear. *And you should see the way he looks at you*. Revulsion and flattery warred within her, though quickly squashed by shame that she had wed the man who defiled their instruments. But Seti had repented. More shame compounded over even thinking such a thought.

"No." She choked and cleared her throat. "I mean … no thank you, Yuval. It's getting late."

The letdown of his smiling face nearly changed her mind, but she forced her focus on Rahel. "I'm tired. Let's go talk."

"I must get back to my parents. You know how it is now after dark." Rahel's gaze drifted to the dagger hilt protruding from a pouch tied to her waist. "It's a wonder they left without me."

Did Rahel share Eliza's unease about navigating a jam-packed valley? Rahel had once been fearless, until that horrid night the giants attacked. Yet here she sported weaponry with pride.

"You should see what's under my skirt," she whispered, a mischievous gleam in her eye.

Eliza raised an eyebrow at the thought of fighting a giant with meager blades. But even she had charged into battle with nothing but a bow far too big and a single arrow. She glanced at Yuval, then at her family, who chatted idly with neighbors drawn in by Adam's presentation. If not for Rahel, Eliza would be sulking in the confines of her tent, alone. Her best friend was not only a welcome distraction from her worries about Seti but a solace to confide in—and she hadn't yet confided anything. "Please, stay a little longer."

"Yes." Zechariah stood, brushing dirt from his tunic. "The girls haven't been sleeping well since you left. They keep asking when you will sing for them again."

Since when did Zechariah care how well the twins slept? He spent his nights beside the firepit, nowhere near them. Yet Rahel's nightly lullabies had truly been missed, if not by Eliza's sisters, then certainly by her. The twins leaped to their feet with squeals and ran to hug Rahel's legs, confirming his words.

Rahel patted their heads. "I'll stay long enough to sing you to sleep, but must go before the sun sets." Her gaze shifted toward the fading light over the darkening mountains.

The cheers of her youngest sisters lifted Eliza's spirit. She squeezed Rahel's hand, accepting that a sweet song from her dear friend might settle her heartache more than voicing her secrets out loud. Though still early for bedtime, Rahel followed the girls into their tent and cocooned them within their blankets. Eliza joined her at the foot of their mats, a candle in hand. As Yuval and his brothers strummed a soft melody outside, Rahel sang. Her voice filled the small space with the sweet notes Eliza had long missed.

The weeks-long journey with the Avaris group on the way to Horeb would never be forgotten. Rahel's voice had been a spring of hope in the desert, a soothing sound during Eliza's worst headaches. It settled her overwhelmed senses, bringing the whirling mess of amplified emotions to order once again. Like Yuval's music, it offered only temporary relief but pointed to something lasting. Rahel would never know the effect she had with something so simple as her voice. When she finished, she locked eyes with Eliza's as if dedicating the song to her.

Eliza sniffled, her heart a puddle. "Please stay." A sadness permeated the air between them. She reached for Rahel's hand.

"I don't want to walk back in the dark."

"Don't go," one of the twins whispered, peeking out from beneath her blanket. "We aren't asleep yet."

"What if I find somebody to escort you? Then would you stay?" Eliza asked.

"I—I—" Rahel's eyes darted away, worry clouding her face.

"Eliza, Seti's here!" Miera squealed from outside.

The twins scrambled from their blankets and tumbled out of the tent as if the lullaby had never occurred. Eliza stiffened, eyes fixed on Rahel. Of all the moments in the day for Seti to appear, why now? Her heart hammered.

Seti cringed at Miera's over-the-top announcement of his arrival. The family had settled around the campfire with several others in attendance. All eyes lifted toward him as Miera bounded over, braids bouncing, arms outstretched. He should've expected the extra faces and ongoing celebrations, but nothing could have prepared him for the presence of The Lank on the far side of the campfire with his brothers. Their music could be heard from a good distance away, but it hadn't crossed his mind then. Seti dropped Chewy's reins. God had set him up.

"I missed you!" Miera barreled into him.

While long overdue for a Miera-style greeting, the sight of Yuval sapped his joy and derailed his plans. Still, he tried to embrace it for her sake. He winced at her strength against his wounds. "I've missed you too. It's been a while."

He straightened, unhinged her grip on him, and looked at the others. Jeremiah, Sarah, and Adam stood in expectation. A knowing grin stretched across Adam's face as he glanced at each of his kin. Zechariah remained on his haunches beside his parents' tent. He shifted awkwardly, gazing between Seti and Adam.

Seti nodded his acknowledgment and gathered his bearings. "I've come to take Eliza to my tent."

A hush swept over the gathering. Sarah gasped and covered her mouth. The music stopped with an abruptness that stilled Seti's pounding heart, and Yuval raised his face for the first time since Seti's arrival. Sabu slowly stood, eyes dead set on Seti. Taking a deep breath, Seti moved closer, hoping Sabu would take note and come to his side. When he didn't respond accordingly, Seti hesitated. Aharon said this should work. But then again, God had other ideas. He glanced back at Chewy, his only escape, standing patiently in the twilight shadows.

Miera took his hand. "You have a tent?"

The twins plowed toward Seti with squeals and arms outstretched. In their wake, Eliza's head peeked out from their tent. A tinge of relief at her sweet face swept through Seti, recomposing his nerves. If only he could grab her and go, escape the staring audience.

But God had made Himself clear with Yuval's presence. Seti would do this—if not for Eliza, then definitely for God. He took a deep breath, squared his shoulders, and locked eyes with her. As the twins wrapped around his legs, he cleared his throat. "I've prepared a place for you."

She stepped out of the tent and straightened, eyes glistening. His stomach flipped. Wisps of hair floated free from her pinned braids, framing her soft, round face. Her betrothal gown hung delicately off her slight shoulders, clinging to her in all the right places, making Seti wonder if her mother had purposefully sewn it that way to torture him. His clenched hands opened, fingers tingling at the mere thought of sliding over those shapely hips. Yes, God definitely set him up.

With the help of Aharon and his wife, Seti had prepared his tent to accommodate Eliza. They sent him on his way with words to declare his intent, but the rest was his idea. He'd make his announcement, take Eliza on Chewy, and whisk her back to his tent, where he'd apologize for everything and promise to make it up to her. It sounded like a good plan at the time, but seeing her now, Yahweh's perfect bride, set a new plan in motion.

Seti had failed to present her to God pure and worthy, yet here God presented her to him in such a way. Though he could freely take her, Yuval's presence made it clear: there was one more thing God required.

As Eliza came forward, Seti beckoned Sabu as well. "And The La…I mean, Yuval. Yuval, I'd like a word with you."

"You want Yuval to play a song?" Miera asked.

"No." Seti bent to her level. "I must speak privately with him. Later, if Eliza allows me, I'll tell you about it."

The dejection on Miera's face surprisingly stung. Refusing to let her unravel him, Seti unlatched the twins from his legs. "I promise. But I need you to do me a favor and take your sisters."

"You tell me your secrets, I tell you mine."

"Right." He rubbed her head and glanced at Yuval, who left his harp with his brothers and made his way around Eliza's family. "I'm sure it won't be a secret for long."

"Seti?" Eliza approached, barefoot, concern clouding her face. She looked at Yuval, then back to Seti, and whispered, "What are you doing?"

"I'm proving to you that I'm serious." Proving to God. He squeezed Miera's hand. "Please, Miera. And could you find me Eliza's sandals?"

When he didn't yield to Miera's exaggerated pout, she rolled her eyes and tugged the twins away. "Come on, girls."

Seti took Eliza's hand and led her toward Chewy, hoping Sabu and Yuval would follow. He wasn't going to do this with an audience. Whether it became public was up to Yuval and Eliza. They met in the darkness on the opposite side of Chewy. Yuval stood silently beside Sabu, as rigid as a statue. He scanned their surroundings as if plotting an escape route.

"Seti?" Eliza whispered.

"What's going on in that head of yours?" Sabu asked, rocking back on his heels.

"I … Well, Yuval …" Sickness roiled in Seti's stomach as Yuval's gaze landed on him, eyes wide with caution. No turning back now. "It was me." His mouth went dry, and nothing else would come out.

A stifled cough burst from Sabu, and he slapped a hand over his mouth, no longer rocking. Seti shot him a look of warning.

"What was you?" Yuval asked, his voice timid.

Seti shifted his weight and wet his lips, though every second chipped away at his resolve. "I'm the one who tossed the spoiled manna in your tent. I ruined your instruments. It was my fault, my idea, and I want to sincerely apologize." He stopped before saying anything he'd regret. If he mentioned Yuval's behavior toward Eliza, it might sound like deflection, and he'd tarnish the sincerity of his apology.

The shock on Yuval's face pushed him a step back. Surely he'd suspected him.

Seti gulped. "Yuval, I'm sorry. If your family can think of a way I can make restitution, I will."

"You can have my lute," Eliza blurted, eliciting a look of horror from Seti.

"You?" Yuval choked. His expression shifted from shock to deep concentration, as if searching his memory for missed clues. "Why?"

How could Seti say it without deflecting blame? This confession of a lifetime had to come with care, as impromptu as it was. He shrank beneath their waiting stares. "When you shared your lute with Eliza and called her Frog Girl…and the way you looked at her … I got defensive." There, keep the blame on his own insecurities.

Yuval scoffed and narrowed his eyes with scorn. "You ruined my father's drums over a look?" He turned to Eliza. "A nickname? And you didn't tell me?"

Seti nudged her gently behind him. "She didn't know until yesterday when I told her. It's my fault. I take sole responsibility. I'll do whatever it takes to make restitution."

"You said it was all your instruments," Eliza said.

"What does it matter?" Yuval snapped. "Most were in their cases. We still burned the drums and the wind instruments that didn't have cases." He closed in on Seti, towering over him, and making full use of his lanky stature. "You can't replace those drums. They were gifts to my abba from Asia. They had sentimental value. And the others were heirlooms. There is no restitution to be made. You think because you're Egyptian that an apology fixes it? That we'll just forgive you? That it does—"

"Obviously not if I'm offering to do whatever it takes," Seti cut in. He puffed his chest, the furthest he'd allow himself on the defensive. If Yuval wanted the high hand, let him have it. Unless things got physical.

"Like I said, there's nothing you can do." Yuval's cheek twitched. "My abba's going to kill you."

"Then he'd be no better than me—ruled by vengeance. Worse, since I apologized—"

Eliza's fingernails digging into his bicep grounded him.

He took a breath. "Take it to your abba. Then take it to Aharon if need be. Let justice be served. I'm willing."

Yuval stared daggers into his soul. Let him. Seti had nothing left to hide. Not anymore. "Sabu is my witness." He nodded toward the mountain. "God is my witness."

Words of a fool. Would death stalk Seti the rest of his days? He had just consigned his life into the hands of a vengeful Hebrew. What better gift to offer an ex-slave? Seti stood down, relief and regret contending in a belligerent battle within him.

Yuval's gaze darted toward Sabu before landing hard on Seti again. "I will. God is *my* witness." He stepped back and shot Eliza a look of disgust before storming away.

Sabu's strong presence proved a wise decision. Though unfair to Yuval, being outnumbered prevented a rash reaction. Now, it was in God's hands. He had proved Himself faithful and trustworthy. Nevertheless, if this would be the death of Seti, at least he'd die an honest man. Foolish but honest.

"Why'd you do that?" Sabu moved in Seti's narrowing line of vision. "They're going to come after you now."

"God wanted me to." Seti blinked his eyes into focus and shrugged it off like he didn't ask himself that exact question. "He'll take care of it, whether it be justice or mercy." He turned to Eliza, whose brown eyes fixated on him to the point he looked away. His heart stuttered. "You're still upset."

"No." Her soft, gentle voice matched the touch of her fingertips running up his arm. Invisible flames shot up to his shoulder where her hand paused, then slowly moved it to his neck. "I—I'm not upset. I'm in love."

That settled it. "Good." Seti grabbed her around the waist and lifted her onto Chewy. He'd done what he had to do. Now it was time to leave.

He faced Sabu. "Thank you, my friend. I'll be back to visit after I'm a married man."

Sabu smiled and slapped him on the back. "Wait, I have something for you." He rounded Chewy, nearly tripping over his crutches. As he returned with a basket of meat, he announced Seti's departure and invited the others to join him in congratulating the soon-to-be official newlyweds.

Eliza's family rushed forward in excitement, gathering around them. Seti took the basket from Sabu, wishing to leave. He'd accept their blessings later. Right now, all he wanted was privacy with Eliza.

Yet, a pull within him drew his eyes to the flaming mountain in the distance. *Savor the moment.* The cheers from the family solidified his acceptance, born the night of the betrothal. Adam's beaming face beside Jeremiah's genuine smile dissolved the months of pain Seti had carried since leaving Egypt. He filled his lungs with satisfaction and let the adrenaline from speaking to Yuval seep out, slowing his hammering heart.

He glanced up at Eliza, who sat awkwardly—yet radiantly—on the woven blanket on Chewy's back. Her cheeks blushed beneath those wisps of hair that always seemed to come loose. She caught his gaze, and her blush deepened.

"Come up here," she whispered, motioning with her hand.

"No. You ride. I'll lead. You are the bride, after all."

"Seriously, Seti. Don't leave me up here alone."

"I'll help you down when we reach our new home." He took Chewy's reins. "And don't jump either."

As her brothers and Sabu offered gentle jokes and pats on the back, Jeremiah stood back, his eyes gleaming. He nodded in approval, his perpetual smile worth a thousand congratulations.

Sarah burst into tears. "Eliza, dear, we could have a ceremony. I can spread the word. You don't have to rush—"

Eliza shook her head, her gaze falling on her best friend approaching. "I don't want a ceremony, Ima. I have everyone who I want right here."

While Miera and Nala fastened Eliza's sandals on her feet, Rahel squeezed her hand. "I'm honored to have witnessed this, Eliza."

Eliza swung her leg over to jump down, but Seti nudged Chewy forward, jerking her off balance and forcing her to grasp Chewy's mane. She flashed him a mischievous grin, then resettled herself on Chewy's back and focused on her friend. "I couldn't ask for a better way to end the night." Her eyes sparkled as they flitted to Seti and back again. "The sealing of the covenant, playing my lute for God, and your being here. I got to hear you sing again." She lifted her face to the darkening sky. "Seti and I can give you a ride back."

Seti tugged on the reins again and shook his head at the notion. "If Rahel needs an escort to her tent, Zechariah's more than capable." He stifled a smirk and nodded toward the boy, whose head jerked up from his bantering with Adam. "He can fight off any perpetrators."

The open-mouthed stares from Eliza and Rahel sobered him, and he hardened his gaze on his wife. "I'm serious. I'm taking you with me, Eliza."

She looked at Rahel. "Zechariah will take you back."

Seti scanned the shadows for Yuval and his band. The entire group had left. Trepidation splintered his nerves until he laid eyes on the fiery mountain in the distance, a volcano of embers pulsating orange through tendrils of blackened smoke. Peace settled over him. He had done what he promised. He obeyed God, and it felt good. Now if God struck him down for his transgression, let his ashes rise with those of the mountain as a pleasing aroma. But hope rested on mercy, whatever that entailed.

451

Chapter 54

Though Eliza sat on Chewy's back—on a rug for that matter, like royalty—it felt wrong. It was a precarious position unsuited for the likes of her. She ducked her head to avoid the burning stares from those they passed. Seti made no effort to avoid the public as he paraded her through the labyrinth of tents and communes. She should be thrilled to be exalted in such a way.

"Look." She leaned forward. "I know you're making a point to warn my enemies, as if I'm some sort of anointed, but—"

"That's what you think this is?" Seti laughed. "Well, if it serves such a purpose, let it be so. But that's not what I intended."

She straightened with a scoff. "Seti, please come up here. This is absurd."

He peered over his shoulder with pride gleaming in his eyes. "Nah. Let the world witness the absurdity then." He faced forward and gestured with his free hand. "Let everyone see how special you are. One of a kind. A lowly Egyptian leading you on his steed is the least I can do."

"You act like you're at fault for everything. Don't forget my part in it all. I am not someone to be exalted. I don't deserve—"

"Don't." He halted and flashed his alluring eyes her way. "You are my bride, Eliza. No bride of mine sets foot in the dirt upon arriving at her new palace."

If he'd quit interrupting, maybe he'd understand. She squeezed a fistful of Chewy's mane and hissed, "You are *not* below me, Seti. Now get up here."

Instead of surprise or sternness, a gentle patience permeated his features. "As your husband, I am not below you. But I can place myself in such a position at my discretion, and I will serve and honor you as long as you are my wife. You're no longer a slave or the big sister, Eliza. You're free to be you." He faced forward. "I want the world to see that."

Stunned, Eliza closed her gaping mouth.

Eliza squinted at a small tent across from the large white one Adam had indicated as Moshe's the day before. Seti moved Chewy aside to let a wagon packed with singing children pass. Chickens fluttered and squawked off the makeshift road. A group of women paused their stroll to gawk and whisper.

She bit back a harsh remark and turned away, wishing to hide. Her new safe haven stood before her—a crisp camelhair canvas supported by twine and bamboo poles. "This is your tent?"

The pride on Seti's face spoke volumes. Who could have imagined the spoiled boy from the villas of On would one day be so proud to call a humble piece of canvas his home?

She swung her leg over Chewy's back to dismount, but Seti held up a finger. He dashed into the tent and returned with a small rug, which he spread on the ground between Chewy and the tent flap.

"Allow me."

She waited, offering a hesitant smile. The gesture added to the list of grand gestures and soul-stirring words he'd racked up that evening, overwhelming her with undeserved kindness. She slid from Chewy's back into his strong arms, landing gently on the rug. He planted a small kiss on her forehead and gently smoothed her frizzed hair from her eyes.

Like a child about to open a gift, Seti hurried to the tent flap. He paused, peering back at her. "Ready?"

His energy was contagious, and Eliza couldn't choose what to be more excited about: stepping into her new home or putting her hands on him with no guilt. For once, she'd freely have him. She licked her lips and rubbed her hands together. "Yes."

He pulled back the flap and stepped aside. A flowery aroma spilled out, halting Eliza before she entered. Not one to burn incense, he was either masking a foul smell or trying to impress her. The thought set her stomach aflutter. She stifled a giggle and stepped inside. An oil lamp burned on a small table near a two-person mat against the wall opposite the flap. Several blankets woven of various materials neatly covered the mat, topped with two pillows.

The giggle escaped. She clapped a hand over her mouth and glanced at Seti. He truly had prepared a place for her, not merely introduced her to a homely tent, ripe with body odor as she half expected.

He raised an eyebrow. "Look around."

Resting on a silk cloth draped over a simple acacia wood chest sat the head-net she'd given him at their betrothal. Frankincense burned beside it. On a thin rope strung along the side wall hung a white tunic smeared in crimson.

"Is that …" Eliza pulled the tunic into the light.

"Yes. From the offerings at the foot of the mountain. I want to keep it, but I'm not sure how to preserve it."

A wave of warmth filled her chest as memories of Seti's bedroom back in Egypt flooded her mind. Each week, she'd spend hours dusting the exotic relics from his journeys abroad with his father. Treasures saved from childhood or tokens from late ancestors joined them, covering his walls and dangling from the ceiling. He'd left all of that for her. For this.

She let the tunic hang and surveyed the rest of her surroundings. A large rug woven of a hodgepodge of materials covered the dirt floor. Another chest sat near the entrance, topped with a silver tray laden with a gold-etched silver cup, an old wineskin, and a small leather water pouch.

She smiled. "You remembered the wine."

His eyes sparkled beneath budding brows. "Of course." He spread his arms wide and spun around. "Plenty of room for your things."

"Which isn't much," she said with a shrug.

Seti plopped onto the mat and snatched Eliza's hand, pulling her off her feet. She fell snug into his lap, laughing. His arms enveloped her, and he dipped her back. Eliza's heart leaped into her throat. She gazed into his eyes as he smoothed the stray hairs from her face with fingers so gentle, they barely brushed her skin.

"You are absolutely stunning in that dress." His boyish smile accentuated his dimples and creased his deep eyes. That smile morphed into a hungry, mischievous grin as his gaze poured over her.

Eliza's heart skipped into a flutter. "Seti." She dug her nails into his arm. Why the panic? She craved this moments ago, days ago, months even. But now, unwarranted fear seized her. "Wait." She clamped her eyes shut in shame.

He immediately sat her up to face him. "I'm sorry."

The sincerity of his words calmed her nerves. "No, I'm sorry. I want this. I do. I just, just …"

Again, a gentle patience softened his features, as did a pink blush. "I'm as new at this as you are. We have all night. All eternity, for that matter. I mean, our betrothal still stands, doesn't it?"

How could he ask such a question? Did he think his foolish antics worthy of divorce? Or her so shallow? "Of course!" She gasped, cupping his face. "I was upset, yes, but I could never … Seti, I love you."

His hands covered hers, as if to pull them from his cheeks, but he paused, hesitant. "Well, you know … I was betrothed before. Lumeri, she …"

With the panic long gone, compassion took over with a surge of arousing sensations. Eliza would show him how far from Lumeri she was. "I know, Seti. But I'm not Lumeri. I will never stop loving you. Plus, Hebrew betrothals are different from Egyptian. We are considered married, minus the consummation. The dowry, the ketubah, all that was binding. If I left you, it'd be divorce."

He let out a heavy breath and released her hands. Then, as if the clouds parted, Seti's face beamed. "Did you know that we are God's bride? Each of us. Betrothed to Him, sealed today with the offerings." His voice rose. "Moshe said marriage was designed after God's relationship with man. At least, it's supposed to be."

He lifted Eliza aside and jumped to his feet. "The Ten Words that He spoke aloud yesterday—that was the ketubah. Everyone agreed to it."

With a renewed energy, he grabbed the silver cup, wineskin, and water pouch from the tray. "And the gifts from Egypt, your freedom … The consecration was more than just a consecration, too. It was the mikvah, like you did before our betrothal." He blinked, as if a new thought struck him. "Like a sign, a pledge to belong to Him."

"What?" Where was he getting all this?

Seti plopped down cross-legged before her and poured wine into the cup. "Aharon let me borrow this." He paused to lock eyes with her. "The elders and Hoshea ascended the mountain with Moshe to have a ceremonial meal with Yahweh. They're going to eat with God!" His eyes widened with such wonder that Eliza laughed, the joy in his words infecting her. "Or maybe God's going to watch them eat. I don't know, but it's a celebration. But there's more."

Eliza lifted her hands, smiling. "More what?"

"God is preparing a place for us, like I have for you." He spread his hand, gesturing around the tent. "Aharon told me to make sure I said that I've prepared a place for you." He laughed, shaking his head. "And obviously your family knew what that meant."

"Right." Eliza nodded, thoughts whirling as she tried to keep up.

"And there's more." He nearly sloshed the wine from the cup.

"More?"

"There's a dowry."

Eliza raised an eyebrow. "A mohar?"

"Not in case He dies—because He can't, of course. But because there's a bride-price."

Enthralled by his fascination, she sifted through the onslaught of Seti's revelation while he waited, holding his breath. Finally, she straightened. "But why? Who's He purchasing us from? Egypt?" Her stomach knotted. "What's the price?"

His breath gusted her face with warmth. "He hasn't paid it yet. Moshe said He will, before the marriage supper, which comes after the seed of the woman."

Eliza's heart nearly arrested. Her mother's words from long ago echoed in her mind, loud and clear. She seized Seti's arms. "The seed of the woman crushes the serpent's head. God purchases us from the serpent." The next words hurt to say. "But the serpent first bruises His heel."

Seti's face went blank. "Huh? How can God be bruised?"

Her mother's stories weren't just tales, no, that much had been proven. If God had yet to pay the bride-price, then the serpent had yet to bruise His heel. And somehow, God must let him. "The curse on all creation," she muttered, sorting through her mother's stories. "The seed of the woman is the cure, so it's a man, but yet God? Or a specific man of God? The Great Yakov calls him Shiloh."

"Wait," Seti said. "Who's the serpent?"

The excitement sapped from Eliza as realization set in. She dropped her gaze. "The one who tempted Eve. Canaan isn't the end. It's only the beginning. This whole betrothal thing is only the beginning."

Seti lifted her chin with a gentle finger. "I know it will be generations before God pays the bride-price. But you and I will be together. And Yahweh is with us just as I am with you. Only more so. We are the beginning of the making of history, Eliza." He lifted the wine glass. "You are my bride. I will love you like Yahweh loves us."

His words fortified her, grounding her in the moment. She covered his hand with hers on the silver cup. "And I you."

Lost in his dazzling eyes, she sipped the wine, then let him do the same. Its searing strength burned her throat, eliciting a gasp for air. Seti handed her the water pouch.

"Sorry. I should've reminded you where it came from." He wiped his mouth on his arm. "You know, we can get drunk and fall asleep together all night this time." He folded his hands in his lap, waiting.

"I've had enough." Eliza fanned her mouth, blinking away tears.

Seti looped his arm around her waist and pulled her close. "You are a treasure, Eliza. Hidden before my eyes until God opened them."

The absurdity of his words made her laugh, but his severe expression stilled her.

"I mean it," he said. "However long it takes for God to complete His mission, I will love you longer."

Her mouth dropped.

He gently closed it with a nudge of his hand and pressed his lips against hers.

His mouth skimmed down her neck in gentle caresses, igniting an array of tingles and jitters down her spine. His grip tightened around her waist.

He paused long enough to breathe. "I want to search you, explore you, discover every facet, every nook …"

This time, she fully relinquished. He laid her back, blew out the lamp, then returned, going straight for the ties on her dress.

As if the evening sun could not be contained, orange rays burst from the canopy cloud, a reflection of God smiling down on His people. A new hope alighted Eliza's in heart. She nestled against Seti, atop a hill overlooking the valley, sharing a large cushion given to them by Sabu. Apparently, Yahweh delighted in shepherding His flock, teaching them, salvaging them from the wreckage of their debauchery and carnality. It pleased Him to bestow mercy and grace, to raise His people in the riches of His kindness.

The peace now encompassing Eliza evaporated the heaviness she had borne for so long. That weight had lifted, signaling the end of a long season of slavery and struggle. A new life lay ahead with new challenges. But knowing God's faithfulness—and His joy in walking beside her—armed her until the day she'd be perfected in Him.

Eliza's family had offered a celebratory meal the day after the consummation and ladened Chewy with her belongings and gifts. Yuval's father had confronted Seti during that time, but upon recognizing Seti from the battlefield, his heart had softened, and he invited him for a covenantal dinner at his camp. Before Yuval and their entire camp, his father and Seti vowed peace and sealed it with the blood of a ram. His father even called on God and the mountain as witnesses—a bold move—setting Eliza's heart at ease. Who would dare break such a vow? Yuval himself had taken no part.

She and Seti began that evening with a new tradition: Every evening of their marriage would end with fellowship and thankfulness, just the two of them, beneath a canvas of colors.

"You like the view?" Seti swept his hand over the valley of a renewed people.

Shadows from the mountains darkened the sprawl of tents and enhanced the glow of campfires as far as Eliza could see. Pockets of music drifted into the air.

She smiled at how her people enlivened the barren desert. "It's perfect."

Seti shifted on the cushion. He draped an arm around Eliza's shoulders and gazed pensively at God's holy mountain, its ever-rolling storm clouds blackening as the sun set behind it. A random lightning flash illuminated portions of the mountain, outlining the edges of the clouds.

"Moshe and Hoshea are up there somewhere."

Was it really a marriage covenant as Seti had suggested? Eliza stared into the inferno as if it were God Himself.

Seti spoke into the breeze. "It amazes me how God touched every single heart that day."

"Everybody's except Yuval's, it seems," Eliza muttered.

Charming Yuval clung to his bitterness. Whether it was rooted in Seti's actions or his indecipherable feelings toward her, she didn't know. All would be perfect if Yuval would just forgive. Or if she would have stayed away from him to begin with. His bitterness and whatever else he held would keep her away, unable to join him in worship with her lute. It'd be a rift she would forever feel somewhat responsible for, regardless of what anybody said.

Before she could turn away, Seti lifted her chin with his thumb and gazed deep into her soul. "And what was it like for you, my little kitten? When God spoke at the foot of the mountain, I mean."

Another mystery to ponder. The beauty of it had faded as quickly as any memory, leaving only the worst parts still so vivid.

"You were right," Eliza whispered, remembering her meltdown in front of Hoshea. "I'm too complicated. God saw right through me, down to my core." She pulled back, not wanting Seti to see her shame. God had exposed every lie she had believed about herself, laying her bare. He then filled her with truth. Yet, already she had reverted to those lies and started rebuilding those walls.

She looked away, swallowing the raw emotion rising in her throat.

"Eliza." Seti lifted her onto his lap, turning her to face him.

She dropped her gaze to her fumbling hands between them.

He cradled her. "You didn't like it, did you?"

"I did …" Her voice trembled. "I … I don't know. He showed me His perspective of me, and it was beautiful. How every phase of growth I pass through pleases Him." She looked away. "It was incredible. But you've changed. Yuval's father had changed. Adam changed. And no matter how hard I try to hold on to those images, I'm still the same emotional, defensive Eliza."

Seti lifted her chin again, gently forcing her to look at him. "Yuval's father arrived with vengeance on his heart, even after the day at the mountain. If it weren't for our encounter on the battlefield, the night could have ended dreadfully different. And I can't say I wouldn't have gone down without a fight. If Adam didn't hear my repentance to God, would he still hate me? A dramatic moment with God is wonderful, yes, but actual change takes time. You know the truth, Eliza. You must believe it. Remember when I wanted you to believe what I said about you? Strengthen yourself in the Lord by focusing on His faithfulness and what

He says."

Seti's eyes grew distant as if searching his own memories. "Strangely, I think it was witnessing God's work on my behalf that really struck me. How He softened hearts. More than the grand demonstrations of His power."

Butterflies erupted in Eliza at the realization. "Because it was personal."

She snuggled against Seti's chest, allowing his warmth to envelop her. She had entered two covenants in a span of a week, and Seti three. One could say she merely exchanged masters, but God's yoke would be light, as would Seti's.

Seti's transformation from an idol-worshipping, self-serving Egyptian to a member of God's flock eclipsed every other miracle. Hopefully, Eliza would also bearYahweh is a personal God. His love, at times, may stir overwhelming feelings, but that comes and goes. The true power of His love lies in truth and everlasting transformation.

A Note from the Author

I love the Old Testament. Like how a book reveals an author's innermost musings, so the Bible, the Old Testament in particular, reveals the inner musings of God. We see it in the way He chooses people, often the humble and lowly. We see it in how He responds to people, particularly those He calls His own. He is merciful, but at the same time uncompromising of His justice in righteousness. He has a heart for the lost, the abandoned, the widow, and the orphan. He's a romantic but untamable, reckless even, a warrior willing to humble himself, to wash the feet of those He loves, to be the bride-price in His unfolding love story.

God, who's magnificent glory is so blinding that we cannot see past it, set this glory aside so we can know what's behind it. Only as the Son, can He come close to us in such an intimate relationship. His desire is to be freely chosen by His bride, the apple of His eye. He is forming a kingdom for this bride, the bride of His son, a home to take her to.

All prophecy is pattern, a play book, often repeating in various ways and types until its ultimate fulfilling. Often, people played roles and parts that they weren't even aware of (like Joseph or Moses). Every ordinance for the Israelites and every player and pattern is a picture of the grand plan. The easiest example is Passover. Another such pattern is the ancient wedding custom. The Israelites lived it out as a community, but it's the same for Christianity. Once betrothed (making our official declaration), we consecrate ourselves for our groom, setting ourselves apart for Him. And as He builds the Kingdom, He prepares us, and we prepare ourselves (yes, it's a messy job with one step forward and two steps back. Thankfully, God sent His Holy Spirit to guide us in this), looking forward to the day He comes for us and for the wedding supper.

If you enjoyed the story of Seti and Eliza, visit my website Ashmoreswildernessbooks.com to learn more about the making of this book, as well as more about God's great love story.

465